Available in Arrow Books by Jean Plaidy

Royal Road to Fotheringay

JEAN PLAIDY

arrow books

Published by Arrow Books 2007

4 6 8 1 9 7 5

First published in the United Kingdom in 1964 by Robert Hale Ltd

The Random House Group Limited
20 Vauxhall Bridge Road, London SW1V 2SA

www.randomhouse.co.uk

Addresses for companies within The Random House Group Limited can be found at:
www.randomhouse.co.uk/offices.htm

The Random House Group Limited Reg. No. 954009

A CIP catalogue record for this book is available from the British Library

ISBN 9780099493341

Typeset by SX Composing DTP, Rayleigh, Essex

The Random House Group Limited supports The Forest Stewardship
Council® (F͟S͟C͟®͟)͟,͟ ͟t͟h͟e͟ ͟l͟e͟a͟d͟i͟n͟g͟ ͟i͟n͟t͟e͟r͟n͟a͟t͟i͟o͟n͟a͟l͟ ͟f͟o͟r͟e͟s͟t͟ ͟c͟e͟r͟t͟i͟f͟i͟c͟a͟t͟i͟o͟n͟ organisation.
Our boo͟k͟s͟   aper.
FSC is   ding

For Mildred Ligonier Johnston

MARY THE QUEEN

🏵 Chapter I 🏵

through the great rooms of the Castle of Stirling five little girls were playing hide-and-seek. They were all in their fifth year and all named Mary.

She, whose turn it was to seek, stood against the tapestry, her eyes tightly shut, listening to the echo of running feet, counting softly under her breath: 'Ten . . . eleven . . . twelve . . .'

It was fair now to open her eyes, for they would all be out of sight. She would count up to twenty and then begin to search. Livy would give herself away by her giggling laughter. She always did. Flem would betray herself because she wished to please and thought it wrong that her beloved Mary should not succeed immediately in everything she undertook. Beaton, the practical one, and Seton, the quiet one, would not be so easy.

'Fifteen . . . sixteen . . .'

She looked up at the silken hangings. They were soft and beautiful because they came from France. Her mother spoke often of France – that fairest of lands. Whenever her mother spoke of France a tenderness came into her voice. In France

3

there was no mist, it seemed, and no rain; French flowers were more beautiful than Scottish flowers; and all the men were handsome.

In France Mary had a grandfather, a grandmother and six uncles. There were some aunts too but they were not so important. The uncles were all handsome giants who could do anything they wished. 'One day,' her mother often said, 'you may see them. I want them not to be ashamed of you.'

'Eighteen ... nineteen ... twenty ...' She was forgetting the game.

She gave a whoop of warning and began the search.

How silent the rooms were! They had chosen this part of the castle for hide-and-seek because no one came here at this hour of the day.

'I am coming!' she called. 'I am coming!' She stood still, listening to the sound of her voice. Which way had they turned – to the left or to the right?

She wandered through the rooms, her eyes alert. Was that a shadow behind the stool? Was that a bulge behind the hangings?

She had now come into one of the bedrooms and stood still, looking about her. She was sure she had heard a movement. Someone was in this room. Yes, there was no doubt. 'Who are you?' she called. 'Where are you? Come out. You are found.'

There was no answer. She ran about the room, lifting the curtains, looking behind the furniture. Someone was somewhere in this room, she felt sure.

She lifted the curtains about the bed and there was little Mary Beaton.

'Come out, Beaton,' commanded the little Queen. But

Beaton did not move. She just lay stretched out on her stomach, resting on her elbows, propped up on her hands.

Mary cried impatiently: 'Come out, I said.'

Still Beaton did not move.

The colour flamed into Mary's face. She remembered that she was Queen of Scotland and the Isles. Great men knelt before her and kissed her hand. Her guardians, those great Earls – Moray, Huntley and Argyle – never spoke to her without first kneeling and kissing her hand. And now fat little Beaton refused to do as she was bid.

'Beaton, you heard me! You're found. Come out at once. The Queen commands you.'

Then Mary understood, for Beaton could no longer contain her emotions; she stretched full out on the floor and began to sob heartbrokenly.

All Mary's anger disappeared. She immediately got on to her knees and crawled under the bed.

'Beaton . . . dear Beaton . . . why are you crying?'

Beaton shook her head and turned away; but Mary had her arms about her little friend.

'Dear Mary,' said the Queen.

'Dear Mary,' sobbed Beaton.

Rarely did the Queen call one of her four friends by their Christian names. It only happened in particularly tender moments and when they were alone with her, for Mary the Queen had said: 'How shall we know which one we mean, since we are all Maries?'

They did not speak for some time; they just lay under the bed, their arms about each other. The little Queen could be haughty; she could be proud; she could be very hot-tempered; but as soon as those she loved were in trouble she wished to

5

share that trouble and she would do all in her power to comfort them. They loved her, not because she was their Queen whom their parents and guardians had commanded them to love and serve, but because she made their troubles her own. It was not long before she was sobbing as brokenheartedly as Beaton, although she had no idea what Beaton's trouble was.

At last Mary Beaton whispered: 'It is . . . my dear uncle. I shall never see him again.'

'Why not?' asked Mary.

'Because men came and thrust knives into him . . . so he died.'

'How do you know? Who told you this?'

'No one told me. I listened.'

'They say it is wicked to listen.'

Beaton nodded sadly. But the Queen did not blame her for listening. How could she? She herself often listened.

'So he is gone,' said Mary Beaton, 'and I shall never see him again.'

She began to cry again and they clung to one another.

It was hot under the bed, but they did not think of coming out. Here they were close, shut in with their grief. Mary wept for Beaton, not for Beaton's uncle, the Cardinal – a stern man, who had often told the Queen how good she ought to be, how much depended on her, and what an important thing it was to be Queen of Scotland. Mary grew tired of such talk.

Now she had another picture of the Cardinal to set beside those she knew – a picture of a man lying on the floor with knives sticking into him. But she could not think of him thus for long. She could only remember the stern Cardinal who wished her to think continually of her duty to the Church.

They were still under the bed when the others found them.

They crawled out then, their faces stained with tears. Mary Fleming began to cry at once in sympathy.

'Men have stuck knives in Beaton's uncle,' announced Mary.

All the little girls looked solemn.

'I knew it,' said Flem.

'Then why didn't you tell?' asked the Queen.

'Your Majesty did not ask,' answered Flem.

Seton said quietly: 'Everyone won't cry. The King of England will be pleased. I heard my father say so.'

'I hate the King of England,' said Mary.

Seton took the Queen's hand and gave one of her solemn, frightened looks. 'You must not hate him,' she said.

'Mary can hate anyone!' said Flem.

'You should not hate your own father,' said Seton.

'He is not my father. My father is dead; he died while I was in my cradle and that is why I am the Queen.'

'If you have a husband,' persisted Seton, 'his father is yours. My nurse told me so. She told me that you are to marry the English Prince Edward, and then the King of England will be your father.'

The Queen's eyes flashed. 'I will not!' she cried. 'The English killed my father. I'll not marry the English Prince.' But she knew that it was easy to be bold and say before her Maries what she would and would not do; she was a Queen and had already been forced to do so many things against her will. She changed an unpleasant subject, for she hated to dwell on the unpleasant. 'Come,' she said, 'we will read and tell stories to make poor Beaton forget.'

They went to a window seat. Mary sat down and the others ranged themselves about her.

But the vast room seemed full of frightening shadows. It was not easy to chase away unpleasant thoughts. They could read and tell stories but they could not entirely forget that Mary Beaton's uncle had been stabbed to death and that one day the Queen would have to leave her childhood behind her and become the wife of some great prince who would be chosen for her.

The Queen-Mother noticed at once the traces of tears on her daughter's face. She frowned. Mary was too emotional. The fault must be corrected.

The little Queen's stern guardians would have noticed the marks of tears.

Since the Cardinal had been murdered there were only three guardians – Moray, Huntley and Argyle.

The Queen-Mother herself could have shed tears if she had been the woman to give way to them. The Cardinal was the one man in this turbulent land whom she had felt she could trust.

She looked about the assembly. There was the Regent, Arran, the head of the house of Hamilton, and of royal blood, longing to wear the crown of Scotland, Arran, who could not be trusted, whom she suspected of being the secret friend of the English, who had hoped to marry his son to the English King's daughter Elizabeth, and who doubtless had hopes of his son's wearing not only the crown of Scotland but that of England. There was false Douglas, so long exiled in England and only daring to return to Scotland after the death of James, Douglas, who had schemed with the King of England. He it was who had agreed, when in the hands of the English, to the marriage between the little Queen and Prince Edward. It was he who had come with soft words to the Queen-Mother setting forth the advantages of the match.

There was the giant Earl of Bothwell who had hopes of marrying the Queen-Mother. Was he loyal? How could she know who in this assembly of men was her friend? Scotland was a divided country, a wild country of clans. There was not in Scotland that loyalty to the crown which the English and French Kings commanded.

And I, she thought, am a woman – a Frenchwoman – and my child, not yet five, is the Queen of this alien land.

All eyes were on the little girl. What grace! What beauty! It was apparent at even so young an age. Even those hoary old chieftains were moved by the sight of her. How gracefully she stood! How nobly she held her head! She had all the Stuart beauty and that slight touch of something foreign which came from her French ancestors and which could enhance even the Stuart charm.

'God protect her in all she does,' prayed her mother.

She raised her eyes and caught the flashing ones of Lord James Stuart – Stuart eyes, heavy lidded, not unlike Mary's, beautiful eyes; and the proud tilt of her head denoted ambition. He was a boy yet in his early teens. But ambition smouldered there. Was he thinking even now: Had my father married my mother, I should be sitting in the chair of state and it would be my hand those men would kiss!

'God preserve my daughter from these Scots!' prayed the Queen-Mother.

Now the little Queen stood while the great chieftains came forward to kiss her hand. She smiled at them – at Arran, at Douglas. They looked so kind. Now came Jamie – dear Jamie. Jamie knelt before her but when he lifted his eyes to her face he gave her a secret wink, and she felt the laughter bubble up within her. It was rather funny that tall handsome Jamie should kneel before his little sister. She knew why of course, for she had demanded to know. It was because although his mother was not the Queen, the King, her father, had also been Jamie's father. Mary had other brothers and sisters. It was a pity, she had said to her Maries, that their mothers had not been queens, for it would have been fun to have a large family living about her – even though she was so much younger.

Now her mother would not allow her to stay.

'The Queen is very tired,' she said, 'and it is time she was abed.'

Mary wanted to stay. She wanted to talk to Jamie, to ask questions about the dead Cardinal.

But although they all kissed her hand and swore to serve her with their lives, they would not let her stay up when she wanted to. She knew she must show no annoyance. A Queen did not show her feelings. Her mother had impressed that upon her.

They all stood at attention while she walked out of the apartment to where her governess, Lady Fleming, was waiting for her.

'Our little Queen does not look very pleased with her courtiers,' said Janet Fleming, with one of her gay bursts of laughter.

'No, she is not,' retorted Mary. 'I wanted to stay and talk to Jamie. He winked when he kissed my hand.'

'Gentlemen winking at you already – and you the Queen!' cried Janet. Mary laughed. She was very fond of her governess who was also her aunt. For one thing red-haired Janet was very beautiful, and, although no longer in her first youth, was as full of fun as her young charge. She was a Stuart, being the natural daughter of Mary's grandfather; and little Mary Fleming was her daughter. She could be wheedled into letting the Queen have much of her own way, and Mary loved her dearly.

'He is only my brother,' she said.

'And should be thankful for that,' said Janet. 'Were he not, it would be an insult to the crown.'

She went on chattering while Mary was prepared for bed; it was all about dancing, clothes, sport and games, and when her mother came to the apartment Mary had temporarily forgotten the grief which Beaton had aroused in her.

The Queen-Mother dismissed all those who were in attendance on the Queen, so Mary knew that she was going to be reprimanded. It was a strange thing to be a queen. In public no one must scold; but it happened often enough in private.

'You have been crying,' accused Marie of Lorraine. 'The traces of tears were on your face when you received the lords.'

Fresh tears welled up in Mary's eyes at the memory. Poor Beaton! She remembered those desperate choking sobs.

'Did your women not wash your face before you came to the audience?'

'Yes, *Maman*, but it was such a big grief that it would not come off.'

The Queen-Mother softened suddenly and bent to kiss the little face. Mary laughed and her arms went up immediately about her mother's neck.

The Queen-Mother was somewhat disturbed. Mary was too demonstrative, always too ready to show her feelings. It was a charming trait, but not right, she feared, in a girl of such an exalted position.

'Now,' admonished Marie, 'that is enough. Tell me the reason for these tears.'

'Men have stuck knives into Beaton's uncle.'

So she knew! thought her mother. How could you keep terrible news from children? Mary had good reason to shed tears. Cardinal Beaton, upholder of the Church of Rome in a land full of heretics, had indeed been her friend. Who would protect her now from those ambitious men?

'You loved the Cardinal then, my daughter?'

'No.' Mary was truthful and spoke without thinking of the effect of her words. 'I did not much like him. I cried for poor Beaton.'

Her mother smoothed the chestnut hair, so soft yet so thick, which rippled back from the white forehead. Mary would always weep for the wrong reasons.

'I share little Beaton's grief,' said the Queen-Mother, 'for the Cardinal was not only a good man, he was a good friend.'

'Why did they kill him, *Maman*?'

'Because of Wishart's death . . . so they say.'

'Wishart, *Maman*? Who is he?'

What am I saying? the Queen-Mother asked herself. I forget she is only a baby. I must keep her from these tales of bloodshed and murder as long as I can.

But Mary was all eager curiosity now. She would find out in some way. Behind those deeply set, beautiful eyes there was an alert mind, thirsting for knowledge.

'Wishart was a heretic, my child, and he paid the penalty of heretics.'

'What penalty was that, *Maman*?'

'The death which is accorded heretics fell to him.'

'*Maman* . . . the flames!'

'How do you know these things?'

How did she know? She was not sure. Had one of her Maries

whispered it? Had she seen pictures in the religious books? She covered her face with her hands and the tears began to flow from her eyes.

'Mary! Mary, what has come over you? This is no way to behave.'

'I cannot bear it. He was a Scotsman, and they have burned him . . . they have burned him right up.'

Marie de Guise was alarmed. A little knowledge was so dangerous, and her daughter was so impulsive. What would she say next? She was precocious. How soon before some of these men began to corrupt her faith? They would do everything in their power to turn her into a heretic. It must not be. For the honour of the Guises, for the glory of the faith itself, it must not be.

'Listen to me, child. This man Wishart met his just reward, but because the Cardinal was a man of the true faith, Wishart's friends murdered him.'

'Then they did right! I would murder those who burned my friends.'

'A little while ago you were crying for the Cardinal.'

'No, no,' she interrupted. 'For dear Beaton.'

The Queen-Mother hesitated by the bedside. How could she explain all that was in her mind to a child of this one's age? How could she expect this baby mind to understand? Yet she must protect her from the influence of heretics. How did she know what James Stuart whispered to the child when he pretended to frolic with her? How did she know what Arran and Douglas plotted?

'Listen to me, Mary,' she said. 'There is one true Church in this world. It is the Church of Rome. At its head is the Pope, and it is the duty of all monarchs to serve the true religion.'

'And do they?'

'No, they do not. You must be careful what you say. If you do not understand, you must come to me. You must talk to no one about Wishart and the Cardinal . . . to *no one* . . . not even your Maries. You must remember that you are the Queen. You are but little yet, but to be a Queen is not to be an ordinary little girl who thinks of nothing but playing. We do not know who are our friends. The King of England wants you in England.'

'Oh, *Maman*, should I take my Maries with me?'

'Hush! You are not going to England.' The mother took her child in her arms and held her tightly. 'We do not want you to go to England. We want to keep you here with us.'

Mary's eyes were wide. 'Could they make me go?'

'Not unless . . .'

'Unless?'

'It were by force.'

Mary clasped her hands together. 'Oh, *Maman*, could they do that?'

'They could if they were stronger than we were.'

Mary's eyes shone. She could not help it. She loved excitement and, to tell the truth, she was a little tired of the castle where all the rooms were so familiar to her. She was never allowed to go beyond the castle grounds; and when she played there were always men-at-arms watching.

Her mother came to a sudden decision. The child must be made to understand. She must be shocked, if need be, into understanding.

'You are being foolish, child,' she said. 'Try to understand this. The worst thing that could happen to you would be for you to be taken to England.'

'Why?'

'Because if you went your life would be in danger.'

Mary caught her breath. She drew back in amazement.

It was the only way, thought the Queen-Mother. There was too much danger and the child must be made aware of it.

'The King of England has said that he wishes you to go to England to be brought up with his son.'

'You do not wish me to marry Edward?'

'I do not know . . . as yet.'

The Queen-Mother stood up and walked to the window. She looked across the country towards the south and thought of the ageing monarch of England. He had demanded the marriage for his son, and that Mary would be brought up in the Court of England as a future Queen of England. A good enough prospect. . . if one were dealing with any but the King of England. But there was a sinister clause in the agreement. If the little Queen of Scots died before reaching an age of maturity, the crown of Scotland was to pass to England. The royal murderer should never have a chance of disposing of Mary Stuart. How easy it would be! The little girl could fall victim to some pox . . . some wasting disease. No! He had murdered his second and fifth wives and, some said, was preparing to murder his sixth. He should not add the little Queen of Scots to his list of victims.

But how tell such things to a child of five years!

Marie de Guise turned back to the bed. 'Suffice it that I shall not allow you to go to England. Now . . . to sleep.'

But Mary did not sleep. She lay sleepless in the elaborate bed – the bed with the beautiful hangings sent to her by her glorious uncles – and thought of that ogre, the King of England, who might come at any moment to carry her off by force.

❀ ❀ ❀

Now the little Queen was aware of tension. She knew that the reason why she must never go beyond the castle walls without a strong guard was because it was feared she would be abducted.

She called the Maries together. Life was exciting. They must learn about it. Here they were shut up in Stirling Castle playing hide-and-seek, battledore and shuttlecock, reading, miming, playing games; while beyond the castle walls grown-up people played other games which were far more exciting.

One day when they were all at play, Flem, who happened to be near the window, called to them all. A messenger was riding into the courtyard, muddy and stained with the marks of a long ride, his jaded horse distressed and flecked with foam.

The children watched – five little faces pressed against the window. But the messenger stayed within the castle and they grew tired of waiting for him to come out, so they devised a new game of messengers. They took it in turn to be the messenger riding on a hobby horse, come from afar with exciting news concerning the King of England.

Later they were aware of glum faces about them; some of the serving men and women were in tears and the words Pinkie Cleugh were whispered throughout the castle.

Lady Fleming shut herself in her apartment and the five Maries heard her sobbing bitterly. Little Flem beat on the door in panic and called shrilly to be allowed to come in. Then Janet Fleming came out and looked blankly at the five little girls. Her own Mary ran to her, and Janet embraced her crying over and over again: 'My child . . . my little Mary . . . I still have you.' Then she went back into her room and shut the door, taking Flem with her.

Mary, left alone with her three companions, felt the tears splashing on to her velvet gown. She did not understand what had happened. She was wretched because her dear Aunt Janet and little Flem were in some trouble.

'What *is* Pinkie?' she demanded; but even Beaton did not know.

It was impossible to play after that. They sat in the window seat huddled together, waiting for they knew not what.

They heard a voice below the window, which said: 'They say Hertford's men are not more than six miles from the castle.'

Mary knew then that danger was close. Hertford, her tutors had told her, was the Lord Protector of England who ruled until Edward – that boy who might very well be her husband one day – was old enough to do so himself, for King Henry had died that very year. To Mary, Hertford was the monster now; he was the dragon breathing fire who would descend on the castle like the raiders on the border and carry the Queen of Scotland off to England as his prize.

That was a strange day – a queer brooding tension filled the castle. Everyone was waiting for something to happen. She did not see her mother that evening and her governess was not present when she went to her apartment for the night.

At last she slept and was awakened suddenly by dark figures about her bed. She started up, thinking: He has come. Hertford has come to take me to England.

But it was not Hertford. It was her mother, and with her were the Earl of Arran, Lord Erskine and Livy's father, Lord Livingstone, so that she knew this was a very important occasion.

'Wake up,' said her mother.

'Is it time to get up?'

'It is an hour past midnight, but you are to get up. You are going away on a journey.'

'What! At night?'

'Do not talk so much. Do as you are told.'

This must be very important, for otherwise even her mother would not have talked to her thus in the presence of these noble lords. She had to be a little girl now; she had to obey without question. This was no time for ceremony.

Lady Fleming – her eyes still red with weeping – came forward with her fur-trimmed cloak.

'Quickly,' said Lady Fleming. 'There is no time to be lost. If your lordships will retire I will get my lady dressed.'

While Mary was hustled into her clothes she asked questions. 'Where are we going? Why are we going now? It's the night . . . the dead of night . . .'

'There is no time for questions.'

It should have been an exciting adventure, but she was too tired to be conscious of most of that journey. She was vaguely aware of the smells of the night – a mingling of damp earth and misty air. Through the haze of sleep she heard the continued thudding of horses' hoofs. Voices penetrated her dreams. 'Pinkie . . . Pinkie . . . Hertford close on our heels. Cattle driven over the Border. Rape . . . murder . . . fire . . . blood.'

Words to make a grown-up person shudder, but to a child of five they were little more than words.

Now she was in a boat and she heard the sound of oars dipping into water. It became suddenly calm and peaceful as though there was no longer the desperate need for haste.

The violent bump of the boat as it touched land awakened her thoroughly. 'Where are we?' she cried. .

'Hush . . . hush!' she was told. *'Maman* is here.' That was her mother talking to her as though she were indeed a baby.

She was taken up and placed in the arms of someone clothed in black. Over his head was a cowl. He might have frightened her had his eyes not been gentle and his voice kind.

'Sleep, little one,' he said. 'Sleep on, little Queen. You have come safely to Inchmahome.'

Inchmahome! The melodious word took the place in her dreams of Pinkie Cleugh and blood . . . murder . . . rape. Inchmahome . . . and peace.

❁ ❁ ❁

It seemed to Mary that she lived for a long time in the island monastery. At first there was much she missed, but it was not long before her four Maries arrived on the island to bear her company. Lady Fleming stayed with her, and because there was need to comfort her aunt, Mary herself was comforted. Lord Fleming had been killed at the terrible battle of Pinkie Cleugh. He was one of fourteen thousand Scots who had died that day.

Mary wept bitterly. First Beaton's uncle and now Flem's father. And both had been killed. There had been no need for either of them to die. 'Why,' she demanded angrily of Lady Fleming, 'could they not all love each other and be friends?'

'It is the accursed English!' cried Lady Fleming. 'They want Scotland for their own. They have killed my Malcolm. I hate the English.'

'But it was not the English who killed Cardinal Beaton,' said Mary.

'They were behind that murder too. They are a heretic people.'

Mary put her arms round her governess and reminded her that she had five sons and there was big James to be Lord Fleming now.

Janet Fleming took the lovely face in her hands and kissed it. 'When you grow up,' she said, 'many will love you. You have that in you which attracts love. There will be men to love you . . .'

Janet's eyes brightened and her sorrow lifted a little, for she could not help knowing that there would still be men to love Janet Fleming too. It was true that she was no longer young but her appeal seemed ageless. She had been born with it and it did not diminish at all. Here in the monastery she would let her grief subside; her wounds would heal and when she again went into the world she would be her jaunty pleasure-loving self, attracting men perhaps because she herself was so easily attracted by them.

So they were able to comfort each other, and the brief rest on the peaceful island was something they were both to remember in the years to come and look back upon with a certain longing.

Mary grew accustomed to the life of the island. She had soon, with her little friends about her, made a miniature court for herself. She was watched with delight – even by the monks – for in her black silk gown, ornamented by the brilliant tartan scarf, held together by the gold agraffe which was engraved with the arms of Scotland and Lorraine, her lovely hair loose about her shoulders, she was a charming sight.

At first the monks in their musty black had not attracted her; she had been startled to come upon them gliding through the cold bare rooms. But when she grew to know them she found a gentleness in them which appealed to her. They answered her only when she spoke to them, but they did not even speak to each other unless it was absolutely necessary.

It was like a world of which she had dreamed – a strange world shut in by granite walls. The bells rang continually, for life on the island in the lake of Menteith was divided into periods, by the bells. Mary went daily with her four friends to the great room with the stained-glass windows; there she prayed to the saints and confessed her sins.

Her curiosity had to be satisfied, and she and the four Maries could not be content until they had wheedled the secret from Lady Fleming.

'Why are we here, Aunt Janet?' asked Mary.

'It is a rest for me . . . after what I suffered.'

'Did they take me out of bed at midnight for that?' asked Mary scornfully.

'It is because of the English,' said Beaton.

'Hertford's men came close to the castle,' added Mary. 'We heard of that.'

Poor Janet! She could never be discreet. 'Well, I do know,' she admitted, 'but nothing would prise it from me.' But the five Maries could, and in a short time Janet was saying: 'If I tell you, you must never mention it to anyone . . . anyone at all.'

She admitted that they had been sent to Inchmahome to escape the English. 'Your mother has plans for you,' she added.

'What plans?' demanded Mary.

'Plans made with the French, so they say.'

'With my uncles?'

'They send messengers to her continually. There are some, my little Queen, who would like to see you sent to England, but your mother has other plans.'

Lady Fleming could not be induced to say what these plans were, so the five little girls, who knew her well, decided that she did not know and that it was no use pestering her further.

When Mary was in her room, which was as bare as a cell, she knelt before the little altar there, but instead of praying she was thinking about plans with the French.

She rose from her knees and studied the ornament her mother had given her and which she always wore to fasten her scarf. Her mother had explained the significance of the emblems on the ornament. The silver eagles were of Lorraine, the double cross was of Jerusalem; and the lilies were of Anjou and Sicily. This was the emblem of Guise and Lorraine. Her mother had said: 'Always remember the emblem when you are afraid or when you are about to do something shameful. It is the emblem of Guise and Lorraine.'

And Guise and Lorraine was France! What had Lady Fleming meant by plans made with the French?

Wherever I go, said Mary to herself, I shall take my four Maries with me. I shall never, never be parted from them.

After a while she grew to love the life of the monastery. There was so much to discover and those black-clad men were so ready to teach. Here she learned to speak and read in French, Spanish and Italian as well as Latin. She could play as she wished in the grounds about the monastery and there was no one to guard her and her little friends. They could go wherever they wished as long as they remained on the island.

Slowly the days passed and it seemed to all the little girls that they lived for a very long time on the island of Inchmahome.

Then one day when they were wandering close to the lake's edge they saw men rowing to the island. They ran back to tell Lady Fleming what they had seen. Mary was in a flutter of excitement because she believed that the English had come to take her away.

The Abbot himself came running in consternation to the water's edge. Mary Fleming had taken the girls into the monastery, but they could not resist watching from a window.

They saw the Abbot was smiling and bowing to the men.

'English!' cried Lady Fleming excitedly. 'They are not English. They are Scottish noblemen. Depend upon it they have come to take us home.'

She was right.

Lady Fleming put the cloak about the dainty little figure and called to Flem to bring the brooch which was emblazoned with the arms of Guise and Lorraine.

'Back to something a little more gay, the saints be praised!' said Lady Fleming.

But oddly enough Mary was not sure whether she really wanted to go. She had now so many friends in this quiet retreat. She thought of the quiet common room in which she and the four Maries had so often sat together taking lessons from the brothers; she thought of the freedom of wandering on the island, of the peace and silence which had frightened them at first but which they had grown to love.

She wept when she said good-bye to some of the brothers who had become her favourites; she threw her arms about them in a most unqueenly fashion and buried her face in the musty robes which had formerly repelled her.

'Farewell to you all,' she cried. 'Farewell, dear brothers. Farewell, dear Abbot. Farewell, dear Inchmahome.'

She stood waving to them as the boat carried her party across the lake.

Her mother was waiting for her at Stirling Castle. With her were the Lords Lindsay, Livingstone, Montrose and Erskine. And there was another – a stranger.

He was tall and his beard was curled as she had never seen a beard curled before; his hands moved expressively; his eyes flashed and sparkled as they rested on the little Queen.

'This is an emissary from the King of France,' said the Queen-Mother, and as she spoke those words she seemed taller and prouder than ever before. 'He comes with greetings from the King and my brothers.'

Mary was enchanted with the newcomer. She decided he was very pretty and unlike any man she had seen before.

He sank to his knees very gracefully, not as the Scottish nobles knelt; he took her hand and raised it to his lips. 'Your Majesty's most humble servant,' he said. He continued to hold her hand.

Then he rose and turned to the Queen-Mother. 'Forgive me, Madame,' he said in French, but Mary's French was good enough to understand him, 'I am struck dumb by such enchanting beauty.'

The Queen-Mother was smiling. She called him Monsieur L'Amiral. There was much talk and laughter and the little Queen saw that other strangers had come into the chamber, and they too had curled beards and gay tongues and spoke quickly – far too quickly – in the French tongue.

She retired to her apartment after a while, but no sooner was she there than her mother entered. Mary had never seen her look so excited.

She too talked French, and so rapidly that Mary had to beg her to speak more slowly.

'This will not do,' cried Marie de Guise. 'What will your uncles say if you cannot speak French fluently? You must do so before you step for the first time on the soil of France.'

Marie de Guise's eyes had filled with tears and, in spite of the fact that there were others present, she abandoned ceremony and taking her daughter in her arms she held her tightly.

Then Mary knew that she was to leave for France – not in the distant future – and that these strange men had come to escort her there.

❀ ❀ ❀

There was a bustle of preparation; there was a packing of baggage; and all this was done at the utmost speed.

Now and then the Queen-Mother found time to talk to her daughter, to tell her of the wonderful future which was being planned for her. 'You are going to my people. The Most Christian King himself will be your father. The Queen of France will be as your mother; and your grandfather, the great Duke of Guise, and your grandmother, who was Antoinette de Bourbon before she became Madame de Guise, will be there, with your uncles, to greet you.'

She had to make this child understand the importance of what was about to happen to her. She was the Queen of Scotland, but a greater throne was coming her way. His Most Christian Majesty was offering her the crown of France through marriage with his son. A great and glorious future was to be hers, and the child would be worthy of it. Surely her beauty must startle even the French.

'Listen to me carefully. The English are close at hand; they have captured some of our towns. They know that our kind friend, the King of France, offers you marriage with his son – and that is the very thing they are anxious shall not take place because they want you for their King Edward. Henri Deux, the King of France has sent ships to Scotland. When we go to Dumbarton you will see those mighty ships, and they have braved the storms and the English fleet to come to us. King Henri is our friend. He is anxious that there shall be great friendship between his country and ours. He has sent these ships to take you back to France.'

'And shall you come with me?'

'I cannot come, my darling. I must stay here. But you will have many of your friends with you. All your little Maries shall go. I shall come to visit you. The King – your new father – will not wish you to be lonely. He wants you to be very happy.'

Mary was too excited to be afraid. She was going to the most beautiful country in the world. But when she looked into her mother's face she was immediately sad. Poor *Maman*, she would stay behind. Poor *Maman*, who must also lose her daughter.

Mary threw her arms about her mother's neck.

'I will not go, dearest *Maman*. I will stay with you.'

'That is nonsense, my child.'

'But you will be unhappy if I go. I would rather never see France than make you unhappy.'

'Why, you foolish child, it makes me the happiest Queen in the world to know you go to France. It is what I wish for you. I shall come to see you soon. The King says I must. He is very kind.'

'I wonder what the Dauphin is like.'

'François? He is the same age as yourself . . . or almost. Your birthday is in December and his in January. Some Queens have to marry men old enough to be their grandfathers and others have to marry those young enough to be their children.'

Mary began to laugh. 'That must be very funny.'

'Royal marriages are never funny.'

'No, *Maman*,' said Mary seriously.

'The Dauphin is not very strong. You will have to be careful not to tire him in your play.'

'Yes, *Maman*.'

Already Mary had decided that she would make the care of the Dauphin her special task.

Her mother took her on board the ship. With them were the four Maries – now very solemn and demure in their heavy capes. Lady Fleming bustled about them, her lovely face flushed with excitement, forgetful of her widowhood, keenly aware of the admiration directed towards herself even when it came from the humblest sailors.

The Queen-Mother made her daughter walk before her on to the King's galley. Behind them came all those who were to form part of the little Queen's entourage in her new country. There would be so many of them, Mary thought, that it would be almost like being at home.

As they stepped aboard, accompanied by Admiral Villegaignon, a tall man came towards them and knelt before the Queen so that his eyes were on a level with hers. Mary knew him, for he was the Sieur de Brézé, the French King's ambassador at the Scottish Court.

'Your Majesty's servant,' he said. 'My master has commanded me to act as your French governor until I have conducted you safely to his presence.'

She answered in her high piping French which, with its faint Scottish accent, delighted all these Frenchmen: 'Rise, Monsieur de Brézé. It give me great pleasure to greet you.'

She held out her hand, from the wrist of which the circles of infant fat had now almost, but not quite, disappeared. He kissed it, and again she was aware of that admiration which all the French seemed to show when they looked her way.

He stood up and she said: 'What does this mean? What will you do as my French governor? Will you teach me?'

'There is only one thing I wish to teach Your Majesty, and that is that all France will take one look at you and fall in love with you.'

It was extravagant talk such as she was unaccustomed to hear, and she was a little bewildered, but delighted all the same. It was true, she was sure, that the French were all that she had been led to believe.

Her mother was smiling, so her French must have passed the test.

Now the Queen-Mother spoke. 'Monsieur de Brézé, I shall wish to know all that happens during the journey. I shall wish to know as soon as possible that my daughter has arrived safely in France.'

He bowed gracefully. 'Madame, I will protect your daughter with my life. Messengers shall be despatched to you; they shall reach you if they have to sink every English ship to do so.'

How vehemently they spoke, thought Mary. How they smiled! How their eyes flashed and how their hands moved with their voices! Strange men! Monsieur de Brézé smelt of violets, or was it roses? His golden beard curled enchantingly. She admired him every bit as much as he admired her.

How happy she could have been if she had not had to part from her mother! But Queen Marie was smiling bravely, although at the last she let affection triumph over ceremony. She held her daughter tightly in her arms, and Mary saw the tears glistening in her eyes.

'The saints preserve you,' were her last words. 'Remember all I have taught you. Never forget that you are a Queen, my dearest, and all will be well.'

'Good-bye, dearest *Maman*.'

'I shall see you soon, I feel sure. And now . . . good-bye.'

The Queen-Mother was escorted off the ship. She stood on the shore gazing after the French fleet, at the fluttering standard bearing the arms of Valois. How small the child looked, wrapped in her heavy cloak, her eyes fixed on the mother she was leaving behind her.

Am I right in letting her go? anxiously wondered Marie de Guise in those moments. What will become of my little one? The King has promised that she shall be as his daughter, but how much can Kings be trusted? What of the Court of France? Is it the right place in which to bring up a child? It was scarcely the most virtuous of courts, but she had heard from her relations that there had been a tightening of morals since the death of François. Was there still that perpetual love-making, seeming so decorous and charming – scented notes bearing verses of poetic merit, delicate compliments overlaying orgies and promiscuity like a gossamer veil? Henri was more *sérieux* than his father had been, and Diane de Poitiers was his faithful mistress, but was Henri's Court so very different from that of his father?

And Mary – so warm-hearted, so eager to love all, so French in many ways – how would she fare in such a Court? Was it right to pass her over to voluptuous Paris? Was that better than sending her to murderous London? But of course it was! In France were her own family, and they were close to the throne. The house of Guise and Lorraine would look after its own.

Marie de Guise stood erect, fighting back tears while the ships set sail; she watched them until she could see them no more. Then she returned to her apartments in Dumbarton and spent long hours on her knees praying that the royal ship and its escort might escape both perilous storms and the English.

It was a wonderful journey. The wind rose and buffeted the ship, but the five Maries, finding themselves free from restraint, first walked sedately about the deck, then ran, calling to each other, taking off their satin snoods and laughing as the wind caught their hair and flung it back across their faces.

Mary's half-brothers, Lord James who was Prior of St. Andrews, Lord John who was Prior of Coldingham, and Lord Robert who was Prior of Holyrood, stood together watching the children.

'Jamie! Jamie!' called Mary. 'Is it not wonderful to be at sea, eh, Robert, eh John?'

The brothers smiled at their little sister, but there was a brooding look in the eyes of Lord James. He could not forget that he, a young man who was strong and healthy, was set aside because he was a bastard. He was merely a rich beneficiary of the Church instead of a King.

The Lords Livingstone and Erskine paced the deck in quiet conversation.

'It will not do to trust them too far,' Livingstone was saying.

'Indeed not,' agreed Erskine.

'Artus de Brézé – ambassador and now the Queen's governor – what manner of man is he? A jewelled perfumed dummy!'

'The Fleming woman seems to be taken with him and cannot hide it even under the eyes of her son – and she but recently a widow.'

Artus de Brézé was in his turn laughing at the Scotsmen. Such gaunt features, such ruddy skins. Paris would be amused with them. Nor were the women too handsome. The little girls were charming, especially the *Reinette*. She was someone whom the French would appreciate – a beauty and aware of it already. But the women – with the exception of Lady Fleming – were of small interest. There would be little trouble on their account.

He wondered whether he could seduce the red-haired lady during the voyage. It would be rather piquant. At night with the darkness all about them, on the high seas, in danger of an English enemy sighting them at any moment. A Scot and a King's daughter at that! Very amusing! thought the Sieur de Brézé.

Now the little one was standing beside him.

'Monsieur!'

It was a pleasure to hear her speak; it was a delight to look into the upturned face at those long eyes thickly lashed, that soft mouth which was meant for tenderness. He could not help but picture her – say in ten years' time.

'I am at Your Majesty's service. You must not cease to call on me at any hour of the day and night. It will be my pleasure to see that your smallest wish is granted.'

She laughed, showing her pretty teeth. 'Ah, Monsieur de Brézé, you say such nice things.'

'I say only that which the beauty of Your Majesty impels and inspires me to say.'

'Monsieur de Brézé, if you would lift me up I could sit on the rail, and that is what I wish to do.'

She was light, and she laughed as he lifted her.

'Why do you regard me in that way, Monsieur?'

'Your Majesty is an enchantress. I see it already.'

'What is an enchantress?'

'It is what you are and what you will increasingly become.'

'Is it a good thing for a Queen to be?'

'It is a good thing for anyone to be – man or woman, queen or commoner. Tell me, what do you think of us Frenchmen?'

'I love you all. And do you think the King of France will love me?'

'He could not fail to do so.'

'And the Queen?'

'The Queen also. The King has said: "The little Queen shall be as my daughter." He says that before he has seen you; but when his eyes fall on you, my little Queen, he will say much more. Where is your governess?'

'The sea has made her ill and she will not show herself.'

'You must tell her that I am desolate.'

'Desolate, Monsieur? But you look so happy.'

'I am desolate to know that she suffers. Will you tell her that?'

'Yes. Put me down and I will tell her at once.'

When she was on her feet she retreated a pace or two. She said with a smile: 'I shall tell her that you *say* you are desolate, and look so happy when you say it.'

She started to walk away.

'Your Majesty,' he called. 'I will explain.'

She stopped, turned and regarded him gravely. Then she said demurely: 'My mother and my guardians have told me that we must quickly learn the ways of the French . . . all of us.'

He watched her skipping away. So beautiful! So young! And already with some knowledge of the ways of the world.

The French galleys were in sight of land, and the dangerous journey was nearly over. Mary stood with Lady Fleming, her three brothers and the four Maries, watching the land as they approached it. None of them was more relieved than Lady Fleming that the journey was over. She declared she had come near to dying. So ill had she been that she had implored Monsieur de Villegaignon to let her go ashore when they were within a few miles of the coast of England; she had felt then that she would rather die at the hands of the English than become a victim of the sea. Monsieur de Villegaignon had forgotten his French manners and peremptorily told her that she should not land; she should go to France or drown by the way. What a mercy it had been that they had brought Scottish navigators with them. These men, accustomed to stormy weather and rocky coasts, had been invaluable during the voyage.

And now, praise the saints, thought Lady Fleming, the peril was wellnigh over.

Mary was unable to feel anything but excitement. She had almost forgotten the terror of seeing English ships on the horizon. It seemed a long time ago when her brothers had stood about her with Lords Erskine and Livingstone, determined to defend her should the need arise. The saints had answered their prayers, and the wind had turned in their favour, so that they were able to speed across the rough waters until the English dropped below the horizon. Now here they were in sight of France, and their galley was drawing in to the little Brittany port of Roscoff.

As soon as she stepped ashore Mary was made aware of the magnitude of the welcome which was to be given to her.

The little port was festooned with gay banners, and the people had come for miles round to line the shore and shout a welcome to *la Reinette*. In this they were obeying the orders of the King, who had said: 'Welcome the little Queen of Scots as though she were already my daughter.'

And when these people saw the little girl – so small and dainty – with her four attendants the same age as herself, in their fur-lined capes, they were enchanted.

'*Vive la petite Reine!*' they cried; and Mary, sensing their admiration, smiled and bowed so prettily that they cried out that she was delightful, this little girl who had come to them from the savages.

The progress across France began. From Roscoff the procession made its way to Nantes, Mary sometimes riding on a small horse, sometimes carried in a litter; and each town through which they passed had its welcome for her. Accustomed to the more restrained greetings of her own countrymen and women, Mary was enchanted by the gaiety of these French who were so ready to drink to her health and make a fête-day of her short stay in their towns or villages.

At Nantes a gaily decorated barge was awaiting her and she, in what proved to be a glorious river pageant, sailed with her entourage up the river Loire through the villages and vine-yards of Anjou and Touraine, where the people lined the river bank to call a welcome to her. When she left the barge and went ashore in her litter, the people crowded round her, their eyes flashing, laughter bubbling from their lips, and she thought them the merriest people she had ever seen. How could she be homesick for those castles which had been nothing more than prisons! Here the people were not only gay but friendly. It was an informal pageant in which the labourers from the vineyard, the tillers of the soil, and plump peasant women, joined merrily.

She had never witnessed anything like it and she was as delighted with the French as the French were with her.

But when they left the barge at Tours, the journey became more of a royal progress, for waiting to greet her was her grandfather Claude Duc de Guise, and her grandmother the Duchesse was with him – she who before her marriage had been Antoinette de Bourbon.

These great personages received her with much ceremony, but when they were alone her grandmother took the child on her knee and embraced her. 'You are indeed a pretty child,' she said; and her eyes gleamed, as did those of the Duke her husband, for the fortunes of the mighty house of Guise and Lorraine rested on this dainty child's shoulders.

'I shall write and tell your uncle François that he will love you,' went on her grandmother.

'Is my uncle François not here then, Grandmother?'

'No, my child, he is much occupied with the affairs of the country. So are his brothers. But they will be delighted, all of them, to hear what a dear little girl you are.'

Her grandfather talked to her too. He reminded her that while she was Queen of Scotland she was also a member of the noble house of Guise and Lorraine.

'We stand together, my little one. One for all and all for each. That is the rule of our family. Soon you will be meeting your uncles. Your Uncle Charles will keep you under his wing.'

Mary listened gravely. She had heard most of it already from her mother.

The Duchesse travelled with the party by river to Orléans where they disembarked and continued by road through Chartres.

'You will be housed,' the Duchesse told Mary, 'with the royal children – the Dauphin and his little sister Elisabeth. The little Princess Claude and Prince Louis are babies still. The King has decided that you shall live at the palace of Saint-Germain as soon as it is sweetened. Meanwhile you will stay near by at Carrières.'

'When shall I see the King and Queen?' asked Mary.

'Ah, you go too fast. The Court is at Moulins, so to begin with you will make the acquaintance of the royal children. The King wishes the meeting to be informal. You understand, my child? The King loves children and thinks tenderly of them – not only his own but others also. He has decided that you shall come to know the children with a complete absence of ceremony. He is anxious that you should love each other. You are to share a room with Madame Elisabeth. She is only three and a half. He hopes that you will be particularly fond of the Dauphin.'

'I shall, I know I shall. I am going to take great care of him.'

The Duchesse laughed. 'Ah, my little one, you have the proud spirit of a Guise. So the Queen of a savage land will take great care of the heir of France, eh?'

'But he is younger than I,' protested Mary. 'And I hear that he is not strong.'

Madame de Guise patted her shoulder. 'You are right, my child. You must take every care of him, for on him will depend your future . . . and that of others. Let it not be too obvious care. Let it be loving tenderness. I know you will be a credit to us. There is another matter. The King is pleased to allow your four little friends to be with you, but he wants them to go away after the first few days at Carrières. No! Do not be afraid. The King has heard of your love for them and he would not for the world part you from them. But for a little while he wishes you to be alone in the royal nursery with François and Elisabeth. He wants no other children to come between you for a little while.'

'It will only be for a little while?'

'For a very little while. You need have no fear, dear child. You will be happy in our royal nurseries.'

'The King is a very good king,' said Mary. 'The Queen . . . is she beautiful?'

'All queens are beautiful,' said the Duchesse lightly.

'Does she too say that she wants me to love François and Elisabeth?'

'The Queen agrees with the King in all things.'

Mary was intelligent. She noticed that the manner of her grandmother changed when she mentioned the Queen of France. Why? wondered Mary.

She was longing to see the Dauphin and his little sister; she was longing to see the King; but oddly enough, as she explained to her Maries, she felt more *curious* about the Queen.

The meeting between the children was unceremonious as it had been intended it should be. In the big room at Carrières

Mary went forward to greet them. With them were their governor and governess, the Maréchal d'Humières and Madame d'Humières. With Mary were her grandmother and the members of her suite.

The Dauphin stared at Mary. She was taller than he was. His legs were thin and spindly and it seemed as though the weight of his body would break them. His head seemed too large for the rest of him and he was very pale.

Mary's tenderness – always ready to be aroused – overwhelmed her. She knelt and kissed his hand. He stared at her wonderingly; and rising she put her arms about him and kissed him. 'I have come to love you and be your playmate,' she said.

The little boy immediately responded to her embrace.

Mary broke away and glanced with some apprehension at her grandmother. They had said no ceremony, but had she been too impulsive in embracing the Dauphin?

The Duchesse was far from displeased. She had noticed the little boy's response. She glanced at Madame d'Humières. What a pity that the King is not here to see this! that glance implied. He would be quite enchanted.

Madame d'Humières nodded in agreement. It was always wise to agree with the Guises, providing such agreement would not be frowned on by the King's mistress.

Mary had turned to the three-and-a-half-year-old Elisabeth, a frail and pretty little girl; and what a pleasure it was for the Duchesse to see a Princess of France kneel to her granddaughter! Madame Elisabeth knew what was expected of her. Had not the King said: 'Mary Stuart shall be as one of my own children, but because she is a queen she shall take precedence over my daughter.'

Mary looked into the face of the little girl and, because the child was so small and because she had embraced her brother, the little Queen could not resist embracing the Princess also.

Her grandmother advanced towards the group, at which the two royal children seemed to move closer to Mary as though expecting she would protect them from her important relative.

But the Duchesse merely smiled at them and turned to the Maréchal and Madame d'Humières.

'So charming, is it not?' she said. 'The King will be delighted. They love each other on sight. Let us leave them together. Then they will be more natural, and when the King slips in unceremoniously he will be delighted with our way of bringing them together.'

When Mary was alone with the two children, she took a hand of each and led them to the window seat.

'I have just come here,' she said. 'First I came in a big ship. Then I rode in a litter. Then I came in another ship. I have come from far . . . far away.'

The Dauphin held her hand in his and clung to it when she would have released it. Elisabeth regarded her gravely. Neither of the French children had ever seen anyone quite like her. Her flashing eyes, her vivacious manners, her strange dress and her queer way of talking overwhelmed and fascinated them. Elisabeth's gravity broke into a quiet smile and the Dauphin lifted his shoulders until they almost touched his big head; and all the time he insisted that his hand should remain in that of the newcomer.

He was already telling himself that he was never going to let her go. He was going to keep her with him for ever.

Mary had lived at Carrières for two weeks. She was the Queen of the nurseries. Elisabeth accepted her leadership in everything they did; François asked nothing but to be her devoted slave.

She was a little imperious at times, for after all she was older than they were; she was so much cleverer. She read to them; she would sit on the window seat her arm about François while Elisabeth tried to follow the words in the book. She told them stories and of games she had played with her four Maries with whom she hoped soon to be reunited; she told of the island of Inchmahome in the lake of Menteith whither she had gone one dark night, wrapped in a cloak, fleeing from the wicked English. She told of the long journey across the seas, of the high waters and the roaring winds and of how the English ships had sighted hers on the horizon, for of course they were on the prowl looking for her.

These adventures made her an exciting person; her age made her such a wise one; and her vitality, so sadly lacking in the French children, made her an entertaining companion; but perhaps it was her beauty which strengthened her power.

Thus it was when one day there came into the nurseries unannounced a tall man with a beard which was turning to silver; he was dressed in black velvet and there were jewels on his clothes. With him came a lady – the loveliest Mary had ever seen.

The children immediately ran forward and threw themselves at the man. This was one of the occasions to which they looked forward. If there had been others present it would have been necessary to bow and kiss hands, but this was one of those pleasurably anticipated occasions when the two came alone.

'Papa! Papa!' cried François.

The big man picked him up and the lady kissed François' cheek.

Elisabeth was holding fast to his doublet and there was love and confidence in the way her little fingers curled about the black velvet.

'This will not do! This will not do!' cried the man. 'My children, what of our guest?'

Then he lowered François to the floor. François immediately caught the lady's hand and they all advanced to the Queen of Scots who had fallen to her knees, for she knew that the big man with the silvering beard was Henri, King of France.

'Come,' he said in a deep rumbling voice which Mary thought was the kindest she had ever heard, 'let us look at you. So you are Mary Stuart from across the seas?'

'At Your Majesty's service,' said Mary.

He laid his hand on her head and turned to the lady beside him. 'I think we shall be pleased with our new daughter,' he said.

Mary flushed charmingly and turned to kneel to the lady. She took the slim white hand and kissed the great diamond on her finger.

'Yes, indeed,' said the lady, 'our new daughter enchants me.'

'I am happy,' said Mary, in her charming French, 'to know that I have not displeased Your Majesties.'

They laughed and the Dauphin said: 'Mary has come across the sea. She came in a boat and then in another boat and she reads to us.'

The King stooped then and picked up the boy, swinging

41

him above his head. 'You must borrow Mary's rosy looks, my son,' he said.

Elisabeth was quietly waiting to be picked up and kissed, and when it was her turn she put her arms about her father's neck and kissed him; then she buried her face in his beard.

The beautiful lady, whom Mary assumed to be the Queen, said: 'Come and kiss me, Mary.'

Mary did so.

'Why, what a fine girl you are!' The soft white fingers patted Mary's cheeks. 'The King and I are glad you have come to join our children.' She smiled fondly at the King who returned the smile with equal fondness over the smooth head of Elisabeth. In a sudden rush of affection for them both, Mary kissed their hands afresh.

'I am so happy,' she said, 'to be your new daughter.'

The King sat in the big state chair which was kept in the apartment for those occasions when he visited his children. He took Mary and the Dauphin on his knees. The lady sat on a stool, holding Elisabeth.

The King told them that there was to be a grand wedding at the Court. It was Mary's uncle who was to be married.

'Now, my children, Mary's uncle, the Duc d'Aumale, must have a grand wedding, must he not? He would be displeased if the Dauphin did not honour him by dancing at his wedding.'

The Dauphin's eyes opened wide with horror. 'Papa . . . no!' he cried. 'I do not want to dance at the wedding.'

'You do not want to dance at a fine wedding! You do, Mary, do you not?'

'Yes, I do,' said Mary. 'I love to dance.' She put out her hand and took that of the Dauphin. 'I will teach you to dance with me, François. Shall I?'

The grown-ups exchanged glances and the King said in rapid French which Mary could not entirely understand: 'This is the most beautiful, the most charming child I ever saw.'

❊ ❊ ❊

The children were alone. Mary was explaining to the Dauphin that there was nothing to be frightened of in the dance. It was easy to dance. It was delightful to dance.

'And the King wishes it,' said Mary. 'And as he is the best King in the world, you must please him.'

The Dauphin agreed that this was so.

While they practised the dance, Elisabeth sat on a cushion watching them. The door silently opened, but Mary did not hear it, so intent was she on the dance. She noticed first the change in Elisabeth who had risen to her feet. The smile had left Elisabeth's face. She seemed suddenly to have become afraid. Now the Dauphin had seen what Elisabeth saw. He too stood very still, like a top-heavy statue.

There was a woman standing in the doorway, a woman with a pale flat face and expressionless eyes. Mary took an immediate dislike to her, for she had brought something into the room which Mary did not understand and which was repellent to her. The woman was dressed without magnificence and Mary assumed that she was a noblewoman of minor rank. Hot-tempered as she was, she let her anger rise against the intruder.

As Queen of the nursery, the spoiled charge of easy-going Lady Fleming, the petted darling of almost everyone with whom she had come into contact since her arrival in this country, fresh from her triumph with the King, she said quickly: 'Pray do not interrupt us while we practise.'

The woman did not move. She laughed suddenly and

43

unpleasantly. The little French children had stepped forward and knelt before her. Over their heads she regarded the Queen of Scots.

'What will you do, Mademoiselle?' asked the woman. 'Are you going to turn me out of my nurseries?'

'Madame,' said Mary, drawing herself to her full height, 'it is the Queen of Scotland to whom you speak.'

'Mademoiselle,' was the reply, 'it is the Queen of France to whom you speak.'

'N . . . no!' protested Mary. But the kneeling children had made her aware of the unforgivable mistake she had made. She was terrified. She would be sent back to Scotland for such behaviour. She had been guilty not only of a great breach of good manners; she had insulted the Queen of France.

'Madame,' she began, 'I humbly beg . . .'

Again the harsh laugh rang out; but Mary scarcely heard it as she knelt before the Queen, first pale with horror, then red with shame.

'We all make mistakes,' said Catherine de' Medici, 'even Queens of such great countries as Scotland. You may rise. Let me look at you.'

As Mary obeyed she realised that there were two Queens: one lovely and loving who came with the King, who kissed the children and called them hers and behaved in every way as though she were their mother, and another who came alone, who frightened them and yet, it seemed, was after all their mother and the true Queen of France.

🏵 Chapter II 🏵

To Mary, life in those first months was full of pleasure. It was true there were times when the Queen of France would come silently into the nursery, laugh her sudden loud laughter, make her disconcerting remarks, and when little François and Elisabeth would, while displaying great decorum, shrink closer to Mary as though asking her to protect them. But Mary was gay by nature and wished to ignore that which was unpleasant.

Often King Henri and Madame Diane came to the nursery to play with them, to caress them and make them feel secure and contented. It had not taken Mary long to discover that if Queen Catherine were Queen in name, Diane was Queen in all else.

Mary noticed that, when Catherine and Diane were together in the nursery, Catherine seemed to agree with all Diane's suggestions. Being young, being fierce in love and hate, young Mary could not resist flashing a look of triumph at the Queen's flat, placid features at such times.

She is a coward! thought Mary. She is not fit to be a Queen. The four Maries were now added to the little Queen's adoring circle, but the Dauphin had become her first care. All those who saw Mary and the Dauphin together – except Queen Catherine – declared they had never seen such a charming love-affair as that between the Dauphin and his bride-to-be. As for little Madame Elisabeth, she became one of Mary's dearest friends, sharing her bedchamber and following her lead in all things.

It was at the wedding of her uncle François Duc d'Aumale that she met this important man for the first time. He looked very like the knight she had pictured during her childhood in Scotland and she was not disappointed in the eldest of her uncles. François de Guise, Duc d'Aumale, was tall and handsome; his beard was curled; his eyes were flashing; and he was gorgeously apparalled. He was ready to become – as he soon was to be – the head of the illustrious family of Guise. He filled the role of bridegroom well, as he did that of greatest soldier in the land. His bride was a fitting one for such a man. She was Anne d'Este, the daughter of Hercule, Duke of Ferrara, and was herself royal, for her mother was King Henri's aunt.

There was a good deal of whispering in the Court concerning the marriage. 'Watch these Guises,' said suspicious noblemen. 'They look to rule France one way or another. Old Duke Claude had not the ambition of his sons; that doubtless came from their Bourbon mother. But Duke Claude, who was content with the hunt, his table and his women, is not long for this world and then this Duc d'Aumale will become the Duc de Guise, and he looks higher than his father ever did.'

Mary heard nothing of these whisperings. To her the marriage was just another reason for merriment, for wearing fine clothes, for showing off her graces, for being petted and admired for her beauty and charm.

So there she was in the *salle de bal*, stepping out to dance with the Dauphin, enchanting all with her grace and her beauty and her tender devotion to the heir of France.

'Holy Mother of God!' swore the Duc d'Aumale. 'There goes the greatest asset of the house of Guise. One day we shall rule France through that lovely girl.'

❁ ❁ ❁

Later he talked with his brother Charles. Charles, five years younger than his brother François, was equally handsome though in a different way. François was flamboyantly attractive but Charles had the features of a Greek god. Charles' long eyes were alert and cynical. François would win his way through boldness, Charles by cunning. Charles was the cleverer of the two, and knowing himself to lack that bravery on which the family prided itself, he had to develop other qualities to make up for the lack.

So Charles, the exquisite Cardinal, with his scented linen and his sensuality, was an excellent foil to his dashing brother; they were both aware of this, and they believed that between them they could rule France through their niece who in her turn would rule the Dauphin.

They had brought rich presents for Mary; they were determined to win her affection and to increase that respect which their sister, the Queen-Mother of Scotland, had so rightly planted in her daughter's mind.

The Cardinal, whose tastes were erotic and who, although he was quite a young man, was hard pressed to think of new sensations which could delight him, was quite enchanted with his niece.

'For, brother,' he said, 'she has more than beauty. There is in her . . . shall we call it Promise? What could be more charming than Promise? She is like a houri from a Mohammedan paradise, beckoning the newcomer to undreamed of delight, inviting him to explore with her that which she herself has not yet discovered.'

François looked at his brother uneasily. 'Charles, for God's sake, do not forget that she is your niece.'

Charles smiled. Blood relationships were of no account in his world of licentiousness. His long slim fingers a-glitter with jewels which put those adorning his brother's person in the shade, stroked his cardinal's robes. Did he enjoy being a man of the Church so much because, in his relationships with charming people, that fact added an extra relish? François was a blunt soldier for all that he was a Guise and destined, Charles was sure, to be one of the great men of his day. Rough soldier – he took the satisfaction of his carnal appetites as a soldier takes them. Charles was selective, continually striving for the new sensation.

'My dear brother,' he said, 'do you take me for a fool? I shall know how to deal with our niece. She is a little barbarian at the moment, from a land of barbarians. We shall teach her until she is cultured and even more charming than she already is. But the material is excellent, François, excellent.' The Cardinal waved his beautiful hands describing the shape of a woman. 'Beautiful . . . malleable material, dear François.'

'There must be no scandal touching her, Charles. I beg of you to remember that.'

'François! My dear soldier brother! You are a great man You are the greatest man in France. Yes, I will say that, for there is none here to repeat my words to his boorish Majesty. But you have lived the life of a soldier, and the life of the soldier, you will admit, is one that lacks refinement. I am in love with Mary Stuart. She is an enchanting creature. Dear brother, do not think that I mean to seduce her. A little girl of six? Piquant . . . yes. But if I want little girls of six, they are mine. It is her mind that I shall possess. We shall possess it between us. We shall caress it . . . we shall impregnate it with our ideas. What pleasure! I have long since known that the pleasure of the body – after the first rough experimenting – cannot be fully enjoyed without the co-operation of the mind.'

François' brow cleared. Charles was no fool. No fool indeed! If he himself was France's greatest soldier, Charles would be the country's cleverest diplomat.

'I feel,' said François, 'that you should watch over her education carefully, and that the Maréchal and Madame d'Humières should not be given too free a hand. The governess, Fleming, is no danger, I suppose?'

'The governess Fleming is just a woman.'

'If you wish to seduce a royal lady of Scotland, why not . . .' began François.

The cynical mouth turned up at the corners. 'Ten years ago your suggestion would have interested me. The Fleming will be a worthy lover. Very eager she will be. She is made for pleasure. Plump and pretty, ripe, but of an age, I fear, for folly, and the folly of the middle-aged is so much more distressing and disconcerting than that of youth. But there are hundreds such as the Fleming. They are to be found in every village in France. Nay, I'll leave the Fleming for some callow boy. She'll bring him much delight.'

'You could, through the woman, keep a firm hand on Mary Stuart.'

'The time is not yet come. Mary, at the moment, is the

playmate of the Dauphin, and as such shares the governor and governess of young François. That is enough for the moment. Let her strengthen that attachment. That is the most important thing. The Dauphin must be completely enslaved; he must follow her in all things. He is willing to do so now, but she must forge those chains strongly so that they can never be broken. He is his father all over again. Would Diane have caught our Henri so slavishly if she had not caught him young? "How charming!" they say. Madame Diane says it. His Majesty says it. "Was there ever anything more delightful than for two children who are destined for marriage to be already such tender playmates?" These Parisians! They are not like us of Lorraine. They talk love and think love. It is their whole existence; it is an excuse for everything. It is typically Valois. But we must be more clever; we must see farther. We know that this love between our niece and the King's son is more than charming; it is very good for the house of Guise. Let us therefore help to forge those chains, chains so strong that they cannot be broken, for depend upon it, sooner or later the Montmorencys – or mayhap our somnolent Bourbons – will awake from their slumbers. They will see that it is not a pretty little girl who has made the King-to-be her slave; it is the noble house of Guise.'

'You are right, Charles. What do you suggest?'

'That she remains at present as she is. The chattering Fleming will be useful. She – herself the slave of love – will be delighted to see her mistress installed in the heart of our Prince. She will chatter romance; she will foster romance; and she will do no harm. Leave things as they are, and in a few years' time I shall take over Mary's education. I shall teach her to be the most charming, the most accomplished lady in France. None shall be as beautiful as she, none shall excel her at the dance, at the lute; she will write exquisite verses, and all France – but most of all the Dauphin – will be in love with her. Her mind shall be given to the art of pleasing others; and it shall be as wax in the hands of the uncles who will love and cherish her, for their one desire will be to keep her on the throne.'

François smiled at his elegant brother.

'By God!' he cried suddenly. 'You and I will conquer France and share the crown.'

'In the most decorous manner,' murmured Charles. 'Through our little charmer from the land of savages.'

The days flew past for Mary. At lessons she excelled; she played the lute with a skill rare in one so young; she was a good horse-woman. In the royal processions she was always picked out for her charm and beauty. The King often talked to her. Diane was delighted with her. When she rode out with the Dauphin she would watch over him and seize his bridle if he was in any difficulty. He would be uneasy if she was not always at his side.

All the great chateaux which had been but names to her she now saw in reality. She thought less and less of her native land. Her mother wrote frequently and was clearly delighted with her daughter's success. She had had letters from the King, she said, which had made her very happy indeed.

Mary's four namesakes were now with her, but they had to take second place. The Dauphin demanded so much of her time. She explained this carefully to them for she was anxious that they should know that she loved them as dearly as ever.

They listened to gossip, and there was plenty of that at the

French Court. Now the talk was all about the Queen's coronation which was about to take place. The King had already celebrated his coronation shortly after the death of his father, and now it was Catherine's turn.

The celebrations were lavish. Mary had never seen anything quite so wonderful. Even the dreamlike pageants which had accompanied her uncle's wedding seemed commonplace when compared with those of the Queen's coronation. Even the Queen looked magnificent on that day. As for the King he was a dazzling sight, resplendent in cloth of silver; his scabbard flashed with enormous jewels, and his silver lace and white satin hat were decorated with pearls. The sheriffs of Paris held over him a blue velvet canopy embroidered with the golden lilies of France as he rode his beautiful white horse.

Mary would never forget the display of so much beauty. She was, she told Janet Fleming, only sorry that it was not her beloved Diane, instead of Queen Catherine, who was being crowned.

'Well, let her enjoy her coronation,' said Lady Fleming. 'That's all she'll get.'

'All! A coronation *all*! Dear old Fleming, what more could she want?'

'She wants much more,' said Lady Fleming. 'Whom do you think the King has presented with the crown jewels?'

'Diane, of course.'

Lady Fleming nodded and began to laugh. 'And she wears them too. She insists. The King is pleased that she should. What a country! The old Maréchal Tavannes complains that at the Court of France more honour is done to the King's mistress than to his generals. Who is the real Queen of this country, tell me that!'

'Diane, of course. And I am glad that it should be so, for I hate Queen Catherine.'

'She is not worth the hating. She is as meek as a sheep. Look at this. It is one of the new coins struck at the coronation and should bear the heads of the King and Queen. But see! It is Diane riding on the crupper of the King's horse. It means that although he has been forced to marry Queen Catherine and make her the mother of his children, there is only one Queen for him – Diane.'

'And more worthy to be!' cried Mary. 'Queen Catherine is not royal. She has no breeding. She is vulgar. I wish she would go back to her Italian merchants so that the King could marry Diane.'

They looked up sharply. The door had opened so quietly that no one had heard a sound. They were relieved to see that it was not Catherine who stood there; it was Madame de Paroy.

'Yes, Madame de Paroy?' said Mary, immediately assuming the dignity of her rank. 'What is it you want?'

'To ask Your Majesty if you would wait on Queen Catherine.'

'I will do so,' said Mary. 'And, Madame de Paroy, when you come to my apartments will you be so good as to be announced?'

'I could find none of your pages or women, Your Majesty. I am sorry that, as you and Lady Fleming were enjoying such mirth, you did not hear me.'

Madame de Paroy curtsied and retired. Mary looked at Lady Fleming who was trembling.

'Why are you afraid, and of what?' demanded Mary.

'I am afraid that she will tell Queen Catherine what she heard you say.'

Mary tossed her head. 'Who cares for that! If Queen Catherine were unpleasant to me I should ask Diane to protect me.'

'There is something about her that frightens me,' said Janet.

'You are too easily frightened, Fleming dear.'

'Do not keep her waiting. Go to her now . . . at once. I shall not rest until I know what she has to say to you.'

Mary obeyed. She returned very shortly.

'You see, you silly old Fleming, it was nothing. She just wished to speak to me about our lessons.'

Diane had fallen ill and had retired to her beautiful chateau of Anet which enhanced the beauty of the valley of the Eure and which Philibert Delorme had helped her to make one of the most magnificent examples of architecture in the country. The King, filled with anxiety, would have dropped all state obligations to be with her, but Diane would not hear of it. She insisted on his leaving her in her chateau with her faithful servants, and continuing with his Court duties.

Everyone in the Court was clearly delighted or anxious – except, of course, the Queen. She, who would surely be most affected, remained as expressionless as ever; and whenever Diane's name was mentioned spoke of her concern for her health.

A melancholy settled over Saint-Germain, and Mary hated melancholy. When the King visited his children he was absentminded. Nothing was as pleasant as it had been when Diane was there.

Then an alarming incident occurred. Mary would not have heard of this but for the cleverness of Beaton who had quickly improved her French and was now a match for anyone.

Beaton took Mary into a corner to whisper to her: 'Someone tried to poison you.'

Mary was aghast. 'Who?' she demanded; and her thoughts immediately flew to the Queen.

'No one is sure. It was the poisoner's intention to put an Italian posset into a pie for you. But it's all right. They have a man whom they have caught, and I expect they'll tie him to four wild horses and let them gallop in different directions.'

For once Mary was too horrified by what might be happening to herself to feel sorry for the victim of such a horrible punishment.

Mary Beaton had gleaned no further information, so Mary tackled Janet Fleming. Janet had heard the story, although, she said, the King wished it not to be bruited abroad, for he was much distressed that danger should have come so near Mary when she was at his Court.

'He says that the vigilance about you must be intensified. You must not let anyone know you have heard of this.'

'Tell me who did this thing.'

'A man is accused who is named Robert Stuart. Oh, do not look shocked. It is not your brother but a poor archer of the guard who happens to bear his name. He was clearly working for someone else. Some say it was the English. Others that he worked for your kinsman the Earl of Lennox . . . a Protestant. And this would seem most likely as Robert Stuart is clearly a fanatic. He has confessed that he did this thing, and will suffer accordingly. Matthew Lennox declares his innocence, but who shall know?'

'So it was not the Queen,' said Mary.

'The Queen! What do you mean?'

'She hates me. Sometimes I am afraid of her.'

'Nonsense! The Queen is but a name.'

❁ ❁ ❁

The King came into the nurseries to see the children, and with him was the Queen. How different were these visits from those of Henri and Diane! The children did not rush to their father and climb over him; they curtsied and, under their mother's gaze, paid their respectful homage to him as their King.

The Maréchal and Madame d'Humières were not present on this occasion, and Janet Fleming was in charge of the children. Mary noticed how particularly pretty she was looking, and that the glance the Queen threw in her direction seemed to be faintly amused.

Mary wanted to know if there was any news from Anet, but under the eyes of the Queen, she dared not ask.

'Lady Fleming,' said the Queen of France, 'now that the Dauphin and the Queen of Scotland and Madame Elisabeth are growing older, and Madame Claude will soon be joining them in the nursery, it seems to me that you will need some assistance.'

'Your Majesty is gracious,' said Janet Fleming, with that abstracted look which Mary had noticed lately.

'I am sure,' said the King, 'that Lady Fleming manages very well . . . very well indeed. I am struck with the great care she has always shown of our daughter Mary.'

The Queen's lips twitched very slightly. 'Like Your Majesty I too am sure that Lady Fleming is admirable, but I do not wish her strength to be over-taxed.'

'Over-taxed?' reflected the King, frowning at his wife.

'By so many children. And the Maréchal and Madame d'Humières have so much with which to occupy themselves. I do not wish dear Lady Fleming to work all the time she is with us, and I should like her to have some little respite from her duties. I should like her to enjoy a little gaiety.'

The King looked sharply at the Queen, but Catherine had laid her beautiful white hands on her stomacher and lowered her eyes. Her smile was almost smug. Mary wondered whether the rumours were true and that she was going to have another baby.

'I know,' went on the Queen, smiling affectionately at the King, 'how greatly Your Majesty esteems those who look after our children. Therefore I would beg for a few privileges for my Lady Fleming. I will send someone to assist her so that she may have a little more time for pleasure. Madame de Paroy is well skilled and most fitted to help in the nurseries. If Your Majesty would agree to her doing so, it would give her the greatest pleasure and, as for myself, I should feel that I had assisted our good Lady Fleming to obtain a little of the pleasure she deserves.'

Madame de Paroy in the nurseries! That hideous old woman with the crafty eyes – the Queen's spy! Mary felt the hot colour rise to her cheeks. Forgetting ceremony she ran to the King and took his hand. 'Please . . . please, dearest Papa, do not send Madame de Paroy here. *Please!*'

The King looked down at her in some astonishment. He ought to be angry with her for thus addressing him on an occasion when it was clear that ceremony was demanded; but he found it difficult to be angry with children, and such a beautiful child as this one, whatever she did, could not arouse anything but his wish to please her.

'My dear child,' he began helplessly; then he smiled. 'Why, how vehement you are!'

The Dauphin had come to the other side of his father. 'Papa,' he said, 'please do not send Madame de Paroy here.'

'Why do you not want her?' asked the King.

The Dauphin did not answer. He looked to Mary for guidance. 'Come,' said the King, 'speak for yourself. Why do you not want her?'

'Because . . . because Mary does not.'

The Queen gave her sudden laugh. 'Ah! So in the nursery Scotland already rules France!'

'And Elisabeth, what does she wish?' asked the King.

Elisabeth came forward and keeping her eyes on her father's face while she elaborately turned away from her mother said: 'I wish what François and Mary wish.'

'So Madame de Paroy is unanimously rejected!' cried the King.

The Queen laughed. 'You see, Lady Fleming, your charges defeat my good intentions.'

'Your Majesty is very gracious,' said Janet. 'I thank you for your solicitude.'

'And these young people will have none of my Madame de Paroy, eh? Well, well! We will forget I suggested it.'

Mary could not help throwing a triumphant glance at the Queen. She knew that Catherine had particularly wished Madame de Paroy to come. What she wants, thought Mary, is to set a woman to spy on us, and she lacks the courage to insist. I despise her.

While the Queen talked to the children about their lessons, Lady Fleming showed the King some of their essays. They were bending over them and the King looked pleased. Janet, flushed and excited to find herself so popular in such exalted company, ventured to say something which had been in her mind for some time.

'Your Majesty, may I make a request?'

The King's smile was very friendly. 'Lady Fleming, please do.'

'It concerns my very personal affairs, and doubtless I should not bother Your Majesty with it at all.'

'I shall be happy to give my attention to your personal affairs, and if there is anything I can do to help you, I shall be well pleased indeed.'

'It concerns one of my sons, Your Majesty. He is a prisoner of the English. He has long been in their hands and I cannot bring about his liberation. I thought that if Your Majesty would intercede for me with the Queen-Mother of Scotland, perhaps she might arrange to exchange an English prisoner for my son.'

'It would please me greatly,' said the King, 'if I could be sure of granting this request. As it is I shall do my utmost. I will write this day to my cousin of Scotland and suggest to her that there might be an exchange of prisoners.'

His eyes were very warm and friendly. Janet was excited. It was a long time since she had had a lover, and now it occurred to her that the next one might be none other than the King of France. No wonder she was excited. No wonder that, in spite of her age, she looked like a young girl in her teens.

Even the children noticed the change in her. The only one who did not seem to notice was Queen Catherine.

Mary lay in bed; she could not sleep. She was suffering from pains which were not unfamiliar to her. She had eaten more than usual. She had such a healthy appetite, and she looked upon it as a duty to set a good example to François and Elisabeth who pecked at their food. The meal, presided over by Madame d'Humières and the Maréchal, had been much as usual. There were joints of veal and lamb; there were geese, chickens, pigeons, hares, larks and partridges; and Mary had done justice to all, with the result that, although there was to be a grand ball, she had to retire early on account of her pains.

There had been some amusement about this ball because it had been arranged by the Queen and, oddly enough, the Constable de Montmorency had helped her with the arrangements. Young as she was, Mary was very intelligent and eager to learn all she could concerning Court matters; and with her four little Maries to assist her she could not help being aware of the tension which was inevitable in a Court where the Queen was submitted to perpetual humiliation, and the King's mistress enjoyed all – and more – of those honours which should have been the Queen's.

With the ageing mistress sick at Anet – some said dying – that tension must increase. Would the Queen seek to regain some of her rights? Would some beautiful and ambitious lady seek to fill Diane's place?

François and Elisabeth and little Claude might have watched the ball from one of the galleries. The French children would have enjoyed that more than mingling with the guests, but Mary would have wished to be with the dancers in a dazzling gown, her chestnut hair flowing, and all the gentlemen paying her laughing compliments and speaking of the enchantress she would become when she grew up. But alas, she was too sick to attend and must lie in bed instead.

Janet Fleming had talked continually of the ball, but Mary

had felt too sick to listen. She had drunk the posset Queen Catherine had given her, and afterwards had felt some misgivings. She had heard rumours about the Queen's Italian cupbearer who had been torn asunder by wild horses when the King's elder brother had died — of poison, some said, and others added: poison administered by Catherine de' Medici. Mary could not rid herself of the idea that Catherine wished her ill.

'Here,' Catherine had said, 'this is what I call my gourmand's dose. Do you know what your Scottish Majesty is suffering from? A surfeit of gooseflesh, like as not. You have been over-greedy at the table.'

Mary had grown hot with indignation as Catherine had bent over to look into her face.

'You're flushed,' said Catherine. 'Is it a fever, or have I upset your dignity? The truth can be as indigestible as gooseflesh, my dear *Reinette*.'

And Mary had had to swallow the hideous stuff and lie in bed nursing a sore stomach while others danced.

It was near midnight but she could not sleep. She could hear the sound of music from the great ballroom.

Before going to the ball Janet Fleming had come into the apartment to show Mary her costume. Everyone was to be masked. Those were the Queen's orders. The idea of the Queen and the Constable planning a ball! The whole Court was rocking with amusement. They would not miss Madame Diane to-night . . . not even the King.

'How I wish I could be with you,' sighed the little Queen.

'Has her Majesty's posset done you no good then?'

'I am not sure that she meant it to. She hates me because I would not have Madame de Paroy in the nurseries.'

'You are a bold creature, darling Majesty, to go against the Queen of France.'

'Would *you* want Paroy in the nurseries?'

'Holy Mother of God, indeed I would not. Why, if she knew that the King had shown me . . . a little friendship, Heaven alone knows what she might tell the Queen. But . . . my tongue runs away with me and I shall be late for the ball.'

Mary put her arms round her aunt's neck and kissed her. 'Come and see me when the ball is over. I shall want to hear *all* about it,' said Mary.

So now she lay in bed waiting for the ball to be over.

She slept for a while, and when she awoke it was to silence. So the ball was over and her aunt had not come as she had promised. Faint moonlight shone through the windows, lighting the room. She sat up in bed, listening. Her pains had gone and she felt well and wide awake. But she was angry; she always was when she suspected she had been treated as a child. Lady Fleming had no doubt come in to tell her about the ball and, finding her asleep, had tiptoed away – just as though she were a baby.

Mary got out of bed and, putting a wrap about her shoulders, crept across the room to that small chamber in which Lady Fleming slept. She drew back the curtains of the bed. It was empty. Lady Fleming had not come up yet, although the ball was over.

Mary got into Janet's bed to wait for her. She waited for a long time before she fell asleep; it was beginning to grow light when she was awakened by Janet's returning.

Mary sat up in bed and stared at her aunt. She was wearing the costume she had worn at the ball, but it appeared to be crumpled and was torn in several places.

'What is it?' asked Mary.

'Hush! For the love of the saints do not wake anybody.' Janet began to take off the costume.

'But what has happened?' insisted Mary. 'You look as though you have been set upon by robbers and yet are rather pleased about it.'

'You must tell no one of this, as you love your Fleming. You should not be here. You should be punished for wandering from your bed in the night. The Queen would punish you.'

'Perhaps she would punish you, too, for wandering in the night. I command you to tell me what has happened to you.'

Janet got into bed and put her arms about Mary. 'What if another has commanded silence?' she said with a laugh.

'I am the Queen . . .'

'Of Scotland, my dearest. What if I had received a higher command?'

'The Queen . . . Queen Catherine?'

'Higher than that!' Lady Fleming kissed the Queen of Scots. 'I am so happy, darling. I am the happiest woman in France. One day I shall be able to serve you as I should wish. One day you shall ask me for something you want, and I will perhaps, through the King's grace, be able to give it to you.'

Mary was excited. Here was one of the mysteries which occurred in the lives of grown-up people; here was a glimpse into the exciting world in which one day she would have a part to play.

'There is one thing I will ask you now,' she said. 'It is never to allow that dreary de Paroy to come near the nursery.'

'That I can promise you,' said Janet gleefully. 'She is banished from this day.'

They lay together smiling, each thinking of the glorious future which lay ahead of her.

❀ ❀ ❀

Mary forgot the excitement of the Court for a while. With her four friends she went to stay with her grandmother at Meudon. Her grandfather, Duke Claude, was very ill and not expected to live. She knew that soon her Uncle François would be the Duke of Guise and head of the house. But she did not see him. It was her uncle, Cardinal Charles, with whom she spent much of her time.

They would walk about the estate together and the Cardinal's eyes would gleam as they watched her. He studied her so closely that Mary blushed for fear he would find some fault in her. There were occasions when he would take her into his private chamber; she would sit on his knee and he would fondle her. He frightened her a little, while he fascinated her; her wide eyes would stare, almost involuntarily, at those long slim fingers which ceaselessly caressed her. She did not know whether she liked or hated those caresses. They fascinated yet repelled. Sometimes he would make her look into his face, and it was as though he were making her subject to his will. His long light eyes with the dark lashes were so beautiful that she wanted to look at them, although she was afraid; they were tender and malicious, gentle and cruel; and beneath them were faint shadows. His mouth was straight and long; it was the most beautiful mouth she had ever seen when it smiled – and it smiled often for her.

There was a delicious odour about his person; it clung to his linen. He bathed regularly; he was, it was said, the most fastidious gentleman of France. Jewels glittered on his hands, and the colours of those jewels were tastefully blended. Her grandparents were in some awe of him and seemed to have almost as much respect for him as they had for Uncle François.

'Always obey your Uncle François and your Uncle Charles,' she was continually told.

That was what they all wished to impress upon her. Even her new brother – whom she discovered in her grandparents' house – the Duc de Longueville, the son of her mother by her first husband, hinted and implied that it was her duty.

Everyone was telling her that the most important thing in the world was the power of the Guises, and as she played with her Maries she could not completely forget it. She felt like a plant in a forcing house on those occasions in the perfumed chamber of the Cardinal when he talked to her of her duty and how she must make young François her completely devoted slave so that he gave way to her in all things.

'When you are older,' said the Cardinal, putting his hands on her shoulders and pressing her small body to his, 'when you begin to bud into womanhood, then, my sweet and beautiful niece, you must learn how to make the Dauphin entirely yours.'

'Yes, Monsieur le Cardinal.'

He laid his cool lips against her forehead, and, when she received his kiss, for some reason she could not understand she began to tremble.

When Mary returned to Court the excitement regarding the King and Diane had reached its zenith, for Diane was recovered and had come back to Court.

Mary overheard strange whispers.

'Now the fun will start.'

'While the cat is away the mice play.'

'And do you know that mice are very fertile?'

'My dear Duchesse!'

'My dear Count, I assure you, I have noticed!'

Lady Fleming, Mary realised, was more excited than ever.

One day when Mary was in her apartment, she heard her governess talking to one of the Queen's ladies. Janet was saying: 'Yes, it is true, and God be thanked for it. I am with child by the King and I feel honoured. I feel so full of health. There is some magical property in the royal blood, I'll swear!'

Mary was astounded. She decided she would seek out Lady Fleming and demand a full explanation; but when she sought her she could not find her. None of the attendants appeared to know what had happened to her. The King was riding with Madame de Valentinois who had returned from Anet. She was somewhat frail but more beautiful than ever, and the King was like a devoted husband who, after a long separation, is able to enjoy the beloved company of his wife. He could not leave the Duchesse's side; he must spend every minute with her. Perhaps he wished to explain a little affair in which he had regrettably indulged during her absence; perhaps he wished to tell her that it should never have happened – and would not, had she been there – that it had been begun in a moment of desperate longing for herself.

And she would understand. She would tell him that she understood him now as she had when he was a shy Prince with no thought of mounting the throne. She had shown him how to act like a great Prince; now she would show him how to act like a great King.

Life would be as it had always been at Court. Queen Diane

would rule through the King; those entwined initials H and D were as firm as they had ever been, as closely entwined. The foolish Fleming woman would have to be banished from Court and then forgotten. It was no indiscretion to bear the King's bastard. The folly lay in boasting of the honour.

The Queen of France agreed with her husband and his mistress. She was eager to help. Would the King allow her to deal with this little matter? He knew how she abhorred scandal. The little peccadillo she accepted. It was inevitable. It was the flouting of Court etiquette that she could not endure.

The King and Diane were grateful to her. Neither of them wished to hear any more of the disposal of the matter, which they felt sure could be left entirely to the Queen's capable handling.

Catherine came stealthily into Lady Fleming's chamber. Janet rose from the bed on which she was lying and fell to her knees before the Queen of France. She lifted fearful eyes to the flat expressionless face.

'You may rise,' said Catherine. She laughed suddenly. 'We should not have known yet,' she added, 'had you not boasted so freely.'

'Your Majesty, I implore your forgiveness . . .'

The Queen lifted her shoulders. 'The King chose to honour you. You should not ask my forgiveness for that. How many times?'

'Your Majesty . . .'

'How many times?' insisted the Queen. Again that laugh. 'So many that you cannot remember? It began on the night of the masque which I arranged. Well, now Madame de

Valentinois has returned, and your services are no longer required.'

'Your Majesty, I will be content to obey your command.'

'My command is that you leave the Court this night.'

'Leave the Court . . .'

'Have no fear. Arrangements have been made. Remember you carry a royal bastard. You will be cared for and doubtless the child will be brought to Court. The King, as you have doubtless heard, had a child by a girl of Piedmont. It happened when he was away from France. You understand? The blood is hot and there is always some wanton at hand who can amuse for an hour until something better can be found.' The Queen laughed again. 'It is the way of all men, my dear Lady Fleming, and kings are no exceptions.'

Janet covered her face with her hands and began to cry.

'Madame,' she sobbed, 'I beg of you, let me stay. I have been sent here to guard the Queen of Scots.'

'I have another guardian for her. Do not weep so. It is bad for the child. Be prepared to leave in an hour. Where you are going you will have women to talk to. You may tell them how you were got with child by a most exalted person, but you shall not mention his name although you may describe all else in detail.'

The door opened and Mary stood on the threshold.

'I have looked everywhere . . .' she began, and saw the Queen of France. She immediately curtsied.

'Ah,' said Catherine, 'here is her Scottish Majesty.'

'I . . . I had no idea that I should find you here, Madame,' said Mary. 'I came to look for Fleming.'

'You are just in time to say goodbye to her.'

'Good-bye!'

Mary forgot ceremony. She ran to her aunt and threw her arms about her.

'Dearest Aunt Janet, what does this mean?'

'I . . . I . . . I am going away.'

'Oh, no, no!' cried Mary. 'Is it . . . because of the King's child?'

Catherine interrupted. 'So the Queen of Scots shares the knowledge of your lechery?'

Mary said: 'Madame, Lady Fleming is my governess.'

'No longer, my child.'

'No longer!'

'Lady Fleming is no longer considered a person fit to hold that position.'

'But who says so?'

'I say so.'

'Madame, Lady Fleming is my aunt.'

'We all have our disreputable relations. Pray do not apologise for her.'

'I . . . I wish to have her with me.'

'My dear *Reinette*, you are in the charge of the King and myself and we have decided otherwise.'

'I . . . I do not understand.'

'I am glad of that. I had feared that under the influence of your lecherous relative you might have become quite depraved.'

'Please, Madame, do not torment us.'

'I? I have nothing but your welfare at heart. Young girls can quickly fall into trouble, particularly if they are fairly handsome and have a good opinion of themselves. I have a new governess for you. She will come to you this day. You will be pleased to hear that Madame de Paroy is taking over those

duties which Lady Fleming has proved unworthy to perform.'
The Queen smiled and turned to Lady Fleming. 'In an hour –
do not forget.' And to Mary: 'Madame de Paroy will be with
you shortly.'

The Queen walked out of the room and Lady Fleming
threw herself on to her bed and gave way to wild weeping.

Mary stood still, her face white and angry, staring at the
door.

The Queen of France brought the woman into the apartment.
Madame de Paroy could not hide her satisfaction, and the
Queen was smiling blandly.

'Ah, Madame de Paroy, here are your charges.'

The four little girls had arranged themselves behind Mary.

'The Queen of Scots waits to welcome you,' said Catherine.

Mary's eyes were sullen. She had seen the King. She had
entreated him not to send Lady Fleming away and had begged
him not to put Madame de Paroy in her place. The King was as
kind as he always was; but he was ill at ease. He had said very
kindly that such matters were the business of ladies. It was not
his province to appoint a governess for his dear daughter of
Scotland. He wished to please her, he wished to make her
happy; but he was sure the Queen had the same intentions
towards her. It had been necessary for her Scots governess to
go away – there were matters beyond the understanding of
little girls – and she must trust her guardians to do what was
best for her.

In despair Mary had sought out Diane. Diane received her
with the utmost affection.

'My dearest child,' said the King's mistress, 'there are

matters which you are too young to understand. Lady Fleming has to leave Court, and Queen Catherine would deeply resent any interference in this matter of choosing your governess. She has your well-being at heart. You may trust her to do what is best for you.'

Mary sensed that neither the King nor Diane were really giving her their attention, and she realised suddenly how impotent she was. They had petted her because it had been easy to pet her, and she had acquired an opinion of herself which was too exalted. She was but a child here as she had been in Scotland; she was at the mercy of the grown-up world, and the love which these charming people had given her was only a minute part of their lives.

She was thinking of these things as she advanced to greet the Queen and Madame de Paroy.

'We wish you to smile for Madame de Paroy,' said Catherine.

But Mary would not or could not smile. Her lips froze; she could only glower at the ugly figure of the new governess. Catherine took Mary's ear and pinched it hard. She smiled as she did so.

'The Queen of Scotland has much to learn, Madame de Paroy,' said the Queen.

Mary wanted to scream because of the pain in her ear. She felt all alone. The King and Diane were riding away from her. They were leaving her to the mercy of these women.

'I have found it necessary,' went on Catherine, 'to chastise my own sons, knowing that one day they may be Kings of France. Kings . . . Queens . . . all have to learn their lessons, and when pride grows to abnormal proportions it can best be subdued with a stick. There is nothing like a stick applied to the

71

body to drive away a false sense of superiority. Do you agree with me, Madame de Paroy?'

'I do indeed, Your Majesty.'

'Now,' said Catherine, 'a smile of welcome for your new governess.'

Mary opened her lips showing her pretty teeth. She had to free her ear or cry out with the pain.

'H'm,' said Catherine, 'not a very bright smile. But it will suffice for the present.'

Mary was repeating under her breath: 'Vulgar . . . beast . . . tradesman's daughter . . . no true Queen . . . I hate you.'

She would say it aloud when she was alone with her Maries.

She was looking at the Queen and the new governess through a haze of tears. Catherine was well satisfied. The Queen of Scotland had just begun to learn what it meant to pit her puny strength against that of the Queen of France.

🏵 Chapter III 🏵

I n the vast room at Saint-Germain the children of the royal household were assembled as was their custom at this hour.

In a window seat sat Mary – one of the eldest and certainly the most beautiful. She was holding court as she loved to do. Monsieur du Bellay was reading one of his poems, and those who gathered about her – among them Ronsard and Maison-Fleur, those great Court poets – knew that it had been written for her.

> *'Contentez vous, mes yeux,*
> *Vous ne verrez jamais une chose pareille'*

Ronsard and du Bellay had been the leaders of that coterie which called itself the *Pleïade* after a group of seven ancient Greek poets, and had been chosen by Marguerite, the King's sister, to be literary tutors of the royal children and those young people who shared the nursery. Their favourite pupil was Mary, not only on account of her beauty which inspired them to lyrical verse, but because of her response to their own work and of that literary talent which she herself possessed.

All eyes were on her now. François the Dauphin openly admired her, and he was anxious that all should remember she was to be his bride. His brother Charles, though only seven years old, was already one of Mary's admirers. There was also Henri de Montmorency, the second son of Anne, the great Constable, and he could not take his eyes from her face.

Mary was content at such times. She needed such adulation. The last six years of her life had not been easy; Madame de Paroy was still with her and had turned out to be all that Mary feared. Mean-spirited, she lost no time in reporting the least misdemeanour, and she and the Queen never allowed the smallest error to go unpunished. Mary had been made to understand that she was as subject to discipline as any of the other children. She had been chastised as they had; but she had suffered far more from the loss of her dignity than from any physical pain.

In vain had she tried to rid herself of the woman. She had implored her mother to appoint a new governess; her uncle, the Cardinal, realising the woman to be a spy of the Queen of France, had added his pleas to Mary's, but in this matter Catherine stood firm, and neither the King nor Diane cared to interfere in a situation which had come about through the indiscretion of the King.

Lady Fleming had never returned to France, although her son remained to be brought up as a royal child; he was often in the nurseries, a bright, intelligent boy who quickly won his father's affection. But Janet had had to take up her residence in Scotland.

So, at such times as this one when she could escape from the supervision of Madame de Paroy, Mary was happy, with

François her constant companion and Charles showing his affection for her. She wished that Charles were not so wild and would grow out of those unaccountable rages of his. When they were on him he would suddenly kick walls, his dogs or his servants, whichever happened to be at hand. It was disconcerting. But she loved both brothers with a deep protective love. That did not mean that she was not becoming increasingly aware of the ardent looks sent in her direction by young Henri de Montmorency.

There were so many people at the Court to tell her how lovely she was. Monsieur Brantôme, the writer, assured her that her beauty radiated like the sun in the noonday sky. Her uncle, François, Duc de Guise, the great soldier and idol of Paris, exclaimed when he saw her: 'By the saints! You are the fairest creature in France!' Uncle Charles, the Cardinal of Lorraine, held her face in his beautiful scented hands and looked long into her eyes declaring: 'Your beauty will charm all France!' The King himself whispered to her that she was the loveliest of his daughters; and it seemed that all men were ready to sing the praises of Mary Stuart. Lately, devoted as she was to her dear François, she had begun to wish that he looked a little more like Henri de Montmorency.

There were now thirty children in the royal nurseries, for many of the sons and daughters of noble houses were being brought up there. It was a world in itself consisting of ten chamberlains, nine cellarers, thirty-seven pages and twenty-eight *valets de chambres*, besides doctors, surgeons, apothecaries and barbers. The amount of food consumed by this community each day was prodigious. Twenty-three dozen loaves were baked each morning and eaten before nightfall; eight sheep, four calves, twenty capons as well as pigeons, pullets, hares and other delicacies went the same way. The Dauphin and Mary had in addition their separate establishments with a further retinue of servants, but much of their time was spent in these main apartments.

The family of royal children had grown considerably since Mary had first come to France. These children were scattered about the room now.

Twelve-year-old Elisabeth and her sister Claude who was slightly younger were in Mary's group. Poor little Louis had died seven years ago and Charles was now the boy next in age to François. There was young Henri, who had been christened Edouard Alexandre but was always called Henri by his mother. He had just passed his sixth birthday and was extraordinarily handsome, with dark flashing eyes and the features of his mother's Italian ancestors. He was the only one of the children whom Queen Catherine spoilt, and consequently he was very vain. Mary watched him displaying the ear-rings he was wearing.

There was little Marguerite, whom Charles had nicknamed Margot, precocious and vivacious and looking older than her five years; and lastly Hercule, the baby, a pretty, chubby boy of three.

Pierre de Ronsard was sitting beside her; he saw that her attention was wandering as she surveyed the children.

'Since Monsieur du Bellay's verses do not interest Your Majesty, may I read some of mine?' he asked.

Mary held up her hand, laughing. 'No more verses just now please. Let us talk of you. Tell us of your early life and how, with your friends, you formed that group of poets called the *Pléiade*.'

They gathered round while Ronsard told, in his clever and

amusing way, of the Court of Scotland whither he had gone long before the birth of Mary, when her father's first wife had arrived from France.

He told how one day he had discovered a gentleman of the Court reading a small volume, how he had taken it, and once he had experienced the magic of those pages he had known that his life would be barren if it were not devoted to literature. He told of Cassandre, the woman he had loved; he quoted the sonnets he had written to her. He went on to speak of his life in the house of Jean Antoine Baïf where there was great poverty but greater love of literature.

'We were worshippers in the temple of literature. It mattered not that we were cold and hungry. It mattered not that we shared one candle between us. We studied Greek and Latin, and literature was food and drink to us – our need and our pleasure. Then we discussed our great desire to make France the centre of learning. We would enrich France; we would make her fertile. Literature was the gentle rain and the hot sun which would ripen the seed and give us a rich harvest. So we formed the *Pleïade* – seven of us – and with myself, du Bellay and Baïf as the leaders, the *Pleïade* was to shine from the heavens and light all France.'

Henri de Montmorency had moved closer to Mary.

His passionate eyes looked into hers.

'Would it were possible to speak with you alone!' he whispered.

She did meet him alone. She had wandered through the gardens of Fontainebleau, through the great courtyard and past the fountains, and had made her way to the walled garden.

Then she saw Henri de Montmorency approaching her. He was the second son of the great Constable of France whom the King loved and who, to his great grief, had been captured by the Imperial troops at the defeat of Saint Quentin and now lay a prisoner of Philip of Spain. How handsome he was, this Henri; he was so elegant in satin and velvet, the colours of which – pink and green – blended so perfectly. The jewels he wore had been carefully chosen. Henri de Montmorency – one of the most favoured young men of the Court because his father had been, and doubtless would be again, one of the most powerful – was a leader of fashion and good taste.

'Your Majesty!' He took Mary's hand and raised it to his lips. The eyes he lifted to hers were ardent.

She had no wish for such love as she believed was customary throughout the palaces of Fontainebleau, Blois, Amboise, Chambord, or anywhere the Court happened to be. The love which François the Dauphin had for her was the love she wished for. She enjoyed the love of the poets – idealistic and remote; she enjoyed the ardent admiration of Charles. There was, also, the strange and somewhat mystic love which her uncle, the Cardinal of Lorraine, bore her. Those caressing hands which seemed to imply so much, those queer searching looks, those lingering kisses, that spiritual love as he had described it, disturbed her; it frightened her too, but she was child enough to enjoy being a little frightened. She was always afraid, when she was with the Cardinal, that his love for her would change and become something wild and horrible; she fancied that he too was conscious that it might, and that he took a delight in holding his passion on a leash which he would, from time to time, slacken so that it came near to her and yet did not quite reach her. She could not imagine what would happen if it did, but something within her told her that it never would because the Cardinal did not wish it; and in all things the Cardinal's will was hers.

All these loves were different from the love of ordinary mortals; pawing, kissing, giggling and scuffling she would not have. She was a Queen and would be treated as such.

Yet here was Henri de Montmorency, beautiful as she herself was beautiful, young as she herself was young, and offering yet another sort of love, a charming and romantic idyll.

'I saw you enter the garden,' he said breathlessly. 'I could not resist following you.'

'We should not be here alone, Monsieur de Montmorency.'

'I must see you alone sometimes. Sometimes we must do that which is forbidden. Does not Your Majesty agree?'

'It is wrong to do that which is forbidden.'

'Can we be sure of that? I am happier now than I have been since I first set eyes on you.'

'But I do not think you should speak thus to me, Monsieur de Montmorency.'

'Forgive me. I speak thus out of desperation. I adore you. I must let you know of my feelings. Many love you, but none could do so with more passion, with more devotion and more hopelessness than your devoted servant Henri de Montmorency.'

He took her hands and kissed them with passion. She tried to withdraw them for she was conscious of emotion never before experienced, and she was afraid. She could not help comparing him with François. I am being disloyal to dear François! she thought in dismay.

'You are not indifferent to me!' cried Henri.

'We should return to the palace,' said Mary uneasily.

'Just a few more moments, I beg of you. I love you and I am wretched because shortly I must see you married to the Dauphin.'

'That must not make you miserable. It is my destiny, and doubtless you have yours.'

'My father, when he returns, will seek to marry me with the granddaughter of Madame de Valentinois. Oh, how wretched is this life! We are counters to be moved this way and that, and our loves and our desires go for naught. You will be married to the Dauphin. Your destiny is to be Queen of France and I . . . mine is a lesser one, but I am to ally my house with that of the King's mistress. I wish we could run away from France . . . to some unknown island far away from here . . . Would you were not a Queen! Would I were not the son of my father! If you were a peasant girl and I a poor fisherman, how much happier we might be!'

Mary could not imagine herself stripped of her royalty. She would never forget that she was a Queen, she believed. But she was moved by his words and the eager devotion she saw in his eyes.

He went on bitterly: 'My father has five sons and seven daughters, and all must be used to favour the fortunes of our house. My elder brother loved a girl – deeply he loved her. He thought he would die of love, and for a long time he stood out against our father's wishes. But now you see he is married to the King's bastard daughter, Diane of France, and our house is made greater by alliance with the royal one. Now if I marry the granddaughter of Madame de Valentinois, I shall strengthen the link. Not only shall we be allied to the royal house but with that of the King's mistress. What strength will be ours! What greatness! And all brought about because we have been moved as counters into the right squares on the board. They are flesh and blood, those counters; they cry out in anguish; but that is unimportant. All that matters is that our house grows great.'

'What are you saying, Monsieur de Montmorency?'

'That I would run away with you . . . far away . . . where all are merely men and women and there is no policy to be served, no great house that is of more moment than our happiness. Dearest Mary, if only we could run away together, far away from the kingdom of France where they will make you a Queen, far away from that land where you are already a Queen. Mary, did you know that in your country many of the nobles have signed the Solemn League and Covenant to forsake and renounce what they call the Congregation of Satan? That means they follow the new religion; they have cut themselves off from Rome. Yours will soon be a land of heretics. Oh, Mary, I see trouble there for you. You . . . a good Catholic . . . and Queen of a heretic land!'

'I know nothing of this,' she said.

'Then I should not have spoken of it.'

'I made my mother Regent of Scotland. I signed the documents some years ago.'

'Oh Mary, they tell you what to sign and what not to sign. They tell you to marry and you marry. Oh dearest and most beautiful, let us dream just for a moment of the impossible. Do you love me . . . a little?'

She was excited by his charm and the wild words he spoke. She was happy in this scented garden. But she knew she should not listen to him and that she could never be happy if she were disloyal to François. She turned away, frowning.

'I see,' he said bitterly, 'that they have moulded you as they wished. You will be their docile Queen. You will sign the documents they put before you; you will sign away your life's happiness when they ask it.'

'When I am the wife of François,' she said angrily, 'I shall be assured of a lifetime's happiness, Monsieur.'

She turned to leave him and as she did so she saw that two people had entered the garden. The rich red robes of the Cardinal of Lorraine were brilliant beside the more sombre garments of Queen Catherine.

Mary heard the sudden burst of laughter which she had grown to hate over the years. Catherine's amusement was, she believed, invariably provoked at someone else's discomfiture.

'Ah, Cardinal, our birds are trapped,' the Queen was saying. 'And what pleasant-looking birds, eh? We might say "birds of paradise". They look startled, do they not? As though they were about to be seized by the hawk.'

'Or by the serpent, Madame,' said the Cardinal.

'Poor creatures! What hope of escape would they have between the two!'

'Very little, Madame. Very little.'

Mary and Montmorency had hurried forward to pay their respects, first to the Queen, then to the Cardinal.

The Queen said: 'So you two charming people are taking the air. I marvel, Monsieur de Montmorency, that you do not do so in the company of another young lady . . . not the Queen of Scotland. And I should have expected to see my son with her Scottish Majesty.'

'We met by chance, Madame,' said Mary quickly, but the colour rose to her cheeks.

The Cardinal was looking at her quizzically. Because he had made her aware of those occasions when she caused him displeasure, she knew now that he was far from pleased at discovering her thus.

As for the Queen, she was delighted. Mary sometimes thought that the Queen did not wish her to marry the Dauphin, and that she would be very pleased if Mary had been seriously attracted by Montmorency.

The Cardinal said: 'Her Majesty and I, as you no doubt did, found the afternoon too pleasant to be spent with walls about us.'

Before Mary could answer, Catherine said: 'The Queen of Scots appears to be in a fever.' Her long slender fingers touched Mary's cheek. 'You are over-heated, my dear.'

'I have a headache. I was about to return to the cool of the palace.'

'Ah yes, the cool of the palace. That is the place for you. The bed, eh . . . with the curtains drawn, and no one to disturb you – that is the best remedy for the sort of fever which possesses your Scottish Majesty.'

Hating the insinuation contained in the Queen's words, conscious of the discomfort of Henri de Montmorency and the displeasure of the Cardinal, Mary said impulsively: 'Your Majesty has vast knowledge of such things. It is due to your keen observation of the conditions of others, rather than your experience of such maladies. But I dare submit you are mistaken on this occasion. It is a slight headache from the heat of the sun.'

The white hand, laden with rings, came down heavily on Mary's shoulder. Mary winced under her grip.

'I am rarely mistaken,' said Catherine. 'You are right when you speak of the keenness of my observation. Little can be hid from me. Now, Monsieur de Montmorency will escort you to the palace.' Catherine released Mary's shoulder. 'And do not forget my remedy. Your bed . . . the curtains drawn . . . the door locked to keep out your women. That is what you need. Go along . . . now. The Cardinal and I will continue our walk in the sunshine.'

Mary curtsied, Montmorency bowed, and the two walked back to the palace. As soon as possible Mary took leave of him and went to her apartments.

Flem and Beaton hurried to her anxiously, but she waved them aside. She had a headache; she would rest and she did not wish to be disturbed.

The curtains about Mary's bed were silently withdrawn. Mary opened her eyes and saw, standing by the bed, the scarlet-clad figure of the Cardinal. She smelt the perfume of musk which accompanied him, and saw the glittering emeralds and rubies on his folded hands.

'Monsieur?' she cried starting up.

'Nay, do not rise, my child,' he said; he sat on the bed and laid a hand on her hot forehead.

She lay back on her pillows.

'How lovely you are!' he murmured. 'You are very beautiful, my dearest. But you are distressed now.'

'I . . . I came here to rest.'

'On the advice of Her Majesty!'

'I did not expect anyone would come in.'

'You would not have your guardian uncle kept out?'

'No . . . no . . . but . . .'

'Rest easily, my dear child. There is no need to be afraid. The Queen was right to suggest you should return to the palace. It is not good for one of your purity and budding beauty to be seen in intimate conversation with a young man of Montmorency's reputation.'

'His . . . reputation!'

'Ah! You are startled. I see that you have more regard for this young man than I believed.'

'I did not know he had an evil reputation.'

'All young men have evil reputations.'

'That, Uncle, is surely not true.'

'Or they would,' went on the Cardinal, smiling, 'if all their deeds and all their thoughts were known. They sport their jewels to show their worldly riches. What if they should wear their experiences to show their worldly wisdom, eh? Then our simple maidens might not so easily become their victims . . . their light-o'-loves to be discussed and dissected for their companions' pleasure. Ah, you should hear the bawdy talk of some of these gallants when they are with others of their kind. You would be horrified. It is quite different from the sweet words which they employ as the prelude to seduction.'

'I will not be included among those simple maidens!'

'Indeed you shall not.' He slipped his arm under her and leaning forward, gazed into her face. He let his lips linger on her throat, and she felt her heart leap and pound. She could not move and it was as though she were bound by invisible cords. In his eyes there was a flame, in his arms a subtle pressure. Now he had unleashed this strange emotion which he had created; now it was about to envelop her. She was terrified, yet fascinated.

He was speaking softly. 'Nay, you are no simple maiden, my dearest, my other self. My Mary, I love you as I have never loved anyone. Together we will explore the world of the spirit.

You and I shall be as one, Mary, and together we will rule France.'

'I do not understand you . . .'

'You cannot expect to yet, but one day you will understand all that you are to me, and how I have preserved you and kept you sweet and pure.'

His mood had changed. The emotions were subdued. He sat up. He was smiling and his eyes were extraordinarily brilliant in his pale face.

'Mary,' he said, 'in your bleak and savage country, I have heard, the men of the Border ravish towns and hamlets. They take the cattle; then take the women. And what do you think they do with these women? They rape them, Mary . . . in the village streets . . . on the village greens. They mock them. They insult and humiliate them in a hundred ways you cannot even imagine. That is your wild country; that is Scotland. Here we are supposed to be a civilised people. But are we? Some of these bejewelled gallants with their pretty looks and their flowery speeches, their odes to your beauty – they are very like your Borderers beneath their exquisite garments and their courtly manners. The Borderer rapes; our gallant seduces. The Borderer takes a woman as he would an apple; he discusses the flavour while he tastes. Our gallants pluck their apples in scented orchards; all is apparently decorous. But afterwards, they discuss the flavour one with another. That is the difference between the Borderers of Scotland and our gallants. One, you might say, is at least candidly licentious; the other, under the cloak of gallantry, is full of deceit.'

'Why . . . why do you tell me this?'

'Because, *ma mignonne*, you are on the verge of woman-hood. It is time you were honourably married. Holy Mother of

God, your uncle François would run the young Montmorency through with his sword if he knew how he had insulted you in the gardens this day.'

'He did not insult me, Uncle. He was most chivalrous.'

'The first steps towards seduction, my dearest . . . the first indication that the scented couch is prepared. Even now we do not know that he will not boast of his success to his friends.'

'He dare not! He has nothing of which to boast.'

'The braggart will do very well on very little. I shall have him warned. As for you, my dearest, you will not be seen in his company alone again. Do not let your manner change. Be friendly with him as you are with others. Only remember that he is another such as your Border raiders; remember that he is doing his utmost to lead you to seduction. Remember that he will note every weakness . . . any attention you may pay to his words. He will boast to his friends of an easy conquest, and we shall have them all trying to emulate him.'

Mary covered her burning cheeks with her hands.

'Please . . . Uncle . . . stop. I cannot bear such thoughts. It was nothing . . . nothing.'

The Cardinal kissed her forehead.

'My darling, I know it was nothing. Of course, it was nothing. My pure, sweet Mary, who shall remain pure and sweet for the heir of France.' He put his arm about her and held her against him. 'If there should be one, other than the heir of France, it shall not be the son of the Constable!'

She caught her breath, for his lips were on hers. It was one of those moments when she sensed danger close. But almost immediately he had stood up and was smiling down on her.

'Rest, my beloved,' he said. 'Rest and think on what I have told you.'

She lay still after he had gone, trying to shut out the thoughts which the Cardinal had aroused in her. She could not. She could no longer picture Henri de Montmorency as he had seemed to her that day in the gardens; he was a different person, laughing and leering, calling to others to come and see how he had humiliated the Queen of Scots.

She buried her face in her pillows trying in vain to shut out those pictures.

The Cardinal, deeply disturbed, sought out his brother.

'We must hurry on the marriage,' he said. 'I am sure it is imperative that we should do so.'

The Duke looked grave. 'With Mary so young and the Dauphin even younger . . .'

'There are two reasons which make it necessary for us to press the King until this marriage is accomplished. I have it from the Dauphin's doctor that his health is failing fast. What if he were to die before Mary has married him?'

'Disaster!' cried the Duke. 'Unless we could secure young Charles for her.'

'He's nearly ten years younger, and it will be long before he is marriageable. No! Mary must be Dauphine of France before the year is out. I have another reason, brother. I saw her walking in the gardens with the son of our enemy.'

'That remark,' said François cynically, 'might indicate the son of almost any man at Court. As our powers grow, so do our enemies. To which one do you refer?'

'Montmorency. The Queen was with me and I have an idea that she was delighted to see those two together. I fancy she tried to make more of the affair than was justified. She was quite coarse, and talked of a bed as the best place to cool Mary's fever.'

'You alarm me, brother.'

'I mean to. There is reason for alarm. You are the hero of Paris, of all France. You have given back Calais to the King; you bear the mark of heroism on your cheek. The people look at the scar you bear there and cry: *"Vive le Balafré!"* At this moment you could demand the marriage, and the King would find it hard to refuse you. Take my advice, brother. This is our moment. We should not let it pass.'

The Duke nodded thoughtfully. 'I am sure you are right,' he said.

❦ ❦ ❦

The King and Queen received the Duke.

François de Guise, the man of action, did not waste time. He came straight to the point.

'Your Majesties, I have a request to make, and I trust you will give me your gracious attention.'

'It is yours, cousin,' the King assured him.

'It is many years since my niece came to France,' said the Duke, 'and it is touching to see the love she and the Dauphin bear towards each other. I know that both these children long for marriage, and my opinion is that it should take place as soon as possible. I am hoping that Your Majesties are of the same opinion.'

The King said: 'I think of them as children. It seems only yesterday that I went to the nurseries and found the little Stuart there with François. What a beautiful child! I said then that I had never seen one more perfect, and it holds to-day.'

'It is a matter of deep gratification to our house,' said the

Duke, 'that one of our daughters should so please Your Majesty. I venture to say that Mary Stuart will make a charming and popular Dauphine.'

Catherine glanced at her husband and murmured: 'All you say is true, Monsieur de Guise. The little Stuart is charming. It seems that she only has to smile in order to turn all Frenchmen's heads. She will indeed be a beautiful Dauphine . . . when the time comes.'

'That time is now,' said the Duke, with that arrogance which was second nature to him.

The King resented his tone, and the Queen lowered her eyes that neither of the men should see that she was pleased by the King's resentment.

She said quickly: 'In my opinion – which I beg Your Majesty and you, Monsieur de Guise, to correct if it seems wrong to you – these are but two children . . . two delightful children whom everyone loves and wishes the greatest happiness in the world. I know that to plunge two young children into marriage can be alarming for them. It might even injure that pretty comradeship which delights us all.' She was looking at the King appealingly; she knew she had turned his thoughts back to their own marriage all those years ago when he was a boy, of much the same age as François was now, with a girl beside him, a quiet, plain Italian girl – Catherine herself – whom he had never been able to love.

The King's lips came tightly together; then he said: 'I agree with the Queen. As yet they are too young. Let them wait a year or so.'

In exasperation the Duke began: 'Sire, I am of the opinion that these two are ripe for marriage . . .'

The King interrupted coldly: 'Monsieur de Guise, your

opinion can be of little moment if, in this matter of our children's marriage, it differs from that of the Queen and myself.'

The Duke was dismissed. He was furious. He had no alternative but to bow and retire, leaving this matter of the marriage as unsettled now as it had been before he had spoken.

❀ ❀ ❀

But the Cardinal and the Duke were not the men to let important matters slide. The Cardinal was quite sure that at all costs the delay must be ended.

He walked with the King in the gardens. He was more subtle than his brother. He talked first of the Protestant party in Scotland, of those lairds who were in league with John Knox and were turning his little niece's realm from the Catholic faith. The King, as an ardent Catholic, could well see the danger that lay in that.

'Your Majesty knows that my niece's bastard brother, Lord James Stuart, is one of these men, and with him are the most powerful men in Scotland – Glencairn, Morton, Lorn, Erskine, Argyle. It is open war against the true faith in Scotland. A sad state of affairs, Your Majesty.'

The King agreed that it was so.

'We shall have them repudiating Mary Stuart next and setting the bastard over them. That, no doubt, is his plan.'

'They'll never allow a bastard to rule them.'

'Who knows what that fanatic Knox will lead them to! They might well say, better a baseborn Protestant than a true Catholic Queen.'

Henri said: 'It shall never happen. We'll send armies to subdue them.'

'Sire, since Saint Quentin we are not as strong as we were.

If you will forgive the boldness, may I suggest that these barbarians could be made to respect my niece more if her status were raised. If she were not merely a Queen of Scotland but also a Dauphine of France they would think twice about flouting her in favour of the bastard.'

'The Queen and I, as I told your brother, consider that as yet Mary and François are too young.'

'The Queen and Your Majesty are as usual right. Ah . . . these little kings-to-be . . . these queens! Sometimes they must be married before their time. How fortunate it is that our Dauphin is affianced to one whom he has loved almost from her cradle. It is a fate, Sire, which befalls few of any royal house.'

'That's true, Cardinal. I would wish to see them married but I am loth to spoil that happy and tender comradeship which warms my heart every time I see them together.'

'Your Majesty is not only their devoted King; he is their beloved father.'

'That is how I would have it, Cardinal.'

'And that is how they would have it, I know. I hope Your Majesty will consider it wise to have the children married before you need the help of Scotland next year against the English . . . as you assuredly will.'

The King was silent. What the Cardinal said was true. He himself was a soldier of some ability and he knew that he might shortly need the help of Scotland. The marriage would make sure of that.

He continued silent and the Cardinal went on: 'Your Majesty, I have drafted an agreement which, if signed, would bring great good to France. It is premature, I know, and could not, of course, be signed by Mary Stuart until the marriage is certain; but thinking of the good of our country, and the depression we felt after Saint Quentin . . .'

'What is this agreement?' asked the King.

'If she could be induced to sign it, it would give her kingdom to the crown of France should she die without heirs; she would also transfer her rights to the crown of England to Your Majesty, or your successors, until a million gold crowns had been paid to France as an indemnity for those monies which France had paid out for the defence of Scotland.'

The King gasped. 'But . . . how can she sign such a document? She has no power to do so without the consent of the Parliament and the Regent.'

'She is the Queen of Scotland. Her signature on the document would make it valid.'

'Would she sign such a document? Poor child, would she understand what she was doing?'

'I will explain it to her.'

The King was uneasy yet desperately tempted. He must be a King first now, and father second. Scotland was an unruly country; it was an unhappy, a tortured country; how much happier it would be, completely depending on France!

'She would sign,' said the Cardinal softly. 'She would be only too happy to give you these rights. She loves you. You are her beloved father. She would be only too happy to repay something of all you have done for her.'

The King nodded. The crown of Scotland was being offered to him and his heirs. He could not turn away from it. The temptation was too great.

'I am sure,' said the smooth-voiced Cardinal, 'that when she knows she is to be in very truth your daughter, gladly will she put her name to the documents which I shall place before her.'

'I think,' said the King, 'that as they love each other and as they have known each other so long, it would please them to know that they are to be married.'

'Soon,' added the Cardinal. 'I will break this wonderful news to my niece. I am impatient to witness her joy.'

'And I will break the news to my son. I know he will be the happiest boy in Fontainebleau this day.'

So the King smothered his conscience; the Cardinal – having none – was spared such pains.

❦ ❦ ❦

The Cardinal came to conduct his niece to that chamber wherein the King was waiting for them with Cardinal de Sens, who was the Keeper of the Seals of France, in attendance.

The Cardinal had explained to Mary that this was merely a formality. All she need do was sign her name.

'What paper is it, Uncle?' she asked. 'Should I not read it before I sign? You have always said that I should read everything before signing.'

'There is no need to tire yourself. It is such a bore – this language of the lawyers. I can tell you all you want to know. It is a little matter concerning Scotland's debt to the King. You see, His Majesty and the French have given much money for the defence of Scotland, and you, as the Queen of that land, are going to sign this paper promising that you will arrange that, when Scotland is able to do so, the King is repaid.'

'That is what I would wish,' said Mary.

'Well, that is all it is.'

'But it seems such a solemn occasion for such a small thing, does it not?'

'Remember you are a Queen, my child, and now that you

94

are growing up there will be many occasions when some formality, which may seem unnecessary to you, will have to be carried out.'

Mary smiled and allowed the Cardinal to lead her to that chamber in Fontainebleau, and there, with the April sunshine streaming through the windows, put her signature to the documents which gave away that which she had no right to give, and which, although she was a girl not yet sixteen years of age and innocent of wrong-doing, brought great dishonour to her name.

Mary was being dressed for her wedding. About her were her four Maries and several attendants who were helping, their eyes bright with admiration and excitement.

Now she stood in her bridal dress; it was so heavy that she could scarcely stand, for its white damask was covered in jewels. Her royal mantle and train of bluish grey velvet was decorated with pearls; her golden crown was studded with pearls and diamonds, sapphires and rubies, and the centre piece was a hanging carbuncle which alone was worth five hundred thousand crowns.

'You are the most beautiful bride there has ever been!' cried Flem; and the others agreed.

Mary laughed gleefully as she touched the priceless necklace she was wearing. The people in the streets would cheer her as she went from the palace of the Archbishop of Paris – where she, with the royal family, had spent the night – to the Cathedral of Notre Dame. They loved her because she was their charming *Reinette*, and her marriage to the Dauphin gave them such a show as they had never witnessed before.

François was happy too. He was not very nervous, he had told her, although he would have been terrified if he had had to marry anyone else. The thought of Charles worried Mary a little. He was so sullen; he seemed almost murderous and in deadly earnest when he declared he longed to marry her.

It was a pity that the Commissioners from Scotland had come to see her married, for they reminded her that she was Queen of a kingdom very different from this one. Their odd speech was so strange to her, though she supposed she herself had once spoken it. Their clothes were rough and lacking in elegance; they were suspicious of the French, and it had to be admitted that the French did laugh at them and mock them when they were not present. Mary was a little ashamed of her rough countrymen.

She was worried too about her half-brother, Lord James, who had come with them. He had changed since she last saw him; outwardly he was as friendly as ever, but he seemed to be watching her furtively all the time; and she knew that James was among those covenanters who were in league with John Knox.

She was not to trust her brother, the Cardinal had warned her. She was to tell no one of the documents she had signed a short while ago. They were of no great importance, of course, but the Cardinal wished them not to be mentioned.

Mary had for years obeyed the Cardinal without question and she did so now.

But all her uneasiness vanished as she walked along the gallery which had been set up between the palace of the Archbishop of Paris and the Cathedral of Notre Dame.

The King – magnificently jewelled – held Mary's right hand as they walked along the gallery, while the Duke of Lorraine held her left. Mary's train was borne by young ladies who could scarcely lift it, so heavy was it with the jewels which adorned it. Behind them came Catherine the Queen and Jeanne the Queen of Navarre, followed by the ladies of the Court in order of precedence.

The King of Navarre walked with the Dauphin, and behind them came the two Princes – Charles, still glowering and sullen, and Edouard Alexandre full of gaiety because he had never worn such jewels as he wore that day.

At the door of the Cathedral the procession halted and Mary was brought to stand beside the Dauphin.

Henri Deux took a ring from his finger and gave it to the Cardinal of Bourbon who was waiting to receive it, and there, under the blue sky, so that the people of Paris might witness the marriage ceremony, Mary Queen of Scots was married to François, Dauphin of France.

She smiled at her bridegroom reassuringly, not forgetting even at that moment that he might be in need of comfort. She knew that the crowds and the shouting would make his head ache. She knew that his jewelled garments would weigh him down and make him very tired.

He held her hand tightly and looked at her continually as though to reassure himself that the beautiful vision, arrayed in such glorious apparel, was after all his beloved Mary.

When the ceremony was over they returned to the Archbishop's palace and sat down to the banquet which had been prepared for them in the grand hall. Mary ate ravenously, for she was very hungry; she urged François to eat, and he did so, saying that although there were so many people about them and the glitter of jewels was almost blinding, and two gentlemen stood behind Mary all the time they ate, holding the crown royal over her head, they were together; they loved each other and everything was the same except that they were married.

Afterwards there was dancing. Mary delighted to dance and was enchanted when the King chose her as his partner. Her hand rested in his as they turned slowly in the stately *pavane*.

'So you are happy?' asked the King.

'Yes, dearest Papa.'

'Then I am happy too. No one in Paris who saw you this day will ever forget you.'

'I shall never forget this day.'

'You and François should be happy. You do not yet know how fortunate you are.'

Mary had caught sight of François who was dancing with his mother. He looked very uneasy. She wished that she could have gone to him, to tell him not to be nervous. The King followed her gaze.

'You will always take care of him, will you not, Mary?' he said very seriously.

'Always, Papa.'

'He will need your care, my dear, and I know I can trust you to give it to him. The saints bless you and keep you.'

'I am happy to be the Dauphine, Papa, but I hope I shall never be Queen of France, for I could not be that while you live – so I would wish never to be.'

'My dear child,' he said, 'I love you very much.'

By four o'clock in the afternoon the ball at the episcopal palace was over, but the celebrations were to continue. The whole company crossed the Seine to the Palais de Justice. Mary was carried in a litter of gold and silver, and the people shouted to her as she passed. 'Long live the Queen-Dauphine!' they cried. And to each other: 'But she is beautiful. What a contrast to the Italian woman!' Catherine did not seem to care what they said of her. She accepted humiliations from the Parisians as she did from her husband, with a resigned and almost patient smile.

How the people cheered the King when he rode by on his magnificently caparisoned war-horse! But the loudest cheers of all, some noticed, were for the man dressed in frosted cloth of gold, ablaze with gems, the man of action whom no amount of fine clothes or jewels could disguise. They knew him at once; his tall figure attracted immediate attention as did the scar on his cheek. '*Vive le Balafré!* Long life to the great Duke of Guise!' shouted the crowds. He knew how to win the hearts of the people. They did not forget that, during the celebrations when the mob had struggled to see the youthful pair but were prevented from doing so by the fine folk on the dais, he had ordered those fine folk to stand aside that the people's view might not be obstructed. 'God bless the Duke! God bless the hero of Metz and the saviour of Calais!'

And so the procession of litters, coaches and prancing horses came to the great hall of the Palais de Justice where a grand supper was waiting, to be followed by such a ball, such masques and mummeries, games and pastimes as were rarely seen even at the Court of France. With relish Mary ate of the dishes which were set before her. This was the happiest day of her life, she told François. He smiled and said that he was happy to be her husband but he would be happier still when they could be alone together.

He laughed with Mary at the children who, led by young Henri de Guise, rode in on hobby horses; each horse – and there were twenty-five of them – was pulled across the hall by a lackey, but the horses were so beautifully decorated with trappings of cloth of gold and silver that they looked more beautiful than real horses. The Princes, looking very charming in their suits of cloth of gold, came to a halt before the bridal pair and sang in praise of marriage and this royal marriage in particular.

Only the Scottish guests were ill at ease. It was clear that they thought the laughter, the dancing, the lavish display of jewels, the fulsome compliments and the soft looks exchanged between the men and women a strange mode of behaviour. They were unable to join in the gaiety and stood apart about Lord James, as though to be ready to protect themselves if the need arose, watching the strange antics of the French through sullen and suspicious eyes.

The peak of the evening was reached with the appearance of the galleons which glided over the floor of the ballroom, the silver gauze sails filled by an artificial breeze; and as the floor cloth had been painted to represent waves, the effect had a certain realism. Lackeys led the ships to the table at which the royal ladies sat, and in the first of these ships the King was disclosed seated on the deck in a chair of state beside which was an empty chair. The King reached for Mary's hand and helped her on to the deck that she might sit beside him. In the next ship was the Dauphin who had been warned he must select his mother to sit beside him; the Prince of Condé, in the next, chose the Duchess of Guise; the Duke of Lorraine followed and chose the Princess Claude; the King of Navarre chose his own wife; and the ships went gracefully down the ballroom over the painted floor cloth to the delight of all who saw them, and the immense pride of the Duke of Guise who had organised the pageantry.

Later Mary and François sat side by side listening to the poems of Ronsard and du Bellay; and all those poems – some set to music – were in praise of the King of France and the newly married pair and of the joy this union of the two countries would bring to them.

'Mary,' whispered François wearily, 'will it never end?'

She pressed his hand and looked down into his pale face. Poor little bridegroom! He was so tired. He was longing for it to be over, but the bride was wishing it could last for the rest of her life.

❀ ❀ ❀

They lay together in the marriage bed divested of their glittering wedding garments.

François was holding her hand tightly. 'I should be so afraid, Mary, if it were anyone but you.'

'So should I,' said Mary, 'if it were anyone but you.'

The Dauphin laughed happily. Mary knew just how to set him at ease. If he was nervous, so was she. How lucky he was to have her for his wife!

'I shall grow stronger, Mary,' he said. 'I'll be like the Duke, your uncle. I will have all Paris shouting for me, and a scar on my cheek. I'll be like my father, quiet and strong. Oh, Mary, how lucky *you* are! You don't have to be like anybody but yourself.'

'Nor do you, François,' she said.

'Mary, I love you so.'

'I love you too, François.'

'Whatever we have to do . . . it will be all right, won't it?'

'Yes, François. But don't worry. Go to sleep now.'

She could see that he was almost asleep. His lids were

pressing down over his eyes. He nestled closer to her and she held him in her arms protectively.

'I am so glad, Mary,' he murmured, 'so glad to be married to you.'

Then he fell asleep.

🏵 Chapter IV 🏵

The King had decreed that the honeymoon should be spent in the lovely old chateau, built by his father François Premier, at Villers-Cotterets. So to this chateau went François and Mary, accompanied by only a few of their attendants, that they might enjoy each other's company in quiet seclusion.

These were the happiest weeks of François' life. The days seemed long and full of sunshine. He would lie on the grassy lawns near the fountains and listen to Mary's reading to him; she read so beautifully. Sometimes she composed verses about their happiness; sometimes they rode in the forest together. It was quite different, riding almost alone with Mary, from riding with the company which always surrounded him when he was at Court. They would walk their horses under the trees or gallop side by side over the grassy stretches.

At Villers-Cotterets he learned not to be afraid of horses. Mary showed him what loving, gentle creatures they were. They were like herself, she said, eager to serve him.

What enchanting things Mary said! And how happy he was

in her company! She made him forget that he was a sickly boy; she made him feel that he was a man.

To his relief their marriage had not been consummated. He was glad of that. He felt unhappy when he remembered that it would have to be one day; he was so uncertain and he sensed that Mary was also, and that she was glad that everything would be as it had been before their marriage, except that she was Dauphine now and they could be together night and day.

How good it was to be away from everybody who alarmed him! His mother was at Les Tournelles with the Court, and that seemed far away. There was another whom he was beginning to fear as much as his mother, another who seemed to be constantly watching him in a manner that was sinister and subtle. This was Mary's uncle, the Cardinal of Lorraine.

Those sunny days were marred slightly because Mary was not feeling well. She had pains and a cough. In her childhood she had been a healthy girl but later certain weaknesses had begun to show themselves. She had a good appetite – perhaps too good, for she was sometimes ill after eating; and she was subject to fainting fits.

Then came a visitor to the honeymoon chateau. When the Dauphin saw who it was he froze with a horror for which he could really find no reason; but Mary ran forward eagerly to greet her uncle.

The Cardinal embraced both children.

'It is a secret visit,' he said. 'I could not resist it. I wished to see how my dear children were enjoying their honeymoon. And when I heard that my dearest Mary was unwell, I found the desire to make the journey irresistible.' The Cardinal looked at her anxiously. Her skin was of waxy pallor like the petal of the magnolia blossom; it was attractive, thought the

Cardinal, but not a sign of robust health. As he had said to his brother, the Duke, when he had heard of Mary's illness, it was a terrifying thought that the power of their house depended on the lives of two frail children.

He told his brother that he had had a secret conference with the Dauphin's doctors and had forced them to admit that the likelihood of the boy's reaching the age of twenty was very remote.

Mary's illness and the reports from the doctors were the reasons for the Cardinal's intrusion on their honeymoon.

He knew the Dauphin and he knew Mary. The Dauphin was a frightened boy; he was so weak and sickly that he would have no normal impulses. As for Mary, one day she would be a passionate woman. The Cardinal was fully aware of that. He thought it was the secret of that immense attraction which was felt by almost every man who came into contact with her. Her expression was gentle; hers was a tender beauty; yet her dormant sensuality was ready to be roused, and it was this readiness which made all men who set eyes on her, long – subconsciously perhaps – to be that one who should kindle the fire. Her reserve, upheld by her great dignity, was like a fine gauze covering the intensely passionate nature. If the gauze could be removed the true Mary would be exposed – eager, voluptuous, abandoned. Passion would sweep away her dignity. The woman in her would make her forget she was a Queen. This connoisseur of human frailty, this man who had experienced every sensation, understood Mary completely.

It was his task to keep the gauze intact. Only he had lifted the corner to peep beneath, and then dropped it quickly. He was too old and wise to let his emotions stand in the way of his ambition. Mary must be handled with the greatest care. She must never know herself as a woman, if there was any risk that such knowledge might come between her and her duty to the house of Guise. He had fancied that Henri de Montmorency might, in due course, have stripped Mary of her queenly dignity, of her innocence and her ignorance, and found the woman beneath. That was why he had – as he so well knew how to do – made the Montmorency repulsive to her.

That had not been difficult. He had formed Mary's mind; he had watched over her. His relationship with her had been his great delight. It gave him more satisfaction than any of those obviously erotic entertainments which he devised from time to time. Mary must remain his guileless niece. Yet it was necessary for her to taste the fruit of the tree of knowledge, for it was imperative to the house of Guise that the Dauphin and Mary should have an heir. Yet he himself, when he had been determined that she should not fall to the house of Montmorency, that great enemy of the house of Guise, had shown her how bitter that fruit could be. He had made her turn shuddering away; that was why the task which now lay before him was such a delicate one.

He listened in an avuncular manner to Mary's account of the pleasures of the chateau. He heard about François' prowess with his new horse. Then he patted Mary's cheek and said that it grieved him to see her not as well as when they had last been together. He wished her to rest and insisted on her lying down.

'Not now you have come!' she protested.

'*Because* I have come! I will not have this hearty husband of yours tiring you.'

François could not help feeling rather pleased to be referred to as the vigorous one. Mary saw his quick smile which was replaced immediately by his look of concern for her.

Mary said: 'We did ride rather far yesterday. It was a little too far . . . for me.'

'Then you shall rest now, and François shall take me to the stables and show me his horses.'

Mary agreed. She was pleased because on other occasions when her uncle had been present, François had sent out distress signals begging not to be left alone with the imposing Cardinal. It was pleasant to feel that François was less afraid since their marriage, and that he was beginning to be fond of Uncle Charles.

When Mary had left them, the Cardinal smiled at the boy. His smile was warm, and affectionately and successfully masked the contempt he felt for the stripling.

'You . . . you would wish to see the stables?' said the Dauphin timorously.

'Why, yes . . . yes,' said the Cardinal. 'We will go alone.'

As he admired the horses he made himself so agreeable that François began to think he had been rather foolish to be afraid; but when they had left the stables and were walking in the grounds about the chateau, the Cardinal said: 'I trust you are being a good husband to Mary.'

'I love her,' said the Dauphin. 'I would die for her.'

'She will need you to do more than die for her.'

'I . . . I would do all that she wished.'

'Poor Mary, she is a little sad.'

'Oh no. She is happy. She says so. She says that this is the happiest time she has ever known. She is happy because of our marriage.'

'She was happy *thinking* of marrying you. I am not sure that she is happy now.'

'I . . . I do not understand.'

The Cardinal smiled. 'You have given Mary a fine title; you have made her Dauphine of France. But there is more to a marriage than that. What Mary needs is a lover. She needs a child.'

The Dauphin flushed scarlet and did not know where to look. He was near to tears. He knew that he had been right to fear the Cardinal who had brought discord into this Eden.

The Cardinal's long mouth sneered. 'Tell me,' he said; 'I am right, am I not, when I say that Mary has been disappointed in her lover?'

'Mary does not want . . .'

'Mary does not want! Of course she wants!'

'But she said . . .'

'Holy Virgin, have you been such a laggard in love as to ask her what she wants in the matter?' The Cardinal laughed aloud. 'Your grandfather, great François, would rise in his grave and come to you with a horsewhip if he knew. You have betrayed the honour of France and the Valois.'

'But if we wish . . . if we do not want . . .'

'Poor Mary! So I now understand why she is sick. She is pining. Holy Mother of God! Holy saints! Listen to the boy. He is a poor impotent weakling who begs his wife not to make any demands on his manhood. My boy, all France will reject you. Are you a Frenchman then? Are you the heir of France? Now I know why Mary is sad. Now I know why she pines and droops. She was promised marriage, and she has been given . . . what? I know not. I dare not think. My poor niece! My poor, poor niece!'

'How . . . dare you!' stammered François. 'Remember you speak to the Dauphin.'

'Remember it! I would to God I could forget it. I would I did not belong to this land, the heir of which is a lily-livered timorous girl, masquerading as a man.'

'I . . . I will tell the King.'

'I beg of you, do not. Do not bring down sorrow on his silver hairs. Do not bring shame to his royal crown. Do not let him know that he has fathered an unnatural monster with whom the most beautiful girl in all France has been unfortunate enough to marry.'

'You *have* come here to torment me then!'

The Cardinal seized the boy's arm. His face was a mask of piety as he raised his eyes to the sky. 'No, my son. I have come here to see that you do your duty, not only to my niece but to your ancestors.'

The Dauphin's face quivered. 'I . . . I . . .'

The Cardinal released him and laid an arm about his shoulders. 'My dear boy,' he said gently, 'my beloved Dauphin, I have been harsh. Sometimes one must be cruel to be kind. I wish to help you. I know how young you are and that you have not had the good health of some of your companions. You have not roamed the countryside with them and partaken in their manly sports and pastimes. My dearest boy, believe me, I wish to help you. I am your confessor, your priest. It is my place to help you. This marriage must be consummated without delay. It is your duty.' He laughed gently. 'Ah, that from which you shrink will give you great joy. Do you remember when you first mounted a horse? You were afraid then. The ground seemed so far away. You were terrified that you would fall. In your heart you hoped that you would never have to ride again. But now you are glad you learned to ride. So it will be in this matter. If you are frightened, if you run away from your duty, you will be ashamed for the rest of your life. Do you understand me?'

'Yes,' said the Dauphin.

The Cardinal pressed his shoulder warmly. 'I knew that you would. You will grow strong and noble. You will be a man, a worthy successor to your father.'

They returned to the palace.

'Do not mention to Mary what I have said,' warned the Cardinal. 'That would be folly. It would not please her to know that it had been necessary to force her husband to his duty.'

The Dauphin's face was set and determined. He was no longer the happy bridegroom. A duty lay before him, the execution of which frightened him.

The Cardinal saw his niece before he left. He did not intend to stay. He never made the mistake of over-emphasis. If, when the honeymoon was over, the marriage had not been consummated, he would have to consider other methods. What he had done so far would suffice and was, he felt sure, almost certain to succeed.

It had been the wish of the King that the young people should be left entirely to themselves. The King was sentimental where children were concerned, and he remembered the trials of his own early marriage. As for the Queen, she had no wish for the marriage to be consummated, but the Cardinal believed that her wishes were not founded on sentiment.

The consummation of the marriage was vital to the house of Guise; therefore that consummation should take place.

'And it shall!' mused the Cardinal, as he rode away from Villers-Cotterets. 'I have injected some manhood into that ungainly mass of corrupting flesh which calls itself Dauphin of France. I am only sorry that my darling should have been given such an unworthy partner in her first excursion into the delights of the flesh.'

❀ ❀ ❀

The King came down to Villers-Cotterets. He had heard that
Mary had been ill and that the Dauphin was less happy than he
had been on his arrival.

The King came without ceremony, riding there on a
hunting expedition.

The young couple were delighted to see him. He scanned
their faces eagerly. He was moved as he gazed at them; they
were such children, and did he not know what it meant to be a
young husband? He remembered even now with a shudder his
first weeks of marriage.

'And how are you both, my dear children?' he asked as he
embraced them.

'We are very happy, Papa,' they assured him.

Mary was pale; that would be explained by her malady, but
the Dauphin seemed shamefaced. They did not tell the King
that their happiness had lasted until they had been compelled to
indulge in a nightly duty which was distasteful to them both.
Henri did not ask. He remembered his own agonies when his
witty father had made brilliant remarks to his young son.

They will grow out of it, he promised himself. They are so
fond of each other. François turns to her for everything, and
she is as ready to comfort him and humour him as she ever was.

Yet so concerned was the King that he decided he would
separate the newly married pair for a few weeks and see what
effect it had.

'François,' he said, 'I wish you to join the camp at Amiens.
Honeymoons cannot last for ever, you know.'

'No, Papa.'

The King saw the fear leap into the boy's eyes. He dreaded

leaving Mary and Villers-Cotterets for the camp where there would be rough soldiers.

'You will be able to show your skill on horseback,' said his father. 'And, my boy, remember you are the Dauphin. Your people will wish to see you. Do not be afraid of them. There is nothing to fear. Remember, one day you will be their King.'

So to the camp at Amiens went François. Mary stayed at Villers-Cotterets, which the King felt would be healthier for her than Paris. He sent her four Maries to her to compensate her for the loss of her husband. He fancied that, while she was sorry to say a brief farewell to François, she was, in a way, relieved. The King believed he understood.

There was a great deal of excitement in the Court because the Queen of England was dead. Her place had been taken – usurped, said the King, the Guises and almost every Frenchman – by the bastard daughter of the concubine Anne Boleyn; and if the throne of England had not been taken by the bastard Elizabeth, it would surely have fallen to Mary, Queen of Scotland, now Dauphine of France.

'Holy Mother of God!' cried the Duke, his eye watering above his scar. 'We'll take men-at-arms across the sea. By God, we'll turn the red-headed bastard off the throne.'

But the King was against war. The memory of Saint Quentin rankled. It was no easy task to take men and arms across the Channel. He was all for making peace now with his Imperial enemies. He wished to see the return of Anne de Montmorency, the Constable whom he loved and revered. Even now he was seeking peace and would make no fresh wars.

'An undertaking doomed to failure,' said the King.

He had a better idea. Mary Stuart was rightful Queen of England; therefore on all documents she should be described as such. The armorial bearings of England should be displayed whenever the Dauphin and Dauphine appeared in public. Mary should be known as Dauphine of France, Queen of England, Scotland and the Isles.

The Cardinal and the Duke talked to Mary about her new dignity.

'What will my cousin say when she hears of my claim to her throne?' asked Mary.

'*Her* throne! *Her* throne!' cried the Duke testily. 'It is *your* throne. And if I had ten thousand men I'd set you on it without delay.'

But Mary was happy in France. She wished to stay in France. Let her cousin have the throne of England.

The Duke was impatient. Not so the Cardinal. He put his arm about Mary and drew her to him.

'Listen to me, Mary,' he said, 'we cannot forsake our duty and your duty is clear. All Christendom is shocked by this usurpation of the English throne. To accept it because it is an easy thing to do is sin in the eyes of God. . . . You know full well that Margaret Tudor, daughter of Henry the Seventh of England, married James the Fourth of Scotland and that their son was James the Fifth, your father. Henry the Eighth had one legitimate son and daughter. That son was Edward the Sixth; that daughter was Mary who has now died. Neither left issue. Your grandmother, Margaret Tudor, therefore provides the next line of succession and consequently the Queen of Scotland is the true Queen of England.'

'Yes, Uncle.'

'So now, dearest, I know you will not shirk your duty. You will not be guilty of foolish weakness. How do you think God and the saints regard this usurpation of the throne by one who is known to be as immoral as her mother was?'

'Yet . . . she is my cousin.'

'The daughter of a concubine!'

'But the daughter of the King as well.'

The Cardinal laughed. 'My dear Mary, her mother lost her head because she was found guilty of adultery. Now, my darling, purge your mind of foolish thoughts which would be displeasing to God. Your uncle commands you. Nay, how could he command the Queen of Scotland who is also the Queen of England! He begs you instead, my dearest. Will you disappoint him? Will you have him feel that he has wasted all these years when he has tried to show you the path of righteousness?'

'Oh no, Uncle.'

'Then, my Queen, all is well. Proudly bear your titles, and one day we will drive the red-headed bastard out of England.'

Mary said obediently: 'Yes, Uncle. Of course you are right.' But she was thinking of the gown she would wear at the coming pageant, and the last thing she wanted was to be Queen of England, for it might mean leaving the land she loved and of whose Court she was the petted darling.

Since his marriage the Dauphin had grown much taller, but although he himself was delighted with this, it was clear that the sudden shooting up had done little to improve his health. He now became possessed with a mad desire to shine in all sports and pastimes. He would ride for long hours and return exhausted. Mary remonstrated but he replied: 'Others do it. Why should not I?'

Mary had ceased to be a child when she had married. She had discovered that there was more to life than wearing fine clothes, dancing, riding, writing verses and listening to compliments, and that masques and pageants were often cover for plots and murderous intentions. Life was only pleasant on the surface, and the surface was as thin as the sheets of ice which had been declared dangerous to skaters last winter at Rambouillet.

She was sixteen. It was not very old but she had to learn quickly. She had to be able to see behind the masks on people's faces; she had to understand what was behind their words.

It was terrifying when François returned from the forest with his brother Charles. François was white and exhausted. She saw them ride into the courtyard; François slipped from his horse; she ran to him and said: 'You're tired, dearest.'

He had smiled wanly. 'No,' he said. 'I am not tired. It was a good day's sport.' His voice was hoarse. The doctors said there was some affliction of the throat.

'Come and rest now,' said Mary.

'Rest!' cried François, aware of Charles' complacent smile. 'I have no need of rest.'

Charles who had leaped from his horse, threw the reins to a groom and cried out: 'Come, François, let us go and shoot at the butts. Mary, come and watch.'

Mary, impulsive as she was, hot-tempered and quick to anger, was even quicker to feel sympathy, particularly where those she loved were concerned. She had the endearing gift of putting herself in the place of anyone who was uncomfortable or who suffered in any way, and she had seen the look of sheer exhaustion on her husband's face as he said: 'Come on then. I'm ready.'

She would not let him tire himself out. She took his arm and said pleadingly: 'Oh, François, I did want to read my verses to you. I have scarcely seen you all day.'

With what tenderness he smiled into her eyes! Perhaps he knew that her desire was not to read her verses aloud but to see those tired limbs of his enjoy the rest they needed, and that his young brother should not have the pleasure of beating him at the butts.

Charles scowled. Mary saw that familiar clenching and unclenching of the hands.

She slipped her arm through that of François. 'Come along. I insist. You must hear my verses.'

They left Charles to scowl after them as he shouted to his attendants: 'Come . . . to the butts. I am not in the least tired. I can spend ten hours in the saddle and feel as fresh as when I started.'

Mary led François into the palace and made him lie down while she read to him. He was happy to be with her; he had ridden with Charles and shown that he could do these things; now he was free to do as he wished, to rest his exhausted body while Mary sat beside him, her hand in his, his subtle protectress who never showed the rest of the world how she stood between him and everything that hurt him.

After a while he slept and Mary drew the coverlet over him and left him.

She met Charles coming from the butts. He was with several of his attendants, but when he saw Mary he signed to them to go on. His eyes were wild as he looked at Mary; his lips curled unpleasantly. 'Poor old François,' he said. 'He was worn out.'

'You rode too far.'

'Not for me. I have something to say to you, Mary. It is very secret. Come to the window seat here. Then we shall not be overheard. Speak low, Mary. I have heard that François is very sick.'

'François is well,' said Mary quickly. 'He has grown too fast in the last months and that tires him.'

'They are saying that he will never live to reach the throne.'

'*They* talk too much.'

'Mary . . . Mary . . . if he does not . . . when my father dies, I shall be King of France.'

'Your father will not die, and François will live.'

'If my father dies and François dies, you can still be Queen of France. I will marry you.'

He had taken her hands and was covering them with quick kisses.

Mary drew back in alarm. Here was another of those shocks which were coming to her too frequently. Charles had been a young boy not quite nine years old a few moments ago; now he was behaving like a man . . . a lover.

'I will love you as François never can,' said Charles. 'He is too sick. Mary, when he dies, I will marry you . . . and he will die soon. I know he will.'

Mary snatched her hands away.

'You do not know what you are saying,' she cried, rising. Then, seeing the red blood tinge his face and begin to show in the whites of his eyes, she said soothingly: 'I am glad you love me, Charles. But I am François' wife and I hope I shall always be. Stay as you are . . . my little brother. That contents me.'

'It does not content me,' mumbled Charles.

The only way in which she could treat such an outburst was

not to look upon it seriously. She smiled and left him, but her heart was beating furiously.

❀ ❀ ❀

The Cardinal came to see her and asked to speak with her alone.

'My dearest niece,' he said, 'you are looking pale. Perhaps there is a reason?'

'I was not very well yesterday, Uncle.'

The Cardinal could not hide his frown. 'I had hoped there might be another reason.'

'What reason?' asked Mary.

'It is time a child was conceived.'

She blushed and the Cardinal said anxiously: 'My child, I trust you do your duty.'

'Oh . . . yes.'

'It is imperative that you have a child. François knows that, does he not? You know it?'

'We both know it.'

'I wish the Dauphin had the manhood of some others. My poor sweet Mary, would to God . . .'

She waited, but he sighed deeply.

He went on after a pause: 'One day you will understand how much I love you. There must be a child, Mary. There must. If François died and there was no child, what would be your position here in France, do you think?'

'I do not know.'

'Dearest, try to remember your duty as I have taught it. This is a matter which concerns not only yourself but our entire house. The family looks to you. Oh, my Mary, I know that that which should be a pleasure to you is a painful duty. I read your mind and you can hide nothing from me. I see it through your eyes . . . the shameful fumblings . . . the inadequate lover. Oh, that you might enjoy one worthy of you! Oh that you might be now, in this glory of your youth, the woman I see behind those gentle eyes. Ah, what pleasure, what transcendent joy for the one who would be fortunate enough to be your lover! Mary, there must be a child. Somehow, there must be a child.'

She trembled. She was frightened by the meaning she read in his words, by the realisation that the world was so different from what it had at first seemed to be.

Henri de Montmorency danced with her in the stately *pavane*.

He complained: 'I have little chance of speaking to you.'

She thought how handsome he was, how elegant. She understood now what his burning glances meant. She feared she had been very ignorant before. Life was not easy and simple and Henri de Montmorency did not cease to desire her because she was the wife of the Dauphin.

'I must tell you this,' he said; 'I love you still.'

He was bold. He came from a bold family.

'Take care, Monsieur de Montmorency,' she said. 'There are many of your enemies who watch you.'

'Dearest lady, it is you who should take care, for you have more enemies than I could ever have.'

'Enemies . . . ? I?'

'At the Court of France many are in love with you. I mean you yourself. But some are deep in hate for the Dauphine of France.'

'I do not know of these.'

'The Queen of England hates you. She will never forgive you. I have had news from England.'

'What have I done to her?'

'What they have made you do. You have questioned her right. You have established your belief in her bastardy and you have called yourself Queen of England. Others did this, I know, but it is you whom she will blame for it.'

Mary tossed her head. 'She is far away and cannot reach me here. Ah, Monsieur de Montmorency, what do I care for the woman who calls herself the Queen of England? Talk of other things, I beg of you.'

'Your wish is a command. I will say that you grow more beautiful every day and that when I see you I am overwhelmed with love for you.'

'I did not mean that you should change the subject to speak to me thus,' said Mary, but she spoke in such a way as to imply that she did not forbid it. What harm was there in listening to such pleasant compliments from such an elegant young man!

During the weeks which followed, Mary refused to think of the unpleasant. It was exciting to be the Dauphine and enjoy greater power than ever before. She had sent Madame de Paroy from her household, and Catherine had made no attempt to send the woman back to her. Catherine paid greater respect to Mary now, for she was conscious of rank; but Mary did not like her any better.

Now Mary had her own little court – her friends among that little circle in which she and François were as Queen and King. She and François rarely left each other, for he depended on her more than ever. The Cardinal and the Duke of Guise were often in their company; her uncles asked Mary to arrange that this was so, for as they said, François was in truth their nephew now. François admired the Duke but he could not overcome his fear of the Cardinal.

The young pair hunted together, and at such times Mary was always watchful that her husband did not tire himself; and when the Dauphin was not with her she was conscious of a relaxation of responsibility, which brought with it some relief. She loved François but she was very happy without him; then she would listen attentively to the compliments which were poured into her ears; and would dance and laugh more gaily than anyone. And, she was more attractive than ever. The Cardinal, watching her, knew that one day some gallant adventurer would seek to discover the true Mary; then he might find the passionate woman who lived within the Queen.

What could that mean for Mary? Lifelong happiness? That was hardly likely, she being a queen. Lifelong tragedy perhaps, for the, as yet, undiscovered Mary was a woman who would count the world well lost for love.

The Cardinal delighted to watch his puppet; he felt he had made of her a fascinating work of art. But the game of politics must be played with care, and the Cardinal's chief interest was the power which would come to him through the advancement of his house.

The Guises were anxiously watching events. They had succeeded in marrying Mary to the Dauphin, but now the King and Diane were showing their displeasure with the Guise arrogance which had by no means diminished since the royal marriage.

The King wished to make peace with Spain. The Duke of Guise was against peace. There were long, angry discussions between the two, during which the King had to remind François de Guise that the marriage of his niece to the Dauphin did not mean that the Duke was ruler of France.

Henri was angry. Diane had been right when she had pointed out that the Guises were becoming intolerable. It was time the Constable de Montmorency, who had helped to keep the balance of power, was back in France. A peace treaty would mean the return of prisoners and among them Montmorency; thus the power of the Guises could be curtailed. The Duke, so great in war, was less useful in peace. Henri was tired of war, tired of the arrogance of the Guises. He therefore consented to make the Treaty of Cateau-Cambrésis with Philip of Spain.

The Duke ranted: 'By this treaty, by a single stroke of the pen, all the Italian conquests of thirty years are surrendered, except the little marquisate of Saluzzo. Sire, shall we throw away Bress, Bugey, Savoy . . . Piedmont . . . all these and others? Shall we restore Valenza to Spain, Corsica to Genoa, Monteferrato to . . .'

'You need not proceed,' said the King coldly. 'We need peace. We must have peace. You would have us go on until we exhaust ourselves in war. It is not the good of France which concerns you, Monsieur, but the glory of Guise and Lorraine.'

'Guise and Lorraine are France, Sire,' declared the bold Duke. 'And France's shame is their shame.'

The King turned abruptly away. It was time that reliable old ally and enemy of the Guises the Constable de Montmorency was back at Court.

There were other good things to come to France through this treaty. When it was signed, Philip of Spain and Henri of

France would stand together against the heretic world. They could make plans for the alliance of their two countries; and such plans would contain, as they invariably did, contracts for royal marriages.

There came that never-to-be-forgotten day in June. There was no one, in that vast crowd which had gathered in the Rue St Antoine near Les Tournelles where the arena had been set up for the tournament, who would ever forget it. It was a day which, by a mere chance, changed the lives of many people and the fate of a country.

The pale-faced Princess Elisabeth was there – a sixteen-year-old bride who had not yet seen the husband she was shortly to join, and whom she had married by proxy a few days earlier. The great Philip of Spain, she had been told, did not come for his brides; he sent for them. So the Duke of Alva had stood proxy for Philip, and the ceremony which had made her Philip's wife had taken place. She was grateful for the haughty pride of Spanish kings which allowed her this small grace.

It was a frightened bride who watched the great events of that summer's day.

Princess Marguerite, the King's sister, was present. She was to marry the Duke of Savoy – which marriage had also been arranged with the signing of the Treaty of Cateau-Cambrésis. The Duke of Savoy was present on this fateful day with his gentlemen brilliant in their red satin doublets, crimson shoes and cloaks of gold-embroidered black velvet, for this tournament was to be held in his honour.

All the nobility of France had come to pay respect to the

future husband of the Princess Marguerite and the Spanish envoys of Elisabeth's husband.

The Dauphin and the Dauphine came to the arena together in a carriage which bore the English coat of arms, and as they rode through the crowds, the heralds cried: 'Make place! Make place for the Queen of England!'

The Constable de Montmorency was back in France, and Henri, his son, had married Mademoiselle de Bouillon, the granddaughter of Diane de Poitiers.

Did Mary care? She was a little piqued. He had sworn he would be bold; he had sworn that he would never marry, since he could not marry Mary.

Mary laughed. It was all a game of make-believe. She had been foolish to take anyone seriously.

Queen Catherine took her place in the royal gallery at the arena. Her face was not quite as expressionless as usual, for during the preceding night she had had uneasy dreams, and although the sun was shining in the Rue St Antoine and the crowd was loyal, she was conscious of a deep depression.

The jousting began and the noble Princes excelled themselves. Mary was proud to watch the skill of her uncle the Duke of Guise and to hear the people's warm acclamation of their hero.

The Duke of Alva, stern representative of his master, sat beside Elisabeth and applauded. The Count of Nassau, William of Orange, who had accompanied Alva, took part in the jousting.

There came that moment when the King himself rode out – a brilliant figure in his armour, his spurs jewelled, his magnificent white horse rearing – to meet his opponent. The people roared their loyal greeting to their King.

How magnificently Henri acquitted himself that day! His horse – a gift from the bridegroom-to-be, the Duke of Savoy – carried him to victory.

The King had acquitted himself with honour. The people had roared their approval. But he would go in once more. He would break one more lance.

The Dukes of Ferrara and Nemours were trying to dissuade him but he felt like a young man again. He had turned to the box in which sat Diane. Diane lifted her hand. The Queen half rose in her seat. But the King had turned away. He had signed to the Seigneur de l'Orges, a young captain of the Scottish Guards. The Captain hesitated, and then the King was calling for a new lance.

There was wild cheering as the King rode out a second time and began to tilt with the young Captain.

It was all over in less than a minute. The Captain had touched the King on the gorget; the Captain's lance was splintered and the King was slipping from his horse, his face covered with blood.

There was a hushed silence that seemed to last a long time; and then people were running to where the King lay swooning on the grass.

The King was dying. He had spoken little since he had fallen in the joust. He had merely insisted that the Captain was not to be blamed in any way because a splinter from his lance had brought about the accident. He had obeyed the King and had tilted when he had no wish to do so; he had carried himself like a brave knight and valiant man-at-arms. The King would have all remember that.

In the nurseries there was unusual quiet, broken only by sudden outbreaks of weeping.

Little Hercule cried: 'When will my Papa be well? I want my Papa.'

The others comforted him, but they could not comfort themselves. Margot, whose grief, like all her emotions, was violent, shut herself into her apartment and made herself ill with weeping.

Mary and Elisabeth, François and Charles sat together, but they dared not speak for fear of breaking down. Mary noticed an odd speculative look in Charles' eyes as he watched his brother. A King was dying, and when one King died another immediately took his place. The pale sickly boy would soon be King of France, but for how long?

Edouard Alexandre – Henri – was with his mother. She needed all the comfort he could give her. As she embraced him she told herself that he would take the place in her heart of the dying man. She was sure that the King was dying, because she knew such things.

And at last came the summons to his bedside. He was past speech and they were all thankful that he was past his agonies; he lay still and could not recognise any of them. They waited there, standing about his bedside until he ceased to breathe.

In a room adjoining the bedchamber all the leading men of France were gathering. The Cardinal was there with his brother, the Duke, and they both noticed that the glances which came their way were more respectful than they had ever been before, and that they themselves were addressed as though they were kings.

When it was all over, the family left the bedside – François first, apprehensively conscious, through his grief, of his new importance. Catherine and Mary were side by side, but when they reached the door, Catherine paused, laid a hand on Mary's shoulder and pushed her gently forward.

That was a significant gesture. Queen Catherine was now only the Queen-Mother; Mary Stuart took first place as Queen of France.

🏵 Chapter V 🏵

The Queen of France! The first lady in the land! She was second only to the King, and the King was her devoted slave. Yet when she remembered that this had come about through the death of the man whom she had come to regard as her beloved father, she felt that she would gladly relinquish all her new honours to have him back.

François was full of sorrow. He had gained nothing but his father's responsibilities, and dearly he had loved that father. So many eyes watched him now. He was under continual and critical survey. Terrifying people surrounded him and, although he was King of France, he felt powerless to escape from them. Those two men who called themselves his affectionate uncles held him in their grip. It seemed to him that they were always present. He dreamed of them, and in particular he dreamed of the Cardinal; he had nightmares in which the Cardinal figured, his voice sneering: 'Lily-livered timorous girl . . . masquerading as a man!' Those scornful words haunted him by day and night.

There was one other whom he feared even more. This was his mother. If he were alone at any time she would come with all speed to his apartments and talk with him quietly and earnestly. 'My dearest son . . . my little King . . . you will need your mother now.' That was the theme of all she said to him.

He felt that he was no better than a bone over which dogs were fighting.

His mother had been quick to act. Even during her period of mourning she had managed to shut out those two men. She had said: 'The King is my son. He is not a King yet; he is merely a boy who is grieving for his father. I will allow no one to come near him. Who but his mother could comfort him now?'

But her comfort disturbed him more than his grief, and he would agree to anything if only she would go away and leave him alone to weep for his father. Mary could supply all the comfort he needed, and Mary alone.

Mary's uncles came to the Louvre. They did not ask for an audience with the Queen of France; there could be no ceremonies at such a time, said the Cardinal, between those who were so near and dear. He did not kneel to Mary; he took her in his arms. The gesture indicated not only affection, but mastery.

'My dearest,' he murmured, 'so it has come. It has come upon us unexpectedly. So my darling is Queen of France. That is what I and your uncles and your grandmother have always wished for you.'

Mary said with the faintest reproof: 'We are as yet mourning the dead King.'

The Cardinal looked sharply at her. Had the great honour gone to her head? Was she, as Queen of France, less inclined to listen to her uncle than she had been as Dauphine?

He would not allow that.

'You will need your family more than ever, Mary.'

'Yes, Uncle, I know. I have often thought of being Queen, and now I think much of the King and how kind he always was and how dearly we children loved him. But he was not kind to everybody. Terrible things happened to those who were not of the true faith, and at his command.'

'Heretics could not be tolerated in this country,' said the Cardinal.

'But, Uncle, I am a good Catholic, yet I feel that it is wrong to torture people . . . to kill them because they wish to follow a different line of thought. Now that I am Queen I should like to promise everyone religious liberty. I should like to go to the prisons where people are held because of their religious opinions, open the doors and say: "Go in peace. Live in peace and worship God in the way you wish."'

The Cardinal laughed. 'Who has been talking to you, my dearest? This is not a matter of religious thought. . . .' He remembered his robes suddenly and added: 'only. Why, these men who lie in prison care little for opinions. They wish to set the Protestant Bourbons on the throne. Religion and politics, Mary, are married to one another. A man meets his death on the Place de Grève, perhaps because he is a heretic, perhaps because he is a menace to the Catholic monarch. The world is divided into Catholics and Huguenots. But you shall learn more about these things. For the time being you will, I am sure, with your usual good sense take the advice of your Uncle François and your Uncle Charles who think of nothing but your good.'

'It is a comfort to know that you are with me.'

He kissed her hand. 'We will make the throne safe for you, dearest, and the first thing we must do is remove all those who threaten us. Where is François? Take me to him. He must send for the Constable de Montmorency at once. The old man's day is over. There you will see disappear the greatest of our enemies; and the other . . .' He laughed. 'I think we may trust the Queen-Mother to deal adequately with Madame de Valentinois.'

'The Constable! Diane!' cried Mary. 'But . . .'

'Oh, Diane was charming to you, was she not? You were her dear daughter. Do not be deceived, my dearest. You were her dear daughter because you were to marry the Dauphin, and it was necessary for all the King's children to be *her* dear children. She is an enemy of our house.'

'But she is your sister by marriage.'

'Yes, yes, and we do not forget it. But she has had her day. She is sixty and her power has been stripped away from her. When the splinter entered the King's eye she became of no importance – no more importance than one of your little Maries.'

'But does not love count for something?'

'She did not love you, child. She loved the crown which would one day be yours. You have to grow up, Mary. You have to learn a great deal in a short time. Do not mourn for the fall of Madame de Valentinois. She had her day; she may well be left to that Queen whom she has robbed of dignity and power for so many years.' He smiled briskly. 'Now, tell the King that you wish to see him.'

She went to the apartment where François sat in lonely state.

He was glad to see Mary, but wished she had come alone; and particularly he wished that she had not brought the Cardinal with her.

He tried to look as a king should look; he tried to behave as his father had. But how could he? In the presence of this man he could only feel he was a lily-livered girl masquerading as a king.

'Your Majesty is gracious to receive me,' said the Cardinal, and as he took the King's hand noticed that it was trembling.

'My uncle the Cardinal has something to say to you, dearest,' Mary announced.

'Mary,' said François, 'stay here. Do not go.'

She smiled at him reassuringly. The Cardinal, signing to them to sit on their chairs of state, stood before them.

'Your Majesty well knows that your enemies abound,' he said. 'Your position has changed suddenly and you will forgive me, Sire, if I remind you that you are as yet very young.'

The King moved uneasily in his chair. His eyes sought Mary's and sent out distress signals.

'There is one,' continued the Cardinal, 'whom it will be necessary for Your Majesty to remove from his sphere of influence without delay. I do not need to tell you that I refer to Anne de Montmorency, at present Constable of France.'

'The . . . the Constable. . . .' stammered François, thinking of the old man who alarmed him only slightly less than the sardonic Cardinal himself.

'He is too old for his office, and Your Majesty's first duty will be to summon him to your presence. Now this is what you will say to him – it is quite simple and it will make the position clear. "We are anxious to solace your old age which is no longer fit to endure the toil and hardship of service." That is all. He will give up the Seals, and Mary is of the opinion that they should be given to the two men whom you know you can trust. Mary has suggested her uncle, the Duke of Guise and myself.'

'But . . .' murmured François, 'the Constable . . . !'

'He is an old man. He is not trustworthy, Sire. He has been in the hands of your enemies, a prisoner after Saint Quentin. What plight would France be in now had not my brother hurried to the scene of that disaster? As all France knows, François de Guise saved Your Majesty's Crown and your country from defeat. Mary, your beloved Queen, agrees with me. She wishes to help you in all things. She wishes to spare you some of the immense load of responsibility. That is so, is it not, Mary?'

The caressing hand was pressed warmly on her shoulder. She felt her will merge in his. He was right, of course. He was her beloved uncle who had been her guide and counsellor, her spiritual lover, ever since she came to France.

'Yes, François,' she agreed, 'I want to help you. It is too big a load for you, because you are not old and experienced. I long to help you, and so does my uncle. He is wise and knows what is best.'

'But, Mary, the Constable . . .? And there is my mother.'

'Your mother, Sire, is wrapped up in her grief. She is a widow mourning her husband. You can understand what that means. She must not be troubled with these matters of state. As yet she could not give her mind to them.'

'You must do as my uncle says, François,' insisted Mary. 'He knows. He is wise and you must do as he says.'

François nodded. It must be right; Mary said so; and, in any case, he wished to please Mary whatever happened. He hoped he would remember what to say.

' "We are anxious to solace your old age . . ." '

He repeated the words until he was sure he knew them by heart.

Mary knew that the carefree days were over. Sometimes, at night, she and François would lie in each other's arms and talk of their fears.

'I feel as though I am a ball, thrown this way and that,' whispered the King. 'All these people who profess to love me, do not love me at all. Mary, I am afraid of the Cardinal.'

Mary was loyal, but she too, during the last weeks, had been conscious of a fear of the Cardinal. Yet she would not admit this. She had been too long in his care, too constantly assured of his love and devotion.

'It is because he is so clever,' she said quickly. 'His one thought is to serve you and make everything right for us both.'

'Mary, sometimes I think they all hate each other – your uncles, my mother, the King of Navarre . . . I think they are all waiting to tear me into pieces and that none of them loves me. I am nothing but a symbol.'

'The Cardinal and the Duke love us both. They love me because I am their niece and you because you are their nephew.'

'They love us because we are King and Queen,' asserted the King soberly. 'My mother loves me because I am the King; she loves Charles because, if I die, he will be King; she loves Elisabeth because she is Queen of Spain. Claude she loves scarcely at all, because she is only the wife of the Duke of Lorraine. Margot and Hercule she does not love as yet. They are like wine set aside to mature. Perhaps they may be very good when their time comes, and perhaps no good at all. She will wait until she knows which, before she decides whether or not she loves them.'

'She loves your brother Henri very much,' Mary reminded him. 'Yet he could not be King unless you and Charles both die and leave no sons behind you.'

'Everybody – even my mother – must do something sometimes without a reason. So she loves my brother Henri. Mary, how I wish we could go back to Villers-Cotterets and live quietly there. How I wish my father had never died and that we were not King and Queen. Is that a strange wish? So many would give everything they have in order to wear the crown, and I . . . who have it, would give away all I have – except you – if, by so doing, I could bring my father back.'

'It is your grief, François, that makes you say that. Papa's death was too sudden.'

'It would be the same if I had known for years that he was going to die. Mary, we are but children, and King and Queen of France. Perhaps if my father had lived another ten or twenty years we should have been wiser . . . perhaps then we should not have been so frightened. Then I should have snapped my fingers at the Cardinal. I should have said: "I wish to greet my uncle, the King of Navarre, as befits his rank. I will take no orders from you, Monsieur le Cardinal. Have a care, sir, or you may find yourself spending the rest of your days in an *oubliette* in the Conciergerie!" Oh, Mary, how easy it is to say it now. But when I think of saying it to him face to face I tremble. I wish he were not your uncle, Mary. I wish you did not love him so.'

'I wish I did not.' The words had escaped her before she realised she was saying them.

There were items of news which seeped through to her. The persecutions of the Huguenots had not ceased with the death of Henri, but rather had increased. The Cardinal had sworn to the

Dukes of Alva and Savoy on the death of Henri that he would purge France of Protestants, not because the religious controversy was of such great importance to him but because he wished to be sure of the support of Philip of Spain for the house of Guise against that of Bourbon. He was eager now to show Philip that he would honour his vow.

This persecution could not be kept from the young King and Queen. The Huguenots were in revolt; there was perpetual murmuring throughout the Court. Never had the prisons been so full. The Cardinal was determined to show the King of Spain that never would that monarch find such allies in France as the Guises.

There was something else which Mary had begun to discover. This uncle who had been so dear to her, who had excited her with his strange affection, who had taught her her duty, who had moulded her to his will, was hated – not only by her husband, but by many of the people beyond the Court.

Anagrams were made on the name of Charles de Lorraine throughout the country as well as in the Court. '*Hardi larron se cèle*,' was murmured by daring men as the Cardinal passed. '*Renard lasche le roi!*' cried the people in the streets.

Prophecies were rife. 'He will not live long, this Cardinal of Lorraine,' said the people. 'One day he will tread that path down which he has sent so many.'

Great men, Mary might have told herself, often face great dangers. Yet she could not fail to know that beneath those scarlet robes was a padded suit, a precaution against an assassin's dagger or bullet. Moreover the Cardinal had, in a panic, ordered that cloaks should no longer be 'worn wide', and that the big boots in which daggers could be concealed should be considerably reduced so that they could accommodate nothing but the owner's feet. Every time Mary noticed the new fashions she was reminded that they had been dictated by a man who dispensed death generously to others while he greatly feared it for himself. It was said that the Guises went in fear of their lives but, while the Duke snapped his fingers at his enemies, the Cardinal was terrified of his.

He is a coward, decided Mary with a shock.

The fabric of romance which she had built up as a child in Scotland and which had been strengthened by her first years in France was beginning to split.

She was vaguely aware of this as she held the boy-King tightly in her arms. They were together – two children, the two most important children in France, and they were two desolate lonely ones. On either side of them stood those powerful Princes, the Guises and the Bourbons; and the Valois, represented by Catherine the Queen-Mother, Mary feared more than either Guise or Bourbon.

The Court was moving south on its journey towards the borders of France and Spain. With it went the little bride of Philip of Spain making her last journey through her native land. At each stage of the journey she seemed to grow a little more fearful, a little more wan. Mary, to whom she confided her fears, suffered with her in her deep sympathy.

François' health had taken a turn for the worse. Abscesses had begun to form inside his ear, and as soon as one was dispersed another would appear. Ambrose Paré, who was considered the cleverest doctor in the world, was kept in close attendance.

Mary herself suffered periodic fits of illness, but they passed and left her well again. Her radiant health was gone, but if her beauty had become more fragile it was as pronounced as ever. There was still in her that which the Cardinal had called 'Promise'; there was still the hint of a passionate depth yet to be plumbed, and this was more appealing than the most radiant beauty, it seemed, for in spite of her impaired health, Mary continued to be the most attractive lady of the Court.

They had travelled down to Chenonceaux, that most beautiful of all French chateaux, built in a valley and seeming to float on the water, protected by alder trees. The river flowing beneath it – for it was built on a bridge – acted as a defensive moat. It had always been a beautiful castle, but Diane had loved it and had employed all the foremost artists in France to add to its beauty. Henri had given it to her although Catherine had greatly desired it; and the Queen-Mother had never forgiven this slight. One of her first acts, on the death of her husband, was to demand the return of Chenonceaux. In exchange, she had been delighted to offer Diane the Chateau de Chaumont, which Catherine considered to have a spell on it, for she swore that she herself had experienced nothing but bad luck there, and while living in it had been beset by evil visions.

As the royal party – complete with beds and furnishings, fine clothes and all the trappings of state – rode towards Chenonceaux, the Queen-Mother talked to the Queen of the improvements she intended for the chateau. She would have a new wing, and there should be two galleries – one on either side, so that when she gave a ball the flambeaux would illuminate the dancers from both sides of the ballroom. She would send to her native Italy for statues, for there were no artists in the world to compare with the Italians, as old King

François had known; the walls should be hung with the finest tapestries in the world and decorated with the most beautiful of carved marble.

'You are fortunate,' said Mary, 'to find something to do which will help you to forget your grief for the late King.'

Catherine sighed deeply. 'Ah yes, indeed. I lost that which was more dear to me than all else. Yet I have much left, for I am a mother, and my children's welfare gives me much to think of.'

'As does this beautiful chateau, so recently in the possession of Madame de Valentinois.'

'Yes . . . yes. We must all have our lighter moments, must we not? I hope that Chenonceaux will offer rich entertainments to my son and Your Majesty.'

'You are so thoughtful, Madame.'

'And,' went on the Queen-Mother, 'to your children.'

'We are very grateful indeed.'

'I am concerned for my son. Since his marriage he has become weaker. I fear he grows too quickly.' The Queen-Mother leaned from her horse and touched Mary's hand. She gave her ribald laugh. 'I trust you do not tire him.'

'I . . . tire him!'

Catherine nodded. 'He is such a young husband,' she said.

Mary flushed. There was in this woman, as in the Cardinal, the power to create unpleasant pictures. The relationship which she and François knew to be expected of them, and which the Cardinal had made quite clear to them was their duty to pursue, gave them both cause for embarrassment. For neither of them was there pleasure. They could never banish thoughts of the Cardinal and Queen-Mother on such occasions. It seemed to them both that those two were present

– the Cardinal watching them, shaking his head with dissatisfaction at their efforts, the Queen-Mother overcome with mirth at their clumsy methods. Such thoughts were no inducement to passion.

'He is so weak now,' said Catherine, 'that I am convinced that even if you did find yourself *enceinte*, no one would believe the child was the King's.'

Again that laugh. It was unbearable.

They came to Chenonceaux, and Mary's anger with Catherine had not left her when her women were dressing her for the banquet that night.

She looked at her reflection in the beautiful mirror of Venetian glass – the first which had ever been brought to France – and she saw how brilliant were her long, beautiful eyes. There was always some meaning behind the words of the Queen-Mother. Mary guessed that, for all her laughter, she was very much afraid that Mary was with child. Mary was beginning to understand why. If she had a child and François died, Catherine's son, Charles, would not be King; and Catherine was longing for the moment when Charles should mount the throne. François had once said: 'My mother loves me because I am the King; she loves Charles because, if I die, he will be King.' But although François was King he was ruled by Mary's uncles, and Catherine wished to reign supreme. That was why she had appointed special tutors for her son Charles. It would seem, thought Mary, in sudden horror, that she *wants* François to die.

She looked round the beautiful room which was her bedchamber. Perhaps here King Henri and Diane had spent their nights, making love in the carved oak bedstead with its hangings of scarlet satin damask. She glanced at the carved cabinets, the state chair, the stools; and she was suddenly glad that she had not Catherine's gift for seeing into the future. She was afraid of the future.

'Bring me my gown,' she said to Mary Beaton, who, with Seton, helped her into it. It was of blue velvet and satin decorated with pearls.

'A dress indeed for a Queen,' said Flem, her eyes adoring. 'Dearest Majesty, you look more beautiful than ever.'

'But Your Majesty also looks angry,' countered Beaton. 'Was it the Queen-Mother?'

'She makes me angry,' admitted Mary. 'How like her to come to this chateau! She says that Chaumont is full of ghosts. I wonder the ghost of the dead King does not come and haunt her here.'

'It is very soon after . . .' murmured Livy.

'She's inhuman!' cried Mary.

One of her pages announced that the Cardinal was come to see her. The ladies left her.

As he kissed her hand, the Cardinal's eyes gleamed. 'Most beautiful!' he declared. 'Everyone who sees you must fall in love with you!'

Mary smiled. Her image looked back at her from the Venetian mirror. There was an unusual flush in her cheeks and her eyes still sparkled from the anger Catherine had aroused. She enjoyed being beautiful; she revelled in the flattery and compliments which came her way. To-night she would dance more gaily than she ever had before, and so banish from her mind the unpleasantness engendered by the Queen-Mother. François had been advised to rest in his bed. It was wrong of her to feel relieved because of this; but nevertheless it was comforting to remember she need not be anxious because he might be getting tired. To-night she could be young and carefree. She was, after all, only seventeen; and she was born to be gay.

'Those who have always been in love with you,' went on the Cardinal, 'find themselves deeper and deeper under your spell. But tell me, is there any news?'

She frowned slightly. 'News? What news?'

'The news which all who love you anxiously wait to hear. Is there any sign of a child?'

Now she was reminded of that which she preferred to forget – François, the lover who could not inspire her with any passion, François, who apologised and explained that it was but their duty. She saw the pictures in her mind reflected in the Cardinal's eyes. She saw the faint sneer on his lips, which was for François.

'There is no sign of a child,' she said coolly.

'Mary, there must be; there must be soon.'

She looked at the sparkling rings on her delicate fingers and said: 'How can you speak to me thus? If God does not wish to bless our union, what can I do about it?'

'You were made to be fruitful,' he said passionately. 'François never!'

'Then how could we get a child?'

His eyes had narrowed. He was trying to make her understand thoughts which were too dangerous to be put into words.

'There must be a child,' he repeated fiercely. 'If the King dies, what will your position be?'

'The King is not dead, and if he does die, I shall be his sorrowing widow who was always his faithful wife.'

The Cardinal said no more; he turned away and began to pace the room.

'I am a very happy wife,' said Mary softly. 'I have a devoted husband whom I love with all my heart.'

'You will hold Court alone to-night?' said the Cardinal, stopping in his walk to look at her. 'You will dance. The most handsome men in the Court will compete for the honour of dancing with you. I'll warrant Henri de Montmorency will be victorious. Such a gallant young man! I fear his marriage is not a very happy one. Yet doubtless he will find many to comfort him, if comfort he needs.'

He looked into his niece's eyes and watched the slow flush rise from her neck to her brow. She would not look at the pictures which he was holding before her; she would not let him have possession of her mind. She feared him, almost as much as François feared him, and she was longing now to break away from him.

'Let us go now,' she said. 'I will call my women.'

There was a satisfied smile about his lips as he left her. But she would not think of him. She was determined to enjoy the evening. She went to see François before going down to the banqueting hall. He lay on his bed, his eyes adoring her, telling her that she looked more beautiful than ever. He was glad that he could rest quietly in his bed, yet he wished that she could be with him.

She kissed him tenderly and left him.

Down to the great hall she went with her ladies about her.

'The Queen!'

All the great company parted for her and fell to their knees as she passed them.

The Cardinal watched her speculatively. If she were in love, he thought, she would know no restraint; then she would turn from a husband who, if not impotent, was next door to it. Then there would be a child. It would be almost certain with one as passionate as Mary would become. It would not be the first time that a King believed the child of another man to be his.

His eyes met those of the Queen-Mother. She composed her features. Ah, thought the Cardinal, you were a little too late that time, Madame le Serpent. You are desperately afraid that she is already with child. That would spoil your plans, Madame. We know that you are waiting for your son François to die, so that your little puppet Charles, his Mother's boy, shall take the throne, and you, Madame, shall enjoy that position behind it which is now mine and my brother's. But he must not die yet. Everything must be done to prevent such a calamity. He must not die until he has fathered Mary's child.

Mary sat at the head of the banqueting table and her eyes glistened as she surveyed the delicacies set before her. The Queen-Mother, in her place at the great table, for the moment forgot her anxiety as to the condition of her daughter-in-law. She relished her food even more than did the little Queen. Fish delicacies, meat delicacies, all the arts known to the masters of cookery were there to be enjoyed. They both ate as though ravenous, and the company about them did likewise.

But when the meal was over and Mary rose, she was beset by such pains that she was forced to grip the table for support; the lovely face beneath the headdress of pearls was waxy pale. Mary Beaton ran to her side to catch her before she fell fainting to the floor.

There was consternation, although all were aware of the attacks which now and then overcame the Queen.

The Cardinal was alert. He had never seen Mary swoon before, although he knew that the pains she suffered, particularly after a meal, were often acute. Could it be that she was mistaken when she had said there was not to be a child? He saw the colour deepen in his brother's face and the eye above the scar begin to water excessively. Could Mary be unaware of her state? Was it the quickening of the child which had made her faint?

In such a moment the brothers could not hide their elation. The Queen-Mother intercepted their triumphant glances. She also was too moved to mask her feelings. This could be as much her tragedy as the Guise brothers' triumph.

She quickly pushed her way to the fainting girl.

Mary Beaton said: 'I will get Her Majesty's *aqua composita* at once, Madame. It never fails to revive her.'

The Queen-Mother knelt down by the Queen and looked searchingly into her face. Mary, slowly opening her eyes, gave a little cry of horror at finding the face of Catherine de' Medici so close to her own.

'All is well, all is well,' said Catherine. 'Your Majesty fainted. Have you the *aqua?* It is the best thing.'

The Queen-Mother herself held the cup to the Queen's lips.

'I am better now,' declared Mary. 'The pain was so sharp I . . . I am afraid it was too much for me.'

They helped her to her feet and she groped for the arm of Mary Beaton.

'I will retire to my apartments,' she said. 'I beg of you all, continue with your dancing and your games. I shall feel happier if you do.'

The Cardinal stepped forward, but Mary said firmly: 'No, my dear Cardinal. I command you to remain. You too, Madame. Come Beaton, give me your arm. My Maries will conduct me to my chamber and help me to bed.'

They who had crowded all about her drew back and

dropped to their knees as, with her four faithful women, she went from the banqueting chamber.

She lay on the oaken bedstead, the scarlet damask curtains drawn about it. The pain had subsided but it had left her exhausted. She would sleep until morning and then rise refreshed from her bed.

She was awakened by a movement at her bedside. She knew that it was not late for she could hear the music from the ballroom. She opened her eyes and turning saw the Queen-Mother standing by her bed.

Mary felt suddenly cold with apprehension. 'Madame!' she cried, raising herself.

'I did not mean to disturb Your Majesty,' said Catherine. 'I came to see if you were at rest.' She laid a hand on Mary's forehead. 'You have a touch of fever, I fear.'

'It is good of you to disturb yourself, Madame, but I know that it will pass. These attacks always do. They are painful while they last, but when they are gone I feel quite well.'

'You have no sickness? You must tell me. Your health is of the utmost importance to me. You know that I have some knowledge of cures. Monsieur Paré will tell you that I come near to being a rival of his. You must let me care for you.'

'I thank you, Madame, but I do not need your care. Where are my women?'

'You must not blame them for letting me come to you. They understand my concern, and they dared not refuse my entry. Although now I have taken a step backward, they remember that, only a little while ago, I stood in your exalted position.' She laughed her loud laugh. 'I still have some authority in the Court, my dear daughter.'

Catherine's long delicate fingers were feeling Mary's body –

the small, not yet fully developed breasts, she was thinking, were not the breasts of an expectant mother.

Mary sprang up indignantly. 'Madame, you concern yourself too much. I am well. I need only rest.'

'I will send Your Majesty a potion. Drink it and I'll warrant you'll feel better in the morning.'

'Madame, I feel better relying on my own remedies. But it is good of you to take such care of me.'

The Queen blew with her lips – a habit of hers. 'And you my own daughter, the wife of my son? Naturally you are my concern. I think continually of your health. I will bring the potion to you at once.'

'Then I pray you leave it with Beaton or one of my women. I will sleep now and do not wish to be disturbed.'

'It will do you so much good that – as your mother – I shall insist on your taking it at once.'

Catherine went out smiling, and Mary lay still, her heart beating wildly.

It was not long before she heard a commotion in the apartment.

Beaton's voice: 'But, Madame, the Queen gave express orders . . .' Catherine's voice: 'Out of the way, my good woman. I myself will see that the Queen takes this dose.'

Mary kept her eyes tightly shut as the curtains were parted and Beaton with Catherine stood at her bedside.

'Her Majesty needs to sleep,' said Beaton in a high-pitched whisper which betrayed her fear.

Mary could picture the scene: Queen Catherine standing there with the goblet in her hand. Poor Beaton terrified, remembering all the rumours she had heard concerning the Italian woman.

What is in the goblet? wondered Mary. She hates me. She hates François. She wants François to die so that Charles will be the King. Could it be that she wishes to poison me, as some say she poisoned her husband's brother? How would that serve her? No! It is not *I* whom she wishes to kill; it is the child she thinks is within me. That goblet will contain nothing deadly enough to kill *me*. There will be just enough poison to put an end to the life of an unborn child.

Beaton said, with great presence of mind: 'I dare not disturb Her Majesty. That was her command.'

There was a pause before the Queen-Mother spoke. 'I will leave this draught beside her bed. See that she takes it as soon as she wakes. It will ease her of her pains more quickly than anything the doctors can give her.'

'Yes, Madame.'

There was silence. Then Mary heard the sound of footsteps passing across the floor, and the shutting of a door.

When all was quiet she sat up in bed. 'Beaton,' she whispered. 'Beaton, are you there?'

Beaton came hurrying to her bedside.

'I was awake,' said Mary. 'I heard all that was said.'

'Do not drink of it,' said Beaton. 'I beg of Your Majesty not to drink.'

'Assuredly I shall not drink. Take it and throw it away . . . quickly, lest she comes back.'

Beaton was only too glad to do so. She returned in a few seconds with the empty goblet.

Beaton – strong practical Beaton – suddenly stepped forward and threw herself into the Queen's arms. She did not speak, but tremors passed through her body.

They had said goodbye to Elisabeth. The parting saddened Mary. It was a sobering thought that her dear little playmate was lost to her, perhaps for ever. There would be letters, but how could letters make up for that almost constant companionship which they had enjoyed over so many years?

There was bad news from Scotland where John Knox was demanding that Scotland seek freedom from the 'Roman Harlot' as he called the Catholic Faith. Elizabeth of England was supporting him and appeared to have forgiven him for writing his 'First Blast of the Trumpet against the Monstrous Regiment of Women'. Lord James Stuart was fretting for the Regency and Elizabeth was encouraging him. William Maitland of Lethington stood firmly with Lord James. The Duke of Châtelherault, with his unbalanced son Arran, was not far behind. They were fighting to establish Protestantism and drive Catholicism from the land.

The French sent aid, but it was not enough. All through the winter months came urgent appeals from the Queen Dowager of Scotland.

Mary was beginning to understand something of these matters; they could not be kept from her so easily now. Her thoughts were often with her mother whom she had not seen for nine years, although many letters had been exchanged between them. Mary smiled now to remember how hers had been full of trivialities.

One day she became more uneasy than ever. This was when Seton came to her and told her – when they were alone together – that she had seen a meeting between the King of Navarre and the English ambassador; and as the King of

Navarre had evidently thought it advisable to go to the rendezvous heavily disguised, it would seem as though some intrigue was afoot between these two.

'But the King of Navarre is our own cousin,' said Mary. 'He could not be involved in plots against us.'

'He is involved in plots against your uncles mayhap,' said Seton. 'So many are . . . since they came to power.'

Mary shivered. There is nothing but intrigue all about us. Seton, what will happen if the English take my Scottish crown from me?'

'Your Majesty will still be Queen of France.'

Mary thought of the sickly boy who was her husband. She thought of Catherine, standing by her bedside with the goblet in her hands.

For how long would she be Queen of France? she wondered. And then what would happen to her?

Mary was sitting on the stone balcony which overlooked the courtyard of the Castle of Amboise. François was beside her and around them were ranged all the notable people of the Court, including the royal children.

It was March and the day was bright and cold. Mary sat shivering, though not because of the weather. These were the most terrible moments through which she had ever lived. She did not believe that she could endure much more. François' face had turned a sickly green. The younger children were staring before them at the spectacle presented to them, with something like astonishment; they could not believe that it could really be happening. The Duchesse de Guise, wife of Uncle François, was fainting in her chair, her face the colour of the balcony stone. She was in danger of falling but none dared go to her; they were afraid of the fury of the Duke.

Mary thought: I can no longer bear this. I cannot look on such things.

Who could be unmoved by such cruelty? The Queen-Mother could. She seemed to be watching with a calm interest. The Cardinal was also unmoved. There was a slight lifting of his lip which implied that he was gratified by the knowledge that those martyrs, who were being slaughtered and tortured before the eyes of the royal household, were not only learning but showing others what happened to those who opposed the house of Guise.

Mary's eyes went involuntarily to the gibbet from which hung the limp figure of the Sieur de la Renaudie. The body swayed slightly in the March breeze; oddly enough it seemed to mock all the sightseers on the balcony; it seemed to be jeering at them. He was dead, he seemed to imply as he swayed indifferently, and nothing further could be done to hurt him.

François took Mary's hand and pressed it. She turned her sorrowing eyes to his; silently they pleaded with him to stop this cruelty. But who were they to stop it? Each day they realised more and more that they were powerless. They bore proud titles; the people bowed and called them King and Queen; that was the extent of their power. When Mary was told: 'You are Queen of England!' she had no alternative but to allow herself to be called Queen of England. When the followers of the Sieur de la Renaudi were brought up from the dungeons of Amboise and slaughtered before the eyes of the women and children of the royal household in the King's name, the King had no power to forbid such brutality.

It had been explained to them. These rebels had planned to kidnap the King and Queen and members of the royal family, to banish the Guises and, if the King refused to become a Protestant, to set up a new King on the throne. But if the Guises had enemies, they also had friends. The plot had been concocted with the aid of the English, but English Catholics had heard of it and warned the Duke of Guise, with the result that it had been foiled and many prisoners had been taken.

'And not a single conspirator shall be spared,' declared the Duke. 'They shall all be brought up from their dungeons. This will be a lesson to traitors.'

Heads, recently severed from living bodies, made ugly the beautiful battlements of the castle. The stench of blood was everywhere. Some of the rebels had been tied in sacks and thrown into the river. The beautiful Loire was stained with blood. There was blood everywhere . . . the sight, the smell of blood.

And the royal House of France – even young Margot and Hercule among them – must look on the slaying of tortured men. They must watch slow and cruel death being meted out.

The Duchesse de Guise had struggled to her feet. She turned and ran from the balcony. Her husband, her brother-in-law and her son watched her with contempt.

Mary said: 'François . . . François . . . I too must go. These sights will haunt me for ever.'

'They will not permit it, Mary,' whispered François. 'The Duchesse may go, but not the King and Queen.'

'It must be stopped. François, you must stop it. I cannot bear it.'

The Duke was looking at her coldly, the Cardinal in astonishment.

'Your Majesty should resume your seat,' said the Cardinal. 'Your Majesty sets a bad example to others present.'

The Duke cried: 'My wife and now my niece! By the saints, this is a sad day for Guise and Lorraine.'

The Queen-Mother came forward and laid a hand on Mary's shoulder. She looked at the Guises with understanding. She had been flirting with the Protestant cause and was anxious to show the powerful brothers – since they were at the moment in the ascendant – that she was with them.

'Your Majesty will never know how to reign if you do not learn how to administer justice,' she said.

François looked at his wife eagerly when she resumed her seat.

He took her hand and tried to soothe her. But she was sickened by the stench of blood. She would never think of Amboise after this, she was sure – dear, beloved Amboise from whose eminence she had looked down on the mingling streams of the Loire and the Amasse – without remembering this terrible day.

She knew, in that moment, that she was afraid not only of Catherine but of her uncles; never, until now, had she realised what an empty title she bore. Her dignity was touched; her anger grew. These terrible deeds were done in her name – hers and that of François. These poor men were crying for mercy to her and to François, and, by sitting here, meekly looking on, she and François were registering their approval of the deeds which were done in their names.

She could not stop the slaughter; she knew that. But she would not sit quietly and see it done.

'I *will not* stay here, François,' she said firmly. 'I *will* not.'

'Hush!' he soothed. 'Hush, dearest! They will hear. We have to stay. They say so.'

'You are the King,' she murmured.

The colour was glowing in her face now as she went on: 'The King may remain if he wishes. The Queen shall not.'

She made to rise. Her uncle, the Cardinal, was beside her; she felt his hands forcing her into her seat.

'François,' she cried, 'you are the King.'

And in that moment – for the first time in his life – François *was* the King.

He rose, and suddenly a new dignity came to him. He said: 'Monsieur le Cardinal, I command you to take your hands from the Queen.'

There was silence on the balcony. In very astonishment the Cardinal had dropped his hands to his sides.

'You wish to go to your apartments?' said François to Mary.

His mother came forward. 'My son,' she said, and there was the venom of the serpent in her cold eyes and her cold voice, 'it is the duty of the King and Queen to see that justice is done. Remember you are the King.'

'I do remember, Madame,' said François. 'And I would ask you to do so. You also, Cardinal. Come, Mary. You wish to retire. Then let us go.'

He took Mary's hand and led her from the balcony. No one attempted to stop them. François, for one short moment, was indeed King of France.

François' glory was short-lived. He had not the courage to sustain his new role. He realised that he had succeeded merely because he had taken those clever enemies of his by surprise.

The Cardinal's long mouth continued to sneer at him, continued to command. His mother was for ever at his side. He was growing weaker. There was an abscess in his ear which caused him great pain, and Monsieur Paré could do little to ease it. Each day his strength seemed to wane.

He knew that the people did not love him and that they blamed him for the terrible things which were happening under the reign of the Guises.

Rumours concerning the young King spread throughout the country.

'The King suffers from a wasting disease,' was whispered. 'It is terrible in its consequences and a miracle that he lives at all. He only does so by drinking the blood of freshly killed babies.'

Wherever the King rode, the people called their children to them in terror; they bolted and barred their doors in the villages through which he passed.

'When my father rode abroad,' said François sadly, 'the people hurried out to greet him. It was the same with my grandfather. Yet they shrink from me; they run from me; they hate and fear me. My father – good man though he was – was responsible for the death of many; my grandfather too. Yet they loved these kings and they run from me who have killed no one. Oh, Mary, life is so unfair. Why was I born like this? Why was I not born tall and strong like my father and my grandfather? Why cannot I be a King, since I am born a King . . . as they were? Why do I have to be the tool of the Cardinal? I hate the Cardinal. I hate him . . . hate him. . . .'

The Cardinal had come into the room. He was smiling slyly, but François' grief was too deep for him to care for the Cardinal's contempt. He ran to the man, grasped his padded robes and shook him.

He cried: 'I believe it is you they hate. I do not believe it is their King. They know I would not hurt them. It is you they hate ... you ... *you*! Why don't you leave us alone? Why don't you go away – then we shall know whom it is the people hate ... you or me ... you or me ...' François' voice rose to a shriek as he cried: '*Renard lasche le roi!*' Then he turned away and covered his face with his hands.

The Cardinal laughed. 'Is this a raving lunatic?' he asked of Mary. 'I had thought to parley with the King of France, and I am confronted by a madman.'

'He is not mad,' said Mary. 'He has just awakened. He is no longer a boy to be led. He has discovered that he is the King.'

'These are wild words,' said the Cardinal sadly, 'and foolish ones. I would not have expected to hear them from you.'

Mary thought of all the care he had given her, but she thought also of the love François had always had for her. She would never forget as long as she lived how, because she had been in distress on the balcony, he had forgotten his fear and in the face of all those whose displeasure he dreaded he had, for her sake, remembered he was a King.

François had begun to sob hysterically. He cried: 'You are afraid . . . you are more afraid than I. You are afraid of an enemy's dagger. That is why your clothes are padded. That is why the fashion of cloaks and boots must be changed. In the fashions we see signs of a Cardinal's cowardice.'

'It would seem to me,' said the Cardinal, 'that the King is deranged. Perhaps I should call the Queen-Mother. I thank God that there are others who could readily take his place should his mind become too deranged for him to wear the crown.'

Mary cried: 'Should you call him deranged because he seeks to remind you that he is the King of France?'

The Cardinal looked at the sobbing boy. 'There is the most cowardly heart that ever beat inside the body of a King,' he muttered.

'I beg of you, do not try him too far,' said Mary.

The Cardinal snapped his sparkling fingers to imply his contempt for the King.

Mary's eyes flashed. 'Do not be so sure that you are right, my uncle. I am not the foolish girl you seem to think me. I know what is happening here . . . and in Scotland. You . . . and my uncle . . . have set the English against me. You may well have lost me my Scottish crown.'

The Cardinal looked at her in horror. His face was stern as he said: 'This I cannot endure. I have given my devotion to you. I have thought of nothing but your welfare since you came to France. I have cherished you. I have loved you more than any living person. And you talk to me like this! You break my heart.'

Mary looked at him in anguish. What had she said? It was true that he had loved her. No one had cherished her as he had. She, remembering those intimate moments which they had shared, could not bear to see his proud head bent.

'Uncle,' she said, 'my dearest Uncle . . .' She ran to him. His face relaxed. She was held in those arms; her body was crushed against the scarlet padded robes. His lips were on her forehead, on her cheek, on her mouth.

'So you love me then, beloved? You love me yet?'

'Dearest Uncle, I shall never forget what you have done for me.'

He took her face in his hands. 'Plans,' he said, 'the best plans go wrong sometimes, Mary. What has happened in Scotland is a bitter blow, I grant you. But have no fear. Your Uncle François is the most powerful man in France. He loves you. I love you. Together we will face the world for your sake.'

'I know.'

'It is what happened at Amboise, is it not, which has turned you from me? That shocked you, my dearest. But it was necessary. You ask yourself, How could we order such things to be done? How could we look on with apparent satisfaction? For this reason, Mary: Because these scoundrels were attempting to harm our beloved niece. We may be hard men; but we love the deeper for that.'

Now she was weeping. He was dominating her once more. Now he was, as he had said, her spiritual lover. Nothing could come between them – certainly not a diseased boy, even if he called himself the King.

All was well, thought the Cardinal. Let her comfort the crying boy now if she could.

Mary was his, and the King was hers; and that meant, of course, that the Duke and Cardinal, since they need fear no opposition from the King and Queen, could continue to rule France.

❋ ❋ ❋

In the antechamber at Saint Germain a young Scots nobleman was waiting to see the Queen of France. He came with letters from the Queen-Regent of Scotland, and he had proved himself to be one of the few men about that Queen whom she believed she could trust.

He was twenty-five years of age. Tall and broad-shouldered, he gave an impression of enormous strength and vitality; his expression was one of cool unconcern; he was arrogant in the extreme, and many of the elegant Frenchmen who had looked askance at this man who had the appearance of a Norse warrior, had turned quickly away lest that indolent stare, which their faint mockery had aroused, might change to something still less pleasing. No man, looking into that granite-like face, sensing the power in those great arms and shoulders, would care to take the consequences of his anger single-handed.

He stood, legs apart, a man who would be noticed in any assembly, dominant, the over-powering vitality showing itself in the coarse springy hair, the bold flashing eyes, the entirely sensual mouth which suggested that he was a man of many adventures, sexual and warlike; and this impression was by no means a false one. He was as hardy as the granite hills of his native land; he was as wild as the Border from which he came. He was James Hepburn, who had been for the last four years — since the death of his father — the Earl of Bothwell.

As he waited he was wondering what good could come to him through this meeting with the Queen. He had heard a few days ago that her mother had died. She had long suffered from a dropsical complaint and her death was not unexpected. Now the girl who had not reached her eighteenth birthday was his Queen; he would offer her his faithful service, but in return he would expect rewards.

He had heard tales of her fascination but he was sceptical. He did not believe that one woman could be as perfect as she was represented to be. His lips curled a little. The beauty of Queens was apt to be overrated. No Hepburn would join the ranks of their idolators. Queens were women and it was folly to forget that all-important fact. No Hepburn should. There was a story in the family that his ancestor, Adam Hepburn, had found the royal widow, Mary of Guelders, most accessible, and that Queen had become, so it had been recorded, 'lecherous of her body' with the Hepburn. His own father, Patrick Hepburn – who had been called the Fair Earl and had had a way with women – had hoped to marry the Queen, Marie de Guise, and had even divorced his wife, James' mother, to make the way clear. It was true that the royal widow had used his desires in that direction to suit her own purposes, but she had been the loser when in his pique and anger against her, he had become friendly with the English.

To James Hepburn Queens were women, and he had yet to meet the woman who had been able to show an indifference to him.

He would ask for some high office, for he was an ambitious man. He would never be like his father, whatever the provocation, for he hated the English and wished to serve Scotland and the Queen faithfully; but he wished to be rewarded for doing so.

He whistled the tune of a border song as he waited. He was glad to be in France. He had spent some of his youth here, for a certain amount of education at the Court of France was considered by the Scots nobility as a desirable part of a young man's upbringing. Scotland was closely united with France and the French had the reputation of being the most cultured Court in the world. To France came young Scotsmen, and so to France some years ago had come James Hepburn.

He was particularly glad to be here at this time; not only because it was an important time politically, but in order to escape the tearful and too passionate devotion of Anna Throndsen. Anna was expecting their child; he had promised marriage, but he grew tired of women very quickly.

His upbringing had aggravated those characteristics which made him the man he was. He did not remember very much of his life before he was nine years old. That must have been because it was so easy and pleasant; his mother had had charge of him and his sister Janet, and the two of them had been tenderly cared for. They were perhaps wild by nature; they needed restraint, for the family traits were strongly marked in both of them. Their ancestors were lusty men, strong, wild and sensual.

It was unfortunate that, when James was nine years old, his father had secured a divorce from his mother. Ostensibly the grounds were consanguinity; actually they were brought because the Fair Earl wished to pay court to Mary of Guise.

The Countess of Bothwell was forced to leave her home and with it her two children. Gone was the restraining hand and the two – red-headed Janet and tawny James – ran wild.

As a boy of nine James saw terrible things. Henry the Eighth had declared war on Scotland and with typical ferocity had instructed his soldiers to put all to the fire and sword.

'Burn and subvert!' cried the tyrant. 'Put all men and women to fire and sword without exception where any resistance should be shown to you. Spoil and set upside down, as the upper stone may be the nether, and not one stick stand by another, sparing no creature.'

The life of adventure had begun. James in his flight from one town to another, saw the soldiers of the English King carry out his orders. As a result the boy was filled with a passionate hatred towards the English, a hatred which burned within him and made him long to act as he saw their soldiers acting. Rape, torture and death were commonplace sights to him. They did not disgust; they were part of the adventurous way of life; he merely longed to turn the tables, and he swore he would one day.

He became a man at an early age. He was cynically aware of his father's alliance with the enemy; he knew of his father's fondness for women.

He spent a great part of his youth in the establishment of his great-uncle Patrick, Bishop of Aberdeen. The Bishop was a merry man, eager to educate his great-nephew in such a way as to bring credit to the name of Hepburn. He was a great drinker; food and drink, he declared, were the greatest pleasures in life, apart from one other. He would slap the boy on the back when he told him this. The one other? Did he not know? The Bishop put his hands on his knees and rocked with laughter. He would wager the boy – being a Hepburn – would soon know what he meant; if he did not, then, by all the saints, he could not be his father's son.

In the Bishop's Palace the young James would lie awake and listen to the nightly perambulations of his great-uncle's friends. There were whisperings and laughter, little screams of pleasure. James thought he understood. Life at Crichton, his father's home, had not been without these phenomena, but never had he known them conducted on the scale they were in the Bishop's Palace of Spynie.

The Bishop was very fond of several comely serving women. He would chuck them under the chin or pinch various parts of their bodies as he passed them. Sometimes young James would be with him, but he did not abstain from his intimate greeting for the sake of the boy. Why should he? The boy was a Hepburn.

'A real Hepburn!' he would say; and if there was a woman at hand he would push the boy towards her and she, taking her cue, would caress him and say that he was indeed a lovely boy.

In the banqueting hall James would sometimes sit with the Bishop and his cronies, listening to their conversation which invariably concerned their amatory adventures.

The Bishop's numerous children often came to visit him, and he was very fond of them all. There were so many Janets and so many Patricks that James could not remember them all. It was the Bishop's delight to have them legitimised, several at a time.

James willingly took to the life at the Palace of Spynie. It was the life for him. He very soon began to swagger with the Bishop and his friends. He learned how to carry his liquor and boast of his adventures. The Bishop was delighted in his great-nephew. A true Hepburn! was his frequent comment.

In France, whither he had gone to complete his education, he found nothing that he had learned at Spynie a disadvantage. He never did and never would like what he thought of as the effeminate manners of the French. He would not abandon his Scottish accent; he would not ape anybody. He was himself and was determined to continue to be. Moreover he found that his methods were as effective as any. There was not a gallant in the Court of France who could boast of so many easy conquests as could James Hepburn, for all that he did not write pretty poems, nor dance and scent himself, nor wear jewels in his ears. His attractiveness lay in his dynamic personality, in that obvious virility. Not for him the graces; he would not attempt to woo. It was his way to take at a moment's fancy, for that was the way to enjoy. Too long deliberation was fatal to pleasure; his passions came quickly and as quickly passed.

His most satisfying love affair had been with Janet Beaton,

aunt to that Mary Beaton who was one of the Queen's Maries. She had had three husbands and was nineteen years older than James, but a wonderful woman, tempering wisdom with passion, friendship with love. It was a very satisfying relationship to both of them. They had become 'handfast', which meant that they were betrothed and that the betrothal was binding. Handfasting involved no actual ceremony. The couple merely lived together and, if after a certain period, they wished to go through the ceremony of marriage, they were free to do so.

The difference in their ages was too great, James realised; Janet realised it also. Janet was the only reasonable woman he had encountered in his amatory life, for he tired so quickly, the women so slowly. Janet had said that though they ceased to be lovers, there was no reason why they should not remain friends. With Janet he had been as nearly in love as he could be.

It was a pity that Anna Throndsen was not so reasonable.

He had set out on an embassy for the Queen-Mother of Scotland. First he was to go to Denmark where he was to use his persuasive powers on King Frederick that he might lend his fleet to Scotland against the English; secondly he must visit the Court of France, taking letters to the Queen from her mother.

He had set off for Denmark with high hopes, and his sojourn there might have been very successful, for he had won Frederick's promise of help; but with the death of the Queen, the political situation had changed. England was ready to discuss peace with France and Scotland, so that Frederick's offer was no longer needed.

Meanwhile James' personal affairs were giving him some anxiety.

Anna was not only attractive, she was clever; she had been outstanding among the women he had met in Denmark, not only because she was dark among so many who were fair-haired, but because she was a shrewd business woman. The eldest of seven daughters and having one younger brother, she was bold and ruled her parents. James was immediately attracted and they very quickly shared the same bed. Anna had ideas about marriage; she understood that James was a lover without much love, but with lust which came quickly and was quickly satisfied. But his virility was overpowering, and even Anna had succumbed and had felt the need to satisfy passion and make arrangements afterwards.

She believed that she could use him in the future. James was less calculating. He had the Borderer's instinct: a successful Lieutenant of the Border it had been his custom to take his choice of the women prisoners, and the affair would be over and done with quickly; he gave it not another thought. He wished it could always be thus, but there were occasions, in a more regulated society than that of a town in the process of ravishment, when certain tiresome preliminaries were necessary.

Anna was attractive enough to occupy his attention for more than one night – or even two. She saw the ambitious man in her lover; she saw the Scots noble from impoverished estates, so she allowed the rumour to be put about that she was an heiress to no small fortune. James swallowed the bait and suggested marriage.

He had never met such a clever woman. In no time she was pregnant. They must be married. She was the daughter of an honourable Danish family.

He had discovered Anna's fortune to be mythical; he had

also discovered that his desire for her was on the wane; but he could not elude her altogether. When he was ready to leave Denmark (and at that time he had not heard of the death of the Queen-Mother of Scotland and was therefore a petitioner in a hospitable land) he must take her with him, the family said; and in view of the delicate political situation he could see no alternative.

So he and Anna left Copenhagen, but when they reached Flanders he reasoned with her.

'Should I arrive at the French Court with a mistress big with child?' he demanded. 'We shall have those dandified ninnies laughing behind our backs.'

'You could arrive with the Countess of Bothwell whose condition is a delight to you,' said Anna quickly.

'A speedy marriage . . . and in a foreign land? Impossible!'

'With a man such as you are nothing is impossible.'

There was some truth in that, he thought, and, by God, I'll not take you farther. Hard as it is to rid myself of your company, you are right when you say that with me nothing is impossible.

He was cunning; he had merely been caught by the unexpectedness of her tactics, for previously he had never been forced to plead with a woman; he had said: 'Come hither!' and they came; he coolly walked off afterwards leaving them weeping and hoping for his return. He should have known Anna was no ordinary woman.

'The French,' he said contemptuously, 'are sticklers for their etiquette. The Queen has been brought up as one of them. I have my future to consider.'

'I shall see to it,' said Anna demurely, 'that it is *our* future.'

But Anna, as her pregnancy advanced, grew less truculent. She wished only to lie and rest half the day. The prospect of an uncomfortable journey across Flanders alarmed her, and she knew that he would not marry her until they reached Scotland and that it would be necessary to have their child legitimised after its birth. But she would know how to find him; he was too prominent a man to be able to lose himself.

So when he continued to urge that she should stay in Flanders while he went on alone to the French Court, she at length agreed.

Her farewell was tender, but it held a warning in it. James remembered that warning now. It was ominous. 'Do not think I am a woman to be lightly taken up and then cast off. If you think that, James Hepburn, you do not know Anna Throndsen.'

This would be a lesson to him in future. But he had no great qualms. He was not one to brood on the future; he let that take care of itself. He had been in too many scrapes to worry about consequences; he had faced death so often that he was not to be alarmed by a persistent woman.

A page came to him and, bowing before him, asked if Lord Bothwell would be so good as to follow him.

He did so until the page threw open a door and announced: 'My Lord, the Earl of Bothwell.'

He started forward expecting to see the young Queen of whom he had heard so much. Instead it was a red-clad figure, tall, dignified and imposing; and he recognised the Cardinal of Lorraine who, he had heard, with the help of his brother ruled France.

The two men took each other's measure. The sensuality of each was his most outstanding characteristic, yet there could not have been two men more different. The Cardinal was the gourmet, Bothwell the gourmand. The Cardinal was subtle; Bothwell was direct. One was a man of physical inactivity, the other a man of action. The Cardinal pandered to his sensual appetites, using aphrodisiac means – mental and physical – to stimulate them; Bothwell needed no such stimulation. The Cardinal was a coward; Bothwell did not know the meaning of fear. They were two strong men, but their strength lay in different directions.

The Cardinal disliked the boldness of the coarse Borderer; Bothwell disdained the arrogance of the elegant gentleman. But they were each aware of the power possessed by the other. The Cardinal, by far the cleverer of the two, was able to hide his resentment the more easily.

'I had thought to see my Queen,' said Bothwell.

'Monsieur,' smiled the Cardinal, 'you have come from Scotland where Court manners are slightly different. In France we await the pleasure of the Queen. We do not present ourselves unless commanded to do so.'

'I have letters from the Queen's late mother. Doubtless she will be eager to receive them.'

'Doubtless. But as Queen of France she has much with which to occupy herself. I know you have come from Denmark where you did good work. I heard from my dear sister, before her unfortunate demise, that you were a worthy young man whom she delighted to honour with her trust. I therefore welcome you to the Court of France.'

'You are gracious, Monsieur le Cardinal, but it is my Queen I have come to see.'

'You have the letters from her mother?' The Cardinal extended his slim white hand.

'My instructions were to hand them to none but the Queen herself.'

'The Queen has no secrets from me.'

'So I have heard,' answered Bothwell. 'But those were my instructions.'

The Cardinal sighed. 'There is one matter I must discuss with you. The Queen does not know of her mother's death. I myself wish to break the news and break it gently. She has suffered from bad health lately and I fear the shock might prove too much for her.'

Bothwell's lips were set in an obstinate line. He did not see why he should take orders from the Cardinal. He disliked taking orders. His policy with the late Queen had been a bold one. He was no Court intrigant and flatterer. Now that her mother was dead it was well for the Queen of Scots to know of the acute danger which such a situation threatened. He had come to warn her of just that; and now, this man, doubtless for reasons of his own, was forcing him to silence on a most important issue.

'I have had no instructions,' declared Bothwell, 'to keep silent on this matter.'

'Until now . . . no,' agreed the Cardinal.

'My Lord Cardinal, this is a matter which I must discuss with others of my countrymen. Lord Seton is here at Saint-Germain. I . . .'

'That gentleman has already received his instructions in the matter.'

'And the King of France?' said Bothwell with a trace of insolence. 'These are his instructions?'

'The King, Monsieur, knows nothing of the tragedy. If he knew of it, he would be unable to prevent himself from imparting it to the Queen.'

'So then the King and Queen are kept in ignorance of certain facts which concern them!'

The Cardinal decided to smile at such insolence. He said: 'The King and Queen are very young – little more than children. It is the express desire of her uncle, the Duke of Guise, and myself as well as the Queen-Mother of France, not to overtax them. We lighten their burdens as best we can. It is our considered opinion, in view of the Queen's failing health, that she should not at present suffer the shock such news would give her. Therefore, my Lord Bothwell, you will say nothing of her mother's death. I myself will break the news to her when I consider she is fit to receive it.'

'You are not afraid that someone's indiscretion may betray the news?'

'We know how to deal with indiscreet people, my lord. And all of us who love the Queen have no wish to do aught which would bring harm to her. Give me your assurance that you will say nothing of her mother's death, and no obstacle shall be put in the way of your meeting the Queen.'

Bothwell hesitated, but only for a moment. He was sharp enough to see that this man could prevent his meeting with the Queen.

'I give my word,' he said.

The Cardinal was satisfied. There was that about the Scottish adventurer which implied that having given his word he would keep it.

James Hepburn, Earl of Bothwell stood before the Queen of France and Scotland.

He had knelt and kissed her hand and had now been bidden to rise. He was acutely aware, among those about her, of the red-clad figure of the Cardinal.

So here was the Queen of Scotland! he pondered. This was the young woman of whom he had heard so much. This was the 'skittering lass' the Hamiltons referred to. She was but a pale and delicate girl.

It was characteristic of James Hepburn that in those few seconds he had stripped her of her royalty and had seen her as a woman. He was aware of curling chestnut hair that gleamed red and gold in places, long – but not large – eyes, a gentle and smiling mouth, a skin that was pale and delicate, a carriage which suggested pride of race and great dignity. He thought her fair enough, but he had been expecting one more dazzling. He thought of Anna's dark beauty; Mary Stuart's was of a different kind.

That underlying, but as yet unawakened sensuality which was the secret cause – far more than her beauty – of Mary's attractiveness, was beyond his perception. He was attracted by the obvious. He thought Mary unhealthy and the unhealthy did not please him. She was French, for all she called herself the Queen of Scots. Her dress and manners – everything about her – was French. She was a fragile and pretty creature – that was all as far as he could judge.

That she was his Queen was quite another matter.

'My Lord Bothwell,' she addressed him, 'you have brought letters from my mother.'

He said this was so and that he was honoured and delighted to have the opportunity of offering them to her.

He took them from the pocket of his doublet and gave them to her. Smiling she took them. Then he saw her charm. A pretty wench, he thought, but, alas, not a bonny one.

The Cardinal was murmuring to the Queen: 'I will relieve Your Majesty of these documents.' Mary handed them to him.

'Later,' went on the Cardinal, 'if it is Your Majesty's pleasure, we will go through them together.'

'That is my pleasure,' said the Queen.

Bothwell's lips tightened. He himself might just as well have handed the documents to the Cardinal. Did she never do anything unless this man allowed her to?

The Queen was smiling at Bothwell. 'Pray sit down,' she said. 'Here beside me. There is much I wish to hear of Scotland.'

He sat down. She threw a sidelong look at him. That virility alarmed while it fascinated. She was not sure whether she found it attractive or repulsive. With the Cardinal hovering beside her she believed she found it repulsive. She had heard of this Bothwell; he was the successful Lieutenant of the Border and would have lived a wild life. She pictured him, ravishing the towns across the Border, driving the cattle before him, herding the women . . . like cattle. She had heard of such things. He would be brutal, this man. He made her shiver.

'You have come by way of Denmark,' she said.

'Yes, Your Majesty. It was the wish of the Queen, your mother, that I should visit the Court of King Frederick to make requests of him.'

'She will doubtless have told me of these requests in the letters you bring.'

Bothwell was astounded. Did she know nothing? Was she left entirely in the dark? He had come to warn her of the state of her Scottish realm. He had come to warn her of the claims of Arran, the treachery she might expect from the Bastard, Lord James Stuart; he had come to warn her of the machinations of Elizabeth of England and her minister Cecil. There was an immediate need to appoint a new Regent. Yet she – a silly, simpering girl – seemed to know nothing of these matters. Could it be true that she gave no thought to anything but dancing prettily and writing and reading verses?

God help Scotland with such a Queen! Bothwell thought with deep regret and affection of the valiant woman who had recently died after enduring continued hardship fighting a desperate battle, not only against the English, but against her own rebel lords, while this girl, the real Queen, mimed and danced in French chateaux, making simpering Frenchmen fall in love with her!

Bothwell was about to speak, but the Cardinal forestalled him.

'Your Majesty, my Lord Bothwell will be at Court for some time. You are tired now. Retire to your apartments and we will read these letters from your mother, the contents of which I am sure you will wish, above all things, to know, and most speedily. Promise Lord Bothwell that he shall have audience to-morrow. Then you will feel strong enough to hear his news.'

Mary hesitated. Then she said: 'Lord Bothwell, please present yourself at this hour to-morrow.'

James bowed. 'Your Majesty's servant.'

The Queen rose and laid her hand on the arm of the Cardinal with whom she went from the chamber.

Mary was thinking of Bothwell while the Cardinal broke the seals of her mother's letters and began to read them aloud to her.

He had made her uneasy. There was a certain insolence in his gaze. She could not complain; he had bowed low enough; he had kissed her hand in the appropriate manner; he had said the right words; but the eyes – that bold glance . . . how could she describe it? Insolent! It was not one of those passionate looks which she so often received and which she understood meant that the one who gave them longed to be her lover. This man was arrogant and cold and yet in a way he seemed to hint that he too imagined himself making love to her. It was too much to endure. Yet how could she complain?

She had not really known whether she wanted to remain with him or dismiss him. She had chosen to dismiss him because she felt he should know that it was for her to command. That was not entirely true. The Cardinal had intervened, had suggested she should retire because she was tired; and she had obeyed.

The Cardinal now saw that her attention wandered. He said: 'What did you think of the messenger? Was he not a crude clown. It is a sad thing that your mother could not find one more worthy of the mission. But, by all accounts, he may be trusted, which is more than can be said for most of these Scotsmen. A rough fellow – but he did good work on the Border. Such works suit him better, I'll vow, than playing ambassador. Murder and rape are his profession. We shall have to warn our ladies. We do not want him to offend them. We shall have to protect our serving girls. I hear he has a fondness for such.'

'I am sorry to hear it,' said Mary. 'My mother says he is a faithful servant. I should not like her ambassador to make trouble here . . . even if it were only with serving girls.'

'I had him watched in Denmark and Flanders. He is in some trouble with a woman now. It is unfortunate. She is the daughter of a retired Admiral – Christopher Throndsen, a man of some standing in Copenhagen. He promised the girl marriage, promptly seduced her, and now there is to be a child and he has left her to fend for herself in Flanders.'

'It is clear that he is a brute,' said Mary.

'He considers, I fancy, that he has behaved with decorum. Seduction is new to him; rape is his business.'

Mary shuddered. 'Dearest Uncle, do you mind if we speak of his affairs no more? I find them distasteful.'

The faintest satisfaction showed in the Cardinal's face. All was well. The man disgusted her. Her womanhood still slumbered.

Lord Bothwell stretched his legs on the bed in the apartment which had been assigned to him. His page, whom he had engaged recently because the fellow's cheeky manners appealed to him, and whom he called 'French Paris' though his name was really Nicholas Hubert, knelt to take off his master's boots.

'Have done!' growled Bothwell. 'I shall be up again in a minute, and then you'd be obliged to put them on again.'

Paris grinned. He enjoyed serving this master. Bothwell's love affairs were Paris' constant delight, and his greatest pleasure was to have some hand in arranging them.

'And what thought my lord of the Queen of France?'

Bothwell was silent for a few seconds. Then he said: 'It would seem to me that she'll not be long for this world. But mayhap it's this Court with its dancing and fancy ways. Mayhap our Scottish breezes would put her on the road to health.'

Paris had not wanted an opinion of the Queen's health. She was, he had heard, the most desirable woman in the world. Surely his lord had noticed that?

'She's a well-formed lass,' went on the Earl. 'But she needs to be taken out of soft wrappings and to rough it as her mother did. She seemed to know nothing of the country she is supposed to rule, and cares, I'll swear, as little. 'Tis as well for her that she's Queen of France and not obliged to live in her own country. We should have to teach her one or two things if she did.'

Paris nodded. 'There's much your lordship could teach her, I doubt not.'

Bothwell was silent for a few moments before he said: 'The Cardinal of Lorraine would seem to be King of this realm . . . with his brother thrown in. "Do this!" "Do that!" he says, and the Queen does it. "Don't listen to this and don't read that!" And she smiles and lets him have his way.'

'He's her uncle, my lord, but his reputation is the worst in the world.'

Bothwell leaped off his bed suddenly. 'And how does hers stand?' he demanded. 'I wonder! It would not surprise me if she were the Cardinal's mistress.'

'My lord!'

'Where I come from we don't mince our words. It would seem to me that she does all the Cardinal asks. And when it is a matter of asking anything of a woman, the Cardinal would not be backward in his demands – niece or no niece, Queen or tavern girl. Moreover I have seen that between them which tempts me to believe it. It would not surprise me at all.'

'And does my lord relish the thought?'

'Our Queen the Cardinal's loose woman to do his commands! What think you?'

Paris came closer and whispered: 'And does your lordship find it hard to stomach the thought for another reason?'

'What reason, fellow?'

'That your lordship would not mind being in the Cardinal's shoes for a spell?'

The Earl cuffed the man, and Paris retired, holding his ears but still grinning.

'A skittering lass!' Bothwell murmured to himself.

Of what could he talk to the Queen? He could tell her of the money he had lost in the defence of Leith; he could ask for the recompense he so sorely needed. He had talked to those men who had been engaged in the defence of Scotland with him and who were now at St Germain-en-Laye — Seton, Martigues and the Sieur d'Oysel. The Queen, they had told him, had been disinclined to grant their claims — on the advice of the Cardinal, of course. They were disgruntled, all of them.

This was not the occasion, Bothwell realised, to talk of his just deserts. He would try then to warn the Queen and to make sure that, when she formed her new government, he was selected to play a prominent part in it.

At this time the Cardinal decided that he could no longer keep the Queen in ignorance of her mother's death.

Mary was stunned by the news. Ignorant as she had been of the state of affairs in Scotland, she realised that, now that her mother was unable to guard her throne, it would be in peril.

She shut herself away to grieve alone, and her grief was great. It was nine years since her mother had visited the Court of France and yet they had remained close through their letters. Mary knew that she had lost one of the best friends she could ever have.

What would happen in Scotland now? Her thoughts went to the Borderer who had disturbed her with his bold personality. He would know, and he had been especially recommended to her by her mother.

It was easier for them to talk of Scotland now that she knew of her mother's death. Bothwell could talk freely of the perilous state of affairs which had sprung up. There was peace with England, it was true; but there were many warring elements within the troubled realm.

She received him in private. She was wan from the past days of mourning.

She said: 'My lord, you have come recently from Scotland. You will have knowledge of how matters go there. How fares my brother? I should like to see him again – dear Jamie! We were always so fond of each other.'

A faint smile curved the Earl's lips. Dear Jamie! The lass was not fit to govern a rough kingdom. Did she not realise that her 'dear Jamie' would never forgive her for being born legitimate when he – older, wiser, stronger and a man – might have been King? These French had made her soft. He could see in her eyes the affection she bore her big brother. It did not seem to occur to her that the crown came between her and any love Lord James Stuart might have for her.

But how tell a sentimental and emotional woman to beware of her brother! How speak to her of those hardy men of intrigue – James Douglas, Ruthven, Morton?

All he could do was advise her to form, without delay, a governing party; and because of his knowledge of her Scottish subjects, he could at least give her the names of those whom she could trust – farther than most, he might add.

He himself would take a prominent part in the governing

body. He believed Huntley and Atholl too could be trusted.

He did not trust the Bastard of Scotland, but it would be impossible to leave Lord James Stuart out of such a governing body.

The Queen was ready to put her faith in Bothwell.

He looked at her with mild contempt. She was Queen of a troublous realm which she did not even wish to see. He understood perfectly. She liked this soft Court where gallants ducked and bobbed and scented themselves and jangled their jewels in their doublets and even in their ears; she liked pretty verses and music and clever conversation.

It was a sad day, decided the Earl of Bothwell, when Mary of Guise had died and left her frivolous young daughter to fend for herself.

The cold winter had set in, and the Court was preparing to leave the Balliage where they had been staying in the City of Orléans. The royal baggage, with the magnificent beds and tapestries, had been loaded, and they were ready to travel to Chenonceaux.

Lord Bothwell had left France, and Mary was glad. When he went he seemed to take with him her uneasy thoughts of her kingdom across the seas.

Lately Mary had been conscious of a growing alertness in the face of Queen Catherine. François' mother rarely left his side. She was solicitous of the throbbing pain in his ear for which she was constantly supplying lotions and potions to subdue his suffering. Paré, the great doctor, was in attendance upon the King.

Mary knew from the grave face of the doctor and the closed

expression on the face of the Queen-Mother, that François was very ill indeed, far worse than he had ever been before.

She was very anxious on this day of departure, for she knew the keen wind would set François' ear throbbing afresh. The swelling was angrily inflamed and the pain almost unendurable.

She and François were about to mount their horses when François, suddenly putting his hand to his ear, fell fainting to the ground.

There was great consternation, for it was clear that the King was very ill indeed. Mary knelt beside François, and a great fear overcame her for she recognised the signs of approaching death.

Catherine was on the other side of her son. For a moment it was as though a shutter had been drawn aside and Mary glimpsed that in the Italian woman's face which she would rather not have seen.

Catherine knew her son was dying, but Mary realised she felt no grief; instead she had betrayed her great exultation.

Mary sat by the bed which had been hastily set up. François was too weak for speech, but he knew she was there and that knowledge comforted him. Occasionally his pain-crazed eyes would be turned to her, and one word formed on his lips, though no sound came: Mary.

Mary knew that her uncles would be hurrying to Orléans, but she felt desperately alone. She wanted to put her arms about her dying husband and protect him from the quiet woman who glided about the apartment, masking her elation, saying soothing words, bringing soothing drinks. Could it be true that a mother could wish her son dead? Could it be true that her personal power meant more to her than the boy who had once been part of her body? Mary could not believe that. But there were such strange stories about this woman.

'Something must be done!' she cried passionately.

She summoned Monsieur Paré to her. She said she wished to be alone with him; but her mother-in-law was in the apartment, calm and determined.

'I am his mother,' she said. 'You cannot shut *me* out.'

'Monsieur Paré,' said Mary, 'there must be something which can be done. I beg of you to do it.'

'Your Majesty, I would attempt an operation but it might fail. But if there is no operation the King will certainly die.'

'I will not have my son suffer unnecessarily,' said Catherine. 'I must speak with Monsieur Paré. I must know exactly what this attempt will mean. I cannot allow my son to suffer unnecessarily. I am his mother. I would do anything in the world to save him unnecessary pain.'

'We are speaking of his life,' said Mary fiercely.

Catherine turned to the door: 'Monsieur Paré, the Queen is a young wife who loves her husband. She is filled with grief and that grief overwhelms her. Monsieur Paré, I am his mother. I must speak with you alone. I must know exactly what this means.'

The surgeon cried out in desperation: 'Madame, there is a chance to save the King's life . . . a frail one. It is by no means certain. Immediate action would be necessary. There is a slight hope of success, but if nothing is done he cannot last more than a few hours.'

'It is because of that that I will not have him suffer unnecessarily. My son . . . my poor little François! He is still that to me, though he may be the King.'

'We waste time,' cried Mary frantically. 'Precious time . . .'

'You are right,' said the Queen. 'There is no time to lose.' She took the doctor's arm. 'I must talk with you first, Monsieur Paré. Before this operation is performed I must have careful speech with you alone.'

Paré looked from the face of the wife to that of the mother. One was a young girl – almost hysterical with grief – the other was a calm woman.

Catherine took him by the arm and led him from the room.

They were a long time gone, and when they returned Mary's uncles had arrived.

Mary sat by the bed in desolation. There was now a rattle in the King's throat. Mary knew, when Paré returned to the apartment with Catherine, that it was too late to do anything more to save François.

The snowflakes were tapping gently on the window; the wind moaned outside. All those about the bed watched the wan face of the dying King.

The Cardinal had taken the young man's hand; he bent closer over the bed. Even the Cardinal was awed in the presence of death; even to this man came a glimmer of remorse for all he had done to the dying boy.

'Say after me,' he commanded, as all through the boy's reign he had commanded, 'say this: "Lord, pardon my sins and impute not to me, thy servant, the sins committed by my ministers under my name and authority."'

The wan lips moved and tried to frame the words.

'Oh God, listen to him,' prayed Mary. 'It was not at his command that the waters of the Loire were stained blood-red.

He had no hand in what was done at Amboise. Remember that and do not blame François.'

Catherine came closer to the bed. She said: 'It is all over. The King is dead.'

She did not say, but she meant: Long live the King . . . the new King.

She was determined to govern Charles as the Guises had governed François and Mary.

Mary watched her fearfully as she stood there, her white hands folded on her black gown, forcing sorrow into the face which was beginning to inspire great fear in Mary's heart.

❀ ❀ ❀

They walked solemnly out of the chamber of death – the widowed Queens side by side.

Tears were running slowly down Mary's face. Her one thought was to make her way with all speed to her own apartments, to lie on her bed, draw the curtains, and demand that she be left alone with her grief.

They were at the door; she would have passed through but there was a slight detaining touch on her arm.

Queen Catherine was beside her, pressing her large body gently forward, reminding her that she, Mary, must stand aside now as once Catherine had stood aside for her.

Queen Catherine wished her to know in this moment of bitter grief that Mary was no longer first lady in the land. Catherine was in the ascendant; Mary was in decline.

🌑 Chapter VI 🌑

In the shrouded chamber the young widow sat alone. Her face was pale beneath the white coif; the flowing robes of her white dress fell to the floor; even her shoes were white. The chamber was lighted only by tapers and it seemed like a tomb to Mary.

She paced the room. She had no tears left. Since her first coming to the Court of France, François had been her friend and her devoted slave. Had she been at times a little too arrogant, a little too certain of his devotion? If she could only have him back now, how she would assure him of this love which she only knew went so deep since she had lost him.

What tragic changes had overtaken her life! She thought of her uncles as they had been on the day of François' death, standing with her, one on either side of her, while the nobles of the Court, led by Queen Catherine, went to the apartments of the little Charles to do homage to the new King.

They had said nothing to her, those uncles; but she knew they were disappointed in her. There should have been a child, their eyes accused her. A child would have changed everything. Their sinister implication was: If François could not give you a child, there were others who could.

What was honour to those uncles of hers? What was morality? All that mattered was the power of Guise and Lorraine; and, according to them, she had failed in her duty towards her maternal house.

What would become of her?

She smoothed the folds of the *deuil blanc*, apprehensive of the unknown doom which must soon overtake her.

During those first weeks of mourning she must see no one except her attendants and members of the royal family.

They came to visit her – Charles, the nine-year-old King, and Catherine, his mother.

Mary knelt before the boy, who, in his new-found dignity, commanded: 'Rise, dear Mary.'

She should have been comforted by the love she saw in his eyes, but she realised that, young as he was, the love he bore her was not that of a brother. The young King's eyes grew feverish as they studied the white-clad figure. It was as though he were saying: 'I am the King of France now that François is dead. There is nothing between us now.'

Could this thing come to pass? Was it possible that she might again be Queen of France? This boy – this unbalanced child who was now the King – wished it; her uncles would do all in their power to bring it about, for if she married Charles the Guises' power would be unchanged. The only difference would be that in place of gentle François, Mary would have a new husband, wild Charles.

Catherine was closely watching her son's face. She said: 'It is sad for you, my daughter, to be thus alone. Forty days and forty nights . . . it is a long time to mourn.'

'It seems a short time, Madame,' said Mary. 'I shall mourn the late King all my life.'

Catherine puffed her lips. 'You are young yet. When you return to your own country you will mayhap have another husband to love.'

Mary could not hide the fear which showed in her face. That was what she dreaded more than anything – to leave the land which she had come to look upon as her own, to sail away to the dismal country of which she had bleak memories and was reminded every now and then when the crude-mannered Scots came to the Court of France. She could not bear to lose her husband, her position and her country at one blow. That would be too much to endure.

'Madame, I should wish to remain here. I have my estates in France. I would retire from the Court if necessary.'

The King said: 'It is not our wish that you should do so. We wish you to stay here, dear Mary.'

'Your Majesty is good to me. It is a great comfort to me to know of your kindness.'

'Dearest Mary, I have always loved you,' said the King.

His mother had gripped his shoulder so hard that he winced and, turning angrily, he scowled at her. Mary watched them and she saw the fear which suddenly came into the boy's face.

Catherine laughed loudly. 'The King feels tender towards you,' she said. 'He remembers the love his brother bore you. We shall be desolate when you leave us.'

'Mary is not going to leave us,' cried the King wildly. He took Mary's hand and began to kiss it passionately. 'No, Mary, you shall stay. I say so . . . I say so . . . and I am the King.'

The red blood suffused the King's cheeks; his lips began to twitch.

'I cannot have the King agitated,' said Catherine looking coldly at Mary, as though she were the cause of his distress.

'Perhaps if he speaks his mind freely,' said Mary, 'he will be less agitated.'

'At such a time! And my little son with such greatness thrust upon him, and he but a child . . . scarcely out of his nursery! Oh, I thank God that he has a mother to stand beside him at this time, to guide him, to counsel him, to give freely of her love and the wisdom she has gleaned through experience . . . for he has need of it. He has need of it indeed.'

'I am the King, Madame,' persisted Charles.

'You are the King, my son, but you are a child. The ministers about your throne will tell you that. Your mother tells you. Your country expects wisdom of you far beyond your nine years. You must listen to the counsels of those who wish you well, for believe me, my son, there are many in this realm who would be your deadly enemies if they dared.'

A terrible fear showed in the little boy's face and Mary wondered what stories of the fate which would befall an unwanted King had been poured into his ears.

Charles stammered: 'But . . . everybody will be glad if Mary stays here. Everybody loves Mary. They were so pleased when she married François.'

'But Mary has her kingdom to govern. They are waiting for her, those countrymen of hers. Do you think they will allow her to stay here for ever? I doubt it. Oh, I greatly doubt it. I'll swear that at this moment they are preparing a great welcome for her. She has her brothers there, remember. James Stuart . . . Robert and John Stuart and hundreds . . . nay, thousands of loyal subjects. Her neighbour and sister across the border will rejoice, I am sure, to know that her dear cousin of Scotland is not so far away as hitherto.'

Mary cried out: 'I am so recently a widow. I have lost a husband whom I loved dearly. And you come to me . . .'

'To tell you of my sympathy. You were his wife, my dear, but I was his mother.'

'I loved him. He and I were together always.'

'He and I were together even longer. He was with me before the rest of the world ever saw him. Think of that. And ask yourself whether your grief can be greater than mine.'

'Madame, it would seem so,' said Mary impulsively.

Catherine laid a hand on her shoulder. 'My dear Queen of Scotland, I am an old woman; you are a young one. When you have reached my age you will doubtless have learned that grief should be controlled – not only for the good of the sufferer but for those about her.'

'You cannot care as I do.'

'Can grief be weighed?' asked Catherine, turning her eyes to the ceiling. 'You are young. There will be suitors and you will find a new husband . . . one who, I doubt not, will please you better than my dear son did.'

'I beg of you . . . stop!' implored Mary.

Charles cried: 'Mary . . . Mary . . . you shall not go. I'll not allow it. I am the King and I will marry you.'

Catherine laughed yet again. 'You see the King of France is but a child. He knows not the meaning of marriage.'

'I do!' declared Charles hotly. 'I do.'

'You shall marry at the right time, my darling. And then who knows who your bride will be.'

'Madame, it must be Mary. It must.'

'My son . . .'

Charles stamped his foot; his twitching fingers began to pull at his doublet and the golden fringe came away in his hand. He flung it from him and turned his blazing eyes on his mother. 'It shall be Mary! I want Mary. I love Mary.'

He threw himself at the young widow, flung his arms about her waist and buried his hot quivering face in the white brocade of her gown.

'It is so touching,' said Catherine. 'Come, my dear little King. If this is your wish . . . well then, you are a King and a King's wishes are not to be ignored. But to speak of this . . . so soon after your brother has died and is scarce cold in his grave . . . it frightens me. You want your brother's wife. I beg of you to keep quiet on such a matter for, with your brother so recently dead it is a sin. Why, you will be afraid to-night when the candles are doused and your apartment is in darkness. You will be afraid of your brother's accusing ghost.'

Charles had released Mary. He was staring at his mother and biting his lips; his hands began to pull once more at his doublet.

Catherine put her arm about him and held him against her.

'Do not tremble, my son. All will be well. Your mother has that which will protect you from evil spirits. But she needs your collaboration in this. Do not put into words thoughts which could bring disaster to you.'

Mary cried out: 'Madame, I am mourning my husband. I would wish to be alone.'

'You poor child. It is true. You are mourning. This is not the time to remind you that, as Dowager Queen of France, you are no longer in a position to order the Queen-Mother of France from your apartment. We understand that it is the extremity of your grief which has made you forget this little detail. We know that when you emerge from your mourning you will fully realise your changed position. There, my child, do not let your grief overwhelm you. You have had many happy years with us here in France. If, by some ill chance, you should have to leave us, remember you will be going to your own country. It is not France, we know, but you will love it the more because it is yours. You will be a neighbour of your cousin of England . . .'

'Who hates me,' put in Mary.

'Hates you! And you her cousin!'

'She will never forgive me for calling myself Queen of England.'

Catherine looked grave. 'Ah! It is a pity that you could not have foreseen this day. I remember well your riding in your litter proudly bearing England's arms. What pride was yours! Not content with two crowns you must have a third!'

'I but obeyed the orders of your husband, the King, and of my own husband.'

'And now they are no longer here to share the blame! Have no fear. You are young and many have told you that you are beautiful. It is a fact which you know full well, so I have no need to remind you of it. I am sure the Queen of England will soon have the same affection for you as you have inspired in me. We will leave you now to your mourning.'

Mary knelt and took the cold hand. What were those expressionless eyes telling her? You have stepped down from your pedestal and I am in control now. Do not expect friendship from one whose friendship you never sought. You have learned one lesson in France, Mary Stuart. You have learned what a fool you have been to flout Catherine de' Medici, that daughter of tradesmen.

Her uncles came to see her. They had changed since François' death. Their power had been stripped from them. Anne de Montmorency had been recalled; the Queen-Mother was now the Regent of France and it was said that she had complete control over the nine-year-old King. Overnight she had stepped into that position which, during the reign of François and Mary, had been filled by the Brothers Guise.

How to recover that position! That was the urgent concern of François de Guise and Charles de Lorraine.

'We have come to discuss the future, Mary,' said the Duke.

'I do not wish to go to Scotland,' said Mary quickly.

'Nor do we wish you to,' the Cardinal assured her. 'If all we have in mind shall come to pass, there would be no need of that.'

'Many suitors are presenting themselves,' the Duke told her. 'There are Frederick of Denmark and Eric of Sweden . . .' began the Duke.

'None of whom we feel are worthy of you,' put in the Cardinal.

'There is Arran, whom his father is urging forward,' added the Duke; 'although he himself is most eager to come.'

'Poor Arran!' murmured Mary.

'They say his brain is soft,' said the Cardinal, 'and has been since he set eyes on you when he was at Court. They say he was first sick with love, and then mad with love for the most beautiful girl in the world. We should not wish you to make so poor a match.'

'Tell her of that other youth,' interrupted the Duke.

The Cardinal's smile was a sneer. 'What impudence! There

has arrived at the Court one whose mother has sent him to offer condolences for your loss. Condolences, indeed! The youth is delighted by your loss! That is, if he has the sense to understand what his mother must have been at great pains to hammer into his head. He comes full of hopes . . . conscious of his royalty . . . a youth of fifteen, a tall, gangling boy, unsure of anything but that he has royal blood in his veins. He comes to offer condolences from his parents to their kinswoman and to express the hope – oh, most subtly – that if Your Majesty should be looking for another husband, you might be enchanted by a fellow like himself.'

'Who is this?' asked Mary.

'Young Henry Darnley, whose mother, Lennox's wife, will have all the world know that as she was the daughter of Margaret Tudor, sister of Henry the Eighth of England, her son is not without some pretension to the throne of England . . . and of Scotland too. Madame Lennox presents her long lean son for your inspection. I dare swear she thinks that, once having clapped your eyes on him, you'll find it hard to refuse him your bed, your crown, and all that is yours.'

'My dear Uncles, I am pained by all this talk of marriage. It is too soon as yet. I have so recently been a wife, so short a time a widow.'

The Duke showed impatience, but the Cardinal laid his arm about her shoulders. 'My dearest,' he murmured, 'there should be no wedding for a reasonable time. But your affairs are of great moment . . . not only to us but to the whole world. Do you want to be treated continually as you have been treated since the death of François? Do not tell me! I know that Catherine has made you feel your position keenly. You are a Queen and queenly. You would never be happy in a lowly state. You were meant to rule. Your proud carriage says so. Your dignity demands it. That is why we have two matches in mind for you – either would bring you great glory. The first is with the King of France.'

Mary cried in terror: 'But Charles . . . *Charles* . . . he is not entirely sane. He . . . he frightens me.'

'Frightens you?' said the Duke. 'A King of France frightens you!'

'A madman frightens me,' she retorted. 'You talk of the children I might have . . . with a madman as their father!'

'Madness is no deterrent to fertility,' asserted the Duke.

'Mary,' soothed the Cardinal, 'you would never shirk your duty . . . I know. You could be Queen of France again. You could stay in the land you love. There is no other Court – save one – worthy of you.'

'The Court of Spain!' put in the Duke triumphantly. 'Don Carlos, son of great Philip, has need of a wife. We have approached the King of Spain and he is not averse to the match. He wishes to see Scotland firmly settled in the Catholic Faith. Think, Mary. One day the crown of Spain may be yours.'

'It is too soon,' pleaded Mary. 'I beg of you . . . leave me now.'

The cardinal put his arm about her and said softly: 'The Queen of Spain . . . the mightiest throne in all Europe . . . a young husband who will adore you. You will be reunited with your dear little friend Elisabeth who is now the Queen of Spain herself. Oh, Mary, some people are born for distinction. You are one of them.'

She closed her eyes. She felt so weary. A terrible depression had come over her. She wished to be alone that she might throw herself on to her bed and weep.

Mary could not help liking the youth who brought such kind messages from his mother. Henry Darnley was handsome. His large blue eyes and fair hair were almost feminine in their charm; and his manners were not without grace, though naturally seeming a little rough compared with those of the French courtiers.

Mary was sorry for his shyness and tried to make him feel at ease, to forget she was the Queen by reminding him that they were cousins.

'Your Majesty is gracious,' he told her.

When she asked him to play the lute for her – she had heard that he was a master of that instrument – he was glad to do so, and she listened with delight; he played quite charmingly.

He told her he wrote poetry also and he brought her some verses he had written for her. She was delighted with them. They made a poor showing against the polished artistry of Ronsard and his fellow poets but they had good feeling in them, as she told him.

He could dance well and was an enthusiastic follower of the chase. His conversation was of sport and pleasure.

When he left after his brief stay at Court, she was sorry to see him go, but in a day she had forgotten him.

When the Court left for Fontainebleau Mary went with it. The Queen-Mother was coolly polite to her, but beneath the veneer of politeness there was an insolence. It was as though she knew some exciting secret which concerned Mary, and which she longed to impart. It must be unpleasant, thought

Mary, otherwise it would not have pleased Catherine so much.

Whenever the King saw Mary he would gaze longingly at her. There were times when it appeared as though he would throw himself upon her, and yet always he seemed to be conscious of the invisible restraining hand. It was almost uncanny, but then the power of the Queen-Mother was uncanny.

She was thinking more and more about the journey to Spain. It was alarming to consider Don Carlos. Was he really as degenerate as rumour suggested? He was but a boy. There had been evil rumours concerning François, but how happy she had been with him!

There was one thing she dreaded more than all others: return to Scotland.

Her optimism, never long absent, returned to her during those difficult weeks. She would not return to Scotland. Everything could be easily arranged. Her brother, Lord James, longed for the Regency. Let him have it. It was his great desire to govern Scotland; it was her great desire to stay away from Scotland. She would face the truth. She loved to be gay, and the Scots looked on gaiety as a sin. There was no comfort in their castles; there were no merry dances, no versifying, no pleasant pastimes. Scotland was straining towards Puritanism and Mary Stuart could never be a Puritan.

Now that her uncles had retired from Court her new position was brought home to her afresh. At Fontainebleau the Earl of Bedford and the English ambassador, Sir Nicholas Throgmorton, called upon her; and there was no one to advise her how to deal with these gentlemen.

They surveyed her with solemn dignity. They were aloof and cool.

Inexperienced as she was, hurt and humiliated by Catherine, she allowed herself to show a haughtiness which was dictated by her hot temper rather than a considered diplomatic attitude. It had been all very well to flout the English when she was the wife of the King of France; now she stood alone; she was merely the Queen of a small country whose affairs were in disorder.

'The Queen of England,' Bedford began, 'requires the immediate ratification of the Edinburgh treaty.'

She knew that the Edinburgh treaty claimed for Elizabeth the sole right to the throne of England and that Mary Stuart should recognise her as such 'for all time coming'.

She was not pleased by the Englishmen's arrogant attitude towards her. They implied that their Queen's will should be Mary's. She was bewildered, inexperienced in dealing with such situations alone, so she obeyed those inclinations dictated by her pride.

Her uncles and Henri of France had assured her that she was the rightful heir to England. At the moment she was in decline but she would not always be so. One day she might be Queen of Spain and then these Englishmen would think twice before addressing her as they did now.

She said: 'My lords, I shall not sign the treaty of Edinburgh.'

'It has been signed in Edinburgh, Madame.'

'But it would seem that it does not become valid until you have my signature.'

This they could not deny.

Here was another of those moments of folly, the result of hurt pride and ignorance.

'Then, my lords, I will say to you that I cannot give you the signature for which you ask. I must have time to ponder the matter.'

Exasperated, they left her. They wrote to their mistress; and Elizabeth of England vowed that she would never forgive – and never trust – her Scottish kinswoman as long as that beautiful head remained on those elegant shoulders.

She travelled down to Rheims to stay for a while with her aunt, Renée de Guise at the Abbey Saint-Pierre-les-Dames. Renée, the sister of those ambitious uncles, was quite unlike them. Perhaps she, a member of that mighty and ambitious family, had felt the need to escape to a nunnery in order to eschew that ambition which was at the very heart of the family's tradition.

There was quietness with Renée, but Mary did not want quiet. She was restless.

Renée, knowing that Mary was troubled, tried to help her through prayer. Mary realised that Renée was suggesting that if she too would shun ambition – as Renée had done – she might find peace in a life of dedication to prayer and service to others.

Mary, emotional in the extreme, thought for a short time – a very short time – of the peace to be found within convent walls. But when she looked in her mirror and saw her own beautiful face, and thought of dancing and masquing with herself the centre of attention, when she remembered the admiration she had seen in the eyes of those men who surrounded her, she knew that whatever she had to suffer in the future – even if it meant returning to Scotland – it was the only life that would be acceptable to her.

With Renée she did become more deeply religious; she was even fired with a mission. Her country was straining towards Calvinism, and she would bring it back to the Church which she felt to be the only true one.

'But not,' she told Renée, 'with torture and the fire, not with the thumbscrews and the rack. Perhaps I am weak, but I cannot bear to see men suffer, however wrong they are. Even though I knew the fires of hell lay before them, I could not torment myself by listening to their cries, and if I ever countenanced the torture, I believe those cries would reach me, though I were miles away.'

Renée smiled at Mary's fierceness. She said: 'You are Queen of a country that is strongly heretic. It is your duty to return to it and save it from damnation. You are young and weak . . . as yet. But the saints will show you how to act.'

Mary shuddered and, when she thought of that land in the grip of Calvin and his disciple Knox, she prayed that King Philip would agree to her marriage with his son, or perhaps, better still, she need never leave her beloved France. If Charles broke free of his mother's influence, his first act would be to marry Mary Stuart.

To Rheims at this time came her relations on a visit to the Cardinal. The Duke arrived with his mother, and there followed Mary's two younger uncles, the Duc d'Aumale and the Marquis d'Elboeuf.

There were many conferences regarding Mary's marriage into Spain.

The Cardinal took her to his private chamber and there he tried to revive their old relationship. But she had grown up in the last month and some of her innocence had left her. The Cardinal seemed different. She noticed the lines of debauchery on his face, and how could she help knowing that his love for her depended largely on her ability to give him that which he craved: Power. She was no longer the simple girl she had been.

She was aloof and bewildered. It was no use his drawing her

gently to him, laying his fine hands on her, soothing and caressing, bringing her to that state of semi-trance when her will became subservient to his. She saw him more clearly now, and she saw a sly man. She already knew that he was a coward; and she believed that his love for her had diminished in proportion to her loss of power and usefulness.

Marriage with France. Marriage with Spain. They were like two bats chasing each other round in his brain; and he was the wily cat not quite quick enough to catch one of them. But perhaps there was another – more agile, more happily placed than he. Catherine continually foiled him. He was wishing he could slip the little 'Italian morsel' into her goblet, as she was no doubt wishing she could slip it into his.

If he could but remove Catherine he would have Mary married to Charles in a very short time.

To Rheims came the news which sent the spirits of the whole family plunging down to deep depression.

Philip of Spain sent word that he would find it inconvenient, for some time to come, to continue with the negotiations for a marriage between his son Don Carlos and Mary Stuart.

Catherine de' Medici stood between Mary and the King of France. She had – by working in secret – insinuated herself between Mary and the heir of Spain.

Catherine was going to bring about that which she had long desired: the banishment from France of the young and beautiful Queen who had been such a fool as to show herself no friend to Catherine de' Medici.

Word came from Lord James Stuart. He was coming to France to persuade his sister that it was time she returned to her realm.

So she was to leave the land she loved. The Court buzzed with the news. This was farewell to the dazzling Mary Stuart.

She tried to be brave, but there was a great fear within her.

She told her Maries: 'It will only be for a short time. Soon I shall marry. Do not imagine we shall stay long in Scotland; I am sure that soon King Philip will continue with the arrangements for my marriage to Don Carlos.'

'It will be fun to go to Scotland for a while,' said Flem.

'They'll soon find a husband for you,' declared Beaton.

While she too could think thus Mary felt almost gay. It would only be a temporary exile, and she would take with her many friends from the Court of France.

Henri de Montmorency, who had now become the Sieur d'Amville since the return of his father to power, whispered to her: 'So France is to lose Your Majesty!'

She was hurt by his happy expression. She said tartly: 'It would seem that you are one of those who rejoice in my departure.'

'I do, Your Majesty.'

'I pray you let me pass. I was foolish enough to think you had some regard for me. But that, of course, was for the Queen of France.'

He bent his head so that his eyes were near her own. 'I rejoice,' he said, 'because I have heard that I am to accompany your suite to Scotland.'

Her smile was radiant. 'Monsieur . . .' she began. 'Monsieur d'Amville . . . I . . .'

He took her hands and kissed them passionately. For a

moment she allowed this familiarity but she quickly remembered that she must be doubly cautious now. As Queen she could more easily have afforded to be lax than now when she was stripped of her dignity.

She said coolly: 'I thank you for your expression of loyalty, Monsieur d'Amville.'

'Loyalty . . . and devotion,' he murmured, 'my most passionate devotion.'

He left her then, and when he entered his suite he was smiling to himself. One of his attendants – a poet, Pierre de Chastelard – rose to greet him.

'You are happy to-day, my lord,' said Chastelard.

D'Amville nodded and continued to smile. 'Shall I tell you why, Chastelard, my dear fellow? I have long loved a lady. Alas, she was far beyond my aspirations. But now I have gone up and she has come down. I think we have come to a point where we may most happily meet.'

'That is worthy of a poem,' suggested Chastelard.

'It is indeed. I have high hopes.'

'The lady's name, sir?'

'A secret.'

'But if I am to sing her praises in verse . . .'

'Well then, I'll whisper it, but tell no one that Henri de Montmorency is deep in love with the beautiful Mary Stuart who is going to be in need of comfort when she reaches her barbaric land. I shall be there to give it. That is why you see me so gay.'

'Now I understand, my lord. It is enough to make any man gay. She is a beautiful creature and was most chaste, it would seem, when married to our King François. Even Brantôme – who can usually find some delicious titbit of scandal concerning the seemingly most virtuous – has had nothing but praise to sing of the Queen of Scots.'

'She is charming,' said D'Amville. 'And it is true that she is chaste. What is it about her . . . tell me that. You are something of a connoisseur, my friend. She is innocent and yet . . . and yet . . .'

'And yet . . . and yet . . .' cried Chastelard. 'My lady fair is innocent and yet . . . and yet . . . and yet . . .'

The two young men laughed together.

'May all good luck attend you,' said Chastelard. 'I envy you from the bottom of my heart.'

'My hopes soar. She will be desolate. She will be ready to love anyone who is French while she is in that dreary land. You shall accompany me, my dear Chastelard; you shall share in my triumph . . . at second-hand, of course!'

When the two young men went out to follow the hunt they were still talking of the charms of Mary Stuart.

Mary had many causes for anxiety as she contemplated the journey ahead of her. The Queen of England declared she would deny her a safe passage until she signed the treaty of Edinburgh. Mary was on her mettle then. She was determined not to let the Tudor see that she feared her ships and sailors. She said so boldly.

'I may pass well enough home into my realm,' she said to Nicholas Throgmorton, 'without your mistress's passport. I remember your late King tried to prevent my arrival in France; but you see, Monsieur, I came safely without his permission. So I shall journey to my kingdom without that of your mistress.'

It was folly, but she felt stronger for committing it. From now on she would act in accordance with her own wishes. She had gathered some notion of the unhappy state of her country when on her way from Rheims to Lorraine she was met by one of the Catholic lords – John Lesley – who had come to tell her that he brought with him the fealty of the Catholics in Scotland. Caithness, Crawford, Huntley and Atholl were firmly behind her, he assured her. Their plan was that she should land secretly in Scotland, enter Edinburgh with a good force behind her and drive the heretic Lord James from his position as the head of the country in her absence.

She was alarmed. James was her brother – her dear Jamie. She had loved James. She knew he was a Protestant and that it would be his wish to make Scotland Protestant as hers was to make the country Catholic; but she was determined not to be a bigot, dearly as she loved her own faith and sure as she was that the Catholic Church was the true one. She could not feel happy, she said, contemplating that, on her arrival in her country, she would have to fight her own brother.

Fortunately she was able to speak with the Sieur d'Oysel, that French officer who had, in Scotland, worked so faithfully for her mother.

He shook his head over the project. 'Your Majesty,' he said, 'if you will deign to hear the advice of one who has campaigned long in your country and knows the temper of the people, he would say this: No doubt you wish to bring the Catholic Faith back to Scotland, but there are many in your land who are faithful to the Protestant cause, and to take arms against it at this time would plunge the whole of Scotland into a civil war. Your brother, Lord James, is a Protestant and you are a Catholic, but you need him. He will be loyal to you for expediency's sake, if for no other reason. If you lost your crown where would he be? As a Stuart he must support a Stuart. His rivals – as yours are – would always be the Hamiltons or the Gordons. Do not be tempted to rash action. Your brother and Lord Maitland of Lethington are the cleverest statesmen in Scotland. They are both Protestants, but Your Majesty needs them. Therefore be discreet. Shelve the problem of religion until you have tested your people, and your brother with them. He could raise an army, so make sure – and this is what he would prefer to do – that he raises it for you and not against you.'

It was advice which she gladly took, for the prospect of civil war horrified her.

It was only a day or so later when Lord James himself arrived. When she saw him she was glad she had not allowed herself to be caught up in any intrigue against him. He was friendly and courteous; he was also very affectionate. He was very much the big brother whom she remembered. He was nearly thirty now and that seemed, to her, a very wise and experienced age.

He told her how happy he was that she was coming home.

'I am glad you will be there, Jamie.'

He smiled at the use of the childhood name.

'Though you hardly seem like Jamie now,' she went on. 'Why, you are looking so wise, so full of knowledge. A deal must have happened to you since we last met.'

'All my experience I place at your service.'

He talked a little of affairs in Scotland, warning her to beware of certain lords. She listened half-heartedly. She was tired of the stories of continual strife.

'Jamie,' she said, 'I wish you had not gone so far along the road to Protestantism.'

'My dear little sister, you have been brought up with Papists. Wait until you return home. Wait till you hear the sermons John Knox delivers in the Kirk at Edinburgh. Mayhap then you'll come along with me on that road to Protestantism.'

'I shall try to make you turn back, Jamie. I shall try to make *you* come with *me*.'

He smiled indulgently. He still looked upon her as the little sister. She was very charming, with such airs and graces that could be so delightful in a ballroom. She had all the necessary gifts to make her a great lady; none, he believed, to make her a great ruler. She was as different from the red-headed Queen below the Border as any woman could be. It was not surprising. Elizabeth had faced a hundred dangers when she was a child; Mary had been petted from babyhood.

'I am sure,' he said, 'that you can discourse most learnedly and charmingly on all subjects. It is one of the accomplishments they have taught you so well in France.'

'Jamie, Rome would be ready to offer you great honours if you would change your mind.'

'My mind is made up, dear sister; and it is firmly turned away from the Church of Rome.'

'Then there is nothing I can say to turn you back to it?'

'Nothing. And there are other and urgent matters to discuss.'

'It will be a comfort to know that you are at my side to help me.'

He took her hand and let his lips rest lightly on it. 'I shall serve you faithfully while you serve Scotland,' he said.

She believed him; there was that about James which made

her believe him. She felt a little happier for her interview with him. But when he had left she still made excuses to stay in France.

❋ ❋ ❋

Often Mary lay sleepless through the night thinking of the perilous journey across the seas. She would dream that the ships of the Queen of England captured hers; she dreamed that she stood before the red-headed virago, who swore she would have vengeance because Mary had denied her right to the crown of England.

Back in Scotland were the quarrelsome nobles. Her brother and Maitland had not been good friends to her mother, she remembered. The Catholic nobles, led by Huntley, the Cock o' the North, were untrustworthy. Yet she must go amongst them; and to reach them she must brave the perils of the English seas.

Suddenly there came to her memory a man – an insolent man, yet a bold one. He was no friend of the Catholic nobles, and no friend of her brother and Maitland; rather had he stood alone, a chieftain of the Border country, ruthless and despotic; yet her mother had said she would rely on his loyalty more readily than on that of any other man in Scotland.

Then Mary made a sudden decision. She would send a messenger to James Hepburn, Earl of Bothwell, instructing him, as Admiral, to arrange for her safe passage to Scotland. She was surprised how much happier she could feel knowing that the arrangement for the voyage would be in the hands of a strong man.

Bothwell was delighted to receive the summons. He believed his fortunes were now on the rise. He would ingratiate himself with the Queen. Moreover the prospect of a battle with the English delighted him. He began to plan for immediate departure.

Anna Throndsen watched him with passionate eyes. Their life together was a battle. She would win one skirmish and lose the next. She was clever, but so was he, and he had all the advantages.

'I depart to-morrow,' he told her gleefully.

'But you have just arrived.'

So he had. She was living in one of his houses and he visited her now and then. He snapped his fingers at her. He would not marry her. But there were times when he liked to visit her; and enjoyed the battles between them and delighted to arouse her anger, to hear her swear that she hated him, that she wished never to see him again; and then have her sobbing out her passionate need of him, caught in one of those weak moments when quite effortlessly he could sweep away all her resistance and leave her quivering with passion. That was his special gift. He had no need to stress it; it was simply there, and his very indifference to it enhanced it.

'I come and go as I please,' he told her.

'And where shall you go this time?' she asked. 'Back to that old hag Janet Beaton? Have you then such a fancy for the aged? Do you prefer grandmothers?'

'I shall not go to Janet this time, but to a young woman. She sends for me because none other will suit her purpose.'

Passion flamed in Anna's face. She ran to him and slapped his cheek. To him the blow was no more than a tap. He laughed aloud and caught her hand.

'Why, Anna,' he said, 'you almost tempt me to stay another night. I like you better in anger than in gentle love.'

'I wish I had never seen you.'

'It might have saved much inconvenience if I had never seen you.'

'I thought you never allowed women to inconvenience you?'

'I do not . . . for long.'

'You are quite heartless. Have you no thought for the child?'

'I have so many children, they tell me. Were I to concern myself with all of them, I should have time for nothing else.'

'Who is the woman you are going to see, if it is not Janet?'

'She is very beautiful. I can tell you that.'

'Who, I asked.'

'Try to guess.'

She struggled in his grip while her eyes blazed. 'I'll tell you,' he said. 'Her name is Mary and she is the Queen of Scotland.'

'The Queen!'

'She sends for me to bring her safely back to Scotland.'

'For you! So she too . . . !'

He laughed. 'Anna, you are a fool. You see passion everywhere. This is a command from a Queen to a subject.'

'But why you . . . why *you*?'

'Because her mother knew she could trust me. She knew I hated the English. Mayhap this Queen knows that I shall serve her well for the reason that I am a Borderer and a natural enemy of those on the other side. There is hardly a man in Scotland of any standing who is not in the pay of the English. Lord James himself . . . Maitland . . . anyone you can name. But I have never taken a bribe from them. I have taken their cattle and I have taken their women. I am their enemy and they know it. The Queen knows it. So she now asks me to arrange her safe passage, and, my dear Anna, I go with all speed.'

'The Queen will reward you,' said Anna.

'Doubtless.'

'And when she does, you will do the right thing by our child? You will do the right thing by me?'

He sighed deeply. 'Who knows, Anna? Who knows?'

Now her eyes began to blaze again with anger, and he laughed. As he had told her, he liked her thus; and it would be a long time before he saw her again.

❀ ❀ ❀

It was August. Through the French countryside passed a brilliant cavalcade at the head of which in a magnificent carriage decorated with cloth of gold and silver and bearing the arms of Guise and Lorraine rode the great Duke and his brother, the Cardinal. There followed in a beautiful chariot Mary Stuart; and behind her came her four Maries with a company of French noblemen, poets and musicians.

Mary knew that at Calais she would say good-bye to those two uncles who had been her guardians since she had set foot in France, but their three brothers, Mary's uncles, Claude the Duc d'Aumale, François the Grand Prior of Lorraine, and René the Marquis d'Elboeuf, were to accompany her to Scotland. She was glad of this; her Uncle René she liked particularly because he had a gay nature and it was a comfort to have him with her.

She was conscious all the time of Henri de Montmorency, the Sieur d'Amville, who made it his delight to be at her side and gratify her smallest wish. He had introduced to her notice a very personable young man who played the lute with charm and wrote verses which fell not far short of those of Ronsard. This was Pierre de Chastelard, and she had made up her mind that she would reward that young man with a good post when they reached Scotland. She liked him; he was so gay and charming; and she was fond of poets. Unfortunately he was a Huguenot, she had heard; but then, so was Henri de Montmorency, and she would not let a person's religious opinions interfere with the friendship she felt.

She was a little happier than she had feared she would be, and that was due to the people who were going with her. She looked round the company. There were many familiar faces.

She was glad to see Lord Bothwell's among them. She was not sure of her feelings regarding him as a person; he was certainly rather crude but he gave such an impression of strength and power that when she contemplated the journey before her and all its perils, she was glad to know that he was with the expedition.

He had come promptly at her summons; he had arranged for her departure with Lord Eglinton. She trusted them both, for their loyalty and their knowledge of the sea.

Flem had said that Bothwell should travel in the galley with Mary and themselves, but Mary would not have it.

'No,' she said, 'suffice it that he is with the party.'

'But,' persisted Flem, 'Your Majesty says that you feel safer because he is of the party.'

'Safer, yes – but it is enough that he is in one of the galleys. He will be at hand to save us from our enemies. And in my galley I wish to have those about me whom I love . . . my dearest friends and those who delight me with their company.'

'And he does not?'

'He is a Scotsman of rough speech, and we shall see enough of such in the months to come. I wish to enjoy cultured society for as long as I can. Only you, my four darlings, and my dear uncles and a few of our chosen friends shall sail in the first galley. The others may follow, and among them the Border-Earl.'

Flem sighed causing Mary to smile. 'You seem to have a fondness for him,' she teased. 'Have a care. I have heard that his reputation is quite shocking.'

'It is simply that he has an air of being able to subdue anyone . . . including the Queen of England.'

'He has a blustering manner, it is true,' agreed Mary, 'but he shall not subdue the Queen of Scotland. No! He shall travel in one of the accompanying vessels with others like himself.'

And so it was arranged.

When Mary stepped into the galley a sense of foreboding had come to her. She looked very lovely, dressed in her mourning costume. Her veil was full and held in place on each shoulder; her headdress was the shape of a scallop shell and set with pearls, and about her neck was a collar of pearls. Her flowing gown was of cloth of silver and most becoming with its sleeves full from elbow to shoulder and tight from elbow to wrist; the ruff of point lace set off her face to perfection.

Her uneasiness was enhanced by the terrible accident which took place before her eyes. The sails had not been completely unfurled and the royal galley had not left the harbour when a ship, entering the port, capsized suddenly and all aboard were drowned, as no help could reach them in time.

Mary cried out to those aboard to turn back, to do something; but the galley could not turn round and there was nothing to be done but watch the struggling bodies in the water or turn shuddering away.

It was a bad omen, said everyone; this meant bad luck for the Queen of Scots.

Mary walked up and down the deck, her eyes fixed on the land she was leaving. She longed to move out of sight of those shores, yet she dreaded the moment when she would no longer see them.

She could not forget the terrible screams of those drowning men. She explored the galley in the hope of turning her mind to other things, but the sadness was not relieved by the sight of the slaves, with their shaven heads and despairing faces, who worked at the oars. She could not bear to look at their naked backs which were marked by the lash. She thought of them, sweating over the oars when the wind was against them; she thought of them exposed to the cruel weather, with the chains about their legs; they were such sad creatures that they must have longed continually for death.

Impetuously she called the Captain to her and said: 'The galley slaves shall not be whipped while I am aboard. No matter what happens . . . no matter what, I say . . . the lash shall not be used. Do you hear me?'

The Captain was amazed and about to protest; but she had turned away, and those who were near saw the tears streaming down her cheeks.

As it grew dark her Maries begged her to leave the deck and go to her cabin, which had been decorated in a manner fitting a Queen; but she could not bear to turn her eyes from the last glimpse of that land which she loved.

'It is now, my dear France,' she said, 'that I have lost you, for the envious darkness like a black veil conceals you from my eyes which are thus deprived of their chief desire. Adieu then, my beloved France! I lose sight of you and I shall never see you again.'

'Dearest Majesty,' pleaded Seton, 'meat and drink await you. You must sleep. You can do no good waiting here.'

But Mary shook her head. She turned to the Captain and said: 'Set up a bed for me here.'

'Here, Madame, on the poop gallery?'

'Yes, here,' she commanded. 'For when it is again light it may still be possible to see the shores of France. I must not be deprived of a last glimpse of them.'

So the bed was set up on the poop gallery, and Mary lay down while her women drew the curtains.

'As soon as the first glimmer of light is in the sky you must awaken me,' she ordered.

The wind died down during the night so that when the dawn came the galley was still close to the French coast.

It was Flem who awakened Mary, and the young Queen started up from her bed, her eyes red from last night's weeping, her sorrow returning as she remembered where she was.

The curtains about her bed were drawn back and, looking out, she saw the receding land of France.

She wept afresh.

'It is over,' she said. 'Farewell beloved land which I shall behold no more. Farewell, France!'

Thus she remained until there was no longer sight of land.

The perilous journey to Scotland had begun.

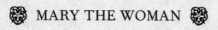

MARY THE WOMAN

🌸 Chapter VII 🌸

Although it was August when Mary first saw Leith again after all her years in France, a thick sea mist hid the countryside. The French shivered in the cold damp air; they looked at each other and shrugged. It seemed that all the warnings about this dismal land were by no means exaggerated.

The foreboding in Mary's heart deepened as she stepped ashore. Her thoughts involuntarily went to Calais and that glittering cavalcade which had accompanied her. How different was her arrival in her own country!

There was no one to greet her as she stepped ashore. She was aware of a bunch of fisherfolk, their rags scarcely covering their bodies, their faces scored with weather. There was no welcome; there was only curiosity. One ragged boy came up boldly to stare at her. A child who might have been boy or girl touched her gown, laughed, and ran back to the group of fishermen and women.

Was this the way to greet the returning monarch?

Elboeuf cried out: 'Good people, here comes your Queen!'

But the people were silent; they nudged each other, and

although they did not laugh, the faint curl of their lips suggested that the Marquis' brilliant garments and mode of speech aroused some kind of mirth in their bleak minds.

Mary said quietly: 'Is it that they do not know me? Is it that they do not want me?'

Her three uncles conferred together.

'Lord James should have been here. Huntley . . . Maitland . . . some of them surely. What savages!'

Mary found her four namesakes beside her. She said: 'It is no use standing here waiting for them to look as though they are pleased to see me. I am tired and would rest. I need food.'

D'Amville was beside her. 'Your Majesty, I will send pages ahead to find out what lodging may be made ready for you.'

'Better send Scotsmen,' said Mary. 'They will more readily procure it.'

'Procure it!' said d'Amville fiercely. 'It shall be given freely by these subjects to their Queen.'

Chastelard caught the Queen's glance. She smiled faintly at his indignant sorrow. She was ashamed of her country then; she was even wishing that there were no French in her retinue. What must they be thinking, who were accustomed to so much splendour, so much honour afforded to their kings and queens!

Men were sent on in advance to warn the townsfolk of the Queen's arrival. Mary glanced over her shoulder to where the galley lay like a ghost-ship in the mist. More people came out of their hovels to look at her, to stare incredulously at the display of glittering jewels. Their low voices mingled with the doleful cries of the sea-birds and Mary could not understand what they said.

And if she, with her beauty and her fine clothes, startled her subjects, what she had seen of them and the hovels in which they lived startled her. Never during her years in France had she been allowed to glimpse such poverty. These people's houses were little more than mud huts; the children, ill-clad and ill-fed, crawled about on the stones while the women sat at the doors mending nets. Mary believed they did not know who she was. Deeply she pitied them and yet she found herself turning from them in revulsion.

But now the pages and heralds were returning, and with them came hurrying some of the chief burghers of the town. These, though rough men, were a little more aware of what was due to their Queen. They knelt before her and kissing her hand swore their loyalty.

They explained to her that their town had been ravaged over and over again by the English hordes. After raids many of the houses were burned to the ground. In these hard days they had scarcely the time or the inclination, even if they had the money, to rebuild. There was no castle in Leith worthy to shelter the Queen. Where she could rest that night, none could say.

One of the burghers, Andrew Lambie, came forward and, kneeling before her, cried: 'Your Majesty, my house is a humble one, but it is at your service. If you will accept a lodging, although I cannot pretend that it is worthy to receive you, the honour will never be forgotten by your humble subject.'

Mary smiled with relief and gratitude. 'Your offer is accepted, good Master Lambie,' she said. 'I thank you. You are the first who has made me feel really welcome in my country.'

So she lay that night on a humble bed in a small room where

the rafters seemed to be pressing down upon her, covered by a homespun blanket. It had been a strange experience.

'It is only for a night,' she said to Beaton. 'Tomorrow we shall ride to my capital, and then everything will be different. I shall ride on my palfrey. Perhaps the mist will lift and all the people will come out to greet me. They will know me for their Queen.'

The Maries exchanged glances. They had decided they would not tell her yet that one of the galleys of their little fleet had been captured by the English. It was the one in which the palfrey was being carried, and with it all the beautiful horses which were used in the processions, together with the rich hangings and canopies and magnificent house furnishings which Mary had decided she could not leave behind.

But Mary had seen their glances and she demanded to be enlightened.

'Then how shall we ride into my capital to-morrow?' she asked.

'Doubtless we shall be able to find horses as fine,' said Livy.

'Where?' demanded Mary.

Livy waved her hand 'Oh . . . here. . . . There are bound to be horses . . . magnificent horses.'

Mary laughed. 'In those mud huts! I doubt if the poor creatures would recognise a fine horse . . . let alone possess one.'

'Let to-morrow's troubles take care of themselves,' said Seton earnestly.

Mary began to laugh. 'I cannot help it. It is funny. Such pomp we enjoyed, did we not? My lord Cardinal . . . my lord Duke in all their robes, and their coaches covered with cloth of gold and silver. What a glittering array! And all to say farewell to me. And then . . . my arrival! That should be a joyous thing, should it not? A Queen comes home . . . but there is no one to greet her . . . no one but a few ragged children who come out of their hovels to see what the tide had thrown up. It is funny. Laugh, Seton. Beaton, you too. Livy! Flem! I command you to laugh.'

They tried to soothe her, but Mary could not stop laughing. The tears were rolling down her cheeks and suddenly her four Maries realised that she was not laughing; she was weeping, wildly and bitterly.

She threw herself on to the burgher's bed which creaked and groaned under her shaking body.

Early next morning, having heard of the Queen's arrival, some Scottish noblemen came riding into Leith.

Mary was delighted to see her brother, Lord James, and with him that man who was his staunchest supporter and of whom she had heard so much – Maitland of Lethington. Immediately on their heels came the Duc de Châtelherault and his son, Arran. She was less pleased to see those two; and the sullen-eyed Arran, whose offer of marriage had been rather curtly refused by her uncles on her behalf, made her very uncomfortable. His brooding eyes did not leave her face; he was already far gone in sickness of the mind.

But she felt more at home to have those men she knew, if only by name, surrounding her. Her brother took command; his clothes might seem shabby beside those of the French, and his horse was by no means a credit to him, yet he had dignity; moreover he was her own flesh and blood.

When he saw the room in which she had spent the night he was greatly disturbed; but she could laugh at it now.

'It was most graciously offered,' she said.

'And was the journey good?' he asked, taking her hand and smiling indulgently at her.

'It could have been worse. Suffice it that we have safely arrived, although we have lost one of the galleys to the English. It contains my palfrey.'

'Then we shall have to find a new one for you. Your subjects wish you to be happy here, but none wishes it more than he who is your most loyal subject . . . your own brother.'

'I know it. Jamie, if you were not a Protestant you would be perfect.'

That made him laugh. He was handsome when he laughed; it was then that the Stuart charm broke through his seriousness.

'You will find Holyrood and Edinburgh Castle very different from Fontainebleau and the Louvre,' he told her. 'You know that, do you not? There are no Gobelins tapestries . . . none of your fountains and flower gardens, no glittering chandeliers nor Venetian mirrors to which you are accustomed.'

'I brought furnishings with me. It is to be hoped the English have not taken all. I can send for more.'

'You must do that,' said James. 'You must make your own Court as you would have it, and you will be its delightful Queen. I doubt not that ere long you will have made a little France of your apartments in Holyrood, and there you will have your songsters and your poets.'

'Jamie, you are my dear brother. You know how I suffer from homesickness . . . for it is hard not to think of the land in which one has lived so many years as home.'

'I understand,' said James. He was pleased with her. She was charming. She was as beautiful as a butterfly, and so should she be, flitting from pleasure to pleasure. Let her have her Little France in Holyroodhouse; let her have her fancy poets and her mincing gentlemen dancers. Let her have all she wanted, provided she left the government of Scotland to Lord James Stuart.

❀ ❀ ❀

They searched every stable in Leith to find a mount worthy of her, but they had set themselves an impossible task. At last they found a weary old nag who had seen happier days; he was mostly skin and bone and had a pathetic expression which made the Queen want to weep for him. On his back was a scratched old saddle.

Alas, it was a poor substitute for her palfrey, but it was the best they could find; and when she saw the mounts provided for the rest of the party she realised that hers was comparatively handsome.

So they left Leith watched by the silent fisherfolk, and a strange sight they were with the Queen of Scotland, richly clad and glittering with jewels, leading the party with her brother Lord James Stuart, and behind them the colourful courtiers dressed in the French manner riding on a collection of horses which, said Mary, might have been rescued from an *abattoir*.

She said to James: 'I cannot ride through the city thus mounted.'

'Remember, dear sister,' was James' reply, 'the people of Edinburgh have never seen your grand French processions. They will think you magnificent enough.'

'I could weep for chagrin. What must my uncles think?'

'They must take us as they find us,' said James grimly. 'Here we are more prone to admire that which is simple in life than lavish spectacles.'

Mary shivered, and not from the damp air.

They were a few miles from Holyrood when, turning a bend in the road, Mary saw before them a crowd of shouting people. At first she thought they were the citizens of Edinburgh come out to welcome her, but as they drew nearer it seemed to her that this was a menacing crowd. They shouted and, although she could not understand what they said, she heard her name mentioned. Their mottled flesh showed through their rags; their feet were bare and bleeding; and to her horror she saw that many of them were brandishing sticks.

'The Queen! The Queen!' shouted the ringleaders, and the crowd rushed forward, surrounding the cavalcade.

Mary was brought to a standstill, but she was not afraid. Rather she welcomed the excitement. She preferred these raucous shouts to the sullen indifference of the fisherfolk of Leith. She discovered in that moment that she was stimulated by danger; instinctively she drew herself up on the worn-out saddle, and nothing at that moment could make her look anything but queenly.

'What do they say?' she demanded of James. 'They are telling me something. Do not spare me, I beg of you. Are they telling me to go back to France?'

James held up his hand. Mary was proud of him as she watched. There was about him that which commanded immediate respect.

'Silence!' he roared. 'Silence in the presence of the Queen!'

There was an immediate hush. Mary looked into the wild faces of the men and women who were pressing so close to her, as James said: 'They do not come to attack you. They come to ask your clemency. They have broken into the prison and rescued one James Kellone who was to have been hanged. They are asking for a free pardon for him and for themselves.'

'What was his offence?' asked Mary.

'He is guilty of masquing on the Sabbath Day, which is against the law,' said Lord James in severe tones.

'But surely not worthy of the death penalty! Indeed I am glad that some of my subjects know how to laugh. I will speak to them.'

'Your Majesty, have a care. Remember the Kirk of Scotland.'

But Mary rarely paused to think. She was with these people of hers. They no longer looked fierce. They had longed for gaiety, for masques and laughter. Dear God! she thought. How I do too, and how I understand their longing!

She forced her horse forward a little so that she was no longer beside Lord James. She lifted her hand and cried: 'Good people of Scotland, bear with me, your Queen, for I have lived in a strange land and, having just come among you, my speech will sound strange to you.'

There was silence all around her, broken only by the squawking of sea-birds. In the crowd it seemed that no one stirred. They stood, their sticks held tightly, their mouths open, waiting for what the Queen would say; and if they did not entirely understand her words, her smile was friendly and her face the fairest they had ever seen.

'You ask pardon for one who has been condemned to die. My subjects, most happily I grant a free pardon to that man and you all.'

A free pardon! That much they could understand. They called out one to another: 'Free pardon! May God bless the Queen.' They cried then as one voice: 'God save the Queen!'

And when the cavalcade pressed on, it was surrounded and followed by a mob of poor people waving their sticks and looking barbarous indeed. The stench, so said the more delicate of the French afterwards, all but made them vomit. But Mary felt happier than she had since she set foot in Scotland. It was pleasant to know that she had made some of her subjects understand her; it was pleasant to know that some – however humble – were proclaiming their loyalty.

Lord James was disturbed. It was a charming gesture, charmingly made, and it might be that she did right to make it at that moment. But as his eyes met those of Maitland of Lethington he knew that the great diplomat agreed with him that Mary Stuart would find trouble in Scotland. The Kirk – and its leader, John Knox – would find good cause to quarrel with her, and the Kirk and John Knox wielded great power in Scotland.

Dusk had fallen before Mary reached her capital city and, as it grew dark, she had the pleasure of seeing the bonfires flare up, first on Calton Hill, then on Salisbury Crag; she saw them burning in the city itself and she could hear the shouts of the people. It was comforting; their welcome might be rough according to French standards, but it was at least a genuine welcome.

Now she could see the fortress which had been built by her father. It looked dark, even menacing. She gazed uneasily at its towers and their crenellated battlements.

Here she would rest, just outside the city's walls; for clearly she could not make her triumphal entry into her capital in darkness.

It was a vast and noble place, but it seemed chill and without comfort. The few tapestries which hung on the walls lacked the brilliance and beauty of those to which she was accustomed; here were no delicate carpets, no carved furniture; everything was plain, heavy and sparse.

Mary had been warmed by the loyal shouts of the mob which had accompanied her to the palace, and soon she would have some of her cherished possessions about her; she would bring warmth and cheer to the place; so that a little discomfort now seemed of small account. She could endure anything, she believed, provided she had the love and loyalty of her people. Even now she could hear the people from the city, crowding about the walls of the palace and calling: 'God Save the Queen!'

Tired as she was, in need of a hearty meal and the comfort she had known at the Court of France, she was not unhappy.

She found Flem beside her. Flem seemed touched with a glowing excitement; she had not noticed before that Flem was growing into a real beauty. Mary noticed also that the stern Lord Maitland had his eyes on Flem, although he was doubtless old enough to be her father.

That served to remind her that now they were home there would necessarily be a few marriages in her suite. She was going to enjoy bringing happiness to those she loved. There would certainly be other marriages to consider besides her own.

Dear Flem! She was not indifferent to the admiring glances of that important statesman. Mary would tease her about it to-morrow.

The meal was served and it seemed more tasty than it was, so hungry were they. And when it was over Mary retired to the apartment which had been prepared for her. While her Maries helped her to disrobe she talked excitedly of the way in which they would refurnish these apartments. It seemed to her then that the nostalgic melancholy of the first day and night had diminished a little. They were not in love with their new life – any of them – but they were becoming reconciled to it.

Then suddenly there broke out beneath her window what seemed to them a caterwauling, a barrage of the harshest sounds they had ever heard. Mary started up in horror, and hastily caused herself to be robed once more. Just as Flem and Livy were fastening her gown, and as the noise had grown louder and wilder and more discordant, there was a knocking on the door of the apartment.

It was Lord James with Lord Maitland, Mary's three Guise uncles and d'Amville.

'What has happened?' cried Mary in alarm. 'Is someone being murdered?'

'The loyal citizens of Edinburgh have come to give you welcome,' said Lord James dryly. 'They are playing the bagpipes in your honour. It would be well for you to appear at your window and say a few words of gracious thanks to them.'

'And,' said Elboeuf in rapid French, 'mayhap that will have the desired effect of putting an end to such ear-splitting sound.'

Mary, listening, began to detect the stirring music in what had at first seemed harsh to her, and she felt angry with those Frenchmen who put their hands over their ears. This was bad manners. To those people below, the old Scottish airs and melodies were sweet music and intended to be a tribute to her.

The bagpipes were subdued as those outside the palace walls began to sing.

'But what sad songs!' cried Mary. 'It would seem as though

they were sorry that I have come. They can hardly be songs of rejoicing.'

'They are the hymns of the Kirk,' said Lord James solemnly.

'Hymns!' cried the irrepressible Elboeuf. 'At such a time! I should have thought sweet madrigals or happy songs expressing joy at the Queen's return would have been more suitable.'

'The people of Edinburgh thank God that the Queen has returned, and they do so sincerely and solemnly. They have been taught that it is sinful to sing profane songs. The Kirk does not allow it.'

'But for the Queen's homecoming . . .'

'They wish to greet her in a godfearing way.'

Elboeuf lifted his shoulders. He was already homesick for Paris and Lorraine. D'Amville and his friend Chastelard were looking at the Queen, and their looks said: 'This is a strange and barbarous country, but we rejoice to be here since you are.'

And while most of the French put their hands to their ears, trying to shut out the sounds, Mary went to a window and cried: 'I thank you all, good people. I thank you with all my heart. You have delighted me with your loyal greetings and I rejoice to be among you.'

The people cheered and shouted. The solemn singing of hymns continued far into the night, and the pipes kept up their stirring strains until far into the morning.

From the windows of Holyroodhouse Mary could look on her capital city. She could see the High Street – the neatest and cleanest in the world – with its stone flags and the channels on either side, made to drain off the rain and filth, and the stone houses with their wooden galleries. There stood the Tolbooth Prison, and as she looked at it she swore none should be incarcerated there during her reign merely for wishing to masque and enjoy laughter; she could see the Lawnmarket and the noble houses and gardens of the Canongate which led to Holyrood.

The great Tron stood in the centre of Market Cross, and there were the stocks and pillories. This was the busiest spot in all Edinburgh, and here, during the days which followed the arrival of the Queen, the people gathered to talk of all that her coming would mean. Apprentices from the goldsmiths' shops in Elphinstone Court, tinsmiths from West Bow, and stall-holders from the Lawnmarket all congregated there in Market Cross to discuss the Queen; and when they discussed the Queen they remembered that other who had told them – and the world – that he was her enemy; the man whom they flocked to hear in the Kirk, the man who swayed them with his promises of salvation and – more often – his threats of eternal damnation.

John Knox ruled the Kirk, and the Kirk was ruling Scotland. Preaching armed resistance to the Devil – and the Devil was everyone who did not agree with John Knox – he had on more than one occasion stirred the people of Scotland to rebellion. With his 'First Blast against the Monstrous Regiment of Women' he had told the world of his contempt for petticoat government, although now that Elizabeth was on the throne of England and promising to do much good for the cause which was John Knox's own, he wished that he had been a little more cautious before publishing his 'First Blast'. He was a cautious man for all his fire. He believed God spoke through him; he believed he owed it to the world to preserve himself that he might the better do God's work. For this reason he had often found it necessary to leave Scotland when his person might be in danger. 'All in God's service,' he would say from the safety of England or Geneva. 'I take a back seat for the better service of God.'

In his absence his actions might be questioned, but when the people saw again the fanatical figure with the straggling beard streaming over his chest like a Scottish waterfall, and heard his wildly haranguing voice, they were converted once more to their belief not only in the reformed religion but in the sanctity of John Knox.

'Have you heard Knox's latest sermon?' was the often-repeated question.

They had. They would not have missed it for all the wealth of Holyroodhouse.

Knox was setting himself against the Queen as he had set himself against her mother. He had preached against the Devil's brood and the congregation of Satan. This included the Queen. Had he not prayed to God to take her mother, declaring to his congregation, when she was smitten with the dropsical complaint which eventually killed her: 'Her belly and loathsome legs have begun to swell. Soon God in His wisdom will remove her from this world.' Had he not rejoiced openly in the Kirk when she had died? Had he not laughed with fanatical glee when he had heard of the death of Mary's husband? 'His ear rotted!' cried John Knox. 'God wreaked Divine Vengeance on that ear which would not listen to His Truth.'

John Knox was no respecter of queens; he would rail against the new one. He would do his utmost to rouse the people against her; unless she cast aside her religion and took to his, he would work unceasingly for her defeat and death as he had worked for her mother's.

The French in the palace were inclined to laugh at the preacher; but Mary did not laugh. The man alarmed her, although only slightly as yet. She looked to those two statesmen, her brother James and Lord Maitland, to help and guide her in what she had to do, although she reminded them that when she had come home she had made no bargain to change her religion. She was a Catholic and would always be so. She would, she said, try to show this man the way of tolerance.

Lord James nodded. He was determined that his sister should leave the government of the country to him and Maitland. They were Protestants, but of a different kind from Knox. Religion was not the whole meaning of their existences; it was something with which to concern themselves when more important matters were not at issue. Maitland and Lord James, while agreeing that a happier state of affairs might have existed had the Queen adopted the religion of the majority of her subjects, were quite prepared to let her celebrate Mass in her own chapel.

Mary, characteristically, wished now to concentrate on what was pleasant rather than unpleasant. She renewed her acquaintance with two more of her half-brothers – John and Robert – handsome, merry boys, slightly older than herself, and she loved them both.

Some of the furnishings had been sent from Leith, and it was a pleasure to set them up in her apartments. The lutes and musical instruments had arrived, so the Court was now enjoying music in the evenings. Mary herself sang and danced under the admiring gaze of many, including d'Amville and Chastelard.

The people of Edinburgh had shown themselves delighted with her youth and beauty. She looked as a queen should; she always had a smile of warm friendliness, and the men whose lives she had saved on the way from Leith to Edinburgh talked of her beauty and wisdom and how, in their belief, she would bring great happiness to her country.

Mary had much to learn of the bitterness and venom which always seemed to attach themselves to religious differences. It did not occur to her that there could be any real reason why she should not continue in her mode of worship, while any of her subjects who wished to follow a different doctrine should do so.

Knox, according to her uncles and d'Amville, was something of a joke, and she did not take him very seriously until her first Sunday in Holyrood Palace. That day she announced her desire to hear Mass in the chapel and, dressed in black velvet and accompanied by her Maries, she was making her way there when she heard the sounds of shouts and screams.

Chastelard came running to her and begged her not to proceed.

'Your Majesty, the mob is at the gates of the Palace itself. They have been inflamed by the man Knox. They swear they will not have the Mass celebrated in their country.'

Mary's temper – always quick – flared up at once. She had intended to play a tolerant role with her people; she was infuriated that they should attempt to do otherwise with herself.

'The mob!' she cried. 'What mob?'

'Knox's congregation. Listen, I beg of you. They are in an ugly mood.'

'I, too, am in an ugly mood,' retorted Mary; but she listened and heard the cries of 'Satan worship! Death to the idolators.'

Flem had caught one of her arms, Seton the other. Mary threw them off angrily, but Chastelard barred her way.

'At the risk of incurring Your Majesty's displeasure, I cannot allow you to go forward.'

She laid her hand on the young man's arm and her anger melted a little as she caught the ardour in his eyes, but she was not going to be turned from her anger. She pushed him aside, but even as she started forward, she saw two men bringing back her priest and almoner. There was blood on their faces.

She ran to them in consternation. 'What have they done to you?'

The almoner spoke. 'It was little, Your Majesty. They wrenched the candlesticks from us and laid about them. But Your Majesty's brothers were at hand, and Lord James is speaking to the people now.'

She hurried on. Lord James was addressing the crowd which had gathered about the door of the chapel.

The crowd would stand back, he ordered. None should come a step nearer to the chapel on pain of death. He himself, Lord James Stuart, would have any man answer with his life who dared lay hands on the Queen or her servants.

There was a hush as Mary approached.

James said to her: 'Say nothing. Go straight into the chapel as though nothing has happened. There must be no trouble now.'

There was something in James' manner which made her obey him. Trembling with indignation, longing to turn and try to explain to these people why she had followed the Church of Rome, yet she obeyed her brother. He seemed so old and wise, standing there, his sword drawn.

He sent Chastelard back to bring the priest and almoner,

that they might celebrate Mass in the chapel according to the Queen's wishes; and after a while Mary was joined by the priest and the almoner, their bandaged heads still bleeding from their wounds.

Mass was celebrated; but Mary was aware of the mob outside. She knew that, but for the fact that her brother stood there to protect her, the crowd would have burst into the chapel.

She sat with her brother in her apartments. Lord Maitland was with them.

She was perusing the proclamation, addressed to the citizens of Edinburgh, which was to be read in Market Cross.

'There,' she said, handing the scroll to James, 'now they will understand my meaning. They will see that I do not like this continual strife. I am sure that with care and tolerance I, with my people, shall find a middle way through this fog of heresies and schisms.'

Maitland and Lord James agreed with the wording of the document. It was imperative to Lord James' ambition that his sister should continue as nominal Queen of Scotland, for the downfall of Mary would mean the downfall of the Stuarts. It was necessary to Maitland that Mary should remain on the throne, for his destiny was interwoven with that of Lord James. They wished for peace, and they knew that the father and mother of war were religious controversy and religious fanaticism.

The proclamation was delivered in Market Cross and then placed where all who wished to could read it.

The citizens stood in groups, discussing the Queen and her

Satan worship, or John Knox and his mission from God. To most men and women tolerance seemed a good thing, but not so to John Knox and the Lords of the Congregation. Mary was the 'whore of Babylon' declared the preacher and 'one Mass was more to be feared than ten thousand men-at-arms.' 'My friends,' he shouted from his pulpit, 'beware! Satan's spawn is in our midst. Jezebel has come among us. Fight the Devil, friends. Tear him asunder.'

After that sermon Maitland declared to the Lord James and the Queen that nothing but a meeting between her and Knox could satisfactorily bring them to an understanding.

Mary was indignant. 'Must I invite this man . . . this low, insolent creature . . . to wrangle with me?'

'He is John Knox, Madam,' said Lord James. 'Low of birth he may be, but he is a man of power in this country. He has turned many to his way of thinking. Who knows, he may influence Your Majesty.'

Mary laughed shortly.

'Or,' added the suave Maitland, 'Your Majesty may influence *him*.'

It was a strange state of affairs, Mary said, when men of low birth were received by their sovereign simply because they ranted against her.

The two men joined together in persuading her.

'Your Majesty must understand that, to the people of Scotland, John Knox's birth matters little. He himself has assured them of that. With his fiery words he has won many to his side. Unless you receive the reformer, you will greatly displease your subjects. And you will weaken your own cause because they will think you fear to meet him.'

So Mary consented to see the man at Holyrood, and John

Knox was delighted to have a chance of talking to the Queen.

'Why should I,' he asked his followers, 'fear to be received in the presence by this young woman? They say she is the most beautiful princess in the world. My friends, if her soul is not beautiful, then she shall be as the veriest hag in my eyes, for thus she will be in the eyes of God. And shall I fear to go to her because, as you think, my friends, she is a lady of noble birth, and I of birth most humble? Nay, my friends, in the eyes of God we are stripped of bodily adornments. We stand naked of earthly adornment and clothed in truth. And who do you think, my friends, would be more beautiful in the eyes of God? His servant clothed in the dazzling robes of the righteous way of life, or this woman smeared with spiritual fornications of the harlot of Rome?'

So Knox came boldly to Holyroodhouse, his flowing beard itself seeming to bristle with righteousness, his face bearing the outward scars of eighteen months' service in the galleys, which into his soul had cut still deeper. He came through the vast rooms of the palace of Holyrood, already Frenchified with tapestry hangings and fine furniture, already perfumed, as he told himself, with the pagan scents of the Devil, and at length he faced her, the dainty creature in jewels and velvet, her lips, hideously – he considered – carmined and an outward token of her sin.

She disturbed him. In public he railed against women, but privately he was not indifferent to them. In truth, he preferred their company to that of his own sex. There was Elizabeth Bowes, to whom he had been spiritual adviser, and with whom he had spent many happy hours talking of her sins; it had been a pleasure to act as father-confessor to such a virtuous matron. There had been Marjorie, Elizabeth's young daughter, who at sixteen years of age had become his wife, and who had borne him three children. There was Mistress Anne Locke, yet another woman whose spiritual life was in his care. He railed against them because they disturbed him. These women and others in his flock were ready to accept the role of weaker vessels; it was pleasant to sit with them and discuss their sins, to speak gently to them, perhaps caress them in the manner of a father-confessor. Such women he could contemplate with pleasure as his dear flock. He and God – and at times he assumed they were one – had no qualms about such women.

But the Queen and her kind were another matter. Every movement she made seemed an invitation to seduction; the perfume which came from her person, her rich garments, her glittering jewels, her carmined lips were outward signs of the blackness of her soul. They proclaimed her 'Satan's spawn, the Jezebel and whore of Babylon'.

There were other women in the room, and he believed these to be almost as sinful as the Queen. They watched him as he approached the dais on which the Queen sat.

Lord James rose as he approached.

'Her Majesty the Queen would have speech with you.'

Mary looked up into the fierce face, the burning eyes, the belligerent beard.

'Madam . . .' he began.

But Mary silenced him with a wave of her hand.

'I have commanded you to come here, Master Knox, to answer my questions. I wish to know why you attempt to raise my subjects against me as you did against my mother. You have attacked, in a book which you have written, not only the authority of the Queen of England, but of mine, your own

Queen and ruler.' He was about to speak, but yet again she would not allow him to do so. 'Some say, Master Knox, that your preservation – when others of your friends have perished – and your success with your followers are brought about through witchcraft.'

A sudden fear touched the reformer's heart. He was not a brave man. He believed himself safe in Scotland at this time, but witchcraft was a serious charge. He had thought he had been brought here to reason with a frivolous young woman, not to answer a charge. If such a charge was to be brought against him, it would have been better for him to have taken a trip abroad before the new Queen came home.

'Madam,' he said hastily, 'let it please Your Majesty to listen to my simple words. I am guilty of one thing. If that be a fault you must punish me for it. If to teach God's Holy word in all sincerity, to rebuke idolatry and to will the people to worship God according to his Holy Word is to raise subjects against their princes, then I am guilty. For God has called me to this work, and he has given me the task of showing the people of Scotland the folly of papistry, and the pride, tyranny and deceit of the Roman Anti-Christ.'

Mary was astounded. She had expected the man either to defend himself or be so overcome by her charm that he would wish to please rather than defy her.

He went on to talk of his book. If any learned person found aught wrong with it, he was ready to defend his opinions, and should he be at fault he was ready to admit it.

'Learned men of all ages have spoken their judgements freely,' he said; 'and it has been found that they were often in disagreement with the judgement of the world. If Scotland finds no inconvenience under the regiment of a woman, then I shall be content to live under your rule as was St Paul under Nero.'

His comparisons were decidedly discomfiting. Not for a moment would he allow any doubt to be cast on his role of saint and God's right-hand man, and hers as tyrant and sinner.

'It is my hope, Madam, that if you do not defile your hands with the blood of saints, neither I nor what I have written may do harm to you.'

'The blood of saints!' she cried. 'You mean Protestants, Master Knox. Your followers stained their hands with the blood of my priest only last Sunday. He did not die, but blood was shed.'

'I thank God he did not die in the act of sin. There may yet be time to snatch his soul for God.'

Thereupon the preacher, seeming to forget that he was in the Queen's Council Chamber, began to deliver a sermon as though he were in a pulpit at the Kirk. The fiercely spoken words rolled easily from his tongue. He pointed out how often in history princes had been ignorant of the true religion. What if the seed of Abraham had followed the religion of the Pharaohs – and was not Pharaoh a great king? What if the Apostles had followed the religion of the Roman emperors? And were not the Roman emperors great kings? Think of Nebuchadnezzar and Darius. . . .'

'None of these men raised forces against his Prince,' said Mary.

'God, Madam, had not given them the power to do so.'

'So,' cried Mary aghast, 'you believe that if subjects have the power, it is right and proper for them to resist the crown?'

'If princes exceed their bounds and do that which God demands should be resisted, then I do, Madam.'

She was furious with him for daring to speak to her as he had; she felt the tears of anger rising to her eyes; she covered her face with her hands to hide those tears.

Knox went on to talk of the communion with God which he enjoyed, of his certainty that he was right and all who differed from him were wrong.

James was at the Queen's side. 'Has aught offended you, Madam?' he asked.

She tried to blink away her tears, and with a wry smile said: 'I see that my subjects must obey this man and not me. It seems that I am a subject to them, not they to me.'

The reformer turned pale; he read into that speech an accusation which could carry him to the Tolbooth. He was off again, explaining that God asked kings and queens to be as foster parents to the Church. He himself did not ask that men should obey him . . . but God.

'You forget,' said Mary, 'that I do not accept your Church. I find the Church of Rome to be the true Church of God.'

'Your thoughts, Madam, do not make the harlot of Rome the immaculate spouse of Jesus Christ.'

'Do yours set the Reformed Church in that position?'

'The Church of Rome, Madam, is polluted.'

'I do not find it so. My conscience tells me it is the true Church.'

'Conscience must be supported by knowledge, Madam. You are without the right knowledge.'

'You forget that, though I am as yet young in years, I have read much and studied.'

'So had the Jews who crucified Christ.'

'Is it not a matter of interpretation? Who shall be judge who is right or wrong?'

Knox's answer was: 'God!' And by God he meant himself.

Mary's eyes appealed to her brother: Oh, take this man away. He wearies me.

John Knox would not be silenced. There he stood in the centre of the chamber, his voice ringing to the rafters; and everything he said was a condemnation, not only of the Church of Rome, but of Mary herself.

For he had seen her weakness. She was tolerant. Had she been as vehement as he was, he would have spoken more mildly, and he would have seized an early opportunity to leave Scotland. But she was a lass, a frivolous lass, who liked better to laugh and play than to force her opinions on others.

Knox would have nothing to fear from the Queen. He would rant against her; he would set spies to watch her; he would put his own interpretation on her every action, and he would do his utmost to drive her from the throne unless she adopted the Protestant faith.

Mary had risen abruptly. She had glanced towards Flem and Livy, who had been sitting in the window seat listening earnestly and anxiously to all that had been said. The two girls recognised the signal. They came to the Queen.

'Come,' said Mary, 'it is time that we left.'

She inclined her head slightly towards Knox and, with Flem and Livy, passed out of the room.

By the light of flickering candles the Queen's apartment might well have been set in Chenonceaux or Fontainebleau. She was surrounded by her ladies and gentlemen, and all were dressed in the French manner. Only French was spoken. From Paris had come her Gobelins tapestry, and it now adorned the walls.

On the floor were rich carpets, on the walls gilt-framed mirrors. D'Amville and Montmorency were beside her; they had been singing madrigals, and Flem and Beaton were in an excited group who were discussing a new masque they intended to produce.

About the Court the Scottish noblemen quarrelled and jostled for honours. The Catholic lords sparred continually with the Protestant lords. On the border the towns were being ravished both by the English and rival Scottish clans.

In the palace were the spies of John Knox, of Catherine de' Medici and of Elizabeth of England. These three powerful people had one object: to bring disaster to the Queen of Scots.

Yet, shut in by velvet hangings and Gobelins tapestry, by French laughter, French conversation, French flattery and charm, Mary determined to ignore what was unpleasant. She believed her stay there would be short; soon she would make a grand marriage – perhaps with Spain. But in the meantime she would make it pass as merrily and in as lively a fashion as was possible; and so during those weeks life was lived gaily within those precincts of Holyrood which had become known as 'Little France'.

❀ Chapter VIII ❀

I n the small room adorned with the finest of her French tapestries, Mary was playing chess with Beaton. Flem was at her embroidery and Livy and Seton sat reading quietly.

Mary's thoughts were not really on the game. She was troubled, as she was so often since she had come to Scotland. There were times when she could shut herself away in Little France, but she could not long succeed in shutting out her responsibilities. These Scots subjects of hers – rough and lusty – did not seem to wish to live in peace with one another. There were continual feuds and she found herself spending much time in trying to reconcile one with another.

Beaton said that Thomas Randolph, the English ambassador, told her that affairs were managed very differently in the English Court, and that the Tudor Queen's frown was enough to strike terror into her most powerful lords. Mary was too kindly, too tolerant.

'But what can I do?' Mary had demanded. 'I am powerless. Would to God I were treated like Elizabeth of England!' She was sure, she said, that Thomas Randolph exaggerated his mistress's power.

'He spoke with great sincerity,' Beaton had ventured.

But Beaton was inclined to blush when the Englishman's name was mentioned. Beaton was ready to believe all that man said.

Mary began to worry about Beaton and the Englishman. Did the man – who was a spy as all ambassadors were – seek out Beaton, flatter her, perhaps make love to her, in order to discover the Queen's secrets?

Dearest Beaton! She must be mad to think of Beaton as a spy! But Beaton could unwittingly betray, and it might well be that Randolph was clever enough to make her do so.

In France, the Cardinal of Lorraine had been ever beside Mary, keeping from her that which he did not wish her to know. Now she was becoming aware of so much of which she would prefer to remain in ignorance. Her brother James and Maitland stood together, but they hated Bothwell. The Earl of Atholl and the Earl of Errol, though Catholics, hated the Catholic leader Huntley, the Cock o' the North. There was Morton whose reputation for immorality almost equalled that of Bothwell; and there was Erskine who seemed to care for little but the pleasures of the table. There was the quarrel between the Hamilton Arran and Bothwell which flared up now and then and had resulted in her banishing Bothwell from the Court, on Lord James' advice, within a few weeks of her arrival, in spite of all his good service during the voyage.

She was disturbed and uncertain; she was sure she would never understand these warlike nobles whose shadows so darkened her throne.

She recalled now that warm September day when she had made her progress through the capital. She had been happy then, riding on the white palfrey which had with difficulty been procured for her, listening to the shouts of the people and their enthusiastic comments on her beauty. She had thought all would be well and that her subjects would come to love her.

But riding on one side of her had been the Protestant Lord James, and on the other the Catholic Cock o' the North; and the first allegorical tableau she had witnessed on that progress through the streets had ended with a child, dressed as an angel, handing her, with the keys of the city, the Protestant Bible and Psalter – and she had known even then that this was a warning. She, who was known to be a Catholic, was being firmly told that only a Protestant sovereign could hold the key to Scotland.

Moreover it had been a great shock, on arriving at Market Cross, to find a carved wooden effigy of a priest in the robes of the Mass fixed on a stake. She had blanched at the sight, seeing at once that preparations had been made to burn the figure before her eyes. She had been glad then of the prompt action of the Cock o' the North – an old man, but a fierce one – who had ridden ahead of her and ordered the figure to be immediately removed. To her relief this had been done. But it had spoilt her day. It had given her a glimpse of the difficulties which lay ahead of her.

She had returned from the entry weary, not stimulated as she used to be when she and François rode through the villages and towns of France. But she had determined to make a bid for peace and, to show her desire for tolerance, had appointed several of the Reformers to her government. Huntley, the Catholic leader, was among them with Argyle, Atholl and Morton as well as Châtelherault. Her brother, Lord James Stuart, and Lord Maitland were the leaders; and in view of the service he had rendered her, she could not exclude Bothwell, though that wild young man had succeeded in getting himself dismissed from Court – temporarily, of course. She had no wish to be severe with anyone.

Beaton looked up from the board and cried: 'Check-mate, I think, Your Majesty. I think Your Majesty's thoughts were elsewhere, or I should never have had so easy a victory.'

'Put away the pieces,' said the Queen. 'I wish to talk. Now that we have our rooms pleasantly furnished, let us have a grand ball. Let us show these people that we wish to make life at Court brighter than it has hitherto been. Perhaps, if we can interest them in the pleasant things of life, they will cease to quarrel so much about rights and wrongs and each other's opinions.'

'Let us have a masque!' cried Flem, her eyes sparkling. She was seeing herself dressed in some delightful costume, mumming before the Court, which would include the fascinating Maitland – surely, thought Flem, the most attractive man on Earth – no longer young, but no less exciting for that.

Livy was thinking of tall Lord Sempill who had made a point of being at her side lately, surely more than was necessary for general courtesy, while Beaton's thoughts were with the Englishman who had such wonderful stories to tell of his mistress, the Queen of England. Only Seton was uneasy, wondering whether she could tell the Queen that one of the priests had been set upon in the streets and had returned wounded by the stones which had been thrown at him; and that she had heard there was a new game to be played in the streets of Edinburgh, instigated by John Knox and called 'priest-baiting'.

The Queen said: 'Now, Seton! *You* are not attending. What sort of masque shall it be?'

'Let there be singing,' said Seton. 'Oh, but I forgot . . . Your Majesty's choir is short of a bass.'

'There is a fine bass in the suite of the Sieur de Moretta,' said Livy.

'And who is he?' asked Mary. 'But he will be of little use, for Moretta will soon be returning to his master of Savoy, I doubt not; and he will take your singer with him.'

'Then Your Majesty is not contemplating the marriage which Moretta came to further?' asked Beaton diffidently.

Mary looked at her sharply. Could it be that she was gathering information for Randolph? No! One look at dear Beaton's open face reassured her

She took Beaton's hand and pressed it warmly. It was a mute plea for forgiveness because she had secretly doubted her. 'No, I shall not marry the Duke of Ferrara, though it was for that purpose Savoy sent Moretta among us – for all that this is reputed to be a courtesy visit. But we stray from the point. What of this singer? Even temporarily he might be of some service to us.'

'He has the voice of an angel!' declared Flem.

'If he is as good as you say, we might ask him to stay with us after his master goes back.'

'Does Your Majesty think he would?'

'It would entirely depend on what position he holds under his master. If it is a humble one, he may be glad of the opportunity to serve me; and I doubt his master would refuse to spare him.'

'Madam,' said Seton, 'I heard him sing yesterday, and I have never heard the like.'

'We will have him brought here to my apartments. He shall sing for us. What is his name?'

'That I do not know,' said Flem.

Mary turned to the others, but none knew his name.

Seton suddenly remembered. 'I fancy I have heard him called Signor David by his fellows.'

'Then we will send for Signor David. Flem dear, send a page.'

The Queen had her lute brought to her, and the five ladies were discussing the music they would sing and play, when Signor David appeared.

He was a Piedmontese, short of stature and by no means handsome, but his graceful manners were pleasing; he bowed with charm, displaying a lively awareness of the honour done to him, while accepting it without awkwardness.

'Signor David,' said the Queen, 'we have heard that you possess a good voice. Is that true?'

'If Your Majesty would wish to judge of it, your humble servant will feel himself greatly honoured.'

'I will hear it. But first tell me – what is your position in the suite of my lord de Moretta?'

'A humble secretary, Your Majesty.'

'Now, Signor David, sing for us here and now.'

She played the lute and rarely had she looked more charming than she did at that moment, sitting there in her chair without ceremony, her delicate fingers plucking at the strings, her eyes shining, not only with her love of music, but because she was about to do this poor secretary a kindness.

And as he sang to her playing, his glorious voice filled the apartment and brought tears to their eyes; it was a voice of charm and feeling as well as power, and they could not hear it and remain unmoved.

When the song ended, the Queen said with emotion: 'Signor David, that was perfect.'

'I am delighted that my poor voice has given Your Majesty pleasure.'

'I would have you join my choir.'

'I have no words to express my delight.'

'But,' went on the Queen, 'when you leave with your master, we shall find my choir will be so much the poorer, that I may wish you had never joined it!'

He looked distressed.

'Unless,' said Mary impulsively, 'you wished to remain in my service when your master goes.'

His answer was to fall on his knees. He took her hand and lifted it to his lips. 'Service,' he stammered, 'to the most beautiful lady in the world!'

She laughed. 'Do not forget you will be choosing this land of harsh winters in exchange for your sunny Italy.'

'Madame,' he replied, 'if I may serve you, that would be sun enough for me.'

How different were the manners of these foreigners, she mused, from those of blunt Scotsmen! She liked the little man with the large and glowing eyes.

'Then if your master is willing, when he leaves Scotland you may exchange his service for mine. What is your name – your full name? We only know you as Signor David.'

'It is David Rizzio, Madame. Your Majesty's most humble and devoted servant henceforth.'

It was Christmas time and the wind howled up the Canongate; it buffeted the walls of Holyrood and the Queen had great logs burning in the fireplaces throughout the palace. To her great regret, most of the French retinue which had accompanied her to Scotland had now returned to France, and of her immediate circle only Elboeuf remained.

There was trouble in the streets, and at the root of that trouble were the lusty Bothwell and the deranged Arran.

Bothwell did not forget that it was due to Arran that he had been dismissed from the Court. Such a slight to a border warrior could not be allowed to pass. Arran, and the whole Hamilton clan, never missed an opportunity of maligning Bothwell and had spread far and wide the scandal concerning him and Anna Throndsen – the poor Danish girl, they called her – whom he had seduced, made a mother and lured from her home merely to become one of those women with whom he chose to amuse himself as the fancy took him.

Arran – a declared puritan and ardent follower of Knox – was not, Bothwell had discovered, in a position to throw stones. Accordingly Bothwell devised a plot for exposing the Hamilton heir in the sort of scandal with which he had conspired to smear Bothwell.

Bothwell had two congenial companions. One of these was the Marquis d'Elboeuf, always ready for a carousal to enliven the Scottish atmosphere, and Lord John Stuart, Mary's base-born brother, who admired the Hepburn more than any man he knew and was ready to follow him in any rashness. Bothwell cultivated Mary's brother for two reasons – one because the young man could do him so much good at Court, and the other because he hoped he would marry his sister, Janet Hepburn, a red-headed girl as lusty – or almost – as her brother, and who had been involved in more than one scandal and had already been lavishly generous with her favours to Lord John.

The followers of Bothwell and Lord John swaggered about the streets of Edinburgh, picking quarrels with the followers of the Hamiltons. But that was not enough for Bothwell's purpose.

'What a merry thing it would be,' he cried, 'if we could catch Arran *flagrante delicto*. Then we should hear what his friend John Knox had to say to that!'

Elboeuf was overcome with mirth at the prospect. Lord John wanted to know how they could do it without delay.

''Tis simple,' explained Bothwell. 'Often of a night he visits a certain woman. What if we broke into the house where they stay, catch him in the act, and drive him naked into the night? Imagine the puritan heir of the Hamiltons, running through the streets without his clothes on a cold night because he has been forced to leave them in the bedchamber of his mistress!'

'Who is his mistress?' asked Lord John.

'There we are fortunate,' explained Bothwell. 'She is the daughter-in-law of old Cuthbert Ramsay who was my grandmother's fourth husband, and lives in his house.'

'Old Cuthbert is no friend to you.'

'No, but in the guise of mummers we should find easy entry into his house.'

''Tis a capital plan!' cried Elboeuf. 'And what of the poor deserted lady? I could weep for her – her lover snatched from her! Will she not be desolate?'

'We'll not leave her desolate!' laughed Bothwell. 'She will find us three adequate compensation for the loss of that poor half-wit. It would seem our game with Arran would be but half-finished if we did not console the lady after dismissing the lover.'

So it was agreed.

The night was bitterly cold as the three conspirators swaggered down to St Mary's Wynd, wherein stood the house of Cuthbert Ramsay. They were dressed as Christmas revellers and masks covered the faces of all three, who were well known as the most profligate men in Scotland.

They found the door of the house locked against them; Bothwell was infuriated because, knowing the customs of Ramsay's house, he realised that there must have been warning of their coming.

'Open the door!' he shouted. He could see the dim lights through some of the windows, but no sound came from behind the door. Bothwell's great shoulders had soon crashed it open and, with the help of his two friends, he forced an entry into the house.

Seeing a shivering girl trying to hide herself, Bothwell seized her and demanded to be shown the apartments of Mistress Alison Craig with all speed. The girl, too terrified to do aught else, ran up the staircase with the three men in pursuit. She pointed to a door and fled.

Bothwell banged on the door. 'Open!' he cried.

'Who is there?' came the instant request. Bothwell turned to his friend and grinned, for the voice was that of Alison Craig.

'It is one who loves you,' said Bothwell, 'come to tell you of his love.'

'My lord Bothwell . . .'

'You remember me? I thought you would.'

'What . . . what do you want of me?'

Still grinning to his companions, Bothwell answered: 'That which I always want of you.'

It was easier to force an entry into Alison's room than it had been into the house. Soon all three of them were in the room, where Alison, half-clothed, cowered against the wall. The open window told its own story.

Lord John ran to the window.

'What . . . do you want here?' demanded Alison.

'Where is Arran?' asked Bothwell.

'I . . . do not understand you. I do not understand why you come here . . . force your way into my room . . .'

'He has made good his escape,' said Lord John turning from the window.

Elboeuf had placed his arm about Alison. She screamed and struck out at him.

'How dare you . . . you . . . you French devil!' she cried.

Lord John said: 'Madam, you would prefer me, would you not? See, I am young and handsome, and a Scot . . . a bold brave Scotsman whom you will find very different from the dastard who has just left you. Do not trust Frenchmen, for as the good people of Edinburgh will tell you, the French have tails.'

'Go away . . . you brutes . . . You loathsome . . .'

Elboeuf interrupted: 'Dear Madam, can you tolerate these savage Scots? He who has deserted you at the first sign of trouble is a disgrace to his nation. I will show you what you may expect from one who comes from a race that is well skilled in the arts of love.'

Alison tried to shut out the sight of those three brutal faces. She had had lovers, but this was a different affair. In vain she tried to appeal to some streak of honour in those three. Perhaps in Lord John, she thought. He was so young. Perhaps the Frenchman whose superficial manners were graceful. Never . . . never, she feared, in Bothwell.

He had pushed the others aside. He said: 'Arran is my enemy and it is meet and fitting that I should be the first.'

Feeling his hands upon her Alison gave out a piercing scream. She slipped from his grip and ran to the window.

'Help!' she cried. 'Good people . . . Help! Save me from brutes and ruffians . . .'

Bothwell picked her up effortlessly. He had played a similar role in many a scene in his border raids. He threw the terrified woman on to the bed.

'Harken!' cried Lord John.

Elboeuf's hand went to his sword.

The servants had not been idle. They had lost no time in making it known that Bothwell and his friends had broken into the house of Arran's mistress. The Hamilton men were rushing up the stairs.

It was a very different matter, attacking a defenceless woman, from facing many armed men, and all three realised that they would be in danger of losing their lives if they hesitated. Already it was necessary to fight their way through those men who were on the staircase. Bothwell led the way, his sword flashing. As for Lord John and Elboeuf – no one cared to wound the Queen's uncle or her brother – and in a short time the three men were clear of the house.

They separated and ran to safety before the streets were filled with the gathering Hamilton clan.

The matter did not end there. The Hamiltons continued to throng the streets, swearing they would do to death their enemy Bothwell. The followers of Elboeuf and Lord John were gathering about them; and it seemed as though a great battle might shortly take place in the streets of Edinburgh.

The Queen, hearing of this, was terrified and uncertain how to deal with the trouble. Once more she was thankful for her resourceful brother, for James acted promptly, and with the Cock o' the North and himself riding at its head led an armed force to disperse the quarrelling clans.

'Every man shall clear the streets on pain of death!' was Lord James' proclamation.

It had the desired effect.

But Bothwell felt the little adventure had not entirely failed. All Edinburgh now knew that, for all his piety, Arran had a mistress, and that was just what he had wished to proclaim.

The Lord James and Maitland were closeted together discussing the affair of Bothwell and Arran.

'Arran,' said Maitland, 'being little more than half-witted, may be the more easily dismissed. It is the other who gives me anxious thoughts.'

Lord James stroked his sparse beard and nodded. 'You're right. Bothwell is a trouble-maker. I would like to see him back in his place on the Border. It may well be a matter for rejoicing, that our Queen has been brought up in the French Court. I fancy she finds us all a little lacking in grace. What she must think of that ruffian Bothwell I can well imagine.'

'Yet he received part of his education in France, remember.'

'It touched him not. He is all Borderer. I think the Queen would be pleased to have him removed from Court.'

'None could be more pleased at that than I. If we can marry the Queen into Spain . . .'

There was no need to say more. Both men understood. Marry the Queen into Spain . . . or somewhere abroad. Leave Scotland for Lord James and Maitland. It was a twin ambition.

'Bothwell would try to prevent such a marriage,' said Maitland. 'He would wish to see the Queen married to a Scot.'

'We will advise the Queen to banish him from Court.'

'What of the others who were equally guilty?'

'Her brother! Her uncle! Let us satisfy ourselves with ridding the Court of Bothwell. He is our man.'

They sought audience with the Queen. She was angry about this brutal outrage which had taken place in the midst of the Christmas celebrations. She was preparing for her brother Robert's marriage to Jane Kennedy, the daughter of the Earl of Cassillis; she had grown fond of Jane and was delighted to do special honour to her. And after that marriage there was to be another: Lord John's to Janet Hepburn. There could be so much gaiety and pleasure, yet these barbarians could not be content to enjoy it – nor would they let others enjoy it in peace.

'Madam,' said Lord James, 'this is a monstrous affair. Such outrageous conduct is a disgrace to our country.'

'Yet it would seem that I am powerless to prevent it.'

'No, no, Your Majesty,' said Maitland. 'The miscreants can be punished – and should be, as a warning to others.'

'How can I punish my Uncle Elboeuf?'

'You can only warn him. It will be said that, as a Frenchman from an immoral land, his sins are not to be taken as seriously as those of honourable Scotsmen. Soon he will be leaving our country. A warning will suffice for Elboeuf. As for our brother, he is but a boy – not yet twenty – and I think led astray by more practised ruffians. He can be forgiven on account of his youth. But there is one, the ringleader, who is not so young and should not be forgiven. Bothwell is the instigator of all the trouble, Madam, and as such should be severely dealt with.'

'I have no doubt that you are right,' said Mary. 'But it seems to me wrong to punish one and let the others go free.'

'While Bothwell remains at Court there will be trouble,' said Lord James.

Mary replied: 'I had thought to give them a severe warning,

to threaten them with stern punishment if they offend again, and then forget the matter. It is Christmastide . . .'

'Madam,' said Maitland, 'these matters cannot be put right by being thrust aside. The Hamiltons were gravely insulted, and for the sake of peace, Bothwell should at least be exiled.'

'Summon him to your presence, dearest sister,' said James. 'Tell him he must leave the Court. I assure you, it is safer so.'

Mary was resigned. 'I suppose you are right,' she said. 'Have him brought here.'

He came into her presence, arrogant as ever; and she was conscious of his veiled insolence.

'My lord Bothwell, you have been guilty of an outrage. You have broken into the house of peaceful citizens and caused much distress. I know that you were not alone. You had two companions. One is a guest in this kingdom – my own guest; the other is a young and impressionable boy. Therefore I hold you responsible for this disturbance.'

'Would you not cast a little blame on the Hamiltons, Madam?'

'From what I hear the trouble started when you forced an entry into a house in St Mary's Wynd.'

'The trouble started long before that, Madam. If you wish for an account of the scores I have to settle with Arran, I shall be pleased to give it.'

Mary waved her hand impatiently. 'Please . . . I beg of you . . . tell me no more. I am tired of your perpetual bickering. You are dismissed the Court. Go back to the Border. Go anywhere, and if you are not soon gone I shall be forced to make your punishment more drastic.'

'Madam,' began Bothwell, 'I appeal to your sense of justice. If you feel I have done aught to deserve blame, then must you cast some blame on Arran. Let me meet him in single combat and settle our affairs thus.'

'No, my lord,' she said sternly, 'there shall be no more bloodshed if I can prevent it.'

She looked up into his face helplessly. Her glance clearly said: What can I do? How can I punish Arran with his father, Châtelherault, and the whole Hamilton clan behind him – to say nothing of his supporter John Knox? Go away. If you must fight, fight the English on the Border. I want Scotland left in peace.

'Leave the Court,' she said. 'Go at once.' She smiled suddenly. 'You will have many preparations to make for your sister's wedding.'

His smile answered hers.

He would retire from Court; he would proceed with his preparations for his sister's wedding; and when the Queen's brother became his brother-in-law, he would be better fitted to pit himself against Lord James and the whole Hamilton clan.

'My sister,' he said, 'will be a sad woman if Your Majesty does not honour us at Crichton with your presence.'

The Queen was still smiling. So he was going. He was not going to plunge into one of those Knox-like arguments which distressed her. 'Of a certainty I shall wish to be present at my brother's wedding,' she told him.

Less than two weeks later Mary set out for Crichton Castle, the chief seat of the Hepburn family.

John Knox thundered against the marriage of these wicked

people who disgusted virtuous Scotsmen with their fornications and lecherous lives. This base-born brother of the
whore of Babylon, he declared, was known to be a whore-
monger; and what of the woman he was marrying? 'A
sufficient woman for such a man!'

Knox was left in Edinburgh reviving old scandals.

'Janet Hepburn, the bride-to-be!' he cried. 'To how many
has she been handfast, I should like to know – or rather I
should shudder to know – before she prepares herself to enter
into this most unholy matrimony with the sanction of the
Queen?'

Mary was glad to put many miles between herself and the
ranting preacher. She was glad to enter the old castle whose
unscalable walls had been built to resist the ruffian raiders from
across the Border. Sternly it faced the Cheviots and the Tyne
– the Hepburns' challenge to marauding Englishmen.

Here she dwelt as the guest of Lord Bothwell. She liked the
wild outspoken girl who was as bold as her brother, and was
not surprised that John wished to marry her.

Lord James, who accompanied her, was more dour than
ever. He did not approve of this alliance with the Hepburns.
The girl was wild, he complained to Mary. John was too young
to be saddled with such a wife. There were nobles of higher
standing who would have been delighted with the honour of
marrying a Stuart.

She refused to listen to his gloomy prophecies. Here was an
occasion for merriment – a wedding, and the wedding of her
own brother at that. Lord Bothwell was making a great
entertainment for her and she was determined to enjoy it.

'James,' she coaxed, 'now that Robert and John are married
you must be the next.'

James listened soberly. He had been thinking for a long time of marriage with the Lady Agnes Keith, who was the daughter of the Earl Marischal. Marry he would, but his marriage would in no way resemble this one between Janet Hepburn and his brother John. For all he knew, John had been caught by the woman at one of the handfast ceremonies where young men and women met round a bonfire and went off to copulate in the woods. Lord James had no desire for such questionable pleasures. When he married Lady Agnes it would be because he had made up his mind that such a match would be advantageous. As yet he was hesitant.

Mary was laughing at him. 'Yes, James,' she said, 'I shall insist. Your marriage shall be the next. You cannot allow your young brothers to leave you behind.'

Lord James pressed her hand in a brotherly, affectionate way. It was impossible not to be fond of her. She was so charming and so ready to take his advice.

Mary gave herself up to the pleasure of being entertained. And what an entertainment Lord Bothwell had prepared for her! She knew that he had sent raiders beyond the Border to procure that which made their feast, but what of that! He was a Borderer with many a score to settle. The eighteen hundred does and roes, the rabbits, geese, fowls, plovers and partridges in hundreds, may have come from the land of the old enemy, but it mattered not at all. They made good feasting. And after the feast there were sports on the green haugh below the castle as had rarely been seen in Scotland, and the leaping and dancing of the bridegroom won the acclamation of all.

Mary now felt better and happier than she had for many weeks.

Could it be true – as her Maries suggested – that her native land was more beneficial to her health than France had been? It was absurd. These draughty castles, so comfortless compared with the luxury of the French chateaux, and food which although plentiful was less invitingly prepared . . . could it be possible that these discomforts could make her better? Perhaps it was the rigorous climate, though often when the mist hung about the rooms she felt twinges in her limbs. No. She was growing out of her ailments – that must be it. Of course her Maries declared it was due to Scotland because they were fast becoming reconciled to Scotland: Flem through Maitland; Livy through John Sempill; Beaton through the Englishman, Randolph; and Seton . . . well, Seton was just happy to see the others happy.

When would Mary's time come; and who would be her husband? It seemed to Mary that every day the name of some suitor was presented to her.

The Queen of England was anxious to have a say in plans for Mary's marriage. If the bridegroom did not please her, she had hinted, she would certainly not name Mary and her heirs as successors to the English throne. That spy Randolph – why was poor Beaton so taken with this man? – always seemed to be at her elbow. She pictured him in his apartment scribbling hard, determined that his mistress should miss little of what went on in Mary's Court.

And now there was to be another marriage. Lord James was at last going to marry Lady Agnes.

Mary wanted to show her gratitude to her brother, and what better time could there be than the occasion of his marriage?

She longed to give him what he craved – the Earldom of Moray; but how could she grant him that Earldom when old Huntley, the Cock o' the North – and not without reason – laid claim to it? Instead she would make him Earl of Mar and beg him to be satisfied with that.

Now for the pleasant occupation of arranging the masques and mummeries. She called her Maries to her, and they fell to discussing the music for the wedding. That led to sending for Signor David whose company never failed to delight Mary. It was always such a pleasure to hear his voice, and now and then she would command him to sing for her.

When he came, all five Maries greeted him warmly.

'Come and sit here,' commanded the Queen. 'Now, Signor David, please sing the new song you brought to me last Monday.'

They listened entranced to his beautiful voice.

'You shall lead the choir for my brother's wedding,' declared the Queen.

He was overwhelmed with delight, as he always was by the slightest favour; that was why it was such a pleasure to do little things for him. If she could give him some small task, the doing of it seemed to please him more than praise. His attitude towards her was one of adoring devotion.

'David,' she said, 'I am going to make you my *valet de chambre*. Then we shall not have to send for you when we want you. You will be here among us. Where do you lodge now, Signor David?'

'In the porter's lodge, Madame.'

'Well, henceforth you shall lodge in the palace, and your chamber shall be near mine, as I shall need your services often. Can you write in the French language, David?'

'Madame, it is as my native language.'

'Then why did you not tell us before!' cried Mary in French. 'Now we shall all speak French. We like to do so when we are alone.'

'Tell us about yourself, David,' said Flem. 'That is if Her Majesty would permit it.'

'Her Majesty permits,' said Mary, 'and is as eager to hear as you are, my dear Flem.'

'There is little to tell,' began David. 'My life was of no great interest . . . until I came to the Court of Scotland. I was born at Pancalieri. We were very poor, but my father was a musician. From my childhood it was singing . . . singing songs . . . and, of course, playing the lute.'

'Then I am glad of that, David,' said the Queen; 'not the poverty, of course, but the singing and the lute-playing. Doubtless it has made you the musician you are.'

'I am glad of it now, Madame, since it brought me to your notice.'

'What else, David?' asked Beaton.

'When I was of an age to leave home, I was sent to serve the Archbishop of Turin. There I played music, sang in his choir, and acted as his secretary.'

'Were you as competent a secretary as a musician?' asked Beaton.

'I think I gave satisfaction, my lady, since from the Archbishop I was able to go to Nice and the Court of the Duke of Savoy.'

'And there became secretary to Moretta,' added Mary. 'Who knows, I might make use of those secretarial qualities also. I will do this, David: I will pay you a salary of sixty-five pounds a year, and, if you please me, I shall increase it.'

'Madame, your goodness overwhelms me. It is sufficient reward to serve Your Majesty.'

'But it is not sufficient for us, is it?' she demanded of her Maries.

'We would have you dressed in velvets, you see,' explained Flem.

Mary said: 'Beaton, my dear, give David money so that next time he comes to us he may be dressed in velvet. And he must have a jewel too.' She looked down at her hands and drew off a ruby ring. 'The colour suits you, David. And I think it will fit your little finger.'

His dark eyes gleamed, and they saw the tears shining there. He fell to his knees, and taking the ring he put it on his little finger; then he pressed it against his lips.

'There it shall remain,' he said, 'until the day I die. A constant reminder of the day Your Majesty gave it to me.'

❁ ❁ ❁

John Knox preached the wedding sermon in the Kirk of St Giles.

Lord James was a favourite of his; he looked to the young man, with high hopes. Naturally there were times when it was necessary to admonish his pupil, but John Knox had declared Lord James to be a friend of God and the true religion, which meant a friend to John Knox; and John Knox, the practical man, while keeping his eyes fixed on his place in Heaven, saw no reason for ignoring advantages which might accrue here on Earth.

He was not sure of Agnes Keith. He did not trust women. So now he spoke out. 'Unto this day the Kirk has received comfort from you. Let God and the Kirk not find you fainter in

265

purpose than you were before, or it will be said that your wife has changed your nature.'

Mary was restless, waiting impatiently for the sermon to be over. When would the odious man finish? Was this the way to preach a wedding sermon? But Jamie was listening intently; and others seemed spellbound by the fire-breathing preacher.

Through the streets, when the church ceremony was over, went the wedding procession. It was magnificent, but Mary remembered another in comparison with which this seemed like a village wedding. Yet it was more grand than any seen before in Edinburgh, and it would show the people how she loved this brother of hers. He was a Protestant and she was a Catholic; but that made no difference to their love, she believed, and she wished her people to take this to heart.

James, now Earl of Mar, still hankered after the Earldom of Moray; but Huntley, who lived in the Northern Highlands like a king, could not be persuaded to give it up. James had said: 'It is a sad thing, my dearest sister, that there should be those in this country who endow themselves with a status above that of the Queen.'

'It is,' Mary agreed. James was referring to Huntley; Mary was thinking of John Knox.

The feasting went on for several days, and the citizens gathered outside Holyrood listening to the music and seeing what they could of the dancers. There were banquets and masques; and Mary had arranged that everything should take place in the elegant French manner.

Through the streets of Edinburgh John Knox stalked, shaking his fist at the palace.

'Within those walls,' he roared, 'the Devil dances. Painted

harlots mingle with seducers. There'll be fornication in the Palace of Holyrood this night.' That subject dominated his mind; it was one on which he seemed compelled to dwell. 'Jezebel calls the tune, and her four handmaidens – Sin, Lechery, Lust and Evil-living – beckon the weak.'

During the revelry, Mary found time to talk to her brother. 'Jamie, on occasions like this I feel at peace with the whole world. I would like to call my enemies to me and speak peaceably with them. I fear John Knox is too far set against me, but what of the Queen of England? If I could have a meeting with her . . . if we could discuss, in person, our differences, would that not be a good thing?'

James smiled at his sister. 'It would indeed.'

James was indulgent. She was so pretty, and so impetuously foolish at times. She would never be a great ruler; she would be no match for the Queen beyond the Border. Elizabeth of England would never have tolerated in her country such a powerful nobleman as James intended to be in Scotland.

But such thoughts made him fonder of her than ever. He liked to see her dancing and enjoying her French games, laughing at the witticisms of her fool, La Jardinière, frittering the days whilst the grown-ups got on with the work.

'I am glad,' she said, 'that you are in agreement with me, Jamie. I will sound Randolph on the subject at the earliest possible moment. Oh, Jamie, I do so long to see her. One hears so many tales of her. Her courtiers say she is dazzlingly beautiful, but we hear different reports sometimes. I should enjoy meeting her face to face.'

James looked into his sister's animated face. 'She would never forgive you if she saw you.'

'Forgive me! For what, James?'

'For being a hundred times more beautiful than herself.'

Mary was delighted. Compliments came rarely from James. Poor frivolous lass! James was thinking. Thinking to set herself against the shrewdest woman in the world!

But it was for her frivolity – and all that it might lead to – that he loved her.

At that evening's banquet, Mary, who had previously had a word with the Englishman Randolph, lifted her golden goblet of wine and, rising to her feet, cried: 'I drink to the health of my sister of England, Queen Elizabeth.' Whereupon all at the table rose and drank with her, to the especial delight of Thomas Randolph who adored his Queen, and Mary Beaton who adored Randolph and so was delighted to see friendly relations between him and her beloved Mary.

And as the bridegroom, James, the new Earl, joined in the toast, he was not thinking of a possible meeting between the two Queens, because he did not believe it would come to pass; he was not thinking of his bride and marriage, because that was something accomplished and he never wasted time in profitless thought; what occupied his mind was how he could openly call himself the Earl of Moray and take possession of the rich lands which went with the title, and he concluded that this could only come about through the downfall of the Cock o' the North.

Bothwell was not pleased by the state of affairs. His prospects had promised to be so fair at that time when the Queen had sent for him to arrange her voyage back to Scotland. Since then he had twice been banished from Court. He was growing ambitious. He knew that James Stuart was against him; he knew too that James Stuart was a friend of the English. The Queen – a foolish woman – did not realise that. In her sentimental way she thought of her dear Jamie merely as her brother, not as the man whose chief aim was to strip her of power that he might add to his own.

He, Bothwell, wanted to see Scotland free from the French and the English. He was ready to serve the Queen; but he wanted a high place for the Earl of Bothwell.

He realised now that he had been foolish to allow his feud with the Hamiltons to put him out of favour. What he had done by his impulsive prank was to play right into the hands of James Stuart and Maitland; but he would beat them at their own game, and to do this he must contrive reconciliation with the Earl of Arran.

How to do this? Bothwell had an idea. He would seek the mediation of John Knox. Knox, of course, would condemn Bothwell for his profligate ways, but even so the Earl would not be so damned in the eyes of the preacher as some were, since he was a professed Protestant; moreover Knox himself came from the Border country and had lived with his parents in a district over which the Hepburns held sway. It was not difficult, therefore, to obtain, through a third party, the desired interview.

Knox received Bothwell in the sparsely furnished room at the manse not far from Market Cross.

'At last,' cried Knox, rising and standing as though he were addressing a meeting, 'you have seen the errors of your ways. You have lived a riotous life and now you have come home . . . like the prodigal son. You wish to leave your sins behind you . . . to lead a better life. You wish to love your neighbour as yourself . . .'

Patience was not one of Bothwell's virtues. He cut the preacher short. 'If I could have Arran's friendship instead of his enmity,' he said, 'I could stay at Court with a mere handful of servants. As it is, I have about me hundreds of men-at-arms. I must be prepared to meet an attack at any time, and it is very expensive.'

Knox was inclined to be lenient. When he was a boy he had been humble before the lords of the estate. This man with the arrogant manner had reawakened that youthful respect. Hard-livers the Hepburns had always been, but they had not been harsh with their own. Moreover, Knox saw in this lusty man one whose friendship could be useful to him.

'My lord,' he said, 'I shall pray for you. I shall pray that I may be given the means of comforting you.'

Bothwell frowned. He had not come for a sermon and he was not going to promise to mend his ways. He interrupted: 'You have influence with Arran. I would have you make him understand that this quarrel between us is fruitless. Arrange a meeting and reconciliation between us. That is what I ask, Master Knox.'

'My lord, the angels are smiling at this moment. Brotherly love, they sing. Rejoice, for he whom we thought to be lost to the Devil has turned to God. You will not lose, my lord, for this night's work.'

Bothwell thanked the preacher and left. He was pleased with what he had done.

He was even more delighted when, at the meeting arranged by Knox, he took Arran's hand in his and, looking into the half crazy eyes, swore eternal friendship.

After that they surprised all Edinburgh. During the next few days wherever Arran was, there was Bothwell. They drank together; they were seen walking arm-in-arm along the Canongate.

❈ ❈ ❈

Mary, with a small train of followers, had travelled up to Falkland Palace to enjoy a little hawking. To the delight of all who saw her, she rode out, a dainty sight, her falcon on her wrist. Beside her rode her brother, the Earl of Mar, and among those who accompanied them were her brother's new wife, Agnes Keith, and the four Maries.

It was when they had returned after an afternoon's sport that a special messenger came riding to the palace. He must see the Queen at once, he declared; he had a despatch for her which was a warning and of the utmost importance.

'Whence comes he?' asked Mar.

'From the Earl of Arran, my lord, who declares that the Queen must, without delay, be made aware of the plots against her.'

James Stuart took the despatch at once to Mary and remained with her while she read it.

'But this is . . . incredible!' she cried. 'It cannot be true. Arran is mad. He says that there is a plot concocted by himself, his father Châtelherault, and Bothwell. They plan to abduct me, carry me off to Dumbarton Castle, murder any who resist, and keep me a prisoner until I marry Arran. They will force me to the marriage, if need be. And Bothwell is to see that all is carried out according to plan.'

'Why does Arran let you into the secret?'

'At the last moment he cannot go on with it. He wishes to warn me against Bothwell who is ruthless enough to attempt anything. James, it is ridiculous. Arran is no longer half-mad; he has completely lost his wits.'

James took the despatch and read it. 'It is coherent enough. It does not read like the words of a madman.'

'Jamie . . . you cannot believe . . .'

'My dearest sister, we cannot be too careful. Arran is mad enough for anything. Châtelherault is ambitious enough and Bothwell is wild enough to attempt to carry out this plan.'

'Seize my person! Keep me prisoner!'

'Aye! And inflict God knows what humiliations upon you.'

'It is a mad notion of Arran's, I am sure. The plan has no meaning outside that poor brain. You will remember he once before talked of kidnapping me . . . and it came to nothing.'

'Mary, you are the Queen. You are also a very desirable woman. Do not lose sight of these facts.'

'What am I to do, Jamie?'

'Have them all placed under arrest. That is the only way to ensure safety.'

'First we should ascertain how deep in madness Arran is.'

'An order should be issued at once for the arrest of Arran, Châtelherault and Bothwell.'

'Let us take Arran first and hear what he has to say.'

'What! And leave his father and Bothwell free to carry out their diabolical plans! Bothwell is at the bottom of this, you may depend upon it. Bothwell and Châtelherault! They are a pair of knaves, using this poor madman to serve their ends.'

'But of what use could my marriage with Arran be to Bothwell?'

'How can we know what plans the Borderer makes?'

Mary was uneasy. She had hoped that the friendship

between Arran and Bothwell would put an end to the strife; could it be possible that the insolent Borderer had arranged it in order to sway poor Arran to his will?

Only a few hours after the messenger from Arran had arrived, a member of the Hamilton family came riding with all speed to the castle of Falkland. He was Gavin Hamilton, the Abbot of Kilwinning, and he declared that his kinsman, the Duke of Châtelherault, had begged him to set out with all speed to Falkland as the Duke feared his son had completely lost his reason. He had come to his father's house of Kinneil with a wild story, and the Duke thought the Queen should know that he had put his son under lock and key.

'Madam,' cried Gavin Hamilton, 'the story of this wild plot to kidnap you is untrue. There never was such a plot. The young Earl imagined it. He threw himself at the Duke's feet, crying that he was possessed by devils and that Bothwell had persuaded him to treason. The Duke threatened to kill his son, and now Arran has escaped through a window by means of knotted sheets. It is not known where he is, but the Duke of Châtelherault considered it expedient to put the whole story before Your Majesty.'

Mary commanded Gavin Hamilton to go to a private chamber where he would be given refreshment. When she was alone with her brother she turned her anxious face to him. Though the plan seemed wild, she feared that it might contain some substance, and she could not help picturing herself the prisoner of Arran and Bothwell.

James said: 'We will at least keep Master Gavin Hamilton under restraint until we have thoroughly probed this matter.'

Before Gavin had finished the meal which was brought to him, Bothwell himself appeared at Falkland Castle.

'Send him to me at once,' said Mary when she heard of his arrival.

He came swaggering in, insolent and arrogant as ever. He showed no sign that he was aware that his plan had miscarried.

James and Maitland were both with the Queen.

'My lord Bothwell,' she began, 'we have had strange visitors this day.'

'Madam?' he questioned. His cool eyes appraised her, stripping her of her jewels, her velvets. She believed that in his mind's eye he set her side by side with the peasant women with whom, she had heard, he amused himself from time to time. His gaze made her uncomfortable.

'I beg of you, do not feign ignorance,' she said with heightened colour.

'I feign nothing, Madam. I am entirely ignorant of the comings of your strange visitors.'

'The Abbot of Kilwinning has been here. Does that suggest anything to you?'

'I do not know the fellow, Madam.'

'You know that he is a Hamilton. He brings me news of the Duke of Châtelherault.'

'Bad news, I assume, from Your Majesty's agitation.'

The cold eyes of James Stuart watched him; the shrewd ones of Maitland never left his face.

'He has exposed your plot, my lord.'

'Plot? What plot? To what plot does Your Majesty refer?'

'The plot which was conceived by you, Arran and Châtelherault, to kidnap me.'

'What is this? I know of no such plot, Madam.'

Mary turned helplessly to James and Maitland.

'You will need to convince Her Majesty of that more

'successfully than you are doing at the moment,' James said.

'I do not understand your lordship.'

'There is a grave accusation against you.'

'Who makes this accusation? Mad Arran?'

'The plot,' said Maitland flippantly, 'does not seem so mad as the man who made it.'

'So Arran has accused me?'

'Arran has laid bare the facts.'

'Bring the fellow here!' cried Bothwell. 'Let him accuse me to my face. By God! I'll challenge him . . . or any who accuse me . . . to single combat.'

'No such combat could serve to elucidate this matter,' said Maitland.

'By God!' cried Bothwell. 'Combat can decide whether a man shall live or die. I give you my word it can be both judge and jury.'

'It shall not be in this case,' said Maitland. 'The Queen is determined to uncover the truth.'

James had given a signal, and six men-at-arms appeared. They knew what they had to do.

Bothwell's hand went to his sword; but deciding this was not the time for violence, he hesitated.

He looked straight at the Queen, and his gaze, which seemed to hold something of contempt in it, made her shiver.

'I demand justice,' he said.

She answered quickly: 'It shall be yours, my lord.'

He allowed himself to be led away.

Mary tried to forget the unpleasant affair. She turned from the subject whenever it was raised.

'I am tired . . . tired of these perpetual quarrels!' she cried.

And then perhaps there would be a wedding at Court to amuse her; then she could briefly forget. She was planning for her meeting with the Queen of England. It should be the most splendid meeting in history. There should be tents set up on the Border and each country should display its chivalry. Her pageants should rival those of the Field of the Cloth of Gold.

But the Queen of England continually found excuses for postponing the meeting.

Meanwhile poor Arran had wandered the countryside, a raving lunatic, and had eventually arrived at the house of an old friend, Sir William Kirkcaldy, in a sorry state, his clothes torn, his body weak from hunger and his mind so distorted that he believed he was the Queen's husband and that, instead of lying in a state of collapse at the door of Hallyards, Sir William's mansion, he was lying in an oak bed at Holyrood with the Queen.

He had wept at the feet of Kirkcaldy and told him he was possessed by devils, that he was the thrall of witches. He was brought to Falkland and later imprisoned in Edinburgh Castle. Bothwell was also imprisoned there. The Duke of Châtelherault had thrown himself at Mary's feet and wept so bitterly that she had embraced him and told him he should not suffer. James, however, had insisted that Dumbarton Castle should be confiscated on the grounds that the son and his confederate could not be imprisoned while the father was held to be guiltless.

'Then,' said Mary, 'let us free Bothwell and Arran.'

'All in good time,' said James.

'Yet should not these men have a speedy trial? Should they be kept imprisoned before they have been proved guilty?'

James smiled tenderly. 'Dearest sister, Arran would have to be restrained in any case, so he suffers no hardship. As for Bothwell, it is as well to keep that rogue out of mischief for a while. Even if he is guiltless in this matter, his sins are many. Let this imprisonment serve to wipe off some of the punishment which is most surely due to him.'

Mary had to be content with that. She was not really sorry. Arran's madness and his preoccupation with marriage to herself perturbed her. Bothwell had a like effect.

Then fresh trouble broke out.

It started when Sir John Gordon, son of Huntley, the Cock o' the North, strolling through the streets of Edinburgh, had come face to face with Lord Ogilvie of Airlie and drawn his sword; in the fight Ogilvie was wounded, and Gordon taken and imprisoned in the Tolbooth.

The story of their feud was then brought to light. Lord Ogilvie had brought an action against John Gordon. One of the Ogilvies – a dissolute youth – had tried to persuade his stepmother to become his mistress, at which his father had been so enraged as to disinherit him and give a portion of his land to Sir John Gordon. Young Ogilvie had called a family conference, and Lord Ogilvie, maintaining that whatever the circumstances, his kinsmen had no right to give away to outsiders that which belonged to his family, had brought a lawsuit in the hope of retrieving the property for the Ogilvies.

Sir John Gordon was infuriated at the bringing of the action. In the Highlands Lord Huntley and all the family of Gordon were regarded as rulers; they did not suffer insults, and if any were offered them it was – as was customary with the Borderer Bothwell – a matter for sword-play. Hence, swaggering through the streets of Edinburgh and meeting Ogilvie, it had seemed right and natural to draw the sword. That he – a Gordon – should be thrust into prison for such an action was an insult.

He had immediately found means of escaping and had fled to the stronghold of the North.

When James Stuart heard of this his eyes glistened and he licked his lips. He remembered the rich lands of Strathearn and Cardel which went with the Earldom of Moray and which were at that time held by the Gordons; he immediately began to see ways in which he could turn this affair to his advantage.

'It is time,' he said to the Queen, 'for Your Majesty to journey North. We must settle this affair with Huntley and his Gordons. You cannot allow young Gordon to flout your authority. We shall have every knave and vagabond breaking prison, believing it is a noble thing to do.'

'Jamie,' she said, 'cannot we ask him to come back and face a trial?'

'Ask him to come back! He never would. He would flout you again as the Gordons have always flouted you.'

'I have not noticed that *they* have done this. There is *one* who has – in the Kirk and the streets of Edinburgh.'

'You may be sure,' said James quickly, 'that that fellow Randolph has given his account of this to his Queen. What, think you, will she say when she hears of it, if you do nothing in the matter? She will say Arran and Bothwell languish in prison, and those are Protestant nobles; Sir John Gordon goes free – but then he is a Catholic! You cannot afford to show the Queen of England that you so favour the Catholics. It is small wonder that she continually postpones your meeting.'

'Then set Arran and Bothwell free so that she cannot make this charge.'

'My dearest sister, you dare not. These two men are dangerous. You know, do you not, that I would protect you with my life?'

'Yes, Jamie.'

'Then Your Majesty must allow me to do so . . . in my own way.'

'Please, Jamie, show me what I ought to do.'

So James showed her. He insisted that they set out for the North.

The people came to cheer, but instead of poets, musicians and courtiers in her train, there rode men-at-arms.

On James' instructions she demanded that the Earl of Huntley should deliver up his houses, Findlater and Auchendown, as a penalty for his son's breach of the law.

Old Huntley, furious to have been disturbed in his domain, and knowing that James Stuart's desire was to wrest not only the title but the lands which went with it from the Earldom of Moray, gathered a strong force of Highlanders together and prepared to repulse the Queen's men. It was civil war in the Highlands, and the result was the capture of John Gordon — the cause of the trouble — and old Huntley himself; but as the latter was taken he was seized with an apoplectic fit, so great was his chagrin, and he died on the spot.

So ended the Queen's first journey to the North. She was depressed, although she had enjoyed riding through the magnificent country at the head of her troops; yet when she contemplated the huge body of the Cock o' the North, she was hard put to it to hide her tears from her brother James, who had now publicly assumed the grand title of Earl of Moray.

Riding south a pleasant surprise awaited Mary.

A young Frenchman joined the party, one whom she had known and liked both in France and on her first coming to Scotland. He had been forced, most regretfully, to return to France with the rest of those who had accompanied her, but now he was back again bringing letters and messages from her friends – and a devotion which had been enhanced by absence.

This was Pierre de Chastelard, the young poet who had been in the train of Henri de Montmorency, the Sieur d'Amville.

Pierre was young and handsome, related to the Chevalier de Bayard whose good looks he had inherited. He came fresh from romantic Dauphiné, and he cherished romantic dreams concerning the Queen of Scots.

He was a little arrogant; so he had been unable to resist talking of his joy at the prospect of seeing Mary again. He thought of her as his lady; and even his lady-love.

He could not have said when he had begun to feel so sure of Mary's response. Perhaps his attitude had begun to change when Catherine, the Queen-Mother of France, had selected him for this mission. Perhaps it was something which she had said to him, something such as: 'I know of your admiration for the Queen of Scots. I remember noting it. And I have heard of the sport you have in these gloomy castles across the sea. Ah, my daughter the Queen of Scots is a most comely woman and she will be glad to see an old friend, I doubt not. I remember how devoted she was to my dear son . . . And think! It is three years since she had a husband. Poor child! Well, Monsieur de Chastelard, you will comfort her.'

'I . . . Madame . . . ?'

'Yes, you. You are a handsome man, are you not?' The

laugh which accompanied the words held a hundred suggestions and was more expressive than words. It could be cruel and mocking but it could arouse such hopes. That coarse face had suddenly been near his own, expression suddenly lighting the eyes which were usually without any. 'Well, Monsieur de Chastelard, remember the honour of France.'

He had thought he understood. She was aware of everything that went on in the chateaux, it was said. In France they were beginning to understand her. She had a new name now – Madame le Serpent. She was telling him something. Was it: 'You love the Queen of Scots. Do not be too backward. Hesitancy never leads to victory.' She knew something. She was telling him that Mary was not inaccessible.

So he had set off full of hope, and now he found himself before the Queen, who was a little older but seemed more healthy and was many times more beautiful than he remembered her.

How warmly she received him!

'Monsieur de Chastelard, I knew you at once. This is a great pleasure indeed. What news . . . what news of my uncles and my dear aunt the Duchesse de Guise? What news of the King and . . . my mother-in-law? What news of Monsieur d'Amville?'

She seized hungrily on the letters which he had brought. She read them at once. Monsieur de Chastelard must stay beside her. He must tell her all . . . all that was happening to her dear friends and relations in her beloved France.

Her eyes filled with tears. She was homesick afresh.

'Yet,' she said, 'I am so happy that you are here.'

There were many to note her pleasure in the young man and the passionate glances he gave her.

As for Pierre, as soon as he was alone, he put his feelings into verse.

> '*O Déesse immortelle,*' he wrote,
> *Escoute donc ma voix*
> *Toi qui tiens en tutelle . . .*'

❦ ❦ ❦

It was pleasant to see Signor David again. His large eyes shone with delight. He did not say how desolate the place had been without her; poor *David le Chante*, as she sometimes called him, was far too modest for that. And with the gallant Chastelard in her train – and what enchanting poems he wrote to her and what a pleasure it was to answer them in verse! – and David showing such decorous devotion, she could almost believe that she was back in France.

She liked to discuss her troubles with David; in some inexplicable way he could so sympathetically suggest the solution she was seeking.

She gave him some of her French correspondence to deal with; she was not sure that she liked Raulet, her French secretary. David was delighted to carry out little tasks, and if she gave him a small present, a jewel or some velvet for new clothes, he would seem almost sorry, preferring, as he said, to do it for love of the Queen and not for payment.

So David had become one of those whom it was a pleasure to find waiting for her.

When she returned from that northern journey, David was sad and reticent, she noticed. She waited until they were alone together, for she had some small matter of correspondence with which she wished him to deal, when she said: 'Are you ill, David?'

'Thank you, Madam. My health is excellent.'

'Then you are in some trouble . . . some little thing has gone wrong for you?'

'Not for me, Madam.'

'For someone you love?'

He turned those brilliant eyes upon her. David's eyes, she thought, were his one beauty.

'Madam,' he said, 'I would speak if I dared.'

'If you dared! You cannot mean that you are afraid of me? Do you think me such a termagant then?'

'No, Madam, the sweetest and most bountiful lady in the world.'

'Then, David, will you give me a chance to be sweet and bountiful over this affair of yours?'

He had risen to his feet. His face was pale. Then he flung himself on to his knees, and taking the hem of her long robe, he raised it to his lips. 'Madam, have I your permission to speak and, if what I say offends you, will you forgive it and wipe it out as though it had never been said?'

'I give you my word, David. Come. Sit down. Sit here beside me. My poor David, it grieves me to see you thus depressed.'

Even so it was some seconds before he spoke. Then he said: 'Your Majesty is in danger. Oh . . . not in immediate danger. How can I – a humble *valet de chambre* – say this? But . . . I have been in the Courts of Europe, and I am constantly on the alert for Your Majesty's welfare. Oh, it is nothing to fear at this moment. It is not a wild plot to kidnap you. It is not an assassin's plan which I have discovered. But, Madam, it is equally dangerous. Your Grace is surrounded by foes. Those who seem to be your friends seek to make you powerless. They take to themselves great power, and with every step they weaken Your Majesty. They will remove from your side all those who would work for your good. They will force you to marry whom they wish. Madam, I beg of you take care.'

'Tell me what you have discovered.'

'Nothing that is not already known to many. It is the interpretation of these things which is significant. My lord Bothwell is in prison. He was loyal to your mother, and it may be that some fear he will be equally loyal to you. And now . . . that very clan is removed which would have set itself at the head of your supporters against the Protestant Knox, the ranting preacher who Your Majesty knows has never pretended to be your friend. I mean the Gordons. They are humbled. They are no longer a power. They are imprisoned or exiled . . . or dead.'

'But David, it was necessary to punish John Gordon.'

David smiled apologetically. 'But not to remove power from the clan. You might have need of their help; they would have rallied to your aid, should you have found it necessary to stand against a rebellion which Knox might raise. Now . . . they are powerless to do so.'

'But the Earl of Moray . . . my own brother . . .' She was staring at David; his brilliant eyes met hers boldly.

'Yes, Madam.'

So David was warning her against Jamie.

He was on his knees now; he was fervently kissing her hands. David was excitable by nature.

'Madam, you promised to forgive and forget. It was merely my desire to serve you . . .'

She put her hand on his thick hair while the tears sprang to her eyes. 'David,' she said, 'I have no doubt of your devotion.

There is nothing to forgive, and I shall never forget. I begin to see that Jamie is ambitious. He has made me his tool. I have suspected it. Oh, David . . . my own brother! What can I do?'

'Madam, have a care. Allow me to serve you. Allow me to keep my eyes ever on the alert. I will serve you with my life if need be. Say nothing. Give no indication that you suspect your brother's motives.'

She nodded. 'You are right, David. I thank you.'

'Madam,' he said, 'I am now the happiest man in Scotland.'

In the light of many candles the apartments at Holyrood were gay. The music was sweet and merry. Mary was dressed in black silk breeches for the part she played in the masque which had just been performed; she made a slender and beautiful boy.

'You are enchanting,' whispered Pierre de Chastelard.

'Monsieur, you repeat yourself.'

'The words escaped me . . . involuntarily . . . sweet Mary.'

He drew back, wondering how she would receive such familiarity. Her answer was a tap on the cheek. His heart leaped with anticipation.

'How liked you that book of my making, the one written in metre . . . the one I wrote for you?'

'It was fair enough,' said Mary.

'Madame, will you dance with me?'

'Come,' cried Mary, 'I long to dance.' She clapped her hands and declared they would dance the new dance which Chastelard had introduced from the French Court. It was considered very daring, for during it the partners kissed.

'It is not a dance which Master Knox would much like, I'll

'swear,' cried Mary, laughing as she tilted her head to receive the kiss of Chastelard.

He was wildly excited that night. The Queen-Mother of France had been right in what she had hinted. If he could but see Mary alone! But she was rarely alone. Even in her most informal moments there would be one or more of her women with her.

The new French dance was a stimulant to the emotions. Again and again they danced it; and there was merry laughter in the apartments. The Queen could be gay on such occasions; it was as though she wished to snap her fingers at the criticisms of herself and her Court.

Why not? mused Chastelard. Why not to-night? Her mood is such that I believe her to be ready.

While Mary was saying her farewells for the night, he slipped away. Mary and her four faithful attendants retired to the sleeping apartments, where the girls began to undress their mistress, chattering of the evening as they did so.

'Would we could have brought Master Knox to the apartment,' cried Flem. 'What fun to watch his fury when he saw Your Majesty dance in these silk breeches!'

'He would have said we were all utterly damned,' said Seton.

'We are already damned . . . according to him!' laughed the Queen. 'As well be damned for a pair of silk breeches as a jewel or two. Seton darling, get my furred robe from the cabinet; I am cold.'

Seton went to the cabinet and, when she opened it, gave a sharp cry. They all turned to stare in amazement at what she had disclosed. There, standing in the cabinet, was Pierre de Chastelard.

'What . . . what are you doing here?' stammered Mary.

'Madame, I . . .'

'Oh!' cried Flem. 'You wicked man!'

Chastelard threw himself on his knees before the Queen.

'Madame, I crave your forgiveness. I was distraught. A madness seized me. I became intoxicated by your beauty. I do not know what possessed me to do such a thing. I cannot imagine . . .'

'I can,' said the practical Beaton.

'Be quiet, Beaton,' said Mary. 'Let him speak for himself. What was your purpose, Monsieur de Chastelard?'

'Madame, I wished to read a poem to you. I had written it . . . and it was for your ears alone.'

All the girls began to laugh.

'A dangerous procedure, Monsieur,' said Flem, 'for the reading of a poem.'

'Where is the poem?' asked Mary. 'Give it to me.'

'Madame . . . in my excitement, I left it in my own apartment.'

Flem could not contain her laughter. Livy had started to shake with hers.

'You are insolent!' said the Queen; but her voice was broken with laughter.

This was the sort of adventure which occurred again and again at the Court of France. It was like being home again.

Beaton said: 'Shall we call my lord Moray and have this man put in chains, Your Majesty?'

Chastelard said: 'Put me in chains . . . it matters not. I am bound by stronger chains . . . the chains of a hopeless passion.'

'Drive him away,' commanded Mary. The four girls began to push him from the room. 'And Monsieur de Chastelard, I shall devise some punishment for you. You have been guilty of a grave indiscretion.'

'Madame, punish me as you will. Set me on the rack. Tear my limbs with red hot pincers . . . but do not deny me your presence.'

'If you were on the rack,' said Beaton grimly, 'you would have little thought of poetry. Get you gone. You embarrass the Queen. Why, if you were seen . . .'

'Madame, your forgiveness. Without your smile I would as lief be dead.'

He was pushed outside and the door slammed; Beaton leaned against it, and the others were all overcome with helpless laughter.

'Still,' said Seton, 'it was a grave offence. What if Your Majesty had been alone?'

'Do you think that I would not have given a good account of myself?'

'I doubt it not; but it would have made pleasing news for the ears of Master Knox.'

'How shall you punish him?' asked Livy.

'How can you punish people because in love they are bold? He has brought a little of France to our grim old Court. Let us set that beside his sins. To-morrow I will speak sharply to him. That will suffice.'

❀ ❀ ❀

A scandal touched the Court about this time. It was unfortunate that the story became known beyond the Court. John Knox learned of it with the utmost pleasure and retold it from his pulpit, roaring at the people of Edinburgh to note the result of Jezebel's rule.

One of the Queen's minor serving women had been seduced by the Queen's French apothecary.

'Both servants of the Queen!' cried Knox triumphantly. 'Does it not speak for itself? Oh, what wickedness goes on within the walls of Holyroodhouse! What revellings to the call of Satan! Fornication is the order of the day in Holyroodhouse, my friends. Women dress as men . . . men as women . . . the better to stimulate their wretched appetites. Satan stands by, calling them to damnation. The servants follow their masters and their mistresses along the road to hell.'

The serving woman had borne a child and, with the help of her paramour, had kept the matter secret. The child had been born in an outhouse and done to death. Its body had been discovered, and the maid, when accused, had broken down and confessed the whole story. She and her lover had paid the penalty of murder; they were publicly hanged.

John Knox was there to see justice done and to lose no opportunity of calling the people's attention to the life of the Court. He blamed the Queen for her maid's seduction; he blamed the Queen for the murder of the new-born child. The apothecary was a Frenchman – a member of that hated race which had captured John Knox and made a galley slave of him; the Queen was half French by birth and all French in her manners. Let the people see what harlotry, what wickedness had been brought into the country by their Queen. Let the people reflect how much happier they would be without her.

'Must I accept the ranting of this man!' demanded Mary; but not to Jamie as she would have done earlier. Now she turned to David. 'Must I, David?'

David's words were comforting. 'For the moment, Madam, yes. But have no fear of that. Between us we will devise some means of clipping the power of that man. We will make the people of Scotland free and happy, and Your Majesty Queen not only in name but in all else.'

'How?' asked Mary.

'We will watch events, Madam. It may be we shall do it through your marriage to a powerful prince – a Catholic like yourself. But patience, Madam, and for the time being – caution!'

You are right. David, I want you to have this ring.'

'But, Madam, it is too valuable.'

'How could it be, for all you have done for me? Take it. I promise you that one day, when I am able, you shall no longer be called my *valet de chambre*, no longer merely David *le Chante*. You shall be my chief adviser, in all things, David . . . in all things.'

He bowed; his great glowing eyes went from her face to the sapphire she was putting on his finger.

A few days later Mary left Holyrood for St Andrews. The Court, among whom was Pierre de Chastelard, stayed a night at Burntisland.

Chastelard had been in a fever of excitement since that night when he had been discovered in the cabinet. He cursed his bad luck. He was sure that if Mary had not required that particular furred robe, and he had succeeded in being alone with her, they would have been lovers by now. Of course she had feigned anger before her women; but it was not real anger; that had been obvious. They had all looked on the matter as a joke. Joke! He would show them that it was no joke.

Mary had scarcely reprimanded him at all, which surely

meant that she expected him to make the attempt again in some way. This time he would do so with more skill; and before the morning he would be her lover.

He had a greater opportunity of concealing himself on this occasion. Mary was closeted with her brother and Secretary of State Maitland, when he went silently to that chamber in which she would spend the night. He examined the bed and gleefully discovered that there was plenty of room for him to hide himself beneath it. It was a pity he was wearing his sword and dagger, for they were rather difficult to manage, but he had not wished to appear before her in anything but his finest array.

He waited in discomfort for a long time, but eventually he heard Mary and two of her women enter the apartment.

'I am tired,' said Mary. 'Come, Flem, hurry. Let me to bed. My feet are so cold. Did you bring my foot polkis?'

'Here they are.' Flem held up the linen foot-bags without which Mary could not sleep on cold nights for her feet would not get warm unless she wore them.

'Such a headache!' said Mary as Livy took off her headdress.

'Dearest,' said Livy, 'I hope you are not going to start your headaches again.'

'It's the cold weather. How I long for summer!'

It was Livy who noticed a faint movement of the bed valance. She stared at it in silence, but then looked closer. With a swoop she lifted it and disclosed a man's boot. The Queen and Flem hurried to her side. Groaning, Chastelard came from under the bed.

'This is too much!' cried Mary.

'The second time!' muttered Flem.

Chastelard, furious at his own folly in allowing himself to be discovered, furious with Livy for discovering him, overcome by pent-up emotions, did not attempt to apologise. Clumsily and without warning, he sprang at the Queen, seized her and, to her horror and that of the two women, began to kiss her passionately.

Mary cried out: 'How dare you!'

Livy and Flem fell upon Chastelard and tried to free their mistress, but his mad desire and determination seemed to lend him the strength of two men. He succeeded in forcing the Queen on to the bed where all four of them wrestled together.

'Help!' cried Mary, really alarmed. 'Quickly!'

Flem broke away and ran to the door calling: 'Help! Save the Queen!'

There was a great bustle in the apartment as guards came rushing in.

'Take this man!' commanded the Queen.

Chastelard was seized, as Moray, the Queen's brother, came into the apartment.

'What means this?' he demanded.

'He was under the bed!' gasped Flem. 'Hiding!'

'Take this man's sword and dagger,' said Moray to the guards. 'Put him under close arrest.'

Chastelard appealed to the Queen. 'Madame, you know my intentions . . .'

'They were clear,' said Mary.

'The love I bear you . . .'

'Take him away!' roared Moray.

Chastelard was dragged, struggling, from the apartment.

Moray turned sternly to his sister. 'Madam,' he said, 'he shall lose his life for this outrage.'

Mary had grown pale but Moray went on quickly: 'I doubt not that he is a tool of your enemies.' He waved his hand to all those who had come into the apartment. 'Your presence is no longer needed,' he added. 'Fortunately the Queen's life has been saved.'

Moray was not slow to note that among those who had come into the Queen's apartment was Thomas Randolph, and his delight in what he was planning to write to his mistress was betrayed by his expression. A nice titbit to send to his mistress in England – the heroine of many a similar story – and one which would naturally be told and retold against the Queen of Scots. There were several firm supporters of Knox who had witnessed this scene; they had good noses for smelling out the scandals. The fact that Chastelard had been found in the Queen's bedchamber would be all over Edinburgh by the morning. They would have it in the Highlands and on the Border within a few hours; and as soon as Master Thomas Randolph could arrange it, Madam Elizabeth would be chuckling over it with her paramour Robert Dudley.

As soon as Moray was alone with the three women he said: 'I must have the truth.'

'Livy found him under the bed,' declared Mary. 'He came out and sprang at me.'

'I fear Your Majesty has given him some encouragement to behave thus.'

'By my appreciation of his poems?' said Mary angrily.

'There has been talk of dances,' growled her brother.

'In France we always danced the latest dances, and none thought the worse of us for that.'

'But Your Majesty is now in Scotland.'

'Jamie . . . what do you propose to do with Chastelard? You spoke of his losing his life. I do not consent to that . . . merely because of a momentary madness, a prank, you might say.'

'He was wearing his sword and dagger. That seems to me significant.'

'What do you mean, Jamie?'

'You must surely know that as Queen of Scotland you have many enemies.'

'Chastelard is no enemy!'

'It would be better for your honour if it could be proved that he is. Get your mistress to bed,' he ordered the Maries. 'Madam,' he went on, turning to Mary, 'we must speak of this matter in the morning.'

When he had gone, Mary said: 'I am sorry we called James in.'

'Madam,' said Flem, 'we had to call for help.'

'Yet . . .' She looked round the room at the shadows cast by the flickering candlelight. 'Well . . . nothing can be done till morning. One of you stay with me. You, Flem . . . sleep in my bed this night.'

'Yes, dearest Majesty.'

'I do not know why I am afraid, my darlings, but I am. See! I am shivering.'

'He upset you, dear Madam,' said Livy. 'Come, let us get you warm, and Flem shall stay the night.'

So Flem and Mary lay in the big bed while Livy drew the curtains and tiptoed away.

Flem noticed that the Queen continued to shiver, and it was dawn before they fell asleep.

❀ ❀ ❀

Mary faced her brother and wished that David were with her at Burntisland. She needed counsel now, because David had opened her eyes and she was beginning to distrust James.

'Does Your Majesty realise,' said James sternly, 'that this day they will be talking in Edinburgh of how your lover was discovered hiding beneath your bed?'

'My lover! A young poet of the Court!'

'All know Your Majesty's fondness for poets.'

'But surely we can say simply that he was *not* my lover. He is a poet and a good dancer.'

'With whom Your Majesty danced in black silk breeches!'

'I'll not be spied on!' said Mary angrily.

'Shall you not, sister? Alas! It is not for you to say whether you will be or not. You *are* spied on, and the whole of Knox's congregation knows that, in black silk breeches, you danced with this man.'

'It was for the purpose of the masque.'

'The Lords of the Congregation have their own ideas as to the purpose.'

'Am I responsible for their evil minds?'

'No, but you must consider them.'

'Chastelard was discovered; he was sent out; there the matter ends. It is of no concern of anyone but myself.'

'There again I must humbly contradict you. It is the concern of Scotland, England, France, Spain, Rome . . . You are a Queen and your actions are watched. Your chances of making an advantageous marriage will not be enhanced by a scandal such as this might well become.'

'Oh, one day I may take it into my head and marry where I please, and it may not be one of these hesitant gentlemen who, with their governments, are calculating whether I shall bring them a big enough dowry.'

'If Your Majesty will pardon my brotherly comment, I must say that you are not speaking with your usual good sense. This man Chastelard has upset you, and understandably so. He must be made an example. We must show the people what happens to those who dare insult the Queen. There is only one thing to be done. He must go to the block.'

'The block! For hiding in a room!'

'In the Queen's bedchamber . . . under the Queen's bed . . . his sword and dagger handy.'

'I would never agree to that. Poor Chastelard! Why . . . I was fond of him.'

'Too fond for his safety, Madam.'

'I shall never consent.' She thought: I shall talk to David. Together we shall find a way to save poor Chastelard.

Moray looked at her quickly. She had changed. He could almost believe there was some influence working against him. He must get her married to some powerful prince; then he would be free to take up the Regency. If she did not marry abroad she would be here for ever; he would be pushed into the background; she must never be allowed to take another adviser. The matter of immediate moment was that there should be no scandal to disturb wedding plans. Nothing must stand in the way of a match with one of the European princes.

'There is something I must tell Your Majesty,' he said. 'You have been deceived in this man. When he played the lover he acted a part. He is a servant of the Montmorencys, and the Montmorencys with the Bourbons are, as you know, the leading Huguenot faction in France. This, my dearest sister, was a plot on your life which your faithful Maries have foiled. There is only one way to deal with such an offence. I beg you to listen to reason.'

'It can't be true!' gasped Mary.

'It is hard for your pride to accept this. It was easy for him to play the role of lover, because so many love you. But I know that he came here to murder you. This I shall tell his judges . . . and I have no doubt of the verdict.'

Mary covered her face with her hands. She remembered the uncontrollable passion of Chastelard when he came from under the bed.

'But . . . it's horrible,' she said. 'Horrible!'

'Mary, have one of your women sleep with you in your bed until we return to Holyrood. The others will be close by, but keep one . . . in your bed. My dear sister, only thus can I feel happy concerning your safety.'

'Flem slept with me last night.'

'Then let her sleep with you until we are in Holyrood once more. Will you do this?'

'Yes, James.'

'I am relieved. Now think no more of this unfortunate business.'

James kissed her hand, and she sat thinking of Chastelard who she had thought had wished only to make love to her, and had come – or may have come – to murder her.

❀ ❀ ❀

A week later in the market place of St Andrews, Pierre de Chastelard laid his head on the block. He looked very handsome, and many who watched his last moments shed tears. There were few in that crowd of spectators who really believed that he had conspired against the Queen.

'It is clear,' they said to each other, 'why he was in her bedchamber. She had not meant her women to discover him. He was to wait there until they had gone.'

Before he died, Pierre de Chastelard quoted Ronsard's

famous Hymn to Death. He stood on the scaffold, his curling hair ruffled by the February wind; the people listened to his beautiful voice and wept afresh, although few understood what he had said.

> *'Je te salue, heureuse et profitable Mort*
> *Des extrêmes douleurs medicin et confort . . .'*

Then smiling he laid his head upon the block and, as the axe descended, he was heard to say: *'O cruelle dame . . .'*

But that was not the end of the scandal concerning Pierre de Chastelard. John Knox had decided that it should not be the end. The drama made too useful a scourge with which to attack the Queen.

' *"O cruelle dame!"* ' screamed Knox from his pulpit. 'You know what that means, my friends. Cruel mistress – that is what is meant by those words. What that complaint importeth, lovers may divine. Ah, my good friends, now is seen the harvest of sin. A woman of the Court murdered her ill-gotten child, and by God's mercy she and her paramour paid the penalty; now in divine justice another of Satan's imps goes to eternal torment.'

And in her candle-lit apartment, although she tried to dance and sing as gaily as before, Mary was haunted by the memory of Chastelard.

🏵 Chapter IX 🏵

*T*wo years after the death of Chastelard, Mary was still unmarried. During that time there had been no lack of suitors; but it seemed that a royal marriage was indeed difficult to arrange. There were so many watching Mary. So the suitors were proposed and dismissed, over those two years.

Mary had suffered one great loss in the death of her uncle François de Guise who had been assassinated at Orléans by a young fanatic, Poltrot de Meroy. The Cardinal wrote often and as affectionately as ever, but he was continually pointing out the advantages of a match with Charles, the Archduke of Austria. This she could not understand. She was hoping for the grandest of marriages with Don Carlos of Spain; and yet she had come to understand – with the help of David Rizzio – that the Cardinal was not working for that match but against it, and it seemed incredible that her uncle should be opposed to that which could bring her so much honour.

'There must be some reason for it, David,' she said.

David knew the reason, and it shocked her deeply.

'Madam, the Cardinal is your uncle and you feel great

affection towards him, but he does not work for your good and your happiness. He works for the power of the Guises in France. A marriage with Don Carlos, while bringing great honour to yourself and to Scotland, would serve to strengthen Spain. France would be less powerful than of yore and, with France, the Guises. No, your uncle as we now know has exerted his strength against the Spanish match for that reason. Now, Madam, a Catholic Scotland with yourself and the Archduke as rulers would be deemed a firm ally of France, but would in fact be a dependant of that country; there would be a strong France to stand against a weakened Spain. That is the Guisian policy. True, it would do you no good; but your uncle's first concern is not with yourself, Madam, but with the Guises in France.'

'But my uncle has done everything for my good . . . always.'

'When your good was his also, Madam.'

This was a tragic discovery, and yet she knew it to be true. She remembered now with humiliation those tender scenes between herself and the Cardinal. Always he had been subduing her will to his, not because he wished to help her, but because he wished to use her in order to increase the power of himself and his family.

David had shown her this as he had shown her the falseness of her brother James; and she knew that David was right.

She stood alone now with no one but David to help her; strangely enough the thought strengthened her. She would cease to listen to the advice of the Cardinal, as she had already to that of James. With David to help her she would arrange her own affairs.

Maitland of Lethington had been back and forth during the past years with messages to and from the Queen of England. Maitland was that politician most likely to find favour with the

English Queen. He was possessed of suave manners, good looks and a clever tongue; and all those qualities appealed to Elizabeth. Now James Melville was also at the English Court and was sending her regular despatches giving accounts of the state of affairs there.

There was one young man who was in the minds of several people as a possible suitor for the Queen of Scots. This was Henry Darnley, a tall, slim youth of nineteen. He was handsome and graceful, with large, blue, rather prominent eyes, a fair complexion and beardless face which made him seem younger than he actually was. He had the additional advantage of royal blood, being a direct descendant of the Tudors. Elizabeth liked him since he was handsome, a good musician and dancer, but she never – or rarely – allowed her personal dislikes to override her political judgement.

She made an open declaration that she would be much against the marriage of Mary and Darnley, but alone with Cecil who shared some of her secrets, she was less emphatic. Although she declared her desire to see Mary's country living in peace and prosperity, that was far from her wish. An internally peaceful Scotland was a threat to England, and Elizabeth would never forget that Mary had dared to display the arms of England, suggesting thereby that Elizabeth was a bastard and had no right to the throne. In their secret sessions, Elizabeth and Cecil were not at all sure that a marriage between Mary and Darnley would be a bad thing for England after all, for they knew Henry Darnley to be a weak, vain and dissolute young man who would not help – but rather hinder – Mary in the governing of her country. But Elizabeth's policy was to make a display of benevolent friendliness towards her cousin over the border.

Darnley remained at the English Court and, though his

ambitious mother, who resided in England where Elizabeth could seize her if she wished, and his equally ambitious father, who had recently been allowed to return to Scotland where he had regained his estates, had high hopes of their son's future, Elizabeth outwardly frowned on these hopes.

There was another young man whom Elizabeth was prepared to offer to Mary. She would not at first disclose his name. Indeed, she declared, she could not bring herself to do so. She offered this man because she loved the Scottish Queen so devotedly and wished to do her so much good, for the man she had in mind was the most perfect man she, Elizabeth, had ever set eyes on, and she could not bear to contemplate his leaving her Court.

But at last she was constrained to whisper the name of this man to Melville, and Thomas Randolph was given instructions to tell it to the Queen of Scots.

When Randolph sought an audience, David Rizzio was with Mary. She had given him more and more work to do, and he was constantly at her side. The Englishman looked askance at the small stunted figure of the Piedmontese, but Mary said: 'You may speak, Master Randolph, before my secretary.'

Randolph then showed her a list of possible suitors suggested by the Queen of England and, on reading the last name on the list, Mary raised her eyebrows and looked full into the Englishman's face.

'Lord Robert Dudley!' she exclaimed.

'The same, Madam.'

'But this man is . . .'

Randolph's look silenced her. He greatly feared she was about to make some indiscreet observation concerning his mistress.

'But this is a man with whom the Queen of England would not wish to part,' said Mary firmly.

'My Queen bids me tell you that she is so desirous for Your Majesty's happiness that she has set herself the task of finding for you the most perfect man she knows. This is Lord Robert.'

Mary was aware of David's eyes upon her; he was pleading: Do not show anger. Do not show that you regard this as an insult. The Queen of England is offering you one who, many would say, is her discarded lover but, Madam, I beg of you, show no anger.

How well she was beginning to co-operate with David. How she delighted in following his lead! He was right, of course. David was always right.

'There are times, Master Randolph,' she said, 'when I think of my dead husband. Although several years have elapsed since he died, the memory of him is still too strong for me to consider re-marriage.'

'But, Madam, a handsome living husband would help you to forget one who is dead.'

'I do not know. There has been too much talk of marriage. Sometimes I think I will follow your Queen's example and remain unmarried.'

'That would entail a grievous loss to Scotland, if you will forgive my saying so, Madam. My Queen assures you that if you marry Lord Robert she will then fix the succession. On her death you or your heirs would be rulers of England if my Queen should die without heirs of her body.'

'It may be that I shall not outlive your Queen, Master Randolph. It is true that I am some years younger, but she is possessed of the better health.'

'My Queen enjoys good health and I thank God for it; but it

is to Your Majesty's interest to consider this important matter of the succession.'

'Indeed, yes. It is a matter near my heart. I must consider my marriage since it involves so much. But there are other suitors mentioned here by your Queen. I should be loth to rob her of one in whom, I have heard, she takes great pleasure. Moreover, I am a Queen, the daughter of Kings, and I should have to consider whether I demean myself by marriage with a commoner; and, for all the excellencies which your Queen knows Lord Robert to possess, he is, alas, of no royal blood. Your Queen, I see, mentions also Ambrose Dudley, the Earl of Warwick, Lord Robert's elder brother.'

'Yes, Madam. She says what an excellent thing it would be if you might have Warwick, and she Lord Robert; although she admits Warwick lacks the beauty and perfection of his brother. She says there could only be one Lord Robert, and if she were not determined to remain a virgin she would marry him herself; but as she is fixed in her determination, she offers him to you.'

'And my lord Robert – what says he?'

'My lord Robert, realising the honour this match would bring him, is eager for it.'

'You must give me time to ponder it, Master Randolph. I should have to give the matter much thought.'

Randolph acknowledged his dismissal and, begging her to let him have her answer as soon as she found it conveniently possible, retired.

When he had gone, Mary let loose her anger.

'How dare she! The insolent woman! Her horse-master! Her paramour! Her confederate in murder! They murdered his wife . . . why did she not then take him as her husband? But she did so . . . of course . . . without the ceremony! And now . . . tired of him . . . she dares to pass him on. It's an insult. David, I should have told Randolph. I have demeaned myself by even pretending to consider this match.'

'Madam, I beg of you to be calm. This is but a trick of the English Queen's. She will not part with him. It is a scheme to cover up some other plot. She has someone else for you, I vow. She wants to make you furious over Dudley, so that you will the more readily turn to the one she wishes you to have.'

'How can you know this?'

'Because, Madam, that woman never follows a straight course. She is full of lies and deceits; she makes a pretence of running in one direction, when all the time she intends to go in another. Be calm, I beg of you. Pretend to consider this match as she herself has pretended to consider so many. We will wait and shall soon see whom the Queen of England really wishes you to marry.'

'I believe she wishes to mock me. He was her lover, is now no longer, and she wishes to rid herself of him, so she offers him to me . . . to *me*?'

'Nay, Your Majesty. She dotes on him as she ever did. Shortly you will be hearing from England that she has greatly honoured him. He is now Earl of Leicester and, during the ceremony of bestowing the earldom upon him, she could not resist putting her fingers between his ruff and his neck and tickling him there before them all. Does that indicate that she has tired of him?'

'Surely she would not be so indiscreet.'

'She is the most indiscreet woman in the world, and the most wily. That is why she succeeds. She hesitates at times; she is reckless at others; therefore she is unaccountable. She covers great schemes with frivolous chatter. Beware of her, Madam. Do not again offend her vanity; you have already done that by assuming the arms of England. That must be lived down. Therefore, thank her for her consideration, pretend to consider Dudley, play her game of coquetry and indecision. It will work as well for Your Majesty as for her.'

'David, you are my wise man. I know it. How did you know that Lord Robert is now Earl of Leicester? How did you know that she tickled his neck?'

David smiled. 'Madam, I took the precaution of sending a servant of mine to the English Court. He went in the role of servant to Melville, and none knew that he worked for . . . us.'

'I cannot imagine what I should do without you.'

'I pray to the saints, Madam, that you will never have to, for if I were dismissed your service there would be no reason for me to live.'

'One does not dismiss those one trusts,' said Mary emotionally. 'One does not dismiss those one loves.'

A few days later she dismissed her French secretary, Raulet, from her service. David had discovered that he was writing to her uncle, the Cardinal, of matters outside French concerns. The man was a Guisian spy, working against the match with Spain on instructions from the Cardinal of Lorraine.

Mary decided that now she would trust only one man – David.

So Rizzio became closer to the Queen; and there were some at the Court who declared that he was fast becoming the Queen's most influential adviser.

It was one of those rare quiet moments when the Queen was sitting alone with Flem while they stitched at their embroidery.

Flem took the opportunity to speak of a matter which had occupied her mind for some time. It concerned the Earl of Bothwell.

Flem had been slightly fascinated by the man. It was something in his courage and manliness which had appealed to her. She knew that he was a rogue, a man of whom to beware, yet she could not help admiring him.

Flem liked to believe that her mistress tempered justice with mercy. Bothwell, she insisted diffidently, had had something less.

Mary raised her eyes from her needle and said: 'How so?'

'Well, first, poor man, he spent four months in Edinburgh Castle, put there on the charge of a man who, we all know, was suspected then of being mad and is now proved to be.'

'Do you not think that there was a real plot to kidnap me?'

'It existed only in mad Arran's brain. And Bothwell, being accused by him, has been made to suffer as though guilty.'

'Has he suffered so? He has escaped from his prison.'

'And why should he not, dear Madam, being wrongfully imprisoned?' Flem laughed. 'Imagine his breaking the bars with his bare hands and swinging down the Castle rock on a rope!'

'It was a bold thing to do, I grant you. I wonder if he has changed. It is a long time since we saw him. Perhaps we shall never see him again.'

'He would give much to return to Court, Madam.'

'We would give much to keep him away.'

'Yet he was not guilty.'

'Flem! Why do you plead for him? Are you in love with the

man and unfaithful to Maitland? You speak so favourably of the Border rogue.'

'I do not like it to be said that injustice has been done in your name.'

'You concern yourself too much with those who are unworthy, Flem. Think of his good fortune. How did he manage to make his way to France, do you think? With the help of women! Janet Beaton is one, that Danish woman another; and there are countless others to whom he is a passionate lover for a night, before he passes on. He escaped in a boat, and was shipwrecked on the English coast before he reached France. And how, I wonder, did he fare at the hands of the Queen of England? We know he was her prisoner in the Tower of London. Did he seduce his jailor's daughter? Flem! You put your reputation in jeopardy by pleading leniency for such a man!'

'Well, Madam, he is now far away in France, and he asks a favour of you.'

'Ah! I thought there was a plea in this. How does it come to you?'

'Through his great-uncle, the Bishop of Moray.'

'That old libertine of Spynie?'

'He is a libertine, it is true, Madam; but he is at least fond of his great-nephew. I think we should remember that Bothwell spent a great part of his life in the Bishop's palace, and it was there mayhap he learned to indulge his passions freely. Madam, we have had the advantage of a happy childhood. Should we judge those who have been less fortunate?'

'My dear Flem, if he was allowed to indulge his passions freely, I have no doubt that is what Bothwell would call a happy childhood.'

'Yes, but it has made him the man he is.'

'So the Bishop has been sounding you, has he?'

'He has spoken to me. He tells me that Bothwell is in dire poverty. He has mortgaged his lands to raise money; he reminds me that he has ever been faithful to Your Majesty.'

'Faithful to me . . . when he planned to kidnap me and force me to marry Arran?'

'A madman's fancy, Madam.'

'How can we be sure of that, dear Flem?'

'At least we know that Arran is mad now. He is put away from the world on account of his madness.'

'And because of this you think Bothwell's sins should be forgiven and he should be invited to return to Court?'

'No, Madam, I do not think that, but . . . the Scottish Captain of the Guard in France has recently died. The post is vacant.'

'And you suggest Bothwell would comfortably fill it?'

'At least it would help him to live, Madam. His finances are in a poor state. He is in exile from his own country.'

'Flem dear, ask someone to bring David here.'

Flem rose. She thought: Nothing is done now without the sanction of this David. The Piedmontese is becoming more powerful than Moray, or my dear lord Maitland.

Rizzio came at once to the apartment. How grand he looked these days! His clothes were as magnificent as anyone's at Court. How polished were his manners, and how subtly he flattered the Queen!

'Davie,' said Mary, and all her affection for the young man was in the Queen's voice as she said his name, 'I have received a request.' She smiled at Flem. 'It is that Bothwell should be given command of the Scottish Guard in France.' In your opinion would that be a worthy appointment?'

Rizzio considered this gravely. Bothwell was regarded as a dangerous man by Moray, and Moray was David's enemy. Moray did not know as yet how deep David Rizzio was in the Queen's counsels, but he was beginning to learn. The very fact that Bothwell was an enemy of Moray seemed to Rizzio a good enough reason for his receiving this sign of the Queen's favour.

'Madam,' he said, 'this is a brave man, whatever else may be said of him. His bravery makes him stand ahead of his fellows, even in this warlike country where courage would seem to come to men as naturally as breathing. He will do you no discredit as Captain of the Scottish Guard.'

So James Hepburn, Lord Bothwell, found his fortunes taking a turn for the better. He was no longer obliged to borrow money, and, although still an exile from his country, he enjoyed some standing in France as Captain of the Scottish Guard.

Moray was displeased by the appointment. He discussed it with Maitland. They both agreed that it had probably been made at the instigation of David Rizzio, and they were becoming more and more disturbed by the presumption of the Italian and the favour shown to him by the Queen.

But at the moment their main concern was with Bothwell.

'You can depend upon it,' said Moray, 'that man has friends in Scotland still. 'Tis witchcraft, I'll swear. He has but to look at a woman, and she's a willing victim. He seduces her and rides away, and if he should return she is ready to be his slave. How could he have got out of the country in the first place, if there had not been a chain of women ready to feed him, offer him a bed for the night – and a bedfellow too – as well as food, money and horses, to speed him on his way!'

'He has friends in the Queen's circle,' admitted Maitland. 'That much is evident.'

'What manner of men are his servants?' asked Moray.

'A parcel of rogues,' replied Maitland.

They smiled at each other. There was no need to say more.

The Captain of the Scottish Guard was not in his house that night. He was, his servants believed, sleeping in the lodging of his latest light-o'-love.

They sat round the table whispering together, listening all the time for his footsteps, though they did not think it likely that he would be home before dawn.

A pity! they all agreed. They had planned the deed for this night.

But was it a pity? In the guttering candlelight, relief showed plainly on every face.

They pictured him, their master. Taller than most men, loud of voice, stronger than two men, his lightest cuff would send any one of them sprawling across the room, and would leave a bruise that would last for days. They feared him and admired him, for he was every inch a man; he was more than a man, they believed. There was magic in him – or some witch-craft. And because he towered above them in all manner of ways, they were conscious of envy; and because of envy they had agreed to carry out instructions which had been given them. Greed too played a part in their willingness, for they would be well paid for their work.

French Paris regarded the Scotsmen about the table. There

was Gabriel Semple, Walter Murray and Dandie Pringle. Paris had no great liking for the task, but he had been drawn into it by the others.

Dandie was in charge of operations. He had arranged with his lordship's barber – who was also in the plot because he understood something of poisons – that the powder should be mixed with his lordship's wine. There was the wine, already poured in the goblet, and mixed with it was the poison; but his lordship, as though Fate had intervened, had not come home that evening.

That was what made superstitious Paris tremble.

'Mayhap he knows!' he muttered, his teeth chattering.

'How could he know, man?' demanded Dandie. 'Unless you've told him.'

'I have told him nothing, but he is no ordinary man.'

'We shall see,' said Dandie Pringle with a sneer, 'where he is so much mightier than ordinary men as that the barber's poison will not affect him. Now, Gabriel, when you take up his lordship's goblet to offer it, you must behave as you always do. You must show no sign that the drink you offer is any different from that which he drinks every day of his life.'

'No . . . no . . .' stuttered Gabriel.

'Would this night's work were done with!' said Murray.

''Twill soon be over,' promised Dandie, 'and then we shall all go back to bonny Scotland where we belong; and there we'll live our lives in luxury for this night's work.'

'I tell you,' said Paris, 'our master is no ordinary man.'

'Is he not then?' sneered Dandie.

'He is not,' persisted Paris. 'You have seen what a way he has with the women. There's none can resist him.'

'There is one I know of,' said Dandie. 'The Queen herself!

Did he not ask her if he might go home, and was he not refused?'

'The Queen, so says the master, is but half a woman,' declared Paris. 'She and the Queen of England between them would not make one woman, so he says.'

'He says that,' put in Murray, 'because they are two who did not immediately invite him to their bedchambers.'

'And he, feeling himself to tower above all men, is therefore piqued,' laughed Dandie.

'He says,' went on Paris, 'that, when she was in France, the Queen was the mistress of her uncle the Cardinal.'

'Nor would it surprise me,' said Dandie, 'for Cardinals are but human behind locked doors. Hark! He returns.'

It was true. The outer door had been flung open and a well-known voice shouted: 'Is no one at home? Where are you? Paris! Semple! I am returned . . . and hungry.'

There was a second's silence, and all eyes were fixed on the goblet in which was the poisoned wine.

'Take it to him, Gabriel,' said Dandie.

Paris had hurried to his master.

'Not abed then!' said Bothwell. 'How comes it that you are abroad at this hour? Have you quarrelled with your kitchen slut?'

'Nay, master,' stammered Paris. 'But I thought you might return, and so waited.'

Paris was trembling under his master's gaze. Bothwell was looking at him as though he knew something was afoot.

'Then bring me food. Bring me wine. I've a thirst that needs quenching.'

'Yes, master . . . yes, master . . .'

Paris hurried into the room where the others waited.

Dandie thrust the goblet into his hands, but Paris was trembling so violently that some of the wine was spilled.

'For the love of God, you'll betray us all!' hissed Dandie. 'Here, Gabriel. You take it.'

Gabriel cried: 'No . . . n . . . no. I dare not. I tell you he will know. He knows such things. He has special powers. That is why he has returned this night.'

The door was flung open and Bothwell himself stood on the threshold looking at his servants.

'What is this?' he demanded. 'A late night session! Some conspiracy, eh? Or just a friendly feast? And not one woman to enliven the company. Is that wine you have there, Semple? Give it here, man. Did I not tell you I had a thirst?'

Gabriel trembled so much that the wine spilled on his hand, as it had on those of Paris. All the servants watched Gabriel.

'What ails you, Gabriel?' demanded the Earl. 'You're trembling like a virgin nun when the soldiers are about her. What is it, man? I say . . . what is it?' His great hand gripped Gabriel by the wrist and the wine spilled on the man's doublet.

''Tis . . . 'tis nothing, my lord.'

''Tis nothing . . . and you shake like a leaf! You're plotting something, man. Out with it. What is it? Out with it, I say.'

''Twas nothing, my lord. 'Twas just that I spilled the wine . . .'

'Give me the goblet.' He took it, and as he did so he looked from it to the faces of his servants. Then slowly, he put his lips to the goblet, still watching them. Paris gave an audible gasp.

Bothwell sniffed the wine. 'It has an odd smell,' he said. 'I like it not. How dare you serve me such filthy stuff! How dare you, you varlets!' He threw the remaining liquid into the face

314

of Gabriel, and the goblet at Dandie Pringle's head. Dandie cried out with the pain as the goblet struck his head, and the Earl laughed.

'Now, you rogues,' he cried, 'bring me good food and good drink. And do not dare serve such stuff to me again. If you do, you'll wish you had never been born, every man of you. I'll see that you're boiled in cauldrons over slow fires. I'll have you cut into collops. I'll make you wish you had never been born to serve another instead of me. Remember it. And Semple . . . go and wake that kitchen girl and bid her bring me food. You know the one – plump, ripe Jeanne – and keep your lecherous hands off her; you understand? Go and wake her and bring her to me.'

Gabriel was glad to escape and, during his absence, Bothwell remained eyeing the others who stood wretchedly before him.

He was no ordinary man, and they knew it. He had uncovered their treachery. That in itself was bad enough; but they understood they had betrayed themselves by their clumsy behaviour. It was not that they lacked the courage to carry out this murderous plan, nor that their master had discovered their treachery, which was so alarming; it was his complete indifference to their power to harm him. They were in no doubt that he had witchcraft to aid him, and they knew that they would never dare make an attempt on his life again.

Gabriel returned with the girl from the kitchens. She was young and comely, and Bothwell's eyes lighted up as they rested on her.

'I am returned hungry, girl,' he said. 'Bring me food and drink . . . at once. Let no hands touch it but yours. You understand, my girl?'

'Yes, my lord.'

'Well, hurry and bring plenty, for my hunger is great. Bring it yourself. And hurry . . . I am waiting for you.'

Then he turned and left them — four guilty men and an excited and expectant girl.

It was February, and that winter was bleak. Even in the far south the weather had been rigorous. The Thames had been so frozen that people could walk across it in safety. The bitter wind buffeted the staunch walls of Wemyss Castle on the Firth of Forth whither the Queen had come to stay with her brother, the Earl of Moray.

The Queen was growing more and more uneasy in her brother's company. She knew that he was against her marriage, either with Don Carlos or one of the French Princes, because neither marriage would serve his plans. He was all for her marrying an Englishman; he was working for Elizabeth and the Protestant Faith.

He had told her that a marriage with Robert Dudley, Earl of Leicester, would be desirable. If Mary married Leicester, he pointed but, the Queen of England would declare Mary and her heirs successors to the English crown.

Did he not see that the idea was ridiculous? Elizabeth's cast-off lover! It was meant to be an insult. Whom else did Elizabeth favour? Mad Arran? Robert Dudley's brother, the Earl of Warwick? Mary smiled to remember the English Queen's comments on Warwick. He was not, of course, as handsome as his incomparable brother, declared Elizabeth, but he was by no means ugly. Nor was he ungraceful. It was only when compared with Robert that he might seem so. If one did not set him side by side with Robert, one would find him a husband worthy of a great princess. Clearly Elizabeth meant to be insulting.

There was one other who was a possible husband. That was Henry Stuart, Lord Darnley; but Elizabeth, being against the match, would not let him come to Scotland. Yet Lord Lennox, Darnley's father, who was in Scotland, continually hoped for a meeting between his handsome son and the Queen; so did Darnley's mother, Lady Lennox, who was in England and at the mercy of Elizabeth.

Mary herself was beginning to wish for the meeting, and she was excited when Lord Lennox sent a message to her.

'My son, Lord Darnley,' ran the message, 'has arrived in Scotland. He had the greatest difficulty in leaving England. The Queen however at last gave her consent, though grudgingly, and my son left at once, fearing to be detained once more before he could make his escape. It seems that no sooner had the Queen given her consent than she regretted it and sought means of detaining him, but my son, greatly desiring to see Your Majesty, had already slipped across the Border. He greatly desires to pay his loyal homage to his gracious Queen, and we shall follow this messenger with all speed to wait upon Your Majesty.'

Mary smiled. So at last she would see this young man of whom there had been so much talk. She vaguely remembered seeing him at the Court of France, but he had been a boy of fifteen then. Now he was nineteen – a man.

She called to her women.

'Come! What shall I wear? What is most becoming? It is a long time since my Lord Darnley and I met. I would not wish him to think that time had wrought havoc with my looks.'

'Madam,' all four Maries assured her, 'time has but enhanced your beauty.'

And, looking into the Venetian mirror brought from Fontainebleau, she believed they were right.

❁ ❁ ❁

Meanwhile Henry Stuart, Lord Darnley, was riding with his father at the head of his retinue on the way to Wemyss Castle.

He was very tall and slim. His face was smooth, for he wore no beard, and because his complexion was so fair this made him seem younger than he really was. His prominent eyes were deep blue in colour, his hair golden, but his chin was weak and his mouth loose. He was so young that the excesses in which he delighted to indulge had scarcely made any mark on his face.

His father was talking to him with great seriousness as they rode along.

'My son, you must act with care. This is the most important moment of your life. It is imperative that you find favour with the Queen. You must curb your drinking habits; and, whilst you are at Court, do not indulge in too much lechery — covertly or otherwise. Make sure that you win the friendship of David Rizzio.'

'That low-born scribe!' said Darnley distastefully.

'Low-born scribe he may be. But what he wills, the Queen *does*.'

'So he is her lover then?' suggested the young man nonchalantly.

'I did not say so. He is her adviser, and she sets store by his counsels. He is an arrogant upstart who must be treated with care.'

'Father,' said Darnley, 'do you think the Queen will take me for her husband?'

'It rests with you, my son. Your looks are fine enough.'

Darnley smirked. He was very vain of his looks.

'But,' went on his father, 'if she should discover your drinking habits and how violent you become when you indulge them; if she learns of your adventures with village girls and tavern sluts . . .'

'She shall not. Father, I will be good. I will be angelic. And then Her Majesty will give me the crown – a present for a good boy.'

❧ ❧ ❧

She received him in her audience chamber. He knelt before her, a tall, slender youth, and she thought: How charming he is! How young!

'Madam,' he said, 'at last I kneel before you. It has been my dearest wish since parting from you in France.'

'My dear Lord Darnley,' she answered, 'you cannot be happier to be here than I am to see you.'

'Madam, your beauty dazzles me. I fear I shall stammer or be speechless.'

'Why, you have made an excellent beginning. Come, sit beside me. I would hear news of the English Court.'

He sat beside her and many watched them. The Earl of Lennox did so with high hopes. Moray did so with annoyance; the last thing he wished for was Mary's marriage with Darnley. The fellow was arrogant and a Catholic. If such a marriage took place the Catholic lords would be rising and driving the Protestants – and with them John Knox and Moray – out of Scotland.

Mary meanwhile was recalling their meeting at the Court of France. 'You played the lute for me.'

'I blush for shame. I trust Your Majesty will give me a chance of showing that I have improved since then.'

'Certainly you must play for me again. You danced well, I remember. You must lead me in the galliard.'

'Madam, nothing could give me greater pleasure.' He was looking at her ardently. 'Forgive me, Madam,' he murmured. 'I had not known that anyone could be so beautiful.'

'We will ask the musicians to play for us, and we will dance. But first there is the banquet.'

She allowed him, as guest of honour, to lead her to the banqueting hall; he sat beside her and she drank from the same goblet to remind him that he was her blood-relation, and to assure him that he was heartily welcome at her table.

She noticed how his eyes kindled as he drank.

'Madam,' he said, 'I fear I disgrace myself. I am intoxicated.'

'On so little wine?'

'On so much beauty, Madam.'

'And you recently from the Court of England! They say Elizabeth's beauty is like the sun.'

'Madam, the Queen of England has no beauty. She is shrewish – an old woman, and the vainest in the world.'

'You are young, my lord. It may be that I, who am twenty-two, seem an old woman to you.'

'I know not what Your Majesty's age may be, but you are the most beautiful and perfect being in the world. That is all I know.'

She had heard similar flattery before, but this seemed different. It was his youth perhaps which appealed so strongly.

The Cardinal of Lorraine, had he been present, would have

realised that the sensual side of Mary was tired of waiting for the gratification so long denied her. Mary was eager to fall in love, and if the ideal lover whom she was beginning to desire so ardently did not come to her, she was ready to invest the nearest and most likely man with the necessary perfection. Mary's sensuality was clamouring for expression, and here was a handsome youth paying extravagant compliments, a youth of the blood royal, a Catholic like herself, and therefore suitable to be her husband.

Mary did not ponder on the qualities of this young man. Outwardly he filled her ideal; she was tremulously eager for passion to overtake her.

They danced. Darnley – by no means inexperienced – realised that he was making a good impression on the Queen. He could, he believed, become King of Scotland if he wished. His ambitions grew as he pictured the future. His father was right. He would step with the utmost care during the coming weeks. He would be modest rather than bold, for he must not forget that she was a Queen. There was more to be gained than a brief pleasure before riding on to the next conquest. If he could continue in the success he had had this night, in a few weeks she would be madly in love with him. And then . . .

These were delightful pictures. Darnley, King of Scotland, the crown matrimonial glittering on his head, and an eager, passionate woman – and a very beautiful one – desperately in love with him.

He was a graceful dancer and the Queen chose again and again to dance with him. The *pavane* and the galliard were danced; and Mary had torches brought that they might dance – as she had in the *salle de bal* at Fontainebleau – the *branle des torches* in which the dancers passed torches from one to the other. Then they danced the *branle des lavandières*, and that other dance, the Purpose, in which the partners kissed. In this last dance Mary was again Darnley's partner, and the kiss they exchanged was full of meaning to them both.

From that moment the Queen was in love. She had made up her mind who her husband would be. She thought it was because he was the most handsome and charming young man she had ever met. She did not stop to count other reasons. She did not remind herself that she must marry, that she was tired of waiting, that too many and strong forces were against a grand marriage into the royal houses of Spain and France. She did not think: Elizabeth of England is against my marriage with Lord Darnley; therefore I wish to marry Darnley. She did not think: I am young; I long for a lover, and I have waited too long.

The Maries discussed the newcomer while they undressed their mistress.

'Very handsome!' was the verdict.

'He dances so gracefully,' said Mary.

'I noticed how he kissed Your Majesty in the dance,' ventured Beaton.

'Well, what of that? It is as necessary to kiss in the Purpose as it is to clap hands in the *branle des lavandières*.'

'Necessary, Madam,' agreed Beaton. 'But not *always* pleasant.'

Mary tapped her cheek with feigned annoyance. 'Livy dear,' she said, to change the subject, 'you are very quiet.'

Livy came forward and, kneeling before the Queen, laid her head in her lap.

'Madam,' she said, 'do you remember that when we were little we all swore we would not marry until you did?'

'I do, darling.'

'You married once . . . and were a widow, but none of us has married. I have often wondered who would be the first. And now this handsome Lord Darnley has come along . . .'

'What are you mumbling into my skirts, Livy? Get up at once and show yourself.'

But Livy continued to kneel.

''Tis clear,' said Flem, 'what has happened. Lord Sempill has been asking her to marry him for these many weeks, and she has put him off by declaring that she has vowed a vow to the Queen.'

'No, Livy! That is ridiculous!' cried Mary. 'You are in love with this tall and handsome Sempill?'

'Yes, Madam, but. . .'

'Rise, Livy. Get up at once. You are to marry Lord Sempill . . . immediately. I insist.'

'Oh, Madam,' said Flem, 'let it not be immediately . . . otherwise Master Knox will have all sorts of suggestions to — make against poor Livy and her Sempill.'

Mary stood up and her eyes flashed. 'Who cares for Master Knox! Let him rave. Livy, my dearest, you shall have the grandest wedding ever seen, and all the world shall know how I love you. We shall have masques and mummeries . . . feasting . . . dancing . . .'

'And you, dearest,' said Flem, 'will dance the Purpose with Lord Darnley.'

'Have done with you!' cried Mary. 'You insolent Fleming! And if I dance with Darnley, you shall partner Maitland. Come! You know how I love a wedding, and what wedding would I rather attend than that of my dear Livy?'

'Your own perhaps?' suggested Beaton.

They were all gay that night. The Queen had never seemed so beautiful, but they had never before seen Mary radiantly in love.

❧ ❧ ❧

They were happy days which followed. Each morning Mary awoke with a feeling of excitement. Each day Lord Darnley waited on her and each day she was a little more in love with him.

What a delightful young man he was! He was so eager to be liked by everyone. It was a charming quality. Moray looked at him with suspicion, but the young Lord Darnley did not seem to be aware of his dislike. He was open and frank with him; he went with him to hear one of John Knox's sermons, and listened so intently to the preacher that even Knox – knowing Darnley to be a Catholic – was flattered. He was deferential to Maitland and to all the lords of the Court. He seemed to imply: I know that I lack your wisdom, but please remember I am young yet and I long to learn.

Mary was glad that he liked David Rizzio and that David liked him. Darnley did not appear even to consider Rizzio's humble birth. He would be seen in the courtyards walking arm-in-arm with the Piedmontese, or begging him to sing or play the lute for him. He had even taken to sleeping in David's bed, which was a symbol of friendship.

'I wish to be as near to Your Majesty as possible,' he told Mary. 'I sleep with my sword beside me. Then, if need be, I could rush to Your Majesty's defence.'

Mary smiled at that. 'No one will harm me.'

'But if they should try . . . I would wish to be the one there to protect you.'

So charming he seemed, so simple and unspoilt. When they were close together she wanted to kiss his smooth cheek. Her senses bounded at the thought of kissing him.

How delightful he was during that game of the bilies he played with her, Thomas Randolph and Mary Beaton.

Randolph was disturbed by Mary's liking for Darnley, for he was working hard to bring about a marriage between her and Leicester. What, wondered Mary, did he think of the favour she showed Darnley whom Elizabeth considered her subject and whom she now, Mary believed, so deeply regretted allowing to leave England?

Randolph and Mary Beaton had won at the bilies against Darnley and the Queen, and Darnley was obliged to present Mary Beaton with fifty crowns' worth of jewellery – a brooch, a ring and two watches – as the stake.

'Madam,' he said to Mary afterwards, 'I humbly ask pardon. I played so badly.'

'You did indeed, my lord,' she agreed. 'You seemed to pay scarcely any attention to the game.'

He lifted those big blue eyes to her face. 'Madam, it was because you were near me. . . .'

She laid a hand, which had begun to tremble, on his shoulder. She moved closer to him. Her body was crying out for him. She wished in that moment that she were not the Queen surrounded by courtiers. She longed to be alone with him, to say: 'I love you. We will marry one day, but for the moment we may be lovers. . . .'

She turned away, dizzy with desire. She heard his voice,

hushed and gentle: 'Madam . . . Madam . . . if I dared . . . if I but dared . . .'

❧ ❧ ❧

Livy was married to Lord Sempill with great pomp – the first of the Queen's Maries to marry.

'It will not be quite the same henceforth,' said Mary sadly. 'Dearest Livy will often be with us, but we must not be selfish. She will wish sometimes to be in her new house with Sempill. How we shall miss her!'

Livy married! thought Mary. So should I be! It is time I married; and here is the one I love; here is the one I will marry.

She could not resist talking of Darnley. 'What think you of my lord?' she asked David.

'Lord Darnley is worthy of Your Majesty's regard.'

'I am so glad you like each other, Davie. He is charming, is he not? I could not have borne it if you two had not been friends.'

She held out her hand. David took it and held it to his lips.

David, who was clever, understood the turmoil within her. He understood the meaning of this new feverish beauty which was hers. She was ripe for marriage; she was longing for the handsome youth; she was all desire, as wise David had always known she could be. David himself had dreamed of arousing that desire; as had others, he had sensed the promise within her. But David was a man of ambition. To be the Queen's lover would indeed have been a dangerous position for a humble musician; as her most trusted secretary and adviser he was much safer.

Everything that David wished for was falling into his hands.

The Pope himself congratulated him on the good work he was doing in Scotland. The Pope sent advice. It seemed incredible that the mighty Pope was sending kind messages to David Rizzio who, when he had first come to Scotland, had slept on a table in the porter's lodge because there was no bed for him. What David wanted, and what the Pope wanted, was to bring Scotland back to the Catholic Faith, while setting her apart from Europe. The Pope did not wish Scotland to be the fief of Spain, nor of France. What the Pope wanted was a Catholic Scotland to stand against Protestant England – yet aloof from the great Continental powers – a Catholic husband for the Queen, yet not a great prince from Europe. Darnley was the suitor favoured by Rome, and therefore by David Rizzio. When the Queen married Lord Darnley more friendly messages would come from the Pope, more rewards would fall to David Rizzio.

David said: 'Madam, there are some in this realm who deplore your interest in that young man.'

'And you are not one of them?'

'Madam, I see that you are happy; and I could never do aught but rejoice in that happiness.'

'And what if I were to marry Lord Darnley, Davie? What would you say then, my faithful secretary?'

'I should say that it was a happy match. I should say: "May the saints guard you. May all happiness and prosperity be yours!"'

'Davie!' she cried. 'You have made me so happy. You always do.'

'I beg of Your Majesty to keep your feelings as secret as possible. There are many who will do their utmost to prevent this match.'

'I will remember.'

And she did remember as she sat with Thomas Randolph watching the dancers at Livy's wedding.

'My Queen is anxious for your happiness, Madam,' said Randolph. 'She hopes soon to see you married.'

'I wish to please your Queen whenever possible,' Mary answered.

'I pray God that when Your Majesty chooses a husband your choice will be a good one.'

'He must be such a one as God would give me.'

'God has made one fair offer to you, Madam.'

'And that is?'

'My lord of Leicester – a perfect man, says my Queen.'

Mary interrupted gaily: 'And one she would have taken herself had she been of a mind to marry.'

'It is true, Madam.'

'Ah, Master Randolph, if your mistress will be a good sister to me, then shall I be a good sister to her. If this were not so – then we must each do as we may.'

Darnley was claiming her for the dance, and she rose and gave him her hand. Thomas Randolph looked after them uneasily.

As they danced, Darnley said: 'How happy those two are – Sempill and Mary Livingstone.'

'They are in love, and it is rather wonderful, is it not, to be in love?'

'It is the most wonderful thing in the world. Madam . . . but I dare not say it.'

'You must say it. Tell me. What is it? I insist.'

'If I could but forget you were the Queen . . . if I might see you alone . . .'

'It is difficult for a queen to receive a young man alone.'

'If you were not the Queen, we could slip away from the ball.'

'And then?'

'Then I might try to explain.'

Mary's eyes were burning as she said: 'I wish to hear these explanations.'

'But alone, Madam? If it were possible . . . But I could not trust myself . . .'

'Why should you not? We are both free.'

'Free, Madam?'

'Free to say what we will.'

'Madam, then you mean . . . Forgive me . . . but I cannot believe I have heard aright.'

He knew that the Queen was in love with him – fiercely and passionately in love with him. He believed that if they were alone she would offer no resistance. And once she had surrendered herself to him the way would be clear; she would not wish to draw back. Once he became the Queen's lover, he would be certain of the crown of Scotland.

What a glorious prospect this was! She was young and beautiful; she was passionate; she would be the prime mover in their love affair. He would allow this to be so, for it was what she wanted; and just how everything must be as she wanted it. She had fallen in love with a young and – as she believed – inexperienced boy. He must play the part of callow youth, of lovesick boy, inexperienced yet eager to be led.

She whispered: 'If you would see me alone, come to my apartments this night. Beaton will let you in. When the palace is quiet . . . and all have retired . . .'

She pressed his hand, but she did not dance with him again.

She was afraid that she was betraying this great passion which was possessing her.

She did not now want marriage with Spain; she did not care for dignity or pride, nor her rank as Queen. She cared for nothing but the immediate fulfilment of her love for Henry Darnley.

Beaton said: 'Madam, is it wise?'

She turned on Beaton angrily. 'Wise! What do you mean? He has something to say to me. Why should I not hear it?'

'But alone, Madam, in your bedchamber?'

'Beaton . . . you are insolent!'

Seton, the calm quiet one, the one perhaps who was most steadfast in her devotion, said nothing, but watched her mistress with a great anxiety in her eyes. Mary would not look at Seton.

Flem could not hide her excitement. The marriage of Livy was responsible for this. It had made the Queen realise that she too was in love, that she too must have a lover.

'Her Majesty will marry him,' soothed Flem; 'then all will be well.'

'You chatter too much,' said Mary. 'Bring me my robe. The white velvet.'

'White velvet becomes Your Majesty more than anything else,' said Flem.

Mary scarcely heard; a feverish excitement possessed her. If he did not come . . . But he would come. He was knocking at the door now.

'Quick, Beaton, quick!'

Beaton was at the door.

'Come in quickly, my lord. Let no one see you.'

Mary stood up, the white velvet draped about her, her long chestnut hair hanging loose about her shoulders.

'Leave us,' she said in a whisper; and silently and swiftly the three Maries left the apartment.

'Madam,' began Darnley, and would have knelt and taken her hands; but she had thrown herself into his arms, her restless fingers caressing his face and neck.

Darnley shyly put his arms about her.

This was success beyond his dreams. He need not plead with her; he need do nothing but obey, for the passionate Queen was commanding him to be her lover.

❁ ❁ ❁

Mary was deep in love and determined to marry Darnley. She thought of little else. David advised caution. All the Protestant lords, headed by Moray, were against the match. Mary could wait for marriage, since she had now found a way to enjoy her lover's society in private.

She was continually thinking of fresh gifts to bestow on him. She sent for her tailor William Hoppringle, and commanded him to make the finest suit which had ever been made; he was to work immediately on black velvet and silver lace. Then he was to make garments of taffeta and silk – and all these were for Lord Darnley. Johnnie Dabrow, the finest hatter in Edinburgh, was to make Darnley's hats, and he was to put as much care into the making as he would if the Queen would be wearing them. Fleming Allyard must get busy making shoes. Shirts and ruffs were ordered; all were to be made of the finest materials available.

The jewellers were called in. The Queen wished rubies,

emeralds and diamonds to be set into the most perfect patterns to enhance the fair beauty of the young man she loved.

As yet she believed that her determination to marry him was her secret.

Darnley grew a little impatient. For the crown he did not care, he assured her; he but wished to let the whole world know that he was her lover.

She believed him. He was so young, so naive and, as she was, a stranger to passion.

There was one unfortunate incident which occurred to mar the joy of those days.

It was brought about through the Borderer, Lord Bothwell. He had given up the post for which he had so earnestly begged, that of Captain of the Scottish Guard in France, and had come back to Scotland. He now sent a messenger to the Queen, begging her to grant permission for him to return to the Court.

'And why should he not come back to Court?' asked Mary. 'He was imprisoned for implication with Arran, but now we all know that Arran was mad. We have been unfair to Bothwell.'

Her brother Moray, who was now becoming very uneasy indeed about her relationship with Darnley, assured her that it would be the utmost folly to bring Bothwell back to Court.

'The man is a born trouble-maker,' he said. 'He sows discord. Scotland has been a more peaceful place without him.'

But the Queen was no longer to be dominated thus. She made her own decisions – with the help of Rizzio; and although she deplored the conduct of the Borderer, there was something in his character which appealed to her.

'I think I shall grant him the permission he seeks,' she said.

Moray was furious. He had loved his sister when she

followed his advice and allowed him to rule Scotland; he could come near to hating her now, for it seemed to him that she was fast becoming his enemy. His resentment flared up against her. Why should she – a foolish lass – wear the crown when he, their father's son, was far more suitable to do so? The incredibly bad luck which had attended his birth was a chafing sore that ate into his character, corroding it, destroying his finer qualities, breeding within him a treacherous determination to take the power from his sister's hands.

He would not have Bothwell back at Court. Bothwell was his enemy. Bothwell might have discovered that he had tried to have him poisoned; clearly there was scarcely room in Scotland for Bothwell and Moray.

But to keep Bothwell out of Scotland was not so difficult to accomplish after all, for the rogue, Dandie Pringle – now dismissed from Bothwell's service and living in Scotland – was the very man to help in this.

Moray commanded him to come to Edinburgh and had him brought before the Queen.

'Before Your Majesty recalls Lord Bothwell,' said Moray, 'I thought you might care to hear the testimony of this man.'

'Who is this man?' asked Mary.

'One who served Bothwell when he was in France and knows something of his private life. He will tell you that the Hepburn is one of the greatest libertines in Scotland.'

'There are many libertines in Scotland, great and small. Should one more make so much difference?'

'No, Madam,' said James, 'it should not. But this man is more than a libertine. He has spoken cruel slander against persons of high degree.'

'You, brother?'

'Perhaps, my dear sister, but I have not heard of it. I meant against you.'

'What has he said?'

'I have brought Pringle here to tell you how he spoke of you before his servants.'

'Am I to listen to the tittle-tattle of servants?'

'If it concerns yourself, you undoubtedly should.'

'Bring him in then and let me hear him.'

Dandie Pringle knelt before the Queen.

'So you served with my Lord Bothwell in France?'

'Yes, Your Majesty.'

'And he spoke often of me in your hearing?'

'Not often, Your Majesty, but now and then.'

'And he spoke ill of me?'

'He did, Your Majesty.'

'What said he?'

'Among other things that you and the Queen of England would not make one honest woman between you. He said that the Queen of England had for paramour Lord Robert Dudley, but that if Your Majesty had taken any other than the Cardinal, your uncle, the matter could have been better endured.'

Mary flushed scarlet with anger. 'Take this man away!' she cried. 'How dare he utter such wicked slander? How dare he even think such things!'

Moray signed to Pringle to hurry away.

'The man but repeats the words of that rogue,' he said as soon as they were alone.

'It is so . . . monstrous!'

Mary, overcome with fury and shame that such a thing could be said of her, threw herself into her brother's arms and wept bitterly.

Moray soothed her. He had won this round. Bothwell would not be allowed to remain in Scotland.

❁ ❁ ❁

The sounds of revelry burst forth at intervals from the palace of Holyrood. The Queen had never seemed so healthy, nor so happy. She must have her lover continually beside her; she could not bear to lose sight of him. The pain in her side had not troubled her for weeks; there was a delicate colour in her usually pale cheeks, and the sound of her laughter frequently rang through the apartment of Little France.

It was true that clouds were gathering about her, but she refused to notice them. She could not spare time to look at them; she had at last let loose her slumbering passion, and it had overwhelmed her, so powerful was it.

She did not realise that she was betraying herself. She would not listen to David's warning that Moray knew the state of affairs between herself and Darnley, and would do his utmost to prevent their marriage. Maitland was back from his English embassy; he was anxious that she should marry to please the Queen of England, but Maitland had one other matter on his mind now for there was one marriage which seemed to him of more importance than the Queen's. His wife had died and he was courting Flem.

Flem and the Queen were closer than the others now. They were both deeply in love; they shared little jokes together; their mingling laughter filled the apartments. Neither would concern herself with what was unpleasant; they were determined to be happy.

David begged the Queen to heed his warning. Moray was garnering together an army for the purpose, he said, of driving

Bothwell from the country. A whole army to drive one man from Scotland when that man had already fled back to France? Why did Moray not disband his army? David knew. He wanted Mary to know too.

But if Mary was reckless, if she was almost submerged in the deep seas of her passion, she had attained an even greater dignity than before. In her love affair with Darnley, she was the leader. She was the Queen; she would protect him from such as Moray who, David said, sought to destroy him. Mary was determined to show all Scotland that she was Queen.

At this time Darnley was confined to his bed with an attack of measles. The Queen was distraught – although he was not seriously ill – and insisted on his staying at Stirling Castle so that she could nurse him herself.

She did not leave the sick room, and if any had doubted her intentions, they could no longer do so.

John Knox, who had called the godly to witness the black mummeries and wickedness that went on in Holyroodhouse, now commanded his flock to observe that the Queen attended her lover in a most immodest manner in his sick room.

God, he declared, was recording Mary Stuart's sins. They should be paid for . . . every one.

The Queen of England heard the news and publicly declared herself shocked by it. She, being a virgin, she said, could scarcely bear to speak of it. A Queen . . . in a sick room . . . nursing a young man! It was wanton behaviour.

'The Queen of England,' said Mary, 'protests her virtue continually. It is understandable that she should protect what is left of her, for that virtue has been much besmirched by rumour.'

Mary did not know that in private the Queen of England exulted at the success of her plan to bring disorder into

Scotland. She laughed with Cecil and Dudley at the accounts of Darnley's good behaviour. 'Let her wait,' said Elizabeth. 'Soon that long lad will begin to show himself in his true colours, once let him be sure that he has secured the Queen in his net.'

It was true that Darnley did become a little peevish during his convalescence. Mary noticed that some of his servants bore bruises; she heard rumours that the spoiled boy beat his servants unmercifully. But she paid little attention to such gossip; she was far too happy to let that happiness be spoiled.

And when he was finally recovered, the Queen was so elated that, with some of her women including her three Maries, she dressed up in the humble garments of citizens' wives and roamed the streets, stopping all the men they met and asking them to give coins towards a ball they intended to give that night.

Laughing through the streets they went and, when it was known that the party of supposedly loose women was headed by the Queen, the gossips increased their scandalous talk, John Knox ranted more than ever, and the Queen of England collected more titbits to gloat over in private and condemn in public.

Now that Darnley had recovered, Mary was determined to wait no longer for her marriage.

It was May now – three months since Darnley had come to Scotland. Mary passionately desired to regularise their union now, for she felt it very wrong that Scotland's strict moral laws, laid down by the Kirk and to which she had given her authority, should be broken by Scotland's Queen.

She called her brother to her and told him that she had determined to marry Lord Darnley. She had prepared a document which she asked him to sign.

'A document?' cried Moray.

'It states that you will give your consent to my marriage with Lord Darnley and do all in your power to bring it about.'

'Madam, this is impossible. It will split Scotland in two.'

'Why so?'

'There are many nobles in Scotland who will not stomach this marriage.'

'You mean yourself.'

'I am one, Madam.'

'Because you fear that we shall bring the Catholic Faith back to Scotland and the Reformed Party and yourself will no longer be in power?'

'You are young, Madam.'

'I am of age now, brother. When you were my age you were planning to rule Scotland. That is what I am planning to do now.'

'You cannot do it through marriage with Darnley.'

'I will be Queen and choose the man I marry.'

'You cannot ignore the nation and your ministers when you make that choice.'

'As Queen the nation will follow me in my choice.'

'Never!' cried Moray in a fury.

'You forget yourself, brother.'

'It is you who forget yourself, sister. You behave like a slut with this pretty boy of yours. He shares your bed. The whole Court knows it. I beg of you, if you prize your crown, give up this evil life while there is yet time.'

'You quote Master Knox. There is another who will find his claws clipped.'

'You do not know what you say.'

'I know very well that I say what I mean. Sign this paper and I shall think of you as my good subject.'

Moray's answer was to fling out of the room.

David came to her later to tell her that Moray had an army gathered about him. Argyle, Châtelherault and Kirkcaldy of Grange were with him. These were the most important noblemen in Scotland; and there was not a general to match Kirkcaldy. Moray had been astute; this was not the sudden move he had intended it should appear to be; he had looked ahead and this was his answer to the suggested Darnley marriage.

She paced up and down the apartment. Civil war threatened, but she was not afraid. She was not a frivolous girl now; she was a woman of deep emotions which brought her great courage.

'The English are with him,' said David. 'Elizabeth has promised him arms and men.'

'I care not if the whole world comes against me!' said Mary. 'I will be Queen of Scotland at last.'

'The Highlanders might well stand by Your Majesty,' said David. 'Bring George Gordon out of prison. Create him Earl of Huntley. Then you will have a new Cock o' the North to stand at your side. And there is one other whom you could trust. Recall Bothwell. He is only waiting for the summons and he will relish the opportunity to take vengeance on your brother. He will willingly serve you – if only for the opportunity of being back in Scotland.'

'That man! Do you not remember what he has said of me?'

'Forget old grudges, Madam. The need is desperate. He is a foul-mouthed ruffian but a good fighter – the most courageous in Scotland.'

So Mary sent for Bothwell and created George Gordon Earl of Huntley. The new earl came down from the Highlands with thousands of followers – all brave men and bold, longing for a chance to settle scores with Moray and rally to the standard of the Queen.

They camped about Edinburgh, and the sound of their pipes could be heard in the palace. Along the streets the kilts and steel bonnets could be seen. From all over Scotland warriors were coming to fight for the Queen against Moray.

John Knox watched the growth in numbers of the encroaching Highlanders with apprehension. In vain did he threaten them with eternal damnation; they played jaunty airs on the pipes in answer to him. Most of them were Protestants, but they believed in a wee bit of fun and laughter, and John Knox's talk of his God's delight in vengeance was losing its appeal.

Mary was in some doubt as to the loyalty of these men. There was the lecherous Morton who, she knew, had weighed her chances of success against those of her brother, and it was, therefore, a good augury that he had chosen to support her. There was Lord Ruthven, who was supporting her because his children by his first wife were Darnley's cousins.

It might be that these lords had their own private reasons for being with her in Edinburgh instead of with Moray's armies; but for the present it was enough that they were with her and she could rely on the new Earl of Huntley and – when he came – on Bothwell.

There was one thing she intended to do before all else and that was legalise her union with her lover. Scandal was rife concerning her; it was more malignant than it had ever been, for Moray, who had previously endeavoured to quash it, now sought to foster it. He had set going a rumour that the Queen was a lewd woman and that David Rizzio and Darnley were both her lovers. He revived the Chastelard scandal. Knox was his ardent supporter in all this.

On her wedding day Mary walked from her apartments to the chapel at Holyrood dressed in the mourning gown of black with a large mourning hood, the costume of a sorrowing widow. She made a sombre bride. It was necessary however for her to observe the strict royal etiquette which demanded that until she was another man's wife she must, on all state occasions, appear as the widow of her first husband.

The Earls of Lennox and Atholl led her to the chapel and then went to fetch Darnley.

What a contrast he made in his glittering costume! Mary's heart leaped with pride as she contemplated him. This was to be the happiest marriage that had ever been.

The Dean of Restalrig performed the ceremony with his priests to help him. Mary's hand lay in that of Henry Stuart, Lord Darnley, and they were indeed husband and wife.

The bridegroom left the chapel in advance, in order that he might retire to her chamber, where she would join him when her women led her there.

'Come!' he cried when he saw her. 'I like not this black *deuil*. You must be a dazzling bride. Cast aside these sorrowful garments and dispose yourself to a pleasanter life.'

Mary feigned reluctance to do this, remembering what would be expected of her, but it was difficult to hide her elation and her desire to be done with reminders of her widowhood.

At last she was persuaded to wear the brilliant wedding garments which had been prepared for her, and her women lost no time in dressing her.

'The most beautiful bride in the world!' whispered Flem; and Mary had a sudden memory of hearing those words before. Then François had been her husband. She fleetingly remembered his adoration. How different was little François from the handsome Darnley!

There followed feasting and revelry. The bridegroom drank more freely than previously, and was inclined to be peevish, but he smiled with pleasure when he heard the proclamation which made it known to the people that he, Henry Stuart, Lord Darnley, was also Lord Ardmarnock, Earl of Ross, Duke of Albany, and should be called, by the express wish of Her Majesty the Queen of Scotland and the Isles, King of this kingdom.

At last they were alone. This was bliss for which Mary had long yearned. Now she was free to indulge her passion with a good conscience. There need be no hurried partings before the dawn, no furtive whisperings.

But to her surprise and chagrin it was not the same Henry Darnley who now made love to her. It was true that he was a little drunk; it was understandable that the great honours which had come to him this day had turned his head a little. He was fiercely demanding; he was arrogant; it was as though he said: 'I am the master now.'

She submitted to this new lover, willingly and happily. But in the morning she began to see that the character he had worn as a mask when he first came to Court had been cast aside.

With apprehension Mary began to understand anew the man to marry whom she had risked civil war.

❁ ❁ ❁

The turn of events forced Mary to concern herself with matters other than this partial disappointment in her husband. There came a chance to subdue Knox, and Mary took it boldly.

Darnley, at her request and on the advice of Rizzio, went to the Kirk of St Giles to hear Knox preach. Mary knew that many of the warriors, who had rallied to her and were now encamped about the capital, were firm upholders of the Protestant Faith. She wished to show them that – Catholic though she was – she still intended to follow the policy of toleration which she had promised when she first came to Scotland.

Darnley had gone sullenly, and the sight of him, sprawling in the pew, sumptuously dressed and glittering with jewels, put Knox into a frenzy of rage against the Queen and her husband. He could not resist preaching at the young man.

' "O Lord, our God," ' he cried, quoting from the book of Isaiah, ' "other lords besides Thee have had dominion over us; but by Thee only will we make mention of Thy name." '

He went on to declare that for the sins of the people tyrants were sent to scourge them. Boys and women were sent to rule over them.

There was nothing that annoyed Darnley more than a reference to his youth. He folded his arms and glared at Knox; but Knox was not the man to be intimidated by a glare in his own kirk.

God justly punished Ahab, he declared, because he would not take order with the harlot Jezebel. In these evil days Ahab joined Jezebel in idolatry.

Darnley, deeply conscious of his new status, could not suffer insults lightly. He stood up and, calling to his attendants that he was going hawking, strode out of the kirk.

Mary was sympathetic when she heard what had happened, and laid no blame on her husband who, so far, could in her eyes do no wrong. Instead – in her new mood of bravado and deeply conscious of the brawny kilted men in their steel bonnets who paraded the town – she sent for Knox.

'Master Knox,' she cried as he stood before her, 'this day you have insulted the King. I therefore forbid you to preach in Edinburgh whilst there are sovereigns in the capital.'

'I have spoken nothing but according to the text, Madam,' answered Knox. 'The King, to pleasure you, has gone to the Mass and dishonoured the Lord God, so shall God, in His justice, make you an instrument of his ruin.'

'How dare you make such wicked prophecies!' cried Mary in panic.

'I but speak as God commands me, Madam.'

'You will abstain from preaching whilst there are sovereigns in the capital or suffer the rewards of treason.'

She dismissed him.

Knox began to harangue the Lords of the Congregation more vehemently than ever, urging them to rise against the Queen. Still Mary did not despair. There seemed little need to, as she surveyed the Highlanders who had pitched their tents about the city. Marching through the streets could be seen the kilted warriors, accompanied by the skirling of the pipes – big men, broad and strong; fierce men who did not know the meaning of fear were rallying to the cause of the Queen.

Bothwell was back in Edinburgh, eager to put his services at the command of the Queen – and there was a saying on the Border that Bothwell was worth an army. Huntley's Highlanders and Bothwell's Borderers made a formidable assemblage; and the Queen's eyes glistened as she watched them.

Knox quailed before the display of might. He had found an adversary, who he had not believed existed, in the Queen herself. When John Knox took a look at the steel bonnets of the North he heard the voice of God advising discretion.

So Mary was now ready to place herself at the head of an army which, it was agreed, could not have a better commander than the Earl of Bothwell.

There was only one who opposed that command and this was the Queen's husband.

He was peevish, for although he was called King of Scotland, the Crown Matrimonial had not been bestowed upon him. He was furious when he thought he detected a lack of respect in those about him. He resented the arrogant Borderer; he had quarrelled with many of the lords and was fast becoming unpopular even among those who had decided to give Mary their support.

He sulked and, when Mary tenderly asked the reason, he flashed at her: 'Madam, it is a sad thing when rogues and adventurers are preferred to honest men.'

'My dearest, what do you mean?' asked Mary.

'That villain Bothwell . . . to command your army! Are you mad? The man's a brigand.'

'He's the best general in Scotland with the exception of Kirkcaldy – and he is with our enemies.'

'The best general! What of my father?'

'But your father cannot be called a great general.'

'You insult my family and consequently me. Mayhap I had

better remove myself from your presence. Mayhap I had better find other friends . . . true friends who love me.'

Mary smiled at the spoilt boy in indulgent exasperation. He was so pretty – even when he sulked – that she could not help softening towards him.

'Henry, come and sit beside me.'

He did so sullenly.

She stroked his golden hair back from his face, but he rudely shook her off. 'What is the use of pretending you care for me, when you insult my family by putting that crude oaf above them?'

'My crown is in danger, dearest.'

'*Your* crown! Yes, that is how it is. *Your* crown which you will not share with me. You promised me all I could wish for, and now that we are married it is a different story.'

Mary sighed. 'It *is* a different story now that we are married. Henry, what has happened to you? You were so modest . . . so gentle . . . before we married. Was it because you were deceiving me, pretending to be the man you were not . . . until we were married?'

A cunning look flickered across his face. He threw his arms about her and kissed her, forcing her back into her chair.

'Mary,' he breathed. 'You do not love me, Mary.' He was smiling secretly. He had power over her through her sensual need of him. He could get what he wanted from his Queen. 'Mary, forgive me . . .'

'My darling!'

'It is . . . these people about you . . . they do not pay proper respect to me. Mary is the Queen, they seem to say, but who is Darnley? Only her consort . . . of no importance at all.'

'That is quite wrong, Henry.'

'Then show them it is wrong. Give the command to my father. Dearest Mary, please me in this thing . . . just to prove to me . . .'

She was weakening; she was sinking into that mood when her senses were in command, when nothing seemed too much to give in return for all the joy and pleasure he gave her.

❀ ❀ ❀

The two men faced each other – the adventurer from the Border and the Queen's pretty husband. Darnley was examining the velvet-lined, perfumed gloves – a present from the Queen – which he was drawing on his hands.

'Her Majesty' said Darnley with a smirk which made Bothwell's fingers itch to draw his sword, 'has appointed my father commander of her armies.'

The colour deepened in Bothwell's ruddy face. He had been certain of the command. He knew that the men would follow him to death if need be, because he had the qualities of leadership and men feared him while they admired him. To set weak Lennox at the head of the armies was folly. Moreover, Lennox was not even on the spot.

'I would wish to hear that from Her Majesty's lips before I believed it,' muttered Bothwell.

'Would an order, signed by the Queen, suffice, my lord?'

Bothwell nodded, and Darnley unrolled the scroll he had carelessly carried under his arm. Bothwell studied it.

The foolish woman! he thought. The lives of loyal Scotsmen are at stake, and she can deny this popinjay nothing!

Yet he was too soon returned from exile to risk being sent back again. He bowed his head, but as his eyes met those of Darnley, there was murder in his heart. The strong fingers twitched. He was imagining them, pressing that scented throat until the silly boy had no breath left. He was certain in that moment that the best way any Scot could serve the Queen was by ridding her of the foolish boy she had married.

Never had the Queen lived through such triumphant days. She herself, wearing a light suit of armour under her scarlet, gold-embroidered riding dress and a steel casque under her hood, rode out with her army behind her. Beside her rode her husband, distinct from all others on account of the gilded armour he was wearing; he had not forgotten to put on his scented velvet-lined gloves.

As she rode south, Mary's subjects rallied to her.

'God save the Queen!' they cried. They were enchanted by the youth and beauty of their King and Queen. Compared with them the stern-faced Puritan Moray seemed very colourless.

'Give the Queen a chance,' murmured the people. 'Why should the bonny lass not choose her own husband if she wishes it! And who is behind this rising of Moray's . . . who but the Queen of England!'

There were many who thought often and bitterly of those raids on their homes, of the marauding hordes from beyond the Border. Those raiders were the friends of Moray. Let Moray keep his friends. Scotsmen were rallying in the cause of their Queen.

And so Moray found a lack of the response which had been expected. Few rallied to his standard, and the English, seeing how matters stood, became evasive. Elizabeth held up the aid she had promised, and Moray's rebellion, which was to have brought him control of Scotland, was crushed without bloodshed. He was forced to flee across the Border, for he dared not remain in Scotland; and with him into exile went his powerful helpers – Châtelherault, Glencairn, Kirkcaldy and many others.

Knox, reproaching God, advised Him to do His duty by the exiles and bring them back to power in Scotland. He found some comfort in whispering evil gossip concerning the Queen and Rizzio. The latter, he declared, was a spy of the Pope's; he was the slave of the Roman Harlot; he had corrupted the Queen's mind while he corrupted her body.

'Was it true,' asked the people of Edinburgh, 'that Signor Davie was the Queen's lover?' It was said that he spent long hours alone with her. He was not handsome, but he had beautiful eyes and he played the guitar with great skill. This guitar in itself was believed to be a magic thing; it was made of tortoiseshell, mother o' pearl, ebony and ivory. It could make any who heard it its slave. When Signor Davie played it before the Queen, he cast a spell upon her so that she was eager for his embrace.

Such were the tales that were circulating through Scotland.

Meanwhile heartening news came from London of Elizabeth's reception of Moray, which had been quite different from his expectations. The Queen had received him with great hostility, upbraiding him for daring to question her 'dear sister's rule'. All knew that this was a ruse of Elizabeth's; all knew that she had promised aid to Moray, and that, had he shown signs of succeeding, it would have been given. But it was a heartening sign to Mary and her friends that Elizabeth should consider it politic to scold Moray for daring to rise against his Queen.

The affairs of the Queen of Scots were more satisfactory

than they had ever been before. She was strong now and, while determined to be tolerant in religious matters, was celebrating the Mass with less caution than hitherto.

Mary could have been happy but for the fact that Darnley was growing more and more ill-tempered and arrogant. Her own temper – always ready to break out – had on several occasions flared up against him. Bickering had broken out between them; even their sexual relationship was no longer completely satisfactory. He had changed; he was no longer the tender lover, and his one thought was to exert his superiority over her. Her dignity was in rebellion and her sensuality could not subdue it.

Often she reflected: I could be quite happy now if Henry were only as he used to be.

But gradually she became aware of that other menace; the growing scandals concerning Rizzio.

In the Canongate Church Lord Bothwell was being married. Outside the kirk the citizens waited to catch a glimpse of the bride and groom as they passed from there to Kinloch House, where the celebrations would take place.

There was a look of satisfaction on the face of the Border Earl. He was pleased with this wedding of his and with the general turn of events. Here he was, after years of exile and imprisonment, rising and likely to become one of the most important men in Scotland.

He liked his bride – Jean Gordon, sister of the Earl of Huntley – who brought him all he wanted. She was rich, of high birth and a good woman.

At the moment she was pale and a little sullen. She was not

as pleased to marry the Earl of Bothwell as he was to marry her; that in itself had provided a certain piquancy, for he was accustomed to being much sought after. Strange that the woman he should honour with his hand in marriage should be one of the few reluctant ones he had ever encountered.

Jean was twenty, very pale, with sandy hair, large eyes and the long Gordon nose. She was proud and cold, he imagined; but that would be a change. Too many had been too warm towards him.

When he had asked her to marry him – having previously obtained the consent of her brother and the Queen – she was cool and distant. Another woman might have been frightened, and he would have known how to deal with such fear; but Jean was too proud to show fear.

She obviously wondered why her brother should have considered a man from the Border, and of such reputation, worthy of her. Only the well arched brows betrayed the thought, but they betrayed it completely.

'I do not see, my lord, how such a marriage could be,' she had replied to his proposal, 'since I have already been promised to Alexander Ogilvie of Boyne.'

'Ogilvie!' Bothwell had cried. 'Let that not trouble you. I will deal with Ogilvie of Boyne.'

'Deal with him? I do not wish you to *deal* with him. I am telling you that he and I are betrothed.'

'I have the consent of your family to the match,' he had told her grimly, and he had taken her proud face in his hands and given her his bold stare. It had not had its usual effect, and the faintest shadow of distaste crossed her face as he kissed her full on the lips with a laugh.

But of course it was useless for her to protest. The marriage had been arranged. The Queen had given her consent and Jean's brother had decided to unite his fortunes with the rising ones of Bothwell.

Bothwell needed this marriage. Lord John Stuart, who had married Janet Hepburn, had died recently, and that marriage, from which Bothwell had hoped much since it brought him the Queen's own brother as his brother-in-law, had availed him little. Now that the Gordons were back in favour Jean was an admirable match, and he was determined that she should be his wife.

So they were married, for Ogilvie was not the man to stand out against the Queen's wishes and those of such a powerful nobleman as Huntley had become. Jean's wishes went for little, and here she was – Bothwell's bride.

Her hand was limp in his. Never mind, he thought. We shall soon change that.

He felt grand and powerful, ready to achieve anything. The Queen had wished the ceremony to take place in the chapel at Holyrood, but Bothwell, declaring that he was a Protestant, had insisted that it should take place in the Canongate Kirk.

The Queen had given way graciously. She was pleased with Bothwell; she had even forgiven him for the slander he had spoken against her, accepting his word that it had been a fabrication of the foul-minded Dandie Pringle.

In Kinloch House the Queen was the guest of honour. The King had accompanied her, but not very graciously. He was grumbling that one of his high estate should be expected to attend celebrations at Kinloch House. It was a large house, a luxurious house, the property of a rich townsman who was a favourite at the Court; but Darnley, newly come to royalty, could not deign to approve of anything that was not entirely royal. Moreover he hated Bothwell for his manliness and for the fact that he would have made a better general than Darnley's father. Darnley knew that had Bothwell commanded the army and acted as he wished, the rebels would now be the Queen's captives and not enjoying their freedom in England, where they were doubtless being encouraged to make fresh plots against the Queen.

Mary found the wedding less enjoyable than others she had attended. The bridegroom made her uneasy. She remembered clearly the first time she had seen him when she was in France, and how his appraising, almost insolent gaze had made her uncomfortable. He had not lost that habit. Now, in his doublet made of gold-coloured silk with its puffed sleeves, its inlets of satin, and with narrow lace ruff about his sunburned neck, he looked more virile in his finery than he did when less splendidly clad, for the colourful, almost womanish garments called attention to his strength and masculinity. Those powerful shoulders, those strong hands, that hard face engraved with the strains of many adventures which had not always turned out happily, that sensual mouth touched with bitterness which must have consumed him during his exile, made of Jean Gordon's husband a complete contrast to the handsome young man whom Mary had married.

Mary felt a qualm of conscience about Jean, who had wanted Alexander of Ogilvie. Jean had been one of her ladies of the bedchamber since Livy had gone and the Gordons had come back into favour, and Mary knew her well. She was a practical girl, and Mary assured herself that she would not allow her disappointment to warp her outlook. She was calm and would prove a steadying influence on the Borderer.

Jean must be proud, continued Mary's thoughts, to see

Bothwell so shine in the jousts. He was undoubtedly the victor of the tournament, which was very satisfactory indeed, since he was the man of the moment on this his wedding day.

What strength! Mary shivered slightly. There was something terrifying about the man. She wondered if the stories she had heard of him were wholly true. Was he really the ruffian he was made out to be? Was it true that he had scores of mistresses?

He was a bold man and a wicked one; she had no doubt of that; yet compared with him, her own Henry did seem somewhat childish and ineffectual.

The Bothwell honeymoon was spent at Seton. To both it was an unsatisfactory honeymoon. Bothwell was bewildered; he could not understand his Jean. She was a Highlander; he was a Lowlander; she belonged to the most important family of the North and her father had been the Cock o' the North. It was clear that she found his manners repulsive; he had laughed at her when she disclosed this, and determined to make no effort to mend them. He had been piqued by her attitude towards him. No woman had aroused his interest so completely before, and she was not even beautiful. Her pale face with its crown of sandy hair was serene beneath the green and gold cap, and the lacy ruff accentuated its oval contours; he found it impossible to disturb that serenity.

She submitted unmoved to his rough love-making. He would have preferred her to protest; then he could have brought into action his famous Border tactics. Her calm expression seemed to say: I am married to you and I will do my duty, no matter how unpleasant that may be.

He had even tried gentleness. Nothing moved her. And once, watching her when she was unaware of it, he imagined by the sadness in her face that she was thinking of Alexander Ogilvie.

'Curse Alexander Ogilvie!' cried the Borderer. 'If I had him here I'd slit his throat, and you would see who was the better man.'

'The slitting of throats cannot decide who is the better man,' she had answered.

'It can decide who is the live one,' he had retorted grimly.

'But we were not discussing life and death.'

She showed no emotion when she arrived at her new home of Crichton Castle. What did she think of those stark stone walls built to stand against the raider from the other side of the Border? How did it compare with the glens and fells, the rushing streams and waterfalls of her beautiful Highlands? She gave no sign. It was as though she shrugged her elegant Gordon shoulders and accepted Crichton as she accepted James Hepburn.

'Well,' he roared, 'do you like my castle?'

'It is my home, so I needs must,' she replied.

He watched her as she busied herself with the alterations she would make. She had brought several of her mother's servants with her and she set them sweeping and cooking, cleaning and sewing. Bothwell was amused; he could see that soon he would have a model home.

This wife of his interested him. Her frigidity was such as he had never encountered. A wifely frigidity, he presumed it to be. One would not tolerate it in a mistress. Yet it intrigued him. Here was the first woman who did not melt before his flaming personality.

He had never been faithful to one woman for so long. He might have gone on being faithful, had he not happened to take a short cut through his wife's sewing-room one day.

Seated on low stools were some of his wife's sewing-maids and among them was one who immediately caught his eye. She was small, her face was pale, and her hair the blackest he had ever seen, and so abundant that no amount of restraint could have kept it in order. He was aware of the girl's brilliant eyes fixed upon him as he sauntered through the room. The older maids modestly kept their eyes on their work.

As he passed the girl he stared at her and boldly she returned his stare. He knew then that he had too long been faithful to one woman, and it was a most unnatural condition.

But he forgot the girl until next day when, on his way to the stables, he suddenly remembered that on the previous day he had passed through the sewing-room. He went there again and saw the girl. She was like an inviting goblet of wine ready for the drinking, and he was a man who suffered from the perpetual thirst which only such wine could assuage.

A girl like that in the house! he mused. Why, if I do not . . . then someone else will!

He sent for French Paris whom he had kept in his service even though he knew the man stole from him and had been in that half-jesting, half-earnest plot to poison him.

'Who is the girl in the sewing-room?' he asked.

'The girl, my lord? You would mean Bessie Crawford, for sure.'

'How are you sure, man?'

''Tis the only girl in the sewing-room that would interest your lordship. Why, I've laid a wager with Gabriel that you would take her before the week was out.'

'You insolent knaves!' grinned Bothwell. 'And when is this week out?'

'Sir, it runs out this very day.'

Bothwell slapped the man's shoulder so hard that French Paris' knees gave way.

'We cannot have that,' said Bothwell.

Paris sniggered. 'Her ladyship, in turning out the rooms, my lord, has discarded furniture which she had sent down to the cellars. It well-nigh killed us. An old couch, my lord, there was among other articles. 'Tis there now . . . old . . . shabby . . . having been in use since before my lady's coming, sir . . . but still a couch . . .'

'Send the girl down to the cellar to get wine,' said the Earl.

'Yes, my lord. And lock the door and bring the key to you?'

'How well you follow my plans, man!'

'My lord, there have been other times.'

'Do it then. I'd like you to win your wager with sly Gabriel.'

Paris went off chuckling.

Bessie had heard much of the Earl and she never tired of listening to stories of him. They whispered of him that no woman was safe if he fancied her.

'Keep your eyes on your work,' said elderly Nan, who sat stitching beside her when the Earl passed through the room. 'Don't go casting them in *that* direction, my girl.'

Bessie did not reply. She sat still, shivering with excitement.

When she left the sewing-room that afternoon French Paris was waiting for her.

'You're to go down to the cellar,' he said. 'You're to bring up a flagon of red wine.'

'Where to?' asked Bessie.

'To me in the kitchen.'

Bessie went down the stone stairs to the cellar, taking the candle which Paris had thrust into her hand.

'Watch your step,' he called after her.

Bessie did not like the cellar very much. It was dark and damp and there were cobwebs which touched her face as she groped her way forward.

Suddenly she heard the door shut behind her and the key turn in the lock.

'Master Paris!' she called shrilly. 'Master Paris!'

She went up the stairs and tried the door. She was right. It had been locked. It was a silly trick, she supposed. Paris was teasing her. She looked round her. She must not be frightened. It was just a joke; she must remember that. The servants liked to play jokes on one another. Well, she would do as she had been bidden. She would get the flask of wine and then, if he had not unlocked the door by then, she would bang on it and call for help.

She went to where the flagons were stored, and picked up one; but as she turned towards the door she saw that it was open. She laughed with relief.

'A silly trick, Master Paris,' she said. 'Don't think to frighten *me*.'

But it was not Master Paris who had turned and was locking the door behind him. Bessie's heart raced as the tall figure of the Earl came towards her.

She dropped the flagon as she heard him laugh.

'My . . . my lord . . .' she stammered.

Then she felt those strong arms seize her.

'I . . . I do not understand, my lord . . .'

'You cannot deceive me, Bessie,' he said. 'You understand very well indeed, as you did in the sewing-room, did you not?'

'No, my lord, I . . .'

'No!' he cried. 'Then I shall have to make you.'

With that he picked her up as though she herself were no heavier than the smallest flagon of wine. He put her on the couch. Then Bessie began to understand.

The Queen was humiliated beyond endurance.

She and her husband had been entertained at the house of one of the rich burghers of the city. Darnley no longer attempted to hide from her the fact that he was a heavy drinker and, worse still, a drinker who could not carry his drink.

He no longer bothered to disguise his true nature. She had to agree with others that he was vain, dissolute and despicable. He would pick quarrels with those who dared not stand up to him; he brawled in the streets, accosting women, demanding that his companions did likewise; he boasted of his mastery over the Queen who, he asserted, was so madly in love with him that she would deny him nothing.

Mary watched him, and as she did so her feelings towards him were first lacerated with humiliation and then began to grow colder.

She had begged him this evening to drink less. He had shouted at her before the company that it was no matter for her to decide what he should drink. She should remember that he was her lawful husband. He knew how to punish her, he said with a leer, if she did not treat him with due respect.

This was more than Mary could endure.

She bade goodbye to her host, and, in tears of humiliation and rage, left the house.

Darnley stayed on to drink himself unconscious and be carried back to Holyroodhouse by his attendants and friends.

She was in her apartment when one of them came to tell her that he had been brought back to the palace and put to bed.

She nodded coldly.

There were no more tears; she was no longer heartbroken, for she had made a strange discovery: she had ceased to care for Darnley.

She did not understand herself. That raging passion which had swept over her had turned completely cold. It had died as suddenly as it had flared. She could not understand how she could have imagined herself in love with the dissolute youth. She began to see him in a new light. The blue eyes which she had thought so beautiful now seemed inane, the soft lips weak and foolish. She had begun to suspect that what she had so desperately needed was not Darnley's love but a lover. She was beginning to know herself.

A great sadness came over her. She had dreamed of the perfect union, and she was discovering most bitter disillusion. Darnley's boyish naïvety was assumed; he was hideously experienced; he was full of vice; he had practised every sort of depravity. How he must have laughed at her for falling such an easy victim to his youthful charm.

There was one other factor – a most important one – which had caused her to decide on the measures she would take: she was pregnant.

Perhaps her pregnancy made her less eager for his embraces; perhaps the slackening of desire had given her a chance to see him as he really was. No matter. She saw; and she had made up her mind.

She rose and sent a page to David Rizzio with a message that she wished to see him at once. It was midnight, but he had not retired. Early hours were never kept at Holyroodhouse.

'David,' she said, 'I have something secret to tell you. I wish no one else to know it. I hate Darnley.'

'Madam!'

'Yes, it is true. It has suddenly come to me. I did not really love him. There had been so much talk of marriages, and they never materialised. I suppose I wanted a lover and he was there. He seemed more eligible than anyone within reach. Now I think him loathly. Oh, David, you wonder. I have been so doting, have I not? You wonder if I really mean what I say.'

'Madam, his behaviour to-night was disgraceful.'

'His behaviour every night is disgraceful. He was quite insincere before the wedding. Now we see him as he really is – an arrogant upstart, a drunkard and a lecher. Let us face the truth, David. How has he behaved towards you? Do not speak. I will tell you. He has been insufferable, although when he first came here, knowing the influence you had with me, he made himself most agreeable. That is the truth, is it not, David?'

'Yes, Madam.'

'And you agree with me that my marriage is the biggest mistake I ever made?'

'It was mine too, Madam. I do not forget that I urged you to this marriage.'

'Dear Davie! You did, it is true. But you could not have urged me to the altar if I had not wished to go. The mistake is mine, not yours. We have both been deceived, but let us not ponder on past errors. I have determined to banish him, right out of my heart and from my bed. He shall never share the crown.'

'No, Madam, he should not.'

'It is great good fortune that I have not already bestowed on him the Crown Matrimonial which could have given him powers equal to my own. Then we should have been too late. In future no documents are to be shown to him. We will have a stamp made with his name on it so that his signature will not be necessary on any documents, and you can affix it without consulting him. Consult him! What would be the good of *his* opinion!'

'Madam, he will be infuriated when he hears of this.'

'Davie, his fury matters not at all. I will show him that any power he wields comes from me. I shall never give him another chance to humiliate me as he has to-night.'

David was smiling; he was well pleased. His dignity was dear to him, and Darnley had insulted him time after time. David had known that the Queen must one day grow out of her infatuation, and he was glad that time had come.

'Madam,' he said at length, 'you do well to cut Lord Darnley out of your policies. He has no conception of the important part you have to play in world politics. His own egoism, his own vanity are so large that they obscure his vision and he cannot see beyond them. Madam, never has your position been so secure. These despatches from the King of Spain make his attitude clear. He is delighted with the turn of events in Scotland, and this happy state of affairs, he knows, has grown out of Your Majesty's prompt action against the rebel lords. With Moray and his friends in England, and with Knox subdued, you have so pleased King Philip that he is planning to help you establish yourself even more firmly on the throne of Scotland, with the

Catholic religion restored. Madam, I know that the King of Spain sees no reason why an attack – providing our affairs continue to improve – should not be made on our enemy beyond the Border. The King of Spain visualises the day when the Protestant bastard is robbed of the crown she has no right to wear, and it adorns your own fair brow.'

'Queen of England and Scotland, David!' Her eyes shone. 'That is what I want. If we were one country, then would these wasteful Border raids be discontinued. We *are* one land; we should stand together. That way lies peace, Davie.'

'Yes, Madam. It will be the happiest day of my life when I see you crowned Queen of England.'

'And Philip will truly further this end?'

'He has said so quite clearly . . . or as clearly as can be expected from one so cautious. I beg of Your Majesty to read this despatch.'

They were bending over the table reading, when the door was burst open. Darnley stood watching them; his nightshirt was open at the neck, his hair disordered, his face blotchy, his eyes bloodshot from his recent carousal. He was still very drunk.

'I knew it!' he shouted. 'So you are there then . . . you two together. I knew I'd catch you. I know it's true what they say of you . . . furtively creeping away together . . . The Queen of Scotland and a low-born music-maker. By God!'

The Queen said haughtily: 'Go back to your apartment at once.'

Darnley laughed. 'Do not think to deceive me, Madam.'

'I have no intention of deceiving you. I will tell you plainly that I am weary of your disgraceful behaviour. Henceforth you and I live apart.'

Darnley reeled and hiccupped. 'Oh . . . so *he* satisfies you, does he . . . this low-born . . .'

Mary rose and strode towards him; she could not control her rage. She took him by the hair and shook him. He stared at her in bleary wonderment.

''Strue . . .' he said. 'He's your lover. That stunted go-by-the-ground, that . . .'

'Be quiet!' cried Mary. 'I will have you taken to the Tolbooth.'

Darnley's mouth fell open. 'Come, Mary,' he spluttered. 'Come to bed . . .'

She pushed him from her and he fell to the floor.

'David,' she said calmly, 'call two of his men. They shall carry him back to bed. Now I shall go to mine. Good night, David.'

She went out, leaving Darnley lying on the floor in his drunken stupor.

❧ ❧ ❧

Darnley swaggered about the Court. If the Queen denied him her bed, others did not. He was watched – though he did not know this – by many lords of the Court. There was Maitland of Lethington, now affianced to Mary Fleming. He was privy to the secrets of the bedchamber. It was not that Flem wished to betray her mistress's secrets; she loved her mistress second only to Lord Maitland himself. But Maitland was the cleverest statesman in Scotland; he had beguiled the English Queen and the English Ambassador with his diplomacy; so it was not difficult for him to discover all he needed from his beloved Flem. Maitland's vanity had been deeply wounded. He had been the Queen's chief adviser, had employed his skilful diplomacy in England, and on returning to Scotland had found another in his place: David Rizzio, the upstart musician.

Clearly Scotland would be a happier place for Lord Maitland of Lethington if Rizzio were no longer there.

There was Ruthven – slowly dying of a wasting disease and determined to enjoy great power before he departed from this life. He too resented the Queen's trust in her musician.

There was James Douglas, Earl of Morton, the most treacherous of them all, the man without scruples, the cruel lecher whose bastards were numerous. He was in touch with Moray who was trying to obtain the Queen's pardon, and return to Scotland. Morton, feigning loyalty to Mary, was also in league with the English. He was fully aware of the Spanish plot to strengthen Scotland before making an attack on the English Queen's throne; Cecil and Elizabeth were also aware of this plot. The unlucky Queen of Scots did not know how many of these gentlemen who surrounded her were spies for the champion of Protestantism, Elizabeth of England.

Moray was waiting to leap back into Scotland. So Morton, Maitland, Ruthven, with Argyle and others, met to discuss the new state of affairs, how to rid themselves of the upstart Rizzio whose foreign policy had led them to this pass, how to restore Moray and the exiled lords to their estates, how, when destroying Rizzio, to destroy also – or at least make impotent – the Queen herself.

Money and support were not lacking from England, for Elizabeth was now genuinely alarmed. Philip of Spain was behind this plot, and he could always alarm the English Queen. Philip sent money to Scotland, but the English, being warned of this through Cecil's clever spy-system, waylaid the ships which carried the treasure, captured it and brought it to London.

Philip's advice to Mary was that, since the operations must be delayed owing to the capture of the treasure, she should feign friendship with Elizabeth and lull the suspicions of the English.

Mary did not know that those noblemen who surrounded her throne were in the main spies for England. These men were Protestants and had no intention of allowing their country to return to the Catholic Faith, but it did not occur to their Queen that they could be so blatantly treacherous.

As for Rizzio himself, clever as he was and faithful to the Queen's interest, he had his weakness. He could not resist strutting a little, each day adding something to his finery. An arrogance had crept into his manner. Were the great lords of Scotland going to endure the arrogance of this upstart? Was a musician, a player of the harp and the guitar, a singer in the Queen's choir, to be set over the chieftains of Scotland?

David Rizzio became even more unpopular than Darnley for while the lords despised Darnley they were forced to admire and envy Rizzio who had risen from obscurity to power.

Morton sat beside Ruthven's sickbed in the latter's Edinburgh house. Ruthven lay back in bed; it was clear that he had not long to live, yet his eyes were brilliantly alive in his yellow face; they burned with a lust for Rizzio's blood. Morton was not surprised, gazing at the strange gaunt face, that many believed Ruthven to be a witch.

Ruthven's hopes lay with Morton. The most ruthless of the lords, it was to Morton's interest to have Moray back in Scotland, and Morton would have no compunction in committing murder to bring that about. He was no newcomer to the art of murder.

'It would be a simple matter to waylay the fellow,' Morton was saying. 'It would be over in a few minutes. He could be hustled into one of the city wynds and two stout men would make short work of him.'

'Nay,' said Ruthven, rising on his pillows and falling back with exhaustion, 'that is not the way. *She* shall see the deed done. She is heavy with her child now. In less than four months it will be born . . . if she lives . . . if she survives. . . . No! Let him be taken when he is closeted with her. Let her see the deed done. She has insulted us by her preference for the low fellow. Besides . . .'

Morton nodded slowly. 'It may kill her,' he said bluntly. 'Her health is not good . . . and a pregnant woman, seeing her lover done to death before her eyes . . . I see your point.'

'There is the hope that it may prove too much for her. But we shall not turn our daggers on the Queen. No . . . no . . . let her death come through shock, through remorse . . . anything you like. There is one other whom we must implicate in this. Neither my lord Moray nor Cecil and his Queen wish it to be known that this is a political murder. So there must be another reason for the death of our little musician, and we have it to hand.'

'Oh yes, we have it at hand. The Queen's pretty husband must be implicated. We are all agreed on that.'

'The murder of Rizzio,' said Ruthven, 'is to be no political murder. It has nothing to do with bribes and instructions from England. It is a *crime passionel*, you understand.'

'Then, he must be with us when the deed is done.'

'He must indeed! You can arrange that. The silly young fool will believe all you tell him. He is like a peevish boy robbed of his toys. She will have nothing to do with him. He whimpers because he finds more pleasure in the bed of a queen than in

367

that of a tavern wench. He'll not be difficult to manage. Then we shall have the whole world shocked by the wanton ways of a queen. And if she does not die of shock, she will be most certainly ruined.'

'And the child will doubtless not survive this.'

Ruthven nodded. 'Go to your work, friend Morton,' he said.

Morton had asked to see the young King and to see him alone.

Darnley scowled when he saw his visitor. He was not fond of the Douglases. But Morton was full of flattery – the sort which could not fail to please.

'What a delightful doublet! Never have I seen such a happy blending of colour. Ah, mayhap it is Your Majesty's fair complexion and golden hair which makes the colour seem so perfect. It is small wonder that the Queen is so madly in love with her husband.'

Darnley's scowl deepened. He was recalling the scene which had taken place early that morning. He had waited for Mary in her apartment, had driven out her women and insisted on seeing her alone. She had come at three in the morning, smiling serenely; she had been playing cards with Rizzio. They had supped together, with one or two others as company; and then had settled to the cards. As the game had been so exciting they had gone on playing until early morning.

Darnley had complained: 'It is a shameful thing that you keep your husband waiting while you play at cards with a low musician.'

'My shame,' she had retorted, 'is that I have such a husband to keep waiting.'

She cared nothing for him, and now she was unkind to him. She kept all secrets from him. He was never allowed to see any state papers.

He had seized her arm and said: 'Madam, I demand my rights.'

'Your rights?'

'To share your life, your bed, your crown.'

She had laughed and pushed him from her. 'You have forfeited those rights, Henry. Now leave me and send my women to me, for I am tired and wish to go to bed.'

'I will not go!' he had declared. 'I shall stay here. You cannot turn me away.'

'I can and I will.'

'I shall shout to the whole palace that you are turning me out of your apartment.'

'Shout all you wish. You will only be telling what is already known.'

'Mary . . . dearest . . . I love you.'

'No,' she had said. 'It is a good thing that neither of us love each other. Now go or I shall have to have you turned out.'

He had ignobly left the apartment, and the memory rankled.

Now he continued to scowl at Morton as he said: 'The Queen is *not* in love with her husband.'

'The Court knows it,' said Morton, 'and resents it.'

'Resents it?' said Darnley alert.

'Do you think, Your Majesty, that we like to look on at the vulgar intrigue between the Queen and this foreign upstart?'

'So there *is* an intrigue!'

'Does Your Majesty doubt it?'

'I . . . yes . . . no . . . I am not sure.'

'They would be very careful in your presence, I doubt not.'

'Very careful! You . . . you mean . . . ?'

'Your Majesty, he is with her night and morning. What are they doing, think you – discussing state secrets all the time?'

Darnley's eyes narrowed. 'It is true. It is shameful. I . . . a King . . . to be treated so! I . . . who have been faithful to the Queen!' He faltered and looked at Morton but Morton was not smiling at the obvious lie. He merely looked sympathetic.

'There are many of us,' said Morton slowly, 'who wonder why you do not do the fellow to death. None could blame you if you did.'

'No!' repeated Darnley. 'None could blame me.'

'I have received news from the Queen's brother in England.'

'Moray! He is no friend to me.'

'But would be. It is a shameful thing, he says, that you should be denied your rights. Not only are you denied the Queen's bed, but the Crown Matriminial. Lord Moray says that if you will restore to him and the exiled lords their estates which have been confiscated, the first thing he will do on his return to Scotland will be to give you that Crown.'

'How could I bring about his return? How could I restore his confiscated estates?'

'Alas, how could you? A short while ago when the Queen doted on you, it might have been possible for you. But now . . . another holds her favour. David Rizzio is the man who enjoys all her favours . . . every one . . . adviser, secretary of state . . . lover . . .'

'I would, I could kill that man!'

Morton smiled. 'Your Majesty,' he said, 'let us leave the palace. Let us be sure that we cannot be overheard. There is something we have to say to each other.'

Bothwell and his household had moved from Crichton to another of his houses, Haddington Abbey. He was finding enough to entertain him in his own household for a few weeks. Jean's attitude towards him had not changed in the least, and he was still intrigued by it. Bessie Crawford supplied the erotic entertainment which he had always found necessary – and life passed pleasantly.

There were matters to be attended to on the estate. Jean was doing for Haddington what she had done for Crichton; she was never idle, even when she sat resting she would have her embroidery in her hands.

He saw Bessie often. Her great eyes would follow him, waiting for the signal. Upstairs in the loft . . . this minute . . . or out in the fields away from the Abbey . . . Bessie would be there – a small, quiet girl who could be aroused at his touch to a passion which equalled his own.

He liked Bessie. Between them they – she and Jean – were responsible for his long stay on his estates. He might have continued to stay but for one thing.

It happened quite simply. He went to the sewing-room because he had been reminded suddenly of Bessie and felt an immediate need of her company. Bessie was there alone; his wife had been with her, for they were working together on the same piece of tapestry; but when he arrived Jean's chair was empty.

He said: 'To the loft! Wait there for me.'

Bessie scrambled up. Her eyes were anxious. She began: 'My lord . . . I cannot . . .'

'Go, my girl. Go up, I say.'

She stammered: 'My lord . . . my lady . . .'

He seized her by the shoulders and pushed her towards the door. She almost fell, laughing on a note of high-pitched laughter that betrayed the rising excitement, that complete abandonment to his will. She picked herself up, dropped a hurried curtsey and ran from the room.

He laughed, and after a few moments followed her to the loft.

Bessie was always inarticulate with him. They had exchanged few words. Words were unnecessary in such a relationship. But now it seemed she was trying to tell him something. She had work to do. She must not be long. He would not listen; he did not want chatter from Bessie. He forced her down on to the dusty floor of the loft. The very fact that she wished to go made him determined to keep her there. He liked resistance; he had come to expect it on the Border.

So he kept her there longer than usual, and Bessie, while she could temporarily forget her anxiety, found that it had returned to her when she was at last released.

She made her way down to the sewing-room. The Countess was there; so were several of the servants.

Bessie, red-faced, her dress dusty, put in a shamefaced appearance.

'And where have you been?' demanded Jean.

'Please, my lady . . . I . . .'

'Look at the dust on your dress. What has happened?'

Bessie stammered: 'I went to the loft . . .'

'You went to the loft when you should have been using your needle. Look at your hands. They're filthy. Go and wash them. You must not do delicate needlework with hands like that. Then I shall want to know why you left the sewing-room to go there.'

Bessie, glad to escape, almost collided with the Earl who was then coming into the room. Bessie ran. The Earl scarcely looked at her. But he was betrayed. His clothes were as dusty as those of Bessie. It was a strange sort of dust. Remains of cobwebs could be seen attached to his doublet as they had been to Bessie's hair.

Jean looked at him sharply. She knew that the servants were looking too. She was aware of suppressed laughter. Knowing the Earl, and understanding Bessie, there was only one conclusion to be drawn.

She said nothing to her husband, but mentioning that she had work for them to do, she commanded the servants whom she would need, to accompany her to the kitchens where she wished to make arrangements for that night's supper.

Half an hour later she returned to the sewing-room where Bessie – the dust brushed from her dress and her hands clean – was diligently working.

'Oh, Bessie,' said Jean, 'your father lives in the smithy outside Haddington town, I believe.'

'Yes, m'lady.'

'That is fortunate for you. Gather your things together and go to him immediately.'

'Go . . . m'lady?'

'Yes, Bessie. I find that I no longer require your services.'

Bessie blushed and stammered, then burst into tears. To leave this wonderful house, to live in her father's wretched smithy, to help at the anvil instead of doing fine needlework, to have as a lover some village lout instead of the great Earl of Bothwell – it was too much to be borne!

'Now, Bessie, it is no use weeping. Get ready. Go at once. I shall expect you to be gone in an hour.'

There was nothing Bessie could do but obey.

Bothwell shrugged his shoulders when he heard what had happened. Then he burst out laughing.

'So you're jealous, eh?' he said. 'Jealous of a sewing-girl!'

'Not jealous,' his wife replied. 'Pray visit her if you wish. I have no objection now that she will be no longer here. It is merely that I cannot have you making demands on her time when she is working for me.'

He was astonished. He had never known such a woman.

After that he had Bessie brought to him on one or two occasions. The tradesmen of the town were obliging, providing rooms where they could meet, and carrying messages to and from the smithy; but he grew tired of such arrangements. His lust always demanded satisfaction without delay. By the time matters could be arranged his ardour had cooled or been slaked elsewhere.

So . . . he returned to Edinburgh.

It was Saturday evening. The March winds howled down the great chimneys as the Queen was taking supper in the small closet next to her bedroom. She was in her sixth month of pregnancy and her physicians had advised her to fortify her strength by eating meat although this was the Lenten season; they had also prescribed quiet for the royal patient. The servants were hurrying into the closet with dishes of meat which they set on the small table. Mary was reclining on a couch and beside her were her bastard sister Jane, Countess of Argyle, and her bastard brother, Lord Robert Stuart. It was a small party in view of the doctor's advice, and the Laird of Creich her master of the household, Arthur Erskine, her equerry, the Queen's doctor, David Rizzio and a few servants completed it.

The beef was delicious, and with it they drank French wine.

'This wine always reminds me of Chenonceaux,' said Mary wistfully. 'Oh, what happy days they were!'

'Would Your Grace go back?' asked Robert.

'Nay, brother. If I went back I should have to return again by the same road, and at times I found the going tedious.'

'Signor Davie looks grand this night,' said the Countess.

David looked down at his damask gown which was trimmed with rich fur. His doublet was made of best satin; and his hose were of russet velvet. There was a fine feather in his cap, and about his neck hung a great ruby, a gift from the Queen.

'Yes, Davie,' said Mary, ''tis true.'

'I should consider it an insult to Your Majesty to appear clad in anything but the best I could assemble,' said David.

'You are right, Davie,' said the Queen. 'I like not drab garments. Sing us something of France, please. I have a longing to hear French songs tonight. Master Erskine, I beg of you pass Davie his guitar.' She turned to one of the serving men. 'Can you pull the curtains a little closer? There is a draught.'

'The wind is fierce to-night, Madam,' said the Laird of Creich.

The servant had gone to the window. For a few seconds he looked out and saw figures moving about below. They were numerous and they were in steel bonnets, with guns, swords, Jedburgh staves and bucklers.

What were these men doing out there? He had heard of no reason why they should be there. They might be troopers. What was afoot to-night? Some exercise, he supposed. He would have mentioned it to the company but, as he turned from the window, Signor David was already playing his guitar and his rich voice was filling the small chamber.

When the song was ended, the servant left the apartment. He was going to make sure that he had interpreted correctly what he had seen. He quickly discovered that there were many – possibly more than a hundred – armed men stationed about the palace.

Almost as soon as he had gone, the door which led to the private staircase was opened and Darnley came in. Mary frowned. He appeared to have been drinking. He came to where she sat and slumped on the couch beside her; he laid a hot hand on her arm.

'Have you had your supper?' she asked coldly.

The company had become silent and tense, waiting for one of those scenes which seemed now inevitable when the Queen and her husband were together.

Darnley had not answered her, and suddenly all except the Queen had risen to their feet, for, standing in the doorway through which Darnley had just come, was Lord Ruthven. His face was yellow above his gleaming armour; his hair was wild and there was a look of death on his face. For a moment they thought they were seeing Ruthven's ghost, as they knew he was near to death and not expected to leave his bed again; moreover he had always been suspected of having magical powers.

No one spoke in those frightening first moments as Ruthven's hollow eyes ranged about the room and came to rest on David Rizzio.

Then Mary saw that Ruthven was not alone. Behind him, through the narrow doorway she caught glimpses of Morton,

Lindsay, Kerr and others. Ruthven suddenly lifted his hand and pointed to David.

'Come out, David,' he said slowly. 'You are wanted without.'

David did not move. His great eyes seemed to have grown still larger; his trembling hand reached for the Queen's skirt.

Ruthven began to shout: 'Come out, David Rizzio. Come out from the Queen's chamber. You have been there too long.'

Mary stood up and confronted Ruthven. 'How dare you, my lord, thus come into my chamber? How dare you! You shall pay dearly for this. What means this intrusion? Who are those who follow you here? Why have you come?'

'We come for David Rizzio, Madam.'

'Then go away,' commanded the Queen. 'If David is here it is my wish that he should be.' She turned fiercely to Darnley: 'What means this outrage, my lord? Do you know aught of this?'

Darnley did not reply for a second or so. Then he mumbled: 'N . . . no. But it is a dishonour that David should sup with you, and your husband be kept out.'

Ruthven caught the hangings to prevent himself falling from exhaustion. Mary looked round at the terrified company. Catching her look, Erskine and the Laird of Creich started forward. Ruthven cried in a hollow voice: 'Let no one touch me. They will regret it.' He looked supernatural in that moment, and the two men stood where they were as though held there by Ruthven's uncanny powers.

Mary cried out: 'Leave at once! Go! I command you to go.'

'I have come for Rizzio,' persisted the grim-faced Ruthven. And with those words he unsheathed his dagger.

It was the signal. His accomplices rushed into the chamber.

Rizzio gave a great cry and, falling to the floor, gripped Mary's skirts and tried to hide himself in their folds. Dishes were swept aside; the table toppled over. The Countess of Argyle picked up the candelabra in time and held it high above her head.

Mary felt the child protest within her; nauseated, she tried not to faint. Rizzio was clinging to her and she made an effort to put herself between him and those men who, she knew, had come to kill him.

George Douglas had twisted Rizzio's arm so that, with a cry of pain, he released his grip on Mary's gown.

She saw their faces vaguely, distorted with blood lust, and the desire to kill not only Rizzio, she believed, but herself and the child she carried.

'Take the Queen,' someone said, and she saw Darnley close beside her. He put an arm about her and held her; she turned from him in revulsion just in time to see George Douglas snatch the dagger from Darnley's belt and drive it into the cowering, shrieking Rizzio.

Hands were clutching the terrified David who was bleeding from the wound. She watched him as they dragged him across the floor, and his terrified eyes never left her face. She stretched out her arms to him.

'Oh, Davie . . . Davie . . .' she sobbed. 'They are killing you, Davie. They are killing us both. Where are my friends? Is this the way to treat the Queen?'

'Be quiet!' hissed Kerr. 'If you are not, I shall be forced to cut you into collops.'

She could hear the shrieks in the next chamber to which they had dragged David; she heard the hideous thud of blows. She heard the death agonies of David.

'His blood shall cost you dear!' she cried; and she slid to the floor in a faint.

When Mary came out of the swoon she was aware of Darnley beside her, supporting her. For a moment she was uncertain what had happened to shock her so; then the sight of the room in the light from the candelabra showed her the upturned table, the spilled food and wine and the carpet soaked with David's blood.

She turned to Darnley and cried out in anguish: 'You are the cause of this. Why have you allowed this wicked deed to be done? I took you from low estate and made you my husband. What have I ever done that you should use me thus?'

'I will tell you, Madam,' cried Darnley. She saw his shifty bloodshot eyes; she smelt the wine on his breath and she knew he was not entirely sober. 'Since yonder fellow David came into credit and familiarity with you, you have had little time to spare for me. I have been shut from your thoughts and your chamber. You were with David far into the night'

'It was because you had failed me.'

'In what way? Am I failed in any sort in my body? There was a time when you were so eager for me that you came to my chamber. What disdain have you for me since you favoured David? What offence have I committed that you should be coy with me? You have listened to David and he spoke against me.'

'My lord, all that I have suffered this night is your doing, for the which I shall no longer be your wife, nor lie with you any more. I shall never rest content until I have made you suffer as you have made me suffer this night.'

She could not bear to look at him. She covered her face with her hands and wept bitterly.

Ruthven returned to the chamber.

He said: 'His lordship is Your Majesty's husband, and you must be dutiful one to the other.' As he spoke he sank into a chair from very exhaustion and called for wine to revive him.

Mary went to him and stood over him. 'My lord,' she cried, 'if my child or I should die through this night's work, you will not escape your just reward. I have powerful friends. There are my kinsmen of Lorraine; there is the Pope and the King of Spain. Do not think you shall escape justice.'

Ruthven grasped the cup which was offered to him. He smiled grimly as he said: 'Madam, these you speak of are over-great princes to concern themselves with such a poor man as myself.'

Mary stood back from him. She understood his meaning. He was implying that they were too great to concern themselves with the troubles of a Queen of a remote country, who could be of little use to them when her nobles had rendered her powerless.

Mary was seized with a great trembling then; for she realised that the folly of Darnley had, by this night's work, frustrated all her careful plans; all her triumphs of the last months were as nothing now.

Others were hurrying into the room. She saw the mighty figure of Bothwell among them, and her spirits lifted. Rogue he might be, but he was a loyal rogue. With him were Huntley and Maitland of whom she was not quite certain, but could not believe they were entirely against her.

Bothwell cried: 'What means this? Who dares lay hands on the Queen?' He seized Ruthven and pulled the dying man to his feet.

'What has been done has been done with the consent of the King,' said Ruthven. 'I have a paper here which bears his signature.'

Bothwell seized it. Mary watching saw the change in his expression and that of Huntley. They at least were outside this diabolical plot.

Morton, who was with them, cried: 'The palace is full of those who have had a share in this night's work.'

Mary's eyes were fixed on Bothwell, but at that moment there came a shouting from below. The townsfolk of Edinburgh had heard that something was amiss in the palace and had come demanding to see the Queen.

With a sob of relief Mary dashed to the window, but Kerr's strong arms were about her. She felt his sword pressed against her side while he repeated his threat to cut her into collops if she opened her mouth.

Ruthven signed to Darnley. 'To the window. Tell them that the Queen is well. Tell them that this is nothing but a quarrel among the French servants.'

'Henry!' cried Mary. 'Do no such thing.'

But Kerr's hand was over her mouth.

Darnley, alarmed and uncertain, looking from the Queen to Morton and his followers, seeing the murderous light in Morton's eyes, remembering the groaning, blood-spattered David, allowed himself to be led to the window.

'Good people,' he cried. 'There is naught wrong in the palace but some dispute among the French servants. 'Tis over now.'

He turned and looked at Mary's stricken face. This was the last act of treachery. He was completely against her now.

She looked for Bothwell and Huntley among those who had

filled the small chamber. They had disappeared. Maitland had left too. His loyalty was doubtful but she could have trusted his courtesy and gentleness.

She realised then that she was alone with her enemies. Nausea swept over her; the child leapt within her; and once again on that terrible night, she fell fainting to the floor.

❦ ❦ ❦

Through the long night she lay sleepless. What now? she asked herself.

There were only a few women in her bedchamber. One of these was old Lady Huntley – Bothwell's mother-in-law. The others had been appointed by her enemies, and her Maries were absent. There was no one to help her then.

She struggled up and Lady Huntley came to her.

'Where are my women?' she asked. 'I wish to get up immediately. I wish to leave the palace.'

'Your Majesty,' whispered Lady Huntley, 'that you cannot do. The palace is surrounded by the armed men of your enemies. My son and Lord Bothwell have left Edinburgh in haste. They could do nothing by staying. It would have been certain death. They were here alone, as you know, with few of their men and only a few servants to do their bidding.'

'So I am a prisoner here? But what of the people of Edinburgh? They will come to my assistance. I know it.'

'Your Majesty, they cannot do so. The King has issued a proclamation. He has dissolved Parliament and commanded all burgesses, prelates, peers and barons to leave Edinburgh immediately. The tocsins are sounding.'

'This is a terrible thing that has come upon me,' said Mary. 'Is there no man in Scotland on whom I can rely?'

'There are my son, Your Majesty, and my son-in-law.'

'They ran away, did they not, when they scented danger?'

'Only because they can serve you better alive than dead. They have hurried away to muster forces to come to your aid.'

'Many have deceived me,' said Mary. 'I trust no one.'

She turned wearily on her side and, being aware of the child, a sudden courage came to her, reminding her that it was not for herself alone she must fight.

The child! She would fight for the child. And in a flash of inspiration she realised that the child might give her the help she needed. They could not deny her a midwife, could they? They could be made to believe that the terrible events of last night had brought about a miscarriage.

She was excited now.

Who could help her in this? Lady Huntley. She was old but she could play her part. Who else ... when the palace was held by her enemies?

But there was one of uncertain loyalty. There was a foolish gullible one. There was one whose craven mind she understood – her husband, Lord Darnley.

She said to Lady Huntley: 'They cannot object to my seeing my husband, can they? Go at once and see if you can bring him to me. Tell him that he will find a submissive wife if he will but come to me.'

Darnley came, and as she looked at him, her hope sprang up afresh. He was afraid; he was afraid of her and he was afraid of the lords who – now that the murder was done and done in his name – had hinted that he would do as they bade him.

'My lord ...' said Mary, stretching out her hand.

He took it hesitantly.

'What is this terrible thing which has come between us?' she asked. 'What has made you take the side of my enemies against me?'

'It was David,' he said sullenly. 'David came between us. He has been your lover. Was I to endure that?'

'Henry, you have allowed these men to play you false. They have tricked you. You must see this now. How have they treated you since the deed was done? They command you to obey them. This was no murder of jealousy. This was a political murder. They wanted David out of the way because David knew how to make us great . . . *us*, you too, Henry . . . you who would have been my King. This was not done because you or they imagined David to be my lover. That was how they used you and how they will continue to use you if you allow them. They promised to make you King, but they will make you powerless. And when my brother returns, they will find some means of despatching *you* . . . as they have despatched David.'

Darnley's teeth began to chatter. He was wavering. When he listened to Morton he believed Morton; but now Mary's version of the motives of these men seemed plausible. They had ordered him to dismiss Parliament. Last night they had ordered him to speak to the people of Edinburgh. He had had no say in either matter. Already he could see the gleam in Ruthven's eyes; he could see Morton's tight, cruel lips sneering at him.

'It is my brother whom they will make their leader,' said Mary.

'He . . . he . . . is riding with all speed to Edinburgh,' stammered Darnley. 'He will be here . . . at any minute.'

'Then you will see how they will treat you. You will not live long to feel remorse for what you have done to David. My brother always hated you. It was because I wished to marry you that he went into exile. We defeated him then; that was because we stood together. Now you have gone over to our enemies who seek to destroy me, our child and you too, Henry. You will not escape. Indeed you will be the first whom they will despatch. Who knows, they may let me live on as their prisoner.'

'Do not speak so . . . do not speak so. Do you realise that they are all about us? There are armed men everywhere.'

'Henry, consider this: Help me, and I will help you. You and I must stand together. We must find some way of getting out of here.'

Lady Huntley had come into the room. She said: 'Madam, forgive me for breaking in on you thus, but I thought you would wish to know that your brother, the Earl of Moray, has arrived at the palace.'

Darnley and Lady Huntley had left her, and her brother would be with her at any moment now. Lady Huntley had given her a message brought by one of Bothwell's men and smuggled in to her. It was the most comforting thing that had happened for many terrible hours.

'Do not despair,' was the message. 'Do not think Bothwell and Huntley have deserted Your Majesty. They left Holyrood in order to gather forces to come to your aid. Bothwell will soon have a Lowland force ready to fight for you; Huntley too will be there with his Highlanders.'

The message went on to say that it was imperative for her to leave the palace as soon as this could be arranged, and Bothwell was forming a plan whereby she would be lowered over the walls by ropes to where he would be waiting for her with horses.

She laid her hands on her heavy body. Bothwell seemed to think she was a hardy adventurer like himself, instead of a woman, six months pregnant. Lowered over walls in her condition! It was impossible.

Still, it was gratifying to know that outside these walls her friends were making plans for her safety.

Nevertheless she must find some way to escape from the palace. She must do it, not by following Bothwell's wild suggestion, but in a subtler manner; her plan was already beginning to take shape.

Her brother came into the apartment at that moment. He knelt before her. He lifted his face to hers and there were tears in his eyes when he embraced her.

'Dear Jamie,' she said.

'My dearest sister, I blame myself for this terrible thing. I should never have left you. Brothers and sisters should not quarrel. Had I been at hand I should never have allowed you to suffer so.'

Those tears in his eyes seemed to be of real emotion, but she was not so foolish as she had once been. Did he really believe that she did not know he had been in the plot to kill Rizzio? Did he really believe that she did not understand that he had returned to Scotland to wrest her power from her and take it to himself? It was with pleasure that she would deceive him now as he had so often deceived her.

'Jamie,' she said, 'you see me a sick woman. My child was to have been born three months from now.'

'*Was* to have been born?'

'I am in such pain, Jamie . . . such terrible pain. I fear a miscarriage.'

'But this is more terrible than anything that has happened.'

'You see, Jamie, they have so far taken only my faithful secretary. Now they will take my child as well.'

'You are sure of this?'

She put her hand to her side and groped her way to the bed. Moray was beside her. He put his arm about her.

'Jamie, you will not let them deny me a midwife?'

'No . . . no . . . certainly you must have a midwife.'

'And . . . Jamie . . . it distresses me . . . all these men about me . . . at such a time. I . . . in my state . . . to have soldiers at my door. Jamie, look at me. How *could* I escape in this condition? How could I?'

'I will have a midwife sent to you.'

'I have already asked my woman to bring one. See that she is not kept back, I beg of you.'

Mary turned her head away and groaned. She was enjoying her triumph; she had successfully deceived her brother.

She gripped his hand. 'And . . . the men-at-arms . . . they distress me so. I . . . a Queen in my own palace . . . a poor sick woman . . . a dying woman . . . to be so guarded. Jamie, it is mayhap my last request to you.'

'No . . . no. You will soon be better. Dearest sister, I will do all that you ask. I will have the midwife sent to you as soon as she comes. I will see what may be done about clearing the staircases about your apartments.'

'Thank you, Jamie. This would not have happened, would it, had you been here? Oh, what a sad thing it is when a brother and sister fall out. In future, brother, we must understand each other . . . if I live through this.'

'You shall live, and in future there shall be understanding between us. You will be guided by me.'

'Yes, Jamie. How glad I am that you are back!'

The 'midwife' had come. She was a servant of the Huntleys and knew that her task was not to deliver a stillborn child but to take charge of letters the Queen had written and see that they were despatched with all speed to Lords Huntley and Bothwell.

Moray and Morton had decided that if Darnley would stay in the Queen's bedchamber all night the guards about her apartments could be withdrawn. They trusted Darnley, and in any case the Queen was considered far too sick to leave her bed.

In the evening all the lords retired from the palace to Douglas House, the home of Morton, which was but a short step from the palace. There they could feast and talk of the success of their schemes and make future plans.

As soon as they had gone and the sentries had been withdrawn, Mary rose and dressed hastily. Darnley had changed sides completely now that she had inspired him with fear and had promised him a return to her favour. After the child was born they would live as husband and wife again. He had learned a bitter lesson, Mary said; she hoped that in future they would trust each other.

She had satisfied him that the lords who held them prisoners represented but a small proportion of the population. Had he forgotten what had happened when they had married and Moray had believed he would raise all Scotland against her! Who had mustered the stronger force then! She assured him that all he had to do was escape with her from the palace and join Bothwell and Huntley, who were mustering their forces at this very time. Darnley would be a fool if he did not join her, for her friends would have no mercy on him if he did not. Those with whom he had temporarily cast in his lot would have no further use for him either.

So, trembling, Darnley agreed to deceive the lords, who were feasting and congratulating themselves in Douglas House; he would escape with Mary from Holyrood and ride away.

'Now,' said the Queen.

She was wrapped in a heavy cloak. She stood up firmly. The child was quiet now; it was almost as though it shared the suspense.

'Down the back staircase,' said Mary. 'Through the pantries and the kitchens where the French are. The French will not betray us . . . even if they see us. We can rely on their friendship.'

With wildly beating hearts they crept down the narrow staircase, through the kitchens and underground passages to one of the pantries, the door of which opened on to the burial ground.

Darnley gasped. 'Not that way!' he cried.

'Where else?' demanded Mary contemptuously. 'Will you come or will you stay behind to share David's fate?'

Darnley still hesitated, his face deathly pale in the moon-light. He was terrified of going on, yet he had no alternative but to follow her, and as he stumbled forward he all but fell into a newly-made grave.

He shrieked, and Mary turned to bid him be silent.

'Jesus!' she cried, looking down into the grave. 'It is David who lies there.'

Darnley's limbs trembled so that he could not proceed. 'It's an omen!' he whispered.

In that moment Mary seemed to see anew the terrified eyes of David as he had been dragged across the floor. Angrily she turned on her husband: 'Mayhap it is,' she said. 'Mayhap David watches us now . . . and remembers . . .'

'No . . . no . . .' groaned Darnley. ''Twas no fault of mine . . .'

'This is not the time,' said Mary, turning and hurrying forward.

He followed her across the grisly burial ground, picking his way between the tombs and shuddering as he caught glimpses of half buried coffins.

On the far edge of the burial ground Erskine was waiting with horses. Silently they mounted, Mary riding pillion with Erskine.

'Make haste!' cried Darnley, now longing above all things to put as great a distance as possible between himself and the grim graveyard. He imagined David's ghost had been startled from his grave and caused him to stumble there. Terror overwhelmed him – terror of the dead and of the living.

They rode on through the quiet night, but Erskine's horse with its royal burden could not make the speed which Darnley wanted.

'Hasten, I say!' he cried impatiently. ''Tis dangerous to delay.'

'My lord, I dare not,' said Erskine.

'There is the child to consider,' cried Mary. 'We go as fast as is safe for it.'

'They'll murder us if they catch us, you fools!' cried Darnley.

'I would rather be murdered than kill our child.'

'In God's name that's folly. What is one child? If it should die this night, there'll be others to replace it. Come on, man. Come on, I say. Or I'll have you clapped in jail as soon as we are out of this.'

Mary said: 'Heed him not. I would have you think of the child.'

'Yes, Madam,' said Erskine.

Darnley shouted: 'Then tarry and be murdered. I'll not.'

And with that he whipped up his horse and went ahead with all speed, so that soon he was lost to sight.

Mary felt the tears smarting in her eyes, but they were tears of shame for the man she had married. She was not afraid any more. In moments such as this one, when she was threatened with imminent danger, she felt a noble courage rise within her. It was at such times that she felt herself to be a queen in very truth. She had duped Darnley; she had lured him to desert her enemies. She had foiled the plots of Moray and the scheming Morton. Once again, she believed, she had saved her crown.

Oh, but the humiliation of owning that foolish boy for a husband! For that she could die of shame. He was not only a fool; he was a coward.

How she wished that he could have been a strong man, a brave man on whom she could rely. Then she would not have cared what misfortunes befell them; they would have faced them and conquered them together.

After many hours in the saddle, just as the dawn was

breaking, Erskine called to her that they could not be far from the safety of Dunbar Castle.

A short while after, he told her that he saw riders. Mary raised her weary eyelids. One man had ridden ahead of the rest. He brought his horse alongside that which carried the Queen. She looked with relief and admiration at his man who reminded her, by the very contrast, of the husband whom she despised.

She greeted him: 'I was never more glad to see you, Lord Bothwell.'

🌼 Chapter X 🌼

T he June night was hot and the Queen lay tossing on her bed. She had suffered much during the last months, but now her greatest ordeal was upon her.

Her women were waiting now, and she knew that they did not expect her to leave her bed alive.

She was weary. Since the death of David she had become increasingly aware of the villainies of those about her; she could put no great trust in anyone. Even now, in the agony of a woman in childbirth who has suffered a painful pregnancy, she could not dismiss from her mind the thought of those hard, relentless men. Ruthven was dead; he had died in exile; but his son would be a trouble-maker like his father. Morton, Lindsay, George Douglas, Boyd, Argyle were all traitors. Moray, her own brother, she knew, had been privy to the plot, and the plot had been not only to murder David Rizzio, but to destroy her. Maitland of Lethington – her finest statesman, a man whose services she needed, a man who had always shown a gentle courtesy which she had not often received from others – was of doubtful loyalty. He had fled to the Highlands with Atholl – surely a proof that he was not without guilt.

These men were dangerous, but there was one, the thought of whom depressed her so much that she felt she would welcome death. Why had she married Darnley whom she was beginning to hate more than she had believed it was possible to hate anyone?

He was loyal to nobody. He betrayed all those with whom he had worked against David. Now he was in a state of torment lest she pardon those lords who were in exile and they return to take their revenge on one who had turned informer. He sulked and raged in turn; he whimpered and blustered; he cringed and demanded his rights. She could not bear him near her.

It was an unhealthy state of affairs. It was true that with the followers mustered by Huntley and Bothwell she had returned triumphant to Edinburgh, and the lords responsible for Rizzio's murder – with the exception of Moray who, she must feign to believe, was innocent of complicity – had all hastened to hide themselves. Some minor conspirators had been hanged, drawn and quartered – a proceeding which she deplored for its injustice, but which she was powerless to prevent. Bothwell was in command and, although he was the bravest man in Scotland, as a statesman he could not measure up to Maitland or Moray.

So she made her will and thought of death without any great regret.

She had failed; she saw that now. If only she could go back one year; if only she could go back to the July day when she had walked into the chapel of Holyroodhouse and joined her future fortunes with those of Darnley! How differently she would act and how different her life might consequently be!

She would have come to understand that she could have rallied her people to her and deprived her brother of his power.

She had to be strong, but there was this terrible burden to hinder her; she had married the most despicable man in Scotland and he had all but ruined her.

But now the pains were on her and it was as though a curtain was drawn, shutting out those grim faces which tormented her; but the curtain was made of pain.

Between bouts of pain she noticed that her dear ones were about her. There was Beaton who suffered with her. Poor Beaton! Thomas Randolph had been sent back to England in disgrace, for he had been discovered to be trafficking with the rebels and exposed – not only as a spy for his mistress, which was understandable – but as one who worked against the Queen with her Scottish enemies. Poor Beaton! thought Mary. Like myself she is unlucky where she has placed her affections. There was dear Flem on the other side of her – heartbroken because Maitland had fled from the Court. Sempill was in disgrace and dearest Livy was with him.

But for the murder of David they would all be happy. And but for Darnley's treachery David would be alive now.

I hate the father of this child! reflected Mary. Evil things are said of me. There is doubtless whispering in the corridors now. Who is the father of the Prince or Princess who is about to be born – Darnley or David? Who is it – the King or the Secretary? That was what people were asking one another.

Darnley might be with them when they whispered, and it would depend on his mood of the moment whether he defended or defamed her.

'Why did I marry such a man?' she asked herself. Now that I am near dying I know that I can only wish to live if he should be taken from me.

Beaton was putting a cup to her lips.

'Beaton . . .' began Mary.

'Do not speak, dearest,' said Beaton. 'It exhausts you. Save your strength for the child.'

Save your strength for the child! Do not fritter away your strength in hating the child's father.

There came to her then that strength which never failed her in moments of peril. She battled her way through pain.

At last, from what seemed far away, she heard the cry of a child.

Mary Beaton was excitedly running from the apartment crying: 'It is over. All is well. The Queen is delivered of a fair son.'

❀ ❀ ❀

Her son was born – that child who, she prayed would unite her tortured land with the kingdom beyond the Border; for she knew that there could be no real peace between them until they were joined as one country under one sovereign. Her kingdom must be held for him as well as for herself.

There was one thing she must make sure of immediately. It should not be said that this little James Stuart was a bastard. Rumours of bastardy meant trouble in the life of a would-be king.

Already she had noticed the scrutiny of those who studied the baby. She saw the faint twitch of the lips, the appraising gaze. Now who does he resemble? Is it Darnley? Are his eyes particularly large? I wonder if he will be a skilled musician?

Her first task was not a pleasant one. She must feign friendship with her husband. She must not allow him to pour poison into people's ears, for he would do that even though it was clear that by so doing he injured himself.

She called Darnley to her in the presence of all the people who crowded the chamber and said in a loud voice: 'My lord, you have come to see our child. Look into his bonny face. God has blessed you and me with a son, and this son is begotten by none but you.'

Darnley bent over the child. She was implying that she knew what slander had been spread. He was afraid of her and all that she could do to punish him. He was afraid of those lords who were implicated in the Rizzio plot. They were now in exile, but once let them return, and he feared that his position would be as perilous as David's had been. He was uncertain how to act. At times he felt he must cringe before his wife; at others he wished to show that he cared nothing for her; but when she confronted him with a serious matter such as this, he was always at a loss.

Mary looked from her husband, who had bent over the child, to those lords who stood by watching. She said in a loud ringing voice: 'I swear before God, as I shall answer to Him on the day of judgement, that this is your son and that of no other man. I wish all gentlemen and ladies here to mark my words. I say – and God bear me witness – that this child is so much your son that I fear the worse for him.'

She turned to the nobleman nearest her bed.

'I hope,' she said, 'that this child will unite two kingdoms, my own and that of England, for I hold that only in such union can peace be established between the two countries.'

'Let us hope,' said Moray, 'that the child will inherit these two kingdoms after yourself. You could not wish him to succeed before his mother and father.'

'His father has broken with me,' said Mary sadly.

Darnley stuttered: 'You cannot say that! You swore that all

should be forgiven and forgotten, that it should be between us as it was in the beginning.'

'I may have forgiven,' said Mary, 'but how can I forget? Your accomplices would have done me to death, remember . . . and not only me . . . but this child you now see before you.'

'But that is all over now.'

'It is all over and I am tired. I wish to be left alone with my son.'

She turned wearily from him, and silently the lords and ladies filed out of the bedchamber.

While Mary slept the whispering continued through the castle.

She had sworn that Darnley was the father. Would she have sworn that if it were not true? Would she have called God to witness if David had been the father?

Surely not, for her condition was not a healthy one; and the chances that she would die were great.

But whatever was said in the Castle of Edinburgh, and whatever was said in the streets of the capital, there would always be those to ask themselves – Who is the father of the Prince – Darnley or David?

She had two objects in life now – to care for her baby and to escape from her husband. He was constantly beside her – pleading, threatening. He was no longer indifferent. He fervently wished to be her husband in fact. She must not lock him from her bedchamber, he cried. She must not set guards at the door for fear he tried to creep on her unaware.

He would cry before her, thumping his fists on his knees like a spoiled child. 'Why should I be denied your bed? Am I not your husband? What did you promise me when you persuaded me to fly with you? You said we should be together. And it was all lies . . . lies to make me the enemy of Morton and Ruthven. You took their friendship from me and gave me nothing in return.'

'I give nothing for nothing,' she said contemptuously. 'They never had any friendship for you.'

'You are cruel . . . cruel. Who is your lover now? A woman like you must have a lover. Do not imagine I shall not discover who he is.'

'You know nothing of me,' she told him. 'But learn this one thing and learn it for all time. I despise you. You nauseate me. I would rather have a toad in my bed than you.'

'It was not always so. Nor would it be so. How have I changed? There was a time when you could scarcely wait for me. Do not think I do not remember how eager you were . . . more eager than I.'

'That is done with. I do not excuse my own folly. I merely tell you that I now see you as you really are, and I shudder to have you near me.'

These quarrels were the talk of the Court. Darnley himself made no secret of them. When he was drunk he would grow maudlin over his memories. He would confide in his companions details of the Queen's passion which had now turned to loathing. Sometimes he wanted to kill somebody . . . anybody. He wanted to kill Bothwell who was now high in the Queen's favour, and had been since the death of David. Some said that Bothwell would take David's place; and it did seem that the Earl was more arrogant than ever. Some said Moray would be the one to take David's place. The Queen did not trust him, but his standing in the country was firm.

Darnley was afraid of Bothwell. The Earl had a habit of inviting his enemies to single combat, so Darnley shifted his gaze from Bothwell to Moray. Moray was a statesman rather than a fighter. Darnley felt that in single combat he would be better matched with Moray than with Bothwell.

He began to brood on the influence Moray had with the Queen; he remembered that Moray had been against the marriage in the first place.

He burst in on Mary one evening in August and cried out that he was tired of being left out of affairs, and he would no longer stand by and allow insults to be heaped upon him.

Mary took little notice of such outbursts. She was playing chess with Beaton, and went on with the game.

Darnley kicked a stool across the apartment.

'Your move, Beaton,' said Mary.

'Listen to me!' roared Darnley.

Mary said: 'I've got you, I think, Beaton my dear. Two moves back you had a chance.'

'Stop it!' cried Darnley. 'Stop ignoring me. Come here. Come here at once. I tell you, I'm tired of being treated thus. You will come with me now . . . and we will resume our normal relations . . .'

'Will you leave this apartment,' said the Queen, rising from the chess-table, 'or shall I have you forcibly removed?'

'Listen to me. If it were not for my enemies I should have my rights. I should be King of this realm. I should be master in our apartments. I would not allow you to turn me out . . .'

'Oh dear,' sighed Mary, 'this is very tiresome. We have heard all this before, and we are weary of the repetition.'

There was one thing which infuriated him beyond endurance, and that was not to be treated seriously. He drew his sword and cried: 'Ere long you will see that I am not ineffectual. When I bring you your brother's bleeding head, you will know what I mean. He is against me. He always has been. I am going to kill Moray. I shall waste no more time.' With that he rushed from the room.

Mary sat down and buried her face in her hands. 'I can't help it,' she sobbed. 'He fills me with such shame. I wish to God I had never seen him. I would to God someone would rid me of him. Beaton . . . I doubt that he will attempt anything, but go at once to my brother and tell him in my name what he has said. He had better be warned for if aught happened to James it would doubtless be said that I had had a hand in it.'

Mary Beaton hurried to do her bidding while Mary sat back and stared helplessly at the chessboard. She might pretend indifference to him, but how could she be indifferent? All that he did humiliated her beyond expression. Oh God, she thought, how I hate him!

Moray knew well how to deal with Darnley and his folly.

Calmly he summoned Darnley to appear before him and a company of the most important of the lords at the Court. Darnley, afraid to refuse to appear, went reluctantly and was put through an examination by Moray himself who forced him to confess that he had uttered threats against him. Darnley blustered and denied this, until witnesses were brought who had overheard his words to the Queen.

Always at a loss in a crisis Darnley lied and blustered and was easily proved to be both lying and blustering. He looked at the cold faces of his accusers and knew that they were his enemies . . . He broke down and sobbed out that everyone was against him.

Had he spoken threats against Moray? they insisted.

Yes . . . yes . . . he had, and they all hated him; they were all jealous of him because the Queen had chosen to marry him; and although she appeared to hate him now, once it had been a very different story.

'I must ask you,' said Moray, 'to withdraw those threats and to swear before these gentlemen that you will not attempt to murder either me or any of those whom you believe to be your enemies. If you will not do this, it will be necessary to place you under arrest immediately.'

He was beaten and he knew it. They were too clever for him. He had to submit. He had to ask Moray's pardon; he had to swear not to be foolish again.

They despised him; they had made that clear. They did not think it worth while to arrest him; they did not want to punish him; they merely wished to make him look a fool.

❀ ❀ ❀

Mary was able to forget her unhappiness for a time. Something rather pleasant had happened. Her dear Beaton, after being miserable on the banishment of Randolph, had fallen in love.

Mary was happy about this. It seemed a charming solution to something which had worried her. She wished she could have overlooked Randolph's perfidy for the sake of poor Beaton. But that could not be, and the man had had to go; but now Beaton was in love again and this time it was with Alexander Ogilvie of Boyne.

This was a particularly happy state of affairs, for Mary had given her consent to the marriage of Bothwell with Jean

Gordon, and Jean Gordon had once been promised to this very Alexander Ogilvie. He must have recovered from the loss of Jean, for now he seemed eager to marry Mary Beaton.

She told Bothwell of this. 'I am so happy about it. Mary Beaton is such a charming girl, and I am glad to see her so happy. I shall have the marriage contract drawn up at once.'

'I see, Madam,' said Bothwell. 'Was this Ogilvie not the man to whom my wife was once promised?'

'Did you not remember then? It is the very same. Ah, my lord, I expect you have made dear Jean forget she ever had a fancy for this man.'

She wondered how Jean enjoyed being married to the man. She had heard rumours that he had not mended his ways since marriage. But, she thought comfortably, Jean would know how to deal with trouble of that sort.

She gave herself up to the pleasure of preparing for Beaton's marriage. There was one who was a little saddened by the prospect of another marriage. Poor Flem! Maitland was still in exile. Flem talked of him, often pointing out to the Queen that he was her best statesman, demanding to know if it was not folly to keep in exile a great man whose one desire was to work for his Queen.

'Dear Flem,' said Mary, 'I can understand your feelings. Maitland *is* charming and clever. I know that. But if he were not involved in the murder of poor David, why did he find it necessary to go away?'

'Madam, he knew that Bothwell was his enemy and he also knew that you trusted Bothwell more than any man.'

'Happily would I have trusted Maitland if he would have allowed me to.'

'Dearest, you could trust him. He is your loyal subject and

you need him. You know that none has his subtle cleverness. You know he is the greatest statesman in this country.'

'I believe you are right in that, Flem.'

'Then, dear Madam, forgive him – if there is anything to forgive. Recall him. You know that he was no friend to Morton and Ruthven. Oh, it is true that he did not care for David. Remember he was your first minister, before David took his place in your trust. And why did David take his place? Only because Lord Maitland was doing you good service in England, to which country you sent him knowing that he could serve you at the English Court more wisely than any of your subjects.'

'You are a good advocate, Flem, and I will think about it. I believe it is very likely that I shall recall the fellow.'

'Dearest . . .'

'Oh, I do not think that he is without blame. But you must keep him in order if I allow him to return, and you must warn him that he must be as faithful to me as his wife is, and that it is due to my love for her that I pass over his disaffection.'

Flem kissed her mistress's hand and went on kissing it.

Bothwell heard rumours that Maitland was about to be recalled. He cursed aloud. He did not like Maitland. The suave courtier was too cunning for him. He feared that if Maitland returned to Court it would not be long – with the influence of Mary Fleming – before some charge would be raked up against Bothwell which might result in his falling from the Queen's favour. He did not forget Maitland's share in bringing about his exile from the Court. He also suspected Maitland had played some part – though perhaps a small one – in the plot to

404

poison him. They were natural enemies, and he must do all he could to prevent his return to Court.

He wondered how he should proceed. What he needed was a secret audience with the Queen. He decided that if he could only be alone with her, he could talk more freely and make his arguments more plausible without interruption. The Queen was but a lass, in his opinion – rather emotional and sentimental. He believed that if he could explain how Maitland had always been his enemy, how the fellow had not always been a faithful supporter of the Queen, how he, Bothwell, had never once failed her when danger threatened, there might yet be time to dissuade her from bringing Maitland back to Court.

He knew that in a few days the Queen would be going to the Exchequer House – a small dwelling in Edinburgh which was next to one occupied by a man who had been a servant of his. To this small house Mary was going to check some of her accounts and make arrangements for the clothes which would be needed for her son's christening. She wanted to be alone for a few days – apart from an attendant woman and one servant – so that she could not only go into this matter of accounts but come to a decision as to who should be given guardianship of the young Prince.

Everything seemed to be working in Bothwell's favour. He believed that at the Exchequer House it would not be a difficult matter to obtain a private interview with Mary.

He would not ask for it in case it should be denied to him. Mary would guess what he wished to say and, characteristically, would not wish him to say it. Doubtless Mary Fleming had swayed her one way, and she would be afraid that he would attempt to sway her another. Mary would wish to please them both and, since she could not in this instance give him his wish, she would do all in her power to avoid seeing him.

He understood her very well – a sentimental lassie who was no match for the wily wolves who prowled about her. Therefore she should have a private interview with him, not knowing that it would take place until it was forced upon her. For his purpose she could not have chosen to go to a better place than the Exchequer House – indeed this idea would not have come to him had she not been going there.

David Chambers, who had been one of his superior servants, was the man who lived next door to the Exchequer House; and the gardens of these two houses were separated by a high wall, but in this high wall was a door which made it easy to pass from one to the other. David Chambers had done good service to his master, and Bothwell had rewarded him well. Many a woman had entertained Bothwell at the house of Chambers; and if Bothwell desired to meet a certain woman he merely told Chambers this, and Chambers arranged a meeting. Chambers' house had proved for some time a useful place of assignation.

Moreover the two servants who were with the Queen at the Exchequer House were the Frenchman, Bastian, and Lady Reres. Bastian need not be considered; he would be lodged in the lower part of the house. As for Lady Reres, by great good fortune, she had been Margaret Beaton, sister to Janet, and on his visits to Janet there had been times when – perhaps he had called unexpectedly – only Margaret had been there to entertain him. Margaret, who was very like her sister, had proved an excellent substitute, a sensible creature, ready for the fun of the moment and not one to bear a grudge. Women, such as the Beaton sisters, were the best friends a man could have.

Passionate women, such as Anna Throndsen, could cause a great deal of trouble. He was thankful now that Anna had gone back to Denmark, leaving their son behind to be cared for by his mother's servants. But he need not think of Anna now. All he need concern himself with was the fact that Margaret Beaton, now Lady Reres, was to be the lady-in-waiting to the Queen in the small house, and that he had easy access to that house through his servant David Chambers.

It was all very easy to arrange. He went through the door in the wall and asked Bastian to bring Lady Reres to him and to keep his coming a secret. Lady Reres soon appeared. She was heartily glad – and very amused – to see him.

She wanted to know what devilment he planned.

'Merely to see the Queen. A matter of some importance. What I want is a secret interview and do not think I can get it when she is living in state. So I chose this time when she is living here in seclusion for a few days. Margaret, could you take me to her?'

'I will ask if she will see you.'

'That will not do. She will say no. She will send for her ministers or her courtiers or someone. This is a secret matter, and I wish none to hear it but herself.'

'My lord, you ask too much.'

'Not from you, Margaret.' He pushed her playfully against the wall. 'Remember the good times we had?'

'Well, they are over,' said plump Lady Reres with a laugh.

'Never to be forgotten by either of us.'

'Why should you choose to remember me out of the six thousand . . . or have I been niggardly in the counting?'

'I have not kept the score, but you are one I remember well.'

Lady Reres laughed again. 'I would, of course, help you all

I could. But how can I let you into her apartment? I tell you she is alone here, apart from myself and Bastian. What will she say to me when she knows I have allowed you to come in?'

'She need not know. You need not let me in. But leave her alone after supper this evening and leave the door open. I will slip up by the back stairs. You will be discussing next day's supper with Bastian in the lower part of the house and thus not hear me.'

'We are responsible for the safety of the Queen.'

'Do you think I would hurt the Queen? I tell you it is a matter of great importance . . . a state matter. It is imperative that I see her . . . for her sake as well as mine. Now, will you keep my secret? Say nothing to her, leave her after supper, and see that the way is clear for me.'

'I don't like it.'

'But you will do it for an old friend?'

'I know nothing of it, remember.'

'Why, bless you, Meggie, you know nothing of it. The fault will all be due to my boldness.'

He gave her a loud kiss of gratitude, and she went away thinking of him nostalgically as he used to be in the old days when he came to see Janet. He had changed, she supposed. He was more interested in state matters. His marriage had mayhap sobered him. Ah! They had been good times. She felt young again thinking of them.

The Queen had supped in her small bedchamber and the remains of the meal were still on the table. She was very tired and glad to be alone, free from ceremony for a few days.

She was wearing a velvet robe – loose fitting – and her

chestnut hair hung loose for the weather was warm. It was a comfort to be able to dress thus.

Suddenly she heard a step on the stair. It must be Margaret returning. She was thinking: We shall be leaving here perhaps the day after to-morrow, but there is still another day in which to live quietly.

The door opened and she started up in amazement, for Lord Bothwell was standing on the threshold.

'Lord Bothwell!' she cried.

'Yes, Madam.' He bowed.

'How did you get in here? Why did you not give notice of your coming?'

'I will explain,' he said.

She was angry because now in this small room in this small house his arrogance seemed more in evidence than ever.

'I wish to hear no explanations,' she said. 'I will call Bastian to show you out.'

He did not move. He stood by the door as though barring her way.

'Lord Bothwell,' she said, 'what is the meaning of this?'

He did not speak. He was looking at her flushed face, her disordered hair. He was looking at her as he had never looked before. In that moment she was afraid of him. She would have pushed past him, but he caught her. His grip hurt her and she cried out, trying to twist her arm free.

She stammered: 'This . . . this unwarranted . . . insolence . . . How . . . how dare you! You will suffer for this.'

He had gripped her by the shoulders and bent her backward.

'Shall I?' he said. His eyes were glazed; they looked dazzling in his sunburned weather-beaten face. 'Then there shall be something worth suffering for.'

'You come here,' she panted. 'You come in . . . unannounced
. . . Release me at once. You shall pay dearly for this.'

Bothwell was the Borderer now; the statesman had fled. He
had forgotten that he had come to talk about Maitland. He had
been in situations of a similar nature before. He had felt this
wild excitement, this demand for satisfaction at all costs. But
this was different; this was piquant; this was more exciting than
those other occasions. Many women had partnered Bothwell in
such scenes, but never a Queen before this.

He cared for nothing now but the surrender of the woman.
If it meant death, it must go on now. It was the first time he had
seen her, stripped of her royalty. It was the first time he had
discovered what a very desirable woman she was.

He pulled her towards him and roughly caressed her body.
Mary was trembling with rage and sobbing with terror. She
knew that this encounter had cast its warning over her many a
time. It was the meaning of those insolent looks. He would
treat her now as he would any peasant over the Border. He
cared nothing for the fact that she was the Queen. There was
only one thing that was of importance to him; the satisfaction
of his vile nature.

She kicked and tried to bite. It was all she could do for she
was pinioned. He had turned and, holding her firmly with one
arm, locked the door.

She stammered: 'This . . . this . . . outrage . . . It is the most
monstrous thing that ever happened to me . . .'

'It will also be the most enjoyable,' he said.

'You will lose your head for this.'

'No,' he said. 'You have never had a lover yet, my Queen.
Wait . . . have patience . . . Don't fight . . . and then the sooner
will you come to pleasure.'

He had torn the robe from her shoulder. She was conscious of her weakness compared with his great strength. He lifted her in his arms then as though he read her thoughts and would stress the fact that she was impotent to resist him.

'It is no use screaming,' he said. 'No one will hear. They'll not break the door down if they do. How could they? Poor Bastian! That feeble Frenchman? Fat Margaret? Have no fear. None shall disturb us.'

'You have gone mad,' she said.

'It *is* a temporary madness, they say.'

'You forget . . . I am the Queen.'

'Let us both forget it. Queens should not bring their royalty to the bedchamber.'

'Put me down. I command you. I beg you.'

'I mean to . . . here on your bed.'

He put her on to it. She tried to scramble up but he had forced her down. She struggled until she was exhausted. The room was spinning round her. She thought afterwards that she fainted for a while. She was not sure. She was aware of his heart and hers beating together . . . heavy, ominous beating.

She had no strength left to hold him off. She lay passive without resistance, without resentment or anger. There was nothing but this extraordinary, overwhelming emotion – this mingling of fury and pleasure, of a terrible shame and an unaccountable joy.

She lay on her bed long after he had gone.

What has happened to me? she asked herself. Why do I not send for Moray? Why do I not order the immediate arrest of Lord Bothwell? On what charge? The rape of the Queen?

She remembered that she would present a strange sight if Lady Reres came to the room. She got up from her bed. She gazed at her torn clothes which he had thrown on to the floor. How explain them? But they would be part of the evidence she would need to bring him to the scaffold. The rape of the Queen! She could hear the words now. She could hear John Knox thundering them from his pulpit. He would say that she had encouraged Bothwell. 'No,' she said aloud as if in answer to his imagined accusation. 'It is not true. I always disliked him. Now I hate him. How dared he? The shame of it . . . the shame of it!'

She could not shut it out of her mind. Every detail was clear in her memory. His face . . . his eyes . . . his hands, tearing her clothes.

'He forced me,' she murmured. 'He dared . . . and I the Queen! By now he will be speeding for the Border. He will be terrified of the punishment, which can be nothing less than death.'

She took the torn clothes and hid them in a closet. She could not bear that anyone else should see the shameful evidence. Hastily she wrapped a damask robe around her, and smoothed her wild hair. Now she felt a little calmer. There were still red patches on her face, on her neck and her body. She touched her left cheek gently. Would those marks never go?

She began to pace up and down the apartment. The Queen who was dishonoured! The Queen who was defiled! He had planned this thing. He had known that she would be here. Moray had said once that David Chambers was his procurer and was known as 'Bothwell's Bawd'. David Chambers brought women to his house and Bothwell went there to visit them. So Chambers had procured the Queen for Bothwell. He would have lent his house for the purpose. Bothwell had clearly come from Chambers' house and, because she was ill-guarded, he had found a way to her apartment.

She would never be able to look the man in the face again. Indeed she would not need to. He would be imprisoned at once and hurried to execution. He should not live to gloat over his conquest. But how could she proclaim the crime to the world? She pictured herself telling Moray. 'He came to my room. I could not hold him off. He forced me . . .' She imagined the smiles, the whispers. 'Why did the Queen go to the Exchequer House? Oh, 'tis next door to David Chambers' and he is Bothwell's Bawd.'

'What shall I do?' she whispered to herself. 'What can I do?' Lady Reres came up to the room. She could reprimand the woman. She had been careless. She and Bastian must have left some door unlatched. But how could she talk to Lady Reres of what had happened? How could she talk of that terrible thing at all?

'Are you disturbed, Madam?' asked Lady Reres.

'Disturbed?' cried the Queen. 'No . . . no. I am feeling tired. I think . . . that I am a little unwell. I feel coming on one of those attacks which I had so often when I was in France.'

'Should I send for a physician, Your Majesty?'

'No . . . no. Rest will suffice. Leave me. I will go to bed. Rest is what I need. I do not wish to be disturbed. Oh . . . but . . . sleep here to-night. I . . . I have a fancy not to be left alone this night.'

Lady Reres drew the curtains and the long night began. She did not sleep at all. She lived through it all again. The opening of the door . . . every detail until that moment when she had found herself alone with her shame and that excitement which made her heart thunder till her body was shaking.

She returned to Holyroodhouse next day. She could not bear to stay in the Exchequer House, although she had not finished the work she had gone there to do.

Bothwell had the effrontery to wait upon her with the other noblemen of the Court.

As he knelt before her, her heart thundered. He had raised his insolent eyes to her face, and his smile was conspiratorial, as though they had shared a charming adventure together.

Her lips kindled; her temper flared and impulsive words rose to her lips.

Arrest that man! she wanted to say, and was almost on the point of doing so. In time she pictured the ensuing scene. Moray would ask: 'On what grounds, Madam?' 'On the grounds of rape.' 'The rape of whom, Madam?' 'The rape of the Queen.'

There was nothing she could do unless she would expose herself to greater humiliation, and the cunning rogue, the violator of the innocent, knew it. She was conquered in her own Court as she had been in her bedchamber. She dared say nothing. She was afraid. That was the truth. She could not publicly own to her shame. She dared not face the calumnies of Knox. Consequently it seemed that he who had committed this great sin would go unpunished.

But she would find other ways to make him suffer for what he had done. She would find some way of banishing him from the Court, for his presence there would be a constant reminder.

Even now she could not prevent her thoughts from going over and over what had happened on that night.

He found an opportunity to speak to her. She was tense as he stood beside her. She could almost feel again his hands tearing her clothes, forcing her on to the bed.

He said: 'Now that we are such friends, Madam, I wish to ask a favour. Do not grant Maitland permission to return to Court.'

She turned her back. But that, in the presence of the others, was too pointed a rebuff. He had been in such high favour before to-day. If her manner towards him so obviously changed people would wonder why. They might even guess. That secret must be kept.

She said in a low strained voice: 'You are no friend of mine and never shall be. You need never again make a request to me, for it shall not be granted. You shall lose your head for what you have done. Do not think that because it is still on your shoulders it shall remain there.' It was difficult to put the vehemence she felt into those words, for she must keep her voice very low in case it should be overheard.

'A pity,' he said. 'I fancied you thought my person rather pleasant when we last met.'

'You fancy, my lord,' she answered, and she forced herself to smile, 'that you have behaved in a clever way. You know that I cannot denounce your conduct because of the great shame it has brought me. But do not imagine that will save you.'

'Madam, do not pretend that last night's encounter brought any less pleasure to you than to me. It was startling . . . unexpected. I myself had not planned it, but how happy I am that it happened. There shall now be no holding back of all the joy we bring to each other.'

'I have never heard such insolence.'

'You have never had a lover worthy of you before, Madam. Startling, is it not? It would be easier to explain if we were alone.'

'I shall see to it that I am never again alone with you. Moreover I shall require you to swear friendship with Lord Maitland when he returns to Court – which he will very soon do.'

He bowed. 'Madam,' he said, 'your wish is law.'

A few days later she returned to the Exchequer House. It was necessary that she should do so for there was much to prepare for the Prince's christening, and as she had undertaken the work, she told herself that she must finish it. She had thought on that never-to-be-forgotten night that she could never bear to lie on that bed. Oddly enough that was just what she now wished to do.

She could not settle down to her task. She could not decide what clothes must be bought for her servants. She could not decide what she herself should wear. She could only think of Bothwell. I did the only thing possible, she kept telling herself. There was nothing else I could do. How could I have told anyone what occurred?

On the first day of her return to the Exchequer House Lady Reres came to announce that Lord Bothwell was below and wished to see her.

She turned away that Lady Reres might not see her face. 'No, Reres,' she said shortly. 'I'm busy.'

'He said it was a most important matter of state, Madam. He begs you to see him.'

She did not answer, but she thought: I must show him that I

have no fear of him. But this time there shall be no locking of the door.

She told Lady Reres that he might come up and state his business if he could do so with brevity.

He stood before her, insolent as ever, towering above her, reminding her of his strength.

'It is a marvellous thing to me,' she said, 'that you dare come to this room again.'

'Madam, I have a fondness for this room. I shall always remember it as the four walls within which I enjoyed the greatest experience of your life.'

'You are unbearably insolent.'

'I but seek to speak the truth, Madam.'

'Lord Bothwell, I will not endure your insolence. I have decided that you shall not escape punishment for what you have done. I cannot proclaim your latest misdeeds to the world since I myself was forced to play such an unhappy part in them.'

'Unhappy! You do not know yourself. You have a great capacity for loving, Madam. You have not realised how great. But I have. Would Your Majesty cast back your thoughts to that night and be entirely honest with yourself? Will you ask yourself whether, when you ceased to fight and began to relax, you found that what I so ardently desired was not Your Majesty's own desire?'

She stared at him. She put out her hands as though to ward him off. He came towards her, ignoring her outstretched hands. There was nothing of the courtier about him. He caught her to him and laughed. Then he bent her backwards and kissed her. Knowledge of the truth came to her then. There was something in herself which called to that in him which was primitive and barbaric.

'Why did you come back to this house?' he whispered. 'Tell me that! Why . . . why?'

She did not answer. She was breathless with agitation and expectation, for it was clear to her now why she had come back. It was to offer this challenge to him. It was to bring him back here again.

He knew her even better than she knew herself.

She had come back because he had set a torch to that desire in her which had been lying dormant. He had provoked a mighty conflagration. She desired him now with an intensity which equalled his. And when two such as they recognised their needs, nothing could restrain them.

She felt herself lifted in his arms. It was happening again . . . not in her imagination, but in reality.

They were lovers now. She could think of little else but Bothwell – the last meeting, the next meeting. The periods between were irksome times of waiting.

Flem had become Lady Maitland of Lethington; Beaton had married Alexander Ogilvie; of the Queen's four Maries there was only Seton left. Yet it did not seem important; no one was important but Bothwell.

Some already knew of the relationship between them. It was impossible to keep it entirely secret; Bastian, her French servant, knew, and so, of course, did Lady Reres. Seton knew. Others whispered that Lord Bothwell seemed to be in high favour with the Queen and it appeared that he would soon be taking the place, in her counsels, of David Rizzio. David's brother, Joseph, was now at Court and Mary had given him a high place. Yet she was scarcely aware of the young man; she was aware of little but Bothwell.

Darnley watched her. He would stay away from the Court, sulking in his father's castle; then he would return, coming to her apartments, demanding his rights. He was more despicable to Mary than he had ever been; he seemed quite repulsive. How could I ever have thought I was in love with such a man! she asked herself again and again. It was inexplicable, especially as Lord Bothwell had so often been there for her to see. She had been blind — blind to life, blind to passion, blind to love.

Now she had miraculously lost her blindness. This was living. This was what she had been born for.

Darnley was frightened. Maitland was back at Court, and Maitland was one of those lords who had felt it necessary to leave Court after the murder of Rizzio. This was but a beginning, thought Darnley. He knew that Moray and Maitland would now urge the Queen to pardon Morton, young Ruthven and the rest of them, restore their estates and bring them back to Court. And when they came, what would be their first action?

Darnley was a fool, but any fool would know the answer.

He had been present at the murder of Rizzio; he had given his support to the murderers; the murder had been done in his name — out of his jealousy of the Queen. Yet he had turned traitor. He had changed sides at the crucial moment, so the plot had failed in some way. Rizzio had died, it was true, but the Queen had escaped. She had gathered her followers about her and, with Huntley and Bothwell, had returned to Edinburgh triumphant; the murderers, in spite of all their elaborate plans, had been defeated and forced into exile. And who was to blame? Darnley!

They would never forget and they would never forgive.

And soon the drama would be enacted all over again; but in place of Rizzio there would be Darnley.

If and when the lords returned, he dared not stay. And Maitland was already back.

He was frantic. He began to make plans. He would get into touch with the Pope; he would write to Philip of Spain. After all, was he not a good Catholic – a better Catholic than Mary with her talk of tolerance. Good Catholics did not talk of tolerance. Why should he not procure the support of the Catholic world? Why should he not usurp Mary's throne? Perhaps one day he would be King, not only of Scotland but of England as well. Moreover he was the father of the undisputed heir.

Lennox, his father, was alarmed on hearing of his plans – for Darnley had to confide in someone, and the only person he could trust was his father.

'But, my son,' said the Earl of Lennox, 'this is ridiculous. The Pope would not aid you, and the King of Spain is a cautious man. He would not support a rebel such as you would be.'

'A rebel! I am the King.'

'In name only. The Crown Matrimonial has never been bestowed on you.'

'It is so unjust. I was promised. And first Rizzio frustrated me . . . and now it is Moray and Bothwell. Maitland is back. My old enemy. He will kill me. I know he will. He will bring the murderer Morton back, and together they will kill me.'

Lennox, in great agitation on account of his son's hysteria, wrote to the Queen telling her that Darnley proposed leaving Scotland for Spain.

Mary sent for her husband. He came, ill at ease. 'What are these wild plans of yours?' she demanded.

'I shall not tell you.'

'Henry, I insist.'

'Why should I stay here?' he screamed. 'What am I? You only want me to stay because you fear the scandal my departure would give rise to. Take me back. I demand to be taken back. I wish to be your husband in very truth. Let me stay with you, share your bed and board. Then you shall not have a more faithful servant.' He threw himself at her and tried to put his arms about her. She drew back in disgust.

'Mary . . . Mary,' he pleaded. 'You used to love me. You used to come to my chamber because, you said, you wanted us to be alone even if it was only for a little while.'

She pushed him away. She hated to remember those times; and even now she was comparing him with another. She would never allow Darnley to touch her.

She said: 'If you attempt to put your hands on me I shall call the guards.'

He whimpered: 'What have I done? How have I changed? You used to be eager for me.'

'If you say that again you will regret it.'

'But I will say it . . . I *will*!'

'Go quietly now or I shall call the guards. In the morning you may state your case before the lords of the Court.'

He had no help for it but to go; and in the morning he faced them nervously – Moray and Maitland among them, those two who hated him and he believed sought to destroy him, those two who would not be satisfied until they had brought his enemies back to Court.

Moray did not intend to spare him, not did Maitland. The

cold eyes of Moray, the sarcastic ones of Maitland frightened him. He scraped his feet on the floor and scowled at his toes.

Why was he going to run away? they demanded.

He did not know. He wanted to leave Scotland, that was all. He did not now think he would go after all. It was just to make the Queen understand how badly she treated her husband.

'It would be a treasonable act,' said Moray, 'to leave Scotland for Spain. For what purpose did you intend to go?'

'To . . . to bring the Queen back to her duty . . . To be received back in her favour . . .'

'It is hardly the way,' said Maitland suavely, 'to win the Queen's favour – by playing traitor to her.'

'I am not a traitor. I am no traitor!' screamed Darnley.

Mary could bear no more. There was nothing she wanted so much as to be rid of Darnley. She was filled with shame whenever she was forced to look at him.

She said: 'If he gives his word not to leave Scotland, we will pardon him . . . providing he returns to his father's castle . . . and stays there.'

Darnley's face was white with rage, but he trembled with fear as he turned from the watching group and, shouting: 'Goodbye, Madam. You shall not see my face for a long time!' he hurried away.

❋ ❋ ❋

It was October and the mist lay thick across the land, when news came of Border fighting near the town of Jedburgh. Bothwell left Court and galloped south at the head of his men.

Mary was desolate. She had begged him to let someone else go, for she could not exist without him; but he had laughed at the idea. The Border was his domain. If there were trouble there, who should be at hand but Bothwell? Then she began to understand the difference in their passion. She realised that she did not mean as much to him as he did to her.

He *wanted* to ride away. The excitement of battle called him as lust called him in the room at the Exchequer House.

She was frantic with anxiety and jealousy. He would doubtless call at one of his castles before returning, and he would see his wife. She visualised Jean Gordon – not exactly a comely woman – oval face, sandy hair, and the long Gordon nose; yet it was said in the early days of his marriage Bothwell had been more faithful to Jean Gordon than to any woman.

But not now, she assured herself. He would come straight back to the Court. He must. Why had she not made him promise not to go to his home? Because one did not, she had also realised, command Bothwell in such matters. She knew that to have asked him not to visit Jean would have put it in his mind to do so. But if he was not the man to make such promises, neither was he the man to deceive her. If he had thought of seeing Jean he would have boldly said so. It was his arrogant and most disconcerting boldness that she loved. These were a symbol of his independence. It showed her clearly that she, the Queen, needed him, more than he needed her.

How long would he stay? Until he wished to return?

Why did I let him go? she asked herself. The answer was: You could do no other. None could hold Bothwell against his wish.

With what joy she discovered that there was an assize at Jedburgh which she could attend! With what joy she set out on the journey!

She had a perfectly reasonable excuse for going to him, for her duties as Queen demanded her presence in Jedburgh. Fate was being good to her at last.

Seton watched her with some anxiety as they set out.

Never, thought Seton, had she looked so beautiful. She had changed since her association with Bothwell; she had become feverishly gay. But would it last? wondered Seton. Bothwell was not the man she would have chosen for Mary. There was no tenderness in him; there was instead a ruthless and a primitive appetite. What did he really feel for Mary beyond his lust? There were times when Seton thought she would like to see the peace of a nunnery because the outside world made her so unhappy.

Meanwhile they rode towards Jedburgh, but before they reached the town the news was brought to them. Mary saw the man as he rode towards them and her heart leaped, for she knew him as one of Bothwell's men.

'What news?' she cried. 'What news?'

'Bad news, Your Majesty.'

Her hand tightened on the reins. 'Bothwell?' she gasped.

It seemed as though the man took a long time to answer. 'It was John Elliot of the Park . . . the notorious highwayman, Your Majesty. My lord heard that he was in the neighbourhood and went out to get him. The highwayman was wounded, but . . . not seriously . . . He turned on my lord and . . .'

'And . . . killed him?' murmured Mary.

Seton was beside her, her gentle eyes pleading: Not here . . . do not betray yourself before these people. You loved him . . . He was everything to you . . . but do not betray yourself here before these witnesses.

'So Bothwell is killed,' said Mary blankly. She looked at

Seton, pleading for help. I am lost. I care for nothing. I wish it were I who had died.

Seton said: 'It is a great shock. Her Majesty has not been well of late. I think we should rest here for a while before continuing our journey.'

Seton escorted her to the chamber which had been prepared for her and lay down beside her on the bed, putting her arms about her; they did not weep; they lay close together while Seton stroked the Queen's hair. At length the Queen said: 'There is nothing to live for, Seton. I wish that I were dead.'

She did not know how she sat through the assize. She supposed she conducted herself with outward calm, for none seemed to realise the tumult within her. The strain was so great at times that she seemed near to fainting. The old gnawing pain was back in her side.

She was lenient as she always was with offenders. She wanted to help all those who suffered. And all the time she was thinking: I wish I were dead instead of him. How I wish it was I who died.

When the assize was over there came a messenger from Bothwell's castle of Hermitage. He was not dead, said the messenger, though so seriously wounded that death seemed inevitable. Then she was filled with hope. She would go to him at once. She would *make* him live. She tried to hide her joy; she said calmly: 'He has received his hurt in my service, and I myself must see that all that can be done for his comfort shall be done.'

So she set out from Jedburgh to the Castle of Hermitage, and there she saw him. He was wounded in the thigh, the head and one of his hands; and so severe were these wounds that they would have killed an ordinary man. But he bore them with ease. He lay looking at her, and the old insolent look was in his eyes. They seemed to grin at her below the bandage.

'Thank God you are alive!' cried Mary.

Even as she spoke she fell fainting to the floor. The strain of the last few days had been too much for her. She had sat through the assizes believing her lover dead; she had not been allowed to show her grief because their union was not a regular one, and the need for secrecy had made her burden the harder to bear. And now that she saw him lying very badly wounded, yet still with more vitality than that of ordinary men, now that she knew she might not lose him, the tension snapped. In the days that followed she was as near to death as he was.

She lay at Jedburgh in the house of Lady Fernyhirst whither she had been carried in a litter, and a terrible melancholy filled her.

I love him, she mused, but what am I to him? One of the thousands who have amused him for a while. I, who am a Queen, am but a light woman to him.

She had a husband; he had a wife. What hope was there that they could ever marry? Marriage with him was what Mary desired beyond all things. Only that could comfort her and give her peace. She longed to end her adulterous association, but she could only end it by making it legal.

During those days at Jedburgh she believed she was dying. So did Moray. He began helping himself to some of the precious silver in Holyrood. For more than a week she lay close to death. Bothwell was brought to the same house, but although he had

426

been severely wounded, owing to his amazing vitality, there was no doubt after the first days that he would live.

Mary lay in the room above his, thinking of him constantly while John Hume, her player on the lute, and James Heron, her player on the pipe, tried to beguile her with sweet music. But the music no longer charmed; she could only think of Darnley and Jean Gordon who stood between her and her lover. She planned the new dress she would have when she rose from her bed; it should contain twenty ells of red silk, four ells of taffaty and three ells of finest black velvet; there should be twenty ells of royal Scotch plaid. But what was the use? Such delights could no longer hold her attention.

Darnley came to see her. He was sulky. He had been sending letters abroad. He had reminded Philip that Mary's friends were Moray, Bothwell and Maitland, who were all Protestants. It was Moray who was doing much harm to the Catholic cause in Scotland. Philip would readily understand how different matters would be if Darnley were King and Mary had no power to harm the Church.

He did not care so much that she turned away from him. She would rarely speak to him. She had not wished him to come, she implied. Soon he rode away. There were other women in the world besides Mary; and his head was teeming with plans for his own greatness.

When Mary rose from her bed she went to visit Bothwell. He was unable to move, for the wound in his thigh had not yet healed.

'Ah,' he said, when he saw her, 'so we both came to grief, eh?'

'I thought you were dead,' she answered quietly. 'They told me so.'

'It would take much more than John Elliot to finish me. I'll be up and about as soon as my flesh heals.'

'And what of your head?' she asked. She lifted the bandage and looked at the head wound. She shivered. 'My dearest . . . I cannot bear to think what might so easily have happened.'

He took her hand and kissed it. 'I am out of action,' he said. ''Tis a pity.'

'You will soon be well. I shall nurse you myself.'

'Mayhap I should go to Jean for the nursing.'

Mary's face flamed. 'That shall not be. I shall nurse you.'

He grinned.

'Did you go to Crichton?' she demanded. 'Did you see her?'

'I did.'

'And did you . . . ?'

That made him laugh. 'I declare I shall break open my wounds afresh if you say such things.'

'Did you? Did you?' she cried.

'My dear Queen, what do you think? I am her husband, am I not? It is long since I saw her.'

Mary's eyes filled with tears of rage and jealousy.

'Sometimes I wonder how I can go on loving you.'

'You should not wonder. It is very clear why you do. Now you must not be jealous. She is my wife; you are my mistress. I am content that it should be so.'

'But I am not!'

'Alas, how can you change it? By breaking away from me, of course. You could do that.'

'You do not care.'

'You will see. As soon as I am on my feet we will meet again in the Exchequer House as we did on that first encounter.'

'You should not have gone to Crichton,' she insisted.

He only shrugged his shoulders.

'You have a greater regard for her than for me!' she went on. 'Yet I hear that she has no great love for you. She wanted Alexander Ogilvie. She preferred him to you and yet . . . you go to see her!'

'I like her,' he said quietly. 'I'm fond of her. There's no one quite like Jeannie.'

'And there are many like the Queen!'

'No. There is only one Queen and only one Jeannie. I am fond of them both.'

'But I . . . can give you so much more than she can.'

'What?'

'My love . . . myself . . . my honour . . . my . . .' She put her arms about his neck. 'Please . . . do not be so cynical. You must love me. How can you go to her . . . when you know my feelings?'

'She might ask, How can I go to you . . . and with more reason. What can she give more than you can, you ask. She could give me children.'

'Could I not?'

'Not legitimate ones. So you see, she can give more than you can. You are two women. You have two eyes, a nose, a mouth, two arms, two breasts . . .'

'Be silent!' cried Mary tense with emotion. Then she added: 'There is one thing I could give you which she never can. A crown.'

A flame leaped into his eyes, the only sign that she had touched his smouldering ambition. She knew – and he knew – that nothing would ever be quite the same between them again.

Mary sat alone in her chamber. She, with her nobles about her, had left Jedburgh and was travelling by stages to Edinburgh. Bothwell, now well enough to travel, was with them. The wound in his thigh was healed, and that was all that he had been waiting for. His head was still bandaged, but he cared little for that if he could be on his feet again.

They had rested at Craigmillar and it was in the castle there that Mary sat.

She knew there were schemes in Bothwell's head. She knew that his attitude towards her had changed in some ways. He was as lusty as ever; he had wished – as she had – to resume their passionate relationship. But there was something else. She had more to offer him than Jean Gordon had; she had said so and he had accepted that.

She could not get Darnley out of her thoughts. Sometimes, in her dreams, she saw him lying on the floor in the supper chamber at Holyroodhouse, clutching at her skirts; and as she turned shuddering from him, his face would change to that of David.

'Holy Virgin,' she often prayed, 'intercede for me. Let me die now, for I believe it were better so. I am an adulteress. Let me die before I sin more deeply.'

The door of her chamber opened, and she thought it was her lover coming to her. But although Bothwell was there, he was not alone. With him were four of the lords – Moray, Maitland, Argyle and Huntley. They stood before her – five men, relentless in their struggle for power, and it was Maitland – the obvious choice as spokesman, suave and persuasive – who addressed her.

He began: 'Madam, much distress is caused, not only to you but to our country, through the evil conduct of one who can bring no good to any. I speak of your husband, Lord Darnley.'

She bowed her head and, when she raised it, caught the burning eyes of Bothwell upon her.

'It is known,' went on Maitland, 'that he has tried to get into communication with Spain and Rome; and his object is to do harm to Your Majesty who has done nothing but good to him. Madam, shall you tolerate such conduct, even though it is that of your own husband?'

'I am powerless to do otherwise. If we keep him under close surveillance, if we see that he does no real harm, it is the best that we can hope for.'

'Not so, Your Majesty. If you will grant pardon to Lords Morton, Ruthven and the rest who are now in exile, we, your servants, shall find means of making a divorcement between you and your husband. This is necessary, not only for Your Grace's comfort, but for that of the realm, for if he remains with Your Majesty, he will not rest until he has done you – and the country – some evil.'

Mary saw her lover's eyes upon her. They were gleaming as they had gleamed at the time of the rape. But this time was it her body he desired to possess, or was it her crown? She tried to be calm. 'I agree with what you say, my Lord Maitland. But if there were a divorce it would have to be made lawful, and I could never agree to anything which would prejudice my son's inheritance of the throne.'

Bothwell said: 'It could be done. It could be done. My father was divorced from my mother but my inheritance was safe.'

'But my son is a Prince, Lord Bothwell.'

'It matters not, Madam. We would arrange this matter to bring no harm to the Prince.'

Moray now spoke: 'The Kirk would be against divorce.'

Bothwell's lips curled; Maitland's eyes were sardonic. He said: 'My lord Moray is a stern Protestant, so we must find a means of ridding you of your husband which will enable him to look through his fingers and, beholding our doings, say nothing.'

Mary caught her breath. What was Maitland's meaning? Was it that Moray was too religious a man to approve of divorce, and therefore murder would be necessary to rid her of Darnley?

She was trembling. She must not look at her lover. Had he persuaded the lords to this action, she wondered; had he started to make plans when she had told him in Jedburgh that she could offer him a crown? She knew now that these ruthless men were determined to murder Darnley. Each had his reason. For some it was because Darnley had betrayed his friends, having agreed to the murder of Rizzio and then turned to the other side and foiled these men's schemes. He was to die for that. But there was one who had been outside the plot. There was one who could reduce her decency, her love of justice, to nothing, and put in its place an overwhelming desire. He wanted to rid Scotland of Darnley, for through Darnley's death he saw a crown for himself.

She was glad there were others present. She must not look at him. She said coolly: 'I wish to do nothing by which any spot might be laid on my honour and my conscience.'

Maitland was smiling subtly. 'Madam, leave this matter in our hands and Your Grace shall see nothing but that which is approved of by Parliament.'

'But remember,' she insisted, 'nothing must be done to cast reflection on my honour and conscience.'

'It shall be as Your Majesty wishes.'

They left her, and when they had gone she lay in bed, her heart pounding, as she reflected on what lay behind the words of those men.

❀ ❀ ❀

The baby was christened James Charles with great pomp at Stirling. That was in the middle of December. Darnley, though in the castle, refused to appear. His attitude was giving rise to much gossip; and the castle was full of foreigners, for representatives from all countries had come to Scotland for the christening of the Prince.

Darnley was hinting that he was not the father of the child. He was whispering that each day the boy was growing more and more like the Italian music-maker. On other occasions he would stoutly declare that there could be no doubt that the child was his and that it was shameful that his wife would not live with him.

Oh to be rid of him! thought Mary. Could there be a divorce? Was it possible?

She had made an alarming discovery. She was to have Bothwell's child. She asked herself how she could explain this pregnancy. Something must be done and done quickly.

She told no one. She must keep her secret until she could find a way out of her trouble. She loved intensely. She could have been happy. But her love was bringing her nothing but misery.

It would have been better if I had died before I knew this love, she told herself continually. It would have been far better if I had never lived to sin as I now sin.

How could she confess her wickedness? How could she seek the comfort of her religion which she dared not confess? How could she promise to reform her ways when she had not the power to do so, when her lover could so easily make her his slave?

On Christmas Eve she signed the pardon which would bring Morton, Ruthven, Lindsay and the other rebel lords back to Scotland. She knew that doing so was tantamount to signing Darnley's death warrant.

Darnley knew it too. When he realised what had been done he lost no time in leaving the Castle of Stirling. He made for Glasgow, that territory which was under his father's domination.

Only there could he feel safe from his enemies.

It was January and the weather was bitter. Mary, alone with her thoughts, told herself again and again: I cannot do this thing.

And every time she answered herself: But I must.

Darnley was suffering from the smallpox, and safe in his father's castle he was carefully guarded by his father's men.

When Mary told Bothwell of the child she was by no means displeased.

'There must be no delay,' he said. 'You must see that. Delay is dangerous for us now.'

'Why do you say these things?' she demanded feeling half demented. 'What good could come to us . . . even if we were rid of him? What of you? You are not free!'

He had laughed. 'I'll be free and ready when you are.'

'And Jean?'

'She will stand aside. There'll be a divorce on the grounds of consanguinity. We are related.'

'So, we shall both be divorced and then . . .'

'Divorced! Divorce takes too long where Kings and Queens are concerned. Do not forget the child. It should not be born out of wedlock and it will not wait.'

She closed her eyes and tried to fight free of the spell he laid upon her. She thought fleetingly: If I could go to a nunnery . . . If I could live out my life there . . . But he had his arms about her; he was giving her those rough caresses which always brought memories of the Exchequer House.

He said: 'He must be brought from his father's territory. He could stay there for months surrounded by Lennox's men, hiding in safety. He must be brought to Edinburgh.'

'Who will bring him?'

'There is only one who can.'

'No . . . !' she cried.

'Yes,' he said smiling. 'He would come if you went to him. You could bring him from his father's territory. We need him here in Edinburgh.'

'He is sick.'

'All the more reason why you should look after him.'

'I have told him that all is over between us.'

'Women . . . even queens . . . change their minds.'

She said faintly: 'You had better speak plainly.'

'Go to him. Promise him anything. But bring him out of his hiding place.'

'Promise him . . . anything?'

Bothwell laughed. 'It is hardly likely that he will be in a condition to ask you to redeem your promises.'

She turned away. 'I cannot do this.'

He seized her, and forced her to look into his face.

'You will do it,' he said. 'You will consider what it means to us, and you will do it.'

She could refuse him nothing. He knew it, and she knew it. Now she cried: 'No, I cannot do this thing. I never want to see him again, but I cannot do this.'

He did not urge her then. He laughed; he caressed her; he reduced her to that state of mind and body when she had no thought or wishes beyond the immediate moment.

'You will,' he said, 'do this for me.'

And she knew she would.

When he had left her she remained alone and in torment.

She picked up her pen and, because she dared not write of the terrible thing which was in her mind, she wrote of her passion for the man who had completely enslaved her. She wrote of the tears she had wept on his account, of that first brutal encounter which had taken place before she had known this overwhelming love.

Riding towards Glasgow in the bitter weather, Mary felt like a woman in a trance. She knew that she would play the part which was desired of her. Her own will was subdued. Her lover had as complete possession of her mind as he had of her body. There was one thing which could help her do this: her hatred of Darnley.

When she reached the castle she was taken at once to Darnley. If he had sickened her before, he did so doubly now. The marks of his disease were on his face and the room was unpleasantly odorous. He wore a piece of fine gauze over his face to hide his disfigurement as best he could. But he was pleased to see her.

'It is good of Your Majesty to come hither and see me,' he said humbly.

'There is much I have to say to you. You are very sick.'

'I shall recover.'

She could not bear to look at him. She said: 'Why have you behaved so badly? If you had not . . . But tell me why you write complaining of the cruelty of "some people". You mean your wife, of course. What have I done to be treated so by you?'

'You will not forgive me. You turn from me. I long to resume our normal married life and you will have none of it. I know that I have acted very foolishly, even wickedly. Madam, I am very young. I am not twenty-one yet. I am younger than you are. Let us try again. There is only one thing I desire: to get back to that happy relationship which was ours. Oh, Mary, you loved me once. Have you forgotten?'

She shuddered. 'It was so long ago. I did not know you then.'

'You knew part of me. I *was* like that. I could be like that again. I have been led astray by my own folly . . . by the folly of others. I think of you constantly . . . as my Queen and as my wife. How could I ever be content without you, having known you?'

'I cannot believe you to be sincere. I know you, remember. If I took you back there would be those hideous scenes . . . that shameful humiliation. I cannot forget what you have said to me, how you have humiliated me – not only in private, but before my subjects.'

'Then you would take me back? You would let me be with you again?'

'How could I trust you?'

'You could! You could!'

'Hush! Do not excite yourself so. It is bad for you. Lie still. Speak calmly.'

'Speak calmly when *you* are here, when you have ridden here to see me?'

'I am uncertain,' she began.

'Mary, I will be a good husband to you. Mary, why should we not be happy together? We have a child . . . a son. We could be happy.'

'If we were different people we might be. I . . . I have brought a horse-litter for you.'

He was pathetically alert. 'Why so? Why so?'

'I wish to take you back with me to Edinburgh.'

'To take me back!' He looked wildly about the room. 'To take me back, Mary? I have too many enemies at the Court. They have sworn to be revenged on me for . . .'

'For David's death,' she said. Her eyes were brilliant as she looked full at him and went on: 'It is just a year since David died.' The memory of David, pulling at her skirts as he was being dragged across the floor, gave her courage. He – this sick and repulsive boy lying in the bed – had had no compunction in sending David to his death. She went on: 'That is what you are thinking of, is it not? You fear them because you plotted with them to kill David and then deserted them and informed against them.'

He nodded slowly and fearfully. He said: 'I hear that they have plotted to do me harm. But I would not believe that you would join them in that. Why do you wish me to go back to Edinburgh?'

'Because so many talk of the strained relations between us. I would have us appear to the world to be living in amity together.'

'Mary,' he said, 'I will come back on one condition. I will rise from my sickbed and come back to Edinburgh if you will give me your promise to be my wife . . . in all things.'

She hesitated.

He went on: 'If not, I shall stay here. I want your solemn promise, Mary. You and I shall be at bed and board as husband and wife. Promise me this, and I will leave with you to-morrow.'

She was silent for so long that he said sulkily: 'Very well then, I remain here. It is far too cold for me to travel.'

'You would be comfortable in your litter. You would have the utmost care. In Edinburgh we should all be together . . . you, I and the child. I would care for you myself.'

'I will come only if you promise me that one thing: we shall be as husband and wife and you will never leave me as long as I live.'

'As long as you live,' she repeated, and the shivering took possession of her again. She went on: 'But it would have to be after you have recovered. We could not be together until then.'

'I will recover quickly,' he said eagerly.

'Very well. We shall start to-morrow.'

'Your promise, Mary?'

'I give it.'

'And never to leave me as long as I live?'

'Never to leave you as long as you live,' she repeated.

'Then let us set out to-morrow.'

Shaken, relieved and horrified, she said to herself: It is done. Soon my task will be over.

Darnley was sleeping deeply, his disfigured face turned away from her. Mary sat in the sick room watching through the long night. She was too distressed to sleep and she could not sit idly; so she took up her pen and wrote to her lover.

'I am weary and sleepy, yet I cannot forbear scribbling as long as there is any paper . . .'

She had been writing for some time without considering what she wrote but setting down her thoughts as they came into her mind. She glanced back over the paper and read:

'He would not let me go but would have me watch with him. Fain would I have excused myself from spending this night sitting up with him. . . .

'I do a work here which I hate much . . .

'Excuse me if I write ill. I am ill at ease and glad to write unto you when others be asleep, seeing that I cannot do as they do according to my desire, that is between your arms, my dear life whom I beseech God to preserve from all ill . . .'

There were tears in her eyes and they fell on the paper.

Will this night never end? she asked herself. She looked at the man in the bed, and she thought of the man whom she loved, and she murmured: 'It were better if I had never been born, better I had died long ago when a child, and so many thought I should, than that I should come to this.'

They left Glasgow next day.

'Are we going to Holyroodhouse or the Castle?' asked Darnley.

'To neither,' she answered him. 'In your state it would not be good to stay at either place. You are sick of a disease which many fear. I have had a house prepared for you, and there you shall rest until you are well enough to come to me at the palace.'

'And share your apartments,' he reminded her.

'And share my apartments,' she repeated.

'Bed and board,' he said, smiling. 'Where is this house?'

'It is one of those on the southern slope of the city. You know the ruins of the Church of St Mary. There are several houses there, and this one belongs to Robert Balfour. He has lent it to us that you may rest there until you are well enough to come to the palace.'

Darnley frowned. 'Among all those worn-out and ruined houses! You would mean Kirk-o'-Field, would you not?'

'Kirk-o'-Field, yes. Close to the ruin of St Mary's.'

'It is an odd place to which to take me.'

'It is near Holyrood, and for that reason it seems suitable. It is an old house, it is true, but we have furnished your apartment royally. When you are within and see the bed I have had set there for you, and the rich hangings I have had put up, you will agree that you are as comfortably housed as in your father's castle.'

'And you . . . will you be at this house in Kirk-o'-Fields?'

'I shall have my bed taken there. I shall sleep in the room below yours, so you will not be lonely. Your man Taylor and a few others will be with you. And I shall be there too.'

He nodded. 'But Kirk-o'-Field! A dismal place!'

'Only outside. Inside it will be as a palace furnished for a king.'

As they came into Edinburgh and Darnley saw the dismal surroundings of the house which had been chosen for him he was uneasy. He looked with distaste at the house itself which had been lent by Robert Balfour, the Provost of Kirk-o'-Field and brother to Sir James. It was a house of two stories. There was a spiral staircase in a turret by means of which it was

441

possible to enter the lower chamber and the upper through two small lobbies. On each of the two floors there were a few rooms which were more like cupboards than rooms – these were the *garderobes* and here the servants would sleep. Sliding panels acted as doors for these *garderobes*. The house had been built over an arched crypt.

'Such a spot!' he said. 'For a King! Ruins all about me and a view of Thieves' Row from the window!'

'Wait until you see your apartment.' She showed him the lower chamber in which was her velvet state bed. 'This is where I shall sleep. I shall be immediately below you. Let me show you your apartment and then food shall be brought.'

He was cheered when he saw his apartment. It was decorated with tapestry and velvet hangings which had been taken from the Earl of Huntley at the time of his disgrace, as had the magnificent bed and most of the furnishings. Darnley could not complain of these.

He lay exhausted on the bed and thought of the future. He believed he had acted wisely in becoming reconciled to the Queen and in showing his trust in her. He would emerge from this sickness a handsome young man again; he would be the Queen's adored husband. He only had to lie in bed and recover his strength and his handsome appearance. Then all that he desired would be his.

Mary had slept in the velvet state bed at the house in Kirk-o'-Field on Tuesday and Friday of that week. On the Friday, late at night, she had heard the sounds of stealthy footsteps close to the house. She had not awakened Lady Reres who had been her companion since she had gone with her to the Exchequer

442

House, but had crept to the window. She had seen French Paris and some of James Balfour's men opening the door of the crypt and carrying in something bulky. She shuddered and went back to bed, wondering what the men were doing.

On the following day when she returned to Holyroodhouse, she had a few moments alone with Bothwell. He had taken her into his fierce embrace.

He said: ''Tis a fine bed you have there in Kirk-o'-Field.'

She looked at him wonderingly. 'I saw it,' he told her. 'I have keys to all doors. A fine velvet bed. I have a fancy for that. We'll share it on our wedding night. Have it brought from the house to-morrow and a less fine one put in its place.'

'Why . . . to-morrow?' she asked.

'Because I ask it, and because you will do anything in the world to please me.'

❀ ❀ ❀

Darnley said: 'Why are they taking away your velvet bed?'

'It is too fine for such a room as the one below this.'

'Yet . . . to take it away . . . after you took such pains to have it brought here!'

'I wish it to be cleaned and prepared.'

'Prepared?'

'For our reconciliation.'

He was smiling. 'It shall be our bridal bed, for it shall be as though we are newly married. You will be here to-night, Mary?'

'I shall come to see you to-night, but I shall have to return to Holyrood as there is a wedding which I am expected to attend. Bastian is marrying Margaret Garwood. You know how fond I am of Margaret — and of Bastian. I promised

Margaret I would dance at her wedding and that I would see that hers was a fine one.'

'Would that I could dance at Margaret's wedding!'

'There was a time when you would have scorned to dance at a servant's wedding.'

'I was so young. I was over-proud! And look to what my folly has brought me!'

She turned away because she knew that if she tried to say more the words would choke her.

After a pause he said: 'This is a strange house. Do you think it is haunted? I hear footsteps. I fancy I hear whispers. There are strange noises in the night. In the crypt, it may be. I seem to hear these sounds.'

'This is such a small house that you would naturally hear noises from without.'

'Perhaps that is it. Mary, I think much of the velvet bed.'

'Yes,' she said faintly, 'the velvet bed.'

'You shall see that I have changed. I was so young, Mary, and the honour done to me was too much. You . . . so beautiful . . . so desired by all, and to be so much in love with me as you were! And then to be the King. Remember my youth. Why do you weep, Mary? Is it for the past?'

She nodded, and she thought: For the past, for the present, for the future.

Robert Stuart, Mary's base-born brother, had come to see his kinsman Darnley. Robert was in a quandary. The Stuart characteristics were strong in him, and the Stuarts, if they were often weak and foolish, hated cruelty and were over-whelmingly tender and generous to their friends.

Robert was disturbed. He had heard rumours and the rumours concerned Darnley.

Why, Robert asked himself, should Darnley have been brought to a house such as this? Darnley was a fool not to see the reason. There was a plot against him and his enemies were all around him. Even the Queen hated him and wanted to be rid of him. Why could not Darnley see what was so clear to others?

'You seem disturbed,' said Darnley.

'I am,' retorted Robert. 'Are you not?'

He signed to the servant to leave them alone together.

'Where does he go when he leaves this room?' asked Robert.

'To the little gallery with the *garderobes*. There are really only two rooms in this house. Mine and the Queen's. It is a very small house.'

'You are isolated here, my lord.'

'I shall not be here long. Plans are being made for removing me.'

That was too much for Robert. 'It is only too true,' he said. 'Plans are being made and you will not be long on this earth if you ignore them.'

'What do you mean?'

'Think, man. Why have you been brought to this desolate spot? If you are reconciled with the Queen why is it not Holyroodhouse or Edinburgh Castle? Why this little house in ruined Kirk-o'-Field?'

'Because . . . because I am sick. Because . . . because many fear my disease. I shall go to Holyrood with the Queen as soon as I am well. She has had her state bed removed this day, that it may be where we can use it together.'

'Jesus!' cried Robert. 'Is it so then? Her state bed removed! Then man, do not wait another hour in this accursed house. Fly now . . . while you have yet time.'

'The Queen is my friend. The Queen has promised me that I shall be her husband.'

'Listen! Bothwell, Morton, Moray, Maitland . . . all are against you. You betrayed so many after Rizzio's murder. They wish to free the Queen from her marriage with you. A plot to do so is afoot. Do not ask me more. Go! I am warning you.'

'I trust the Queen,' stammered Darnley.

'Then you are a fool. Hush! Someone comes.'

'It is the Queen herself,' said Darnley, rising from his bed.

'Say nothing of what I have told you,' said Robert.

But Darnley had not yet learned enough wisdom.

'Mary,' he cried as she came into the room. 'I have just heard a terrible tale. Robert says there is a plot to kill me.'

The Queen grew pale. She looked at her brother.

Robert thought: Why did I try to help the fool? Let him wait here to die. He deserves death for his folly, if for nothing else. He laughed and protested: 'I . . . ! You have misheard me, brother. I know of no plot.'

'But you have just said . . .' began Darnley.

Robert shrugged his shoulders. He looked at his sister. 'It would seem that he wanders in his sickness.'

Darnley cried out in anger: 'But you have just warned me. Mary, what does he mean? Is there some plot?'

'I . . . I do not know of what you speak,' said Mary.

Robert smiled patiently. 'You misunderstood, my lord. I spoke of no plot.'

'It . . . it was meant to be a . . . joke?'

Oh, you fool, thought Robert. A joke! When the Queen

446

wishes to be rid of you. When there is not a nobleman at Court who does not hate you, who has not some score to settle. Robert said coldly: 'You have completely misunderstood me.'

'So . . . it was nothing . . .' began Darnley.

'It was nothing.'

'I do not like such jokes,' said Darnley angrily.

'Robert,' interrupted the Queen reprovingly, 'you should remember that Henry is very weak as yet. You should not distress him so.'

Robert lifted his shoulders and smiled his charming Stuart smile. He began to talk of Bastian's wedding.

On Sunday evening Mary took supper at the house of Sir James Balfour, and for company she had with her Lords Huntley, Bothwell and Cassillis. Bothwell was anxious that Mary should be where he could keep an eye on her. He had heard that Robert Stuart had warned Darnley. He could see that she was frightened to-night. She knew that her brother Moray had some reason for leaving Edinburgh other than the fact that his wife was slightly unwell. Moray – the sancti-monious man who could not look at evil except 'through his fingers' – had always thought it advisable not to be on the spot when some deed was to be done which, though necessary to him, might earn the condemnation of all decent people. Moray's departure was a sure sign that trouble was coming very near. None knew that better than the Queen.

She rose from the supper table saying that she had promised to call that night at the house in Kirk-o'-Field to see Darnley.

'Your Majesty has not forgotten the wedding?' asked Bothwell.

'Oh no. But I must see him first, for I have given him my promise to do so.'

'Then,' said Bothwell, 'let us all go now to his apartment.'

'Shall we not be intruding on their Majesties?' asked Cassillis.

'Nay,' said Bothwell, 'we three will play dice in a corner while the Queen talks with her husband.'

The party left, and guided by the flare of torches, passed through Black Friars Wynd to Kirk-o'-Field.

Mary was deeply aware of her lover's presence. She knew that what happened to-night was of the utmost importance to him, and therefore to her.

Darnley was pleased to see her, but not so pleased to see her companions.

'We came, my lord,' said Bothwell, 'to escort the Queen.'

'Come, sit beside me,' said Darnley eagerly to Mary.

Bothwell smiled. 'Your Majesties may forget our presence. We shall be playing dice in this corner.'

Mary sat by the bed and Darnley said in a low voice: 'Would you were staying the night.'

'I would, but I must attend the wedding, and there will be dancing till three of the morning. I could not come then.'

'To-morrow night then?'

'To-morrow night . . . if possible,' promised the Queen.

He began to talk then of his plans for the future, when he would leave this house and how happy they would be together. Mary listened, yet aware of the men playing in the corner; now and then looking up to find her lover's eyes upon her.

She wondered: Was ever woman asked to play such a part?

She rose at length and said: 'I must not forget the wedding.'

'So soon!' complained Darnley.

She nodded and turned to the players. 'My lords, I would go back now to dance at the wedding.'

They rose, bade farewell to the sick man and left him with his attendant Taylor.

As they came out of the house, Mary noticed with surprise the face of French Paris who was waiting with his master's horse.

'How begrimed you are, Paris!' she exclaimed.

'Yes, Your Grace,' said the man, with an evil grin.

By the light of torches they rode back to Holyrood, where the wedding celebrations were in progress. Mary joined in the gaiety – dancing, singing and seeming as gay as any; but just after midnight she declared that it was a shame to keep the newly married pair from their nuptials, and she would conduct Margaret to her *coucher* at once that she might in person assist in the custom of breaking the benediction-cake over the bride's head, present her with the silver posset-cup and throw the stocking.

When these ceremonies had been completed the Queen retired to her own chamber, and as soon as her women had prepared for her sleep, she lay on her bed, exhausted.

❀ ❀ ❀

Darnley could not sleep. His room seemed to be filled with gloomy menacing shadows. He kept thinking of Robert's words and of the uneasiness of the Queen. He had noticed the glances which Bothwell had sent in her direction from the dice table in the corner of the room. It was almost as though Bothwell were the King and Mary his humble subject. What had given him that impression? What had given him these uneasy thoughts? Was it this lonely, isolated house? Was it the thought of all his enemies? Was he remembering the hatred he had once seen in Mary's eyes? He could sense evil near him. Those voices in the night – what did they mean? Were there evil spirits in the crypt below the house? Were his enemies hiding there in order to spring upon him in the dead of night? He raised himself on his elbow. He could make out the figure of Taylor lying at the foot of his bed.

'Taylor!' he whispered.

Taylor started up in alarm. 'My lord?'

'I cannot sleep. I hear noises. Taylor, there is someone prowling about the house.'

Taylor was listening. 'It is but the wind, my lord.'

'No, Taylor. I think not. Quiet! Listen with me.'

'My lord, shall I wake the servants?'

'How many are there in this house, Taylor?'

'Only the three, my lord: Nelson, Symonds and my own servant.'

'Have they said aught of noises in the night?'

'No, my lord.'

'They sleep deep in their little gallery. But then . . . any who prowl about the house would not come for them. Jesus! I shall be glad when we leave this house. I like it not. I shall leave it to-morrow.'

'My lord,' said Taylor in a whisper, 'there is someone on the stairs.'

Darnley was out of bed. Taylor had seized his wrap and would have put it about him, but Darnley was at the door.

'Quick, Taylor. We must get out of this house. They come to murder me.'

'Your robe, my lord.'

But Darnley could not wait. He drew Taylor behind the

door just as it was being cautiously pushed open; and two men came stealthily into the room.

They did not see the two behind the door and, as they approached the bed, Darnley, with Taylor behind him, speedily ran down the staircase and out into the garden.

Darnley heard someone cry: 'After them!'

He recognised the voice as that of Archibald Douglas.

The cold night air made him gasp as it cut across his lightly covered body; he was wearing nothing but his nightgown. Dark figures moved towards him; he was caught and held in strong arms.

He gasped: 'You . . . you could do this to a kinsman!' He was weak from his illness, but it was surprising what strength there could be in a sick man when he was fighting for his life. A damp rag was slipped across his mouth. He could scarcely breathe. He smelt vinegar as he fell unconscious to the grass.

Taylor was being suffocated by the same methods. Before he died he heard a voice ask: 'Shall we take them back?'

'Nay . . .' came the answer. 'They're too heavy and time is short. We must be well away from Kirk-o'-Field in ten minutes' time. Leave them here. They're near enough to the house and there'll be no trace of them by morning.'

Stealthy figures moved about the house.

The plans had gone awry. Darnley and his man, Taylor, were to have been strangled in their room. There was no time to take them back. There was only time to put a safe distance between the conspirators and the house in Kirk-o'-Field. They started towards Holyrood, but before they reached the palace they heard the roar of the explosion. The citizens were running out of their houses. The guards of the palace saw men with blackened faces entering it; and there was one of these whose bulk betrayed him; and on the night that Darnley was murdered and the house in Kirk-o'-Field blown sky-high, Bothwell was seen by many with his guilt upon him.

The Queen was startled out of her sleep by the explosion. She rose in her bed crying out in terror. Seton was beside her.

'What is it, Seton?' demanded Mary. 'What is it?'

Seton answered: 'I know not.' And she ran to the window. 'It looks like a great fire. The sky is brilliant and there is much smoke.'

'Where, Seton, where?'

Mary was now beside her at the window. She knew before she looked that the explosion had occurred in Kirk-o'-Field. Her teeth chattered and her body shook as with an ague.

🏵 Chapter XI 🏵

There was tumult throughout Edinburgh. The citizens were in the streets. There was speculation throughout the palace.

Bothwell had to be roused from slumber by his servants. He appeared to be sunk in a deep sleep, though he lay in his bed still dressed and with the grime on his clothes and face.

'Jesus!' he cried, rushing to the window. 'What is this? It would seem as though the city is ablaze. 'Tis an explosion, I'll warrant, somewhere near Kirk-o'-Field.'

He rode out with his followers.

'Keep clear of the fire, good people,' he cried. 'Stand back and keep your distance.'

The good people of Edinburgh looked at him, and looked quickly away. Rumour travelled fast.

The guards of Holyrood had already whispered that one of those who came hurriedly into the palace soon after the explosion was Lord Bothwell himself.

453

In the dawn light men searched the spot. The house was now a smouldering ruin. How explain the mighty explosion which had rent the place? Was it gunpowder? Explosives could easily have been stored in the crypt. And who had done this? Who would have dared stack gunpowder below a house in which the Queen's husband lay sick?

Two men were certainly suspected of foul play! Bothwell who had been seen returning by the guards, and Archibald Douglas whose shoe had been found, marvellously intact, close to the ruins.

But there was a discovery yet to be made. The charred bodies of three servants had been found by those who searched, but where were the bodies of the King and Taylor? Could they have been completely destroyed?

It was not long before they were found. They were lying in the garden, in their nightgowns. Beside them was Darnley's velvet gown as though it had been dropped hurriedly.

It was certain that the explosion had not touched them, but nevertheless they lay lifeless on the grass – most mysteriously dead. The plot became clear now. Darnley and Taylor had been murdered and the explosion which had been arranged to hide the crime had completely failed to do so.

All Edinburgh was aroused to indignation. Who murdered the King? was the question to which the citizens were determined to find an answer.

The Queen was numb. She did not know how to act. The whole of Scotland was talking of the murder of the King. Soon the whole world would be talking. The murderers must be found, said the people. But could Mary join with them when she knew that the murderer-in-chief was her lover?

Bothwell swaggered about the town with thousands of his men within call. No one dared show his suspicion if he had any respect for his life.

The Queen should have been plunged in mourning; but instead she was merely dazed. She took no measures for twenty-four hours to bring the murderers to justice. How could she? She was too deeply concerned. Edinburgh knew it. All Scotland knew it. And the news was being carried with all speed to England and the Continent of Europe.

'You must do something,' said Seton. Poor Seton was aghast. She knew too much, yet she could not believe that her beloved mistress would have agreed to the murder of her husband. Yet Seton knew that Bothwell could do what he wished with Mary; she knew that Mary was in love with her husband's murderer.

'What can I do?' said Mary. 'I wish I were dead. I wish I were in Darnley's place.'

'You must do something to show the people that you wish for justice,' Seton implored. 'You must show them that you wish this crime to be solved.'

Mary broke into hysterical laughter which ended in sobbing.

The next morning there were crowds at the Tolbooth reading the placards which had been affixed there during the night.

The biggest of these bore the inscription: 'Who is the King's murderer?' And beneath it was a drawing of Bothwell.

There were other placards. One said: 'The King's

murderers are Lord Bothwell . . .' and there followed a list of servants – Mary's servants – and among them was David's brother Joseph Rizzio.

The implication was clear. Bothwell was the murderer-in-chief, but the Queen's servants had helped him in his crime.

Bothwell came to see the Queen. Without asking permission he dismissed her attendants. He showed greater arrogance than ever now, being sure of his power. He was the most powerful man in Scotland, for the Queen was his to command. His eyes gleamed with excitement. He was unafraid though he knew himself to be in constant danger. He was ready to face all the lords of Scotland, all the judges. He was completely sure of himself. But they must plan carefully now, he warned. It was inadvisable for the Queen to stay in Edinburgh. The people were growing restive. Darnley should without delay be laid in the royal vault.

'We'll offer a reward of two thousand pounds and a free pardon to any who can give information regarding the murder. And we'll have those servants of yours sent out of the country immediately, for how can we know what they will divulge if they are captured and put to the torture?'

'What of you?' she asked.

'I'll take care of myself,' said Bothwell. He caught her to him and laughed. 'And of you,' he added.

She knew her conduct was wrong but she could act in no other way. She could only live the weeks that followed by striving to pretend the tragedy had not happened. She did not appear to be mourning. She even attended a wedding. She shocked the citizens by her almost feverish pursuit of gaiety. They did not know that in her own apartments, night after night, she was near to collapse.

Bothwell hurried her off to the Castle of Seton, accompanied by himself, Maitland and a few of the lords. All were on tenterhooks, all uncertain of what was to happen next – with the exception of Bothwell whose intentions were perfectly clear in his mind.

In the streets of Edinburgh the cry against him rose more shrilly, now that he was not there to strike terror into the populace.

'Let Bothwell be tried for murder!' shouted the people. 'Bothwell . . . with his servants and the Queen's . . . killed the King.'

The Earl of Lennox raised his voice. He demanded that the suspected Earl of Bothwell be brought to trial.

❋ ❋ ❋

At Seton the lovers could be alone together, but Bothwell was more interested in plans for the future than making love.

'Now,' he said, 'you are free to marry. You are free from that troublesome boy.'

'Free!' she cried. 'I shall never be free from him. He will always be with me. I can never forget him.'

Bothwell was impatient. 'He is dead and that is an end of him. Did you not want him dead? Did you not long to be my wife?'

'If we had met long ago . . .'

'Oh, have done with your "ifs"! We could marry now and there is nothing to stop us.'

'There is your wife.'

'I have told you that I can rid myself of her.'

'Not . . .'

'By divorce,' he said impatiently. 'Jean will agree. There must be no delay. Remember, we have a child to think of.'

'How could we marry now? How could we marry soon? The whole world will know that we are guilty.'

'We must marry,' said Bothwell. 'We shall marry.'

'I dare not. I long to be your wife but I dare not. There is no way out of this. You are accused of the murder. My servants are accused, and that means the people believe they acted in my name. Should we marry, all the world would say that we killed Darnley to bring this about.'

Bothwell took her by the shoulders. He said: 'We shall marry. I tell you we *shall* marry. Whatever happens, I am determined to marry you.'

'Then you must force me to it in some way. I must seem to surrender against my will. That is very necessary or the whole of Scotland will be against me. Oh, my dearest, what have we done! What have we done!'

'What we set out to do – rid ourselves of our encumbrances. What do you wish? To tell the whole world that I ravished you and therefore you consider it necessary to marry me?'

'It is true,' she murmured.

'And that is the only reason why you wish to marry me. Ah! You were no reluctant partner . . . after the first shock!'

She protested: 'You do not love me. You care more for Jean Gordon than for me.'

'I am ready to divorce her, am I not. And all for love of you!'

'Rather for love of my crown,'

He laughed. 'Let us not make such fine distinctions. You are the Queen and royal. Your crown is part of you, and if I would do what I have for the sake of a crown, yet it is for love of you too. You are my mistress, my concubine in private; but in public you must be my Queen. You must be royal. You must distribute the favours. That is how you would have it. When we are alone, I am the master; but when we are in public, you will be the Queen, I the servant.' He paused and seemed to consider awhile. Then he went on: 'Mayhap you are right. Mayhap that is how the people would have it. I will seize your person. I will hold you captive. The whole world shall believe that you are my captive and I ravished you. You therefore feel that the only way in which you can redeem your honour is through marriage, and for that reason you will seek the earliest opportunity to bring it about. You are a widow now. I shall soon be free of Jean. Nothing will stand in our way. That is our next move, my Queen. Leave it to me.'

'There is nothing else I can do,' she said. 'My whole life, my entire happiness is in your hands.'

She would think of nothing but her love of Bothwell. She would put her whole trust in him. He would bring them safely through this danger in which they found themselves. She had sent out of the country Joseph Rizzio and those of her servants who were suspected; she was relieved to know that they were safe. Bothwell and James Balfour would know how to defend themselves.

Bothwell had ridden through the streets of Edinburgh calling on any who accused him to come out and do it openly. He was ready, he declared, to wash his hands in their blood. He had his men – thousands of them in their steel bonnets thronging the streets of Edinburgh – but he would take on any of his challengers single-handed.

Mary wanted to show him how much she loved him; she could not give him enough. She had already bestowed on him the Castle of Blackness; and all the rich furs and jewels which Darnley had amassed were given to Bothwell. She wrote poems expressing her love for him, betraying the depth of her feelings, her desire for him, her bitter jealousy of his wife.

Bothwell himself was ready and eager to face a trial. It was arranged that he should do so, and, ostentatiously filling the town with his followers, he prepared to make his journey to the Tolbooth where the trial was to be held.

He was confident of the result. The Justice was that old and warm supporter of his, Argyle; the jury was picked. Every man among them knew that only fools would support Lennox in his weakness against the might of Bothwell.

It was not that the lords did not fear Bothwell; it was not that they were unaware of his rising power. They were suspicious of his relationship with the Queen, but he now had five thousand men in the city, and the guns of Edinburgh Castle were under the command of one of his men. The strength of Bothwell was much in evidence and the lords could not but quail before him. Bothwell was in charge of events and they were afraid of him.

The citizens watched him ride to the Tolbooth, magnificently clad in velvet hose passamented and trussed with silver and with his black satin doublet similarly decorated; he wore jewels presented to him by the Queen, and his great figure mounted on a fine horse had all the bearing of the King he was determined to become. His exultation was obvious.

The Queen could not resist looking out of a window of Holyrood to watch his departure. She felt there was no need to pray for his safety; he would look after himself; he was invincible.

The trial was conducted in a solemn manner, just as though it were a real trial. The lords considered the evidence brought forward by Lennox; they retired and after long discussion declared the verdict.

'James, Earl of Bothwell, is acquitted of any art and part of the slaughter of the King.'

Triumphantly he rode through the streets of Edinburgh. He galloped along the Canongate and shouted to the people: 'People of Edinburgh, I have been acquitted of that of which I was accused. I have been pronounced guiltness. If there is any man among you who doubts that verdict to be a true one, let him come forward now. I challenge him to single combat. Let him fortify his accusations with the sword.'

People listened behind bolted doors; no one ventured forth, though there was scarcely a man or woman in Edinburgh who did not believe Bothwell to be the King's murderer.

Up and down the streets he galloped, pausing now and then to call to his accusers to come out and fight with him. None came. And at length he returned to Holyroodhouse to tell the Queen that events were moving in their favour.

Mary's life was divided between periods of delirious joy and dreadful remorse. She was more passionately in love with him than ever. He was without hypocrisy, whatever other faults he might have. He would never pretend. He enjoyed their relationship; her passion was as fiercely demanding as his; he found great pleasure in their union, but he was less sentimental than she. She differed from other women in one respect as far as he was concerned; she had a crown to offer him. He would not have been the man he was if he could have hidden this fact. Mary knew it and it caused her many bitter tears.

Often after he had left her she would read through some of the sonnets she had written for him. There was one which described her feelings without reserve.

> *'Pour luy aussi j'ay jette mainte larme,*
> *Premier qu'il fust de ce corps possesseur,*
> *Duquel alors il n'avoit pas le cœur . . .'*

She read it through again and again, thinking of all the bitter tears she had shed for him. She read that line which was as true now as it had been when she had written it.

'Brief, de vous seul je cherche alliance.'

Within a few days he decided he must go to see his wife.

'I must persuade her to the divorce,' he said.

'I hate your going to her!' she cried.

He laughed aloud. 'I go to ask her to release me. What cause for jealousy is there in that?'

The only comfort she could find was in pouring out her thoughts in verses – verses which he would read and smile over before he locked them into his casket, there to lie forgotten.

But he did not go to see Jean then. He discovered that it would be unwise to leave Mary – not for love of her but because he feared that his enemies might capture her and keep her their prisoner. He talked instead to Jean's brother, Huntley. Huntley, aware that Bothwell was the strongest power in the land, decided that it would be worth while setting aside a sister in order to share in that power.

The divorce must be speedy. Bothwell told Huntley that it could be brought about on the grounds of consanguinity as he and Jean were distantly connected.

It was impossible to silence the rumours. The Queen's husband dead. Bothwell seeking to divorce his wife. The inference was obvious.

Great events were about to burst on Scotland. Danger lay ahead. This was certain, for the Earl of Moray had left Scotland for France. He wanted no part in what was about to take place; he only wanted to partake of any good which might come within his reach through the ruin of the Queen, which more than ever seemed to him inevitable.

Bothwell was triumphant. He had been the chief instigator of Darnley's murder and had gone unpunished. His men swaggered through the streets clanging their bucklers and broadswords. They commanded the fortress. All the nobles were invited – or ordered – to take supper with Lord Bothwell at the Ainslie Tavern.

At the closing of the recent parliament he had carried the Queen's crown and sceptre for her, back to the palace. Now there was not a man among them who dared refuse his invitation, while there was not one who was completely easy in his mind.

The revellers were feasting and making merry in the tavern when they were suddenly aware that the inn was surrounded by Bothwell's men who stood on guard at the doors.

Bothwell called to his guests: 'My very good lords, I thank you for your company, and now that we are all together and you know me for your friend, I would know you for mine. I have a bond here and I shall ask you, one and all, to sign it.'

Only the Earl of Eglinton, who was sitting near a window which was unguarded, managed to slip away unnoticed. The others were caught, intensely aware of the armed men surrounding the inn.

Morton cried: 'What is this bond, friend Bothwell?'

'I will read it to you.' Bothwell stood on a table and taking the scroll in his hand read aloud:

'James, Earl of Bothwell, being calumniated by malicious reports and divers placards as art and part in the heinous murder of the King, has submitted to an assize, and been found innocent of the same by certain noblemen his peers and others barons of good reputation. We, the undersigned, oblige ourselves upon our faith and honour and truth of our bodies, will answer to God, that in case hereafter any manner of persons shall happen to insist farther on the slander and calumniation of the said heinous murder we and our kin, friends and assisters, shall take true and plain part with him to the defence and maintenance of his quarrel with our bodies, heritage and goods. And as Her Majesty is now destitute of husband, in which solitary state the Commonweal cannot permit Her Highness to continue, if it should please her so far to humble herself by taking one of her own born subjects and marry the said Earl, we will maintain and fortify him against all who would hinder and disturb the said marriage. Under our hands and seals at Edinburgh this day of April the 19th, in the year 1567.'

The lords were dumbfounded.

They had expected to be asked to stand beside him in the event of his accusers' rising against him, but this proposed marriage with the Queen was a feat of daring which they had not expected, even from Bothwell.

They hesitated. They were aware of the men-at-arms outside. The ferocity of Bothwell's men was well known. And here they were, caught in a trap, befuddled with wine, heavy with feasting.

Morton stepped forward and said: 'It is true that Lord Bothwell was acquitted and therefore every man should stand beside him should he be attacked on this matter of the King's death. I will give my signature to the bond. It is true that Her Majesty is left a widow and that for the good of this country she should marry. If Her Majesty should humble herself and take one of her born subjects and that should be the Earl we see before us, then I say that will be for Scotland's good and I hereby sign the bond.'

Bothwell was taken aback. He had not expected such ready support from Morton.

One by one the lords came up to sign the bond. They knew they must do it or die. Bothwell would have no mercy.

While they were uneasy, Bothwell was triumphant. But there was one who was far from displeased by what he had witnessed in the tavern; he was sly Morton.

By God! he swore to himself, little do these oafs know when they reluctantly sign this bond that they are doing just what they would wish to do; they are signing Bothwell's death warrant. And he, poor fool, is too drunk with ambition to know it. Should he marry the Queen they are both doomed. Such a marriage would expose them to the world as Darnley's murderers. The most foolish step they could take at this point is to marry.

He decided he would send word at once to Moray. It would not be long before James Stuart would return to Scotland to take the Regency.

There was at least one other who agreed with Morton. This was Elizabeth of England. She herself had been in a similar position seven years ago when her lover's wife had been found mysteriously dead at the bottom of a staircase, and Elizabeth with her lover Robert Dudley had appeared to be guilty of the murder. Mary had a shining example of royal behaviour in such a delicate situation. To marry Bothwell now would be to destroy herself, as to have married Dudley at the time of Amy Robsart's death would have destroyed Elizabeth.

The Queen of England had no love for her Scottish rival but she had a strong desire to preserve the dignity of royalty. She wrote warningly to Mary, but her warning meant nothing to the Queen of Scots. The Queen of England was governed by ambition; the Queen of Scots by her emotions which were now concentrated on the passion she felt for one man. Her hand was in that of her lover, and if he were dragging her down to destruction, he was with her and nothing else seemed of any real importance.

On a bright April day Mary set out for Stirling Castle in order to visit her son. She did so at the secret command of Bothwell. He himself had declared his intention of going to Liddesdale where fighting had broken out and his firm hand was needed.

She took with her a small retinue in which were included the lords Maitland and Huntley and Sir James Melville. As she rode out of Edinburgh the people came out to look at her. They were pleased that Bothwell had left the capital; Mary's lovely tragic face softened the hearts of the people to such an extent that they could not believe her to be guilty of murder.

'God bless Your Grace!' called the citizens; but they added: 'If you be innocent of the King's murder.'

If she be innocent! Mary shuddered. What would she not give to be innocent? Everything she possessed but one thing – the love of Bothwell.

Lord Maitland, riding beside her, was filled with fury against her and Bothwell. He saw clearly now how Bothwell had duped the lords, how he had secured their help in the murder of Darnley – not to rid Scotland of an encumbrance, but to remove the Queen's husband that he, Bothwell, might marry her.

That he should have been so used was galling to Maitland. He determined now that if Bothwell married the Queen they should never rule Scotland together. Maitland and Bothwell could never be anything but enemies.

Maitland had wished to serve the Queen. His wife was a very dear friend of the Queen's. He had worked faithfully for her until that time when she had taken Rizzio into her confidence and set him above Maitland. Now he saw that he had, with others, been Bothwell's dupe, and he was determined that he would never accept that man's domination.

Huntley looked sly. Maitland wondered what plans he had made with Bothwell, and as Bothwell was his brother-in-law, Maitland could guess. Bothwell would need Huntley's help if he were to break free from his wife.

Maitland must be on his guard. He had seen too much; he had been too clever. Bothwell, who had so cleverly rid the Queen and himself of Darnley, would have little compunction in being equally ruthless with others who threatened their schemes.

These were uneasy thoughts for Maitland on the road from Edinburgh to Stirling.

The Earl and Countess of Mar, who were the guardians of the little Prince, greeted the Queen with suspicion. News had travelled and they knew of the paper Bothwell had more or less forced the lords to sign. It occurred to Mar that it might be the plan of the Queen and her lover to kidnap the Prince. Mar was not going to lose his precious charge, and he made that quite clear.

Mary held the baby in her arms. He was ten months old, a solemn-faced, wise-looking little boy. He gazed with wonderment at his mother and she, smiling, let his little hand curl about her finger. He was placidly curious as she covered his face with kisses.

If she could take him away with her, live quietly in a nunnery with him, perhaps she would in time forget that she had any desire but to care for him. But such would never be allowed. Already the Earl of Mar was watching her suspiciously; insistent hands were stretched forward to take the baby from her. She was not allowed to be alone in the nursery.

'I am sorry, Madam,' said the Earl. 'The Prince has been accorded to my care and I have sworn to watch over him, night and day.'

'Even when he is with his mother?'

'At all times, Madam.'

So this was the state to which she was reduced – a mother

who might not be alone with her child! She told herself fiercely: Soon it will be different. When I marry, my husband will stand beside me and there shall not be a lord in Scotland who dares treat me thus.

They left Stirling on the third day. Her spirits were high, for she had always been happy in the saddle and she knew what was waiting for her on the road.

It was arranged between them. He would be there . . . towering above all men, striking terror into her escort, seizing her person, taking her as his prisoner to Dunbar, and there boldly – as the world would think – forcing her to submit to him. All would be well, for her future was in his hands.

But as they came nearer to Edinburgh she grew uneasy. He should have appeared before this. They were within a mile of Edinburgh Castle itself and unless he arrived almost immediately their plan would miscarry. But he did not disappoint her. She heard the sound of horses' hoofs pounding on the quiet earth as she rode into Foulbriggs, the small hamlet between Coltbridge and West Port; and as she was about to cross the foul stream – from which the place took its name and which was swollen with the filth from the city – Bothwell's strong force came into view. Blades gleaming, pikes aloft, they surrounded the Queen's small company. Bothwell rode up to her.

'What means this?' she asked.

'Madam,' said her lover. 'I must ask you to turn your horse and ride with me to Dunbar. You are my prisoner; but have no fear. No harm shall come to you if you obey.'

A young captain rode forward and prepared to do battle with Bothwell for the sake of the Queen.

'Put your sword away, my friend,' said the Queen. 'I command you to do so.'

'I'll take care of the young fool,' growled Bothwell.

'There shall be no bloodshed,' said the Queen.

The young soldier turned to Mary, his eyes alight with that devoted admiration which she so often inspired. 'Madam, I would die to save you.'

She smiled, and her smile was her answer. The young man knew that she was by no means disturbed by this adventure, that she was Bothwell's very willing prisoner.

Maitland cried: 'What means this?'

Bothwell flashed a brilliant smile in his direction. 'Patience, my lord Maitland. Soon you will know.'

He then dismissed most of her retinue, but kept Lord Maitland, Lord Huntley and Sir James Melville with him; and the journey to Dunbar began.

The Queen rode ahead and Bothwell was beside her.

Mary waited in the apartment at Dunbar Castle which had been prepared for her.

Soon he would join her. She could close her eyes and imagine that she was in the Exchequer House on that evening before it all began. It would be just like that. They would enact that scene once again, and the whole world should believe that it was the first time it had taken place.

Bothwell would stand exposed to the world as the Queen's ravisher, and as his innocent victim she would declare that she must marry him. As for the unborn child – that would have to be explained later. It was imperative that she marry hastily, that the whole world should not be too shocked by her marriage, and that suspicions that she had been an accomplice in her husband's murder should be allayed.

It was a desperate scheme but their position was desperate. When she had glanced at his stern profile as he rode beside her from Foulbriggs to Dunbar Castle, she had revelled in his strength, in that power within him. How willingly would she surrender! How happily she waited for her ravisher!

In a room below, Melville was remonstrating with Bothwell. Maitland stood aloof; he knew too much. He understood that the Queen and Bothwell were already lovers. He knew that this was just another bridge which they had to cross together.

Melville said: 'Bothwell, know you not that this is treason? You are unlawfully detaining the Queen. For what purpose?'

'I shall marry the Queen,' said Bothwell.

'She will never consent,' said Melville.

'I will marry her whether she will or not. And it may be that by the time I release her from this castle she will be willing enough.'

Melville was aghast at the implication of those words.

Bothwell laughed and went to the Queen's apartment.

Melville turned to Maitland. How could Maitland appear so calm? Had he not heard Bothwell express his intention to ravish the Queen?

Maitland's smile was cynical. Should they be perturbed, it implied, because what was about to take place would be but a repetition of what had been happening for several months?

Maitland shrugged his shoulders. He was concerned with preserving his own life. He was secretly convinced that if he could keep alive for a few more weeks, he need never fear Bothwell again . . . nor the Queen.

Bothwell came to the Queen's apartment and he stood on the threshold of the room, smiling at her as he had smiled in the Exchequer House.

She cried out in feigned alarm: 'My lord . . . what means this?'

He smiled. As though she did not know! But he enjoyed the masquerade as much as she did. Of late she had perhaps been over-eager, and a certain amount of resistance had always appealed to him.

So she protested but her heart was not in the protest, and she was glad when she could surrender freely to his passion.

For twelve days he kept her at Dunbar Castle – his passionate mistress and his most willing slave.

At the end of that time the Queen was escorted back to Edinburgh. She rode into the city with Bothwell beside her, he holding her horse's bridle that the city might know that she was his captive.

Maitland was with them, plans forming in his clever mind. They would marry – those two foolish people – and they would ruin themselves. Morton was already in secret touch with Moray. The country was going to be roused against the King's murderers; and the hasty marriage, the threadbare plot of abduction and seduction would be seen through; the Queen would have none but Bothwell to stand beside her. When she took Bothwell she would lose all else.

Bothwell and Mary could think of little beyond their marriage which would make him King of Scotland and her the wife of her lover. Neither of them could look very far beyond their greatly desired goals.

There was one obstacle yet to be overcome. Bothwell was not free to marry; but he had already set in motion negotiations which would bring him a divorce on the grounds of consanguinity. The Archbishop of St Andrews signed the nullity agreement, but Jean was not satisfied with this. She had been truly married to Lord Bothwell, she declared; and that marriage had been entirely legal. She would not have it said otherwise. She would be happy to be free of Bothwell who had been no good husband to her, but she herself would seek a divorce on the grounds of adultery.

This caused a slight hitch. Bothwell had a reputation as a murderer, and all Scotland knew that he was an adulterer, but the whole world including the fanatical Philip in his Escorial, sly Catherine de' Medici in the Louvre, subtle Elizabeth in Greenwich, would now see him brought low through his wife's allegations. Jean was determined to have her revenge for the slights she had suffered. She named Bessie Crawford, the daughter of a blacksmith, as the partner in Bothwell's adultery.

The scandals grew. The story of Bothwell and Bessie became common knowledge. A Haddington merchant explained how he had one afternoon, on the instructions of Lord Bothwell, taken Bessie to the cloisters of Haddington Abbey; there he had locked her in and given the key – on Lord Bothwell's instructions – to his lordship. There Bessie and the Earl had remained together for a considerable time.

Is this the man who would be King of Scotland? people were asking each other. There were many ready to pry into the affairs of Bessie Crawford and Lord Bothwell and ensure that the whole world should know of them.

His enemies were already at work, but the bold Earl cared nothing for this. What mattered it how the divorce was brought about as long as his marriage with Jean was severed? He had the lords' consent on a document; he was free; Mary was free; and they would wait no longer.

John Craig, the preacher who had taken Knox's place in the Kirk when the latter, after the murder of Rizzio, had thought it wise to go to England and remain there, was loth to publish the banns.

Bothwell threatened him, but the man stood his ground. He begged the Earl to consider the Church's law against adultery and ravishment; he warned him of the likely suspicion of collusion between Bothwell and his wife, the too sudden divorce and above all, his and Mary's complicity in Darnley's murder.

'Read the banns!' roared Bothwell. 'Or by Jesus I'll have you strung up by the neck.'

But John Craig turned away. His courage was high. 'There is only one thing which would make me do it – a written order from the Queen.'

Bothwell laughed. A written order from the Queen! What could be easier?

But he was disturbed. The preacher had boldly stated what was being said in secret.

According to the law, rape was punishable by death, and it was alleged that as Bothwell had raped the Queen, she felt in honour bound to marry him even though it was such a short time since her husband had died.

There were no ends to the twists and turns which must be made to extricate themselves from the position in which they found themselves.

Now Mary must declare that rape was forgiven if the woman subsequently acquiesced; and this, he declared, was what had happened in the case of herself and Lord Bothwell. To show her feelings for him she gave him fresh honours. He was made Earl of Orkney and Lord of Shetland. But the whispers were becoming louder throughout the land, and all were discussing the loose behaviour of the Queen and her paramour. The Queen was no better than Bessie Crawford, and nothing she could say or do would make the people believe that the man she proposed to make their King was anything but a seducer, an adulterer and a murderer.

The night before their marriage was due to take place, a placard was pinned on the door of the palace. It ran:

'Mense malas Maio nubere vulgus ait.'

It was alarming to be reminded through these words of Ovid's that wantons married in the month of May.

Nevertheless on that May morning, accompanied by Huntley, Glamis, Fleming, Livingstone and others – all of whom attended her with restrained feelings – Mary was, in the chapel at Holyrood, married to Bothwell.

But where was that bliss for which she had looked? He had never pretended, but now he had no time to play the lover. Now he must consolidate his position, and already the lords all over the country were making their animosity felt. He was ready. He loved a fight. And now he was preparing to fight for the crown of Scotland.

Mary began to realise the enormity of what she had done. She had married her lover, notorious as the seducer of Bessie Crawford; she had debased her royalty – an unforgivable sin in

475

the eyes of all those who were royal. Her relatives in France were numbed by the shock. Catherine de' Medici in public declared herself shocked and saddened beyond expression, but in private gave full vent to her delight and satisfaction; Philip of Spain had nothing to offer but contempt, and that he showed by silence. Elizabeth of England, while pleased at the prospects of the inevitable result, was genuinely shocked that the Queen should so betray herself and her crown. Elizabeth could not help but remember how near to disaster she had come in circumstances so similar; but she had been wise; she had known when to draw back.

There was less contentment now for Mary than ever before, since she could not help knowing that her lover was out-growing his passion. To him she was but a woman with a crown – and now the crown was his. If she could have fallen out of love with him as she had with Darnley she would have suffered far less. But she could do no such thing; his indifference could not turn her from him.

He neglected her and absented himself for long periods, during which she believed he saw Jean Gordon. She would lie awake at night picturing them together. She believed that sly sandy-haired Jean merely pretended not to be in love with him.

She reproached him on his return but he merely laughed at her, neither admitting nor denying that her surmise was correct.

'You can talk of Jean Gordon when we are in such danger!' he cried. 'Do you know that our enemies are massing their forces against us?'

'But you have visited her. I believe you still think of her as your wife!'

'There is that in her which makes me think of her so. You have always seemed as my mistress.'

Did he mean that or was it part of his brutality? She did not know.

She was exhausted from sleepless nights. Darnley's ghost seemed to mock her. 'You have changed husbands. I died that you might do so. But has it proved to be a change for the better?'

She could not bear his indifference, his cold matter-of-fact passion.

Once she withdrew herself from his arms and, half clad as she was, rushed to the door of her apartment calling to Jane Kennedy to bring her a knife.

'A knife, Madam? A *knife*!'

'That I may pierce my heart with it. I cannot endure to live this life. I would rather be dead.'

Then she flung herself on to the bed and gave way to passionate weeping.

All over the country the lords were gathering. Moray was watching from some distance, waiting to leap forward and seize the Regency when the Queen was defeated. Morton called together Argyle, Atholl and Mar, and told them that Kirkcaldy of Grange was ready to lead an army against Bothwell and the Queen; and that Glencairn, Cassillis, Montrose, Caithness, Ruthven, Lindsay and others were with them. Maitland was still at Holyrood, but waiting his opportunity to escape and join the rebels. Maitland had made up his mind. Mary was unfit to rule. Her conduct of the past year had shown that clearly. The woman who had gathered an army together at the time she had married Darnley and marched against Moray with the country rallying to her, was not the same woman as this love-sick creature. At that time Mary could have risen to greatness; her future might have been assured; but alas, steadily she had taken the downhill road which could only lead to eventual defeat.

Bothwell was aware of the forces gathering against him. He left Sir James Balfour holding Edinburgh Castle and departed with Mary for Borthwick.

It was not for love of her that he was with her constantly now, but because he feared that the rebels might seek to capture her. She reproached him for this, but he made no effort to console her.

Before they had been many days in that solid fortress which was built on a steep mound, surrounded by a moat, and possessed towers so strongly fortified as to discountenance invaders, Lord Hume arrived and demanded the surrender of Bothwell. Awaiting the arrival of his Borderers the Earl roared forth his defiance, but as the days passed and his men did not come he began to calculate how long he could withstand a siege. The castle, with its central fortress, its winding passages, its low arches, its windows which were thirty feet from the ground, was a stronghold, but he had no intention of starving to death. He decided he must break out of the castle.

'Take me with you,' begged Mary.

He shook his head. 'Impossible. One of us might get through. Two would surely be caught. If I can break through the guards I shall ride with all speed to Dunbar. Then I shall muster my men, and, by God, I'll have Hume's head. I'll have the heads of all rebels.'

'Oh my dearest, make sure that it is not they who take your head.'

'My head and shoulders are as firmly wedded as we are!' he cried.

She clung to him, all tenderness, begging him to take care.

He put her from him and, in spite of the enemy guard surrounding the castle, he managed to break out.

Those who had been set to guard the castle, on discovering that Bothwell had eluded them, were afraid to touch the Queen, and they started off towards Edinburgh believing that Bothwell had returned there. Then, dressed in the clothes of a boy – for she dared not attract attention to herself – Mary was lowered from the window of the banqueting hall on to the grass some thirty feet below, and hurried down the mound where she found a horse, saddled and waiting for her. Then began her ride through that wild country of glens and swamps, moorland and mountain. It was many long hours before she reached Dunbar. Bothwell, hearing of her approach to the castle, came out to meet her. He lifted her from her horse and held her at arms' length.

'You make a bonny boy!' he said. And he slung her across his shoulder and carried her into Dunbar Castle.

For the rest of that night she was ecstatically happy. Everything seemed worth while. They made love and afterwards they made plans, and then made love again.

He said at length: 'We cannot remain here. We shall have to ride forth to meet them.'

'We shall win, my dearest,' she cried. 'We shall win and be happy together. You could not fail. Anything you desired you would win.'

'Thrones are not such easy prey as queens.'

'Queens are not easy prey,' she answered, 'except for those whom they love. And to those whom Fortune loves, thrones may come more easily than the love of a queen.'

He kissed her and they were fiercely passionate lovers again. She wondered whether it was because he feared there would be little time left for loving.

❁ ❁ ❁

She determined to ride with him at the head of the army.

She had come to Dunbar as a boy and there was none of her own garments at Dunbar Castle. No women's clothes could be found except that of a citizen's wife. She put on a red petticoat; and the sleeves of her bodice were tied with points; a black velvet hat and a scarf were found for her. And so, dressed as a tradesman's wife, she rode out to meet those who had rebelled against her. Her spirits were high, for beside her rode Bothwell.

The armies met at Musselburgh and the Queen's encamped on Carberry Hill close to that spot where some twenty years before the famous battle of Pinkie Cleugh had been fought; but now that the two armies were face to face they both appeared reluctant to fight.

For a whole day inactivity reigned, each side anxious not to have the sun facing them during battle, and now that they had come to the point, the rebels had no wish to fight against the Queen nor had the Queen to fight against her own subjects.

So the long day passed – each side alert and waiting, watching each other from opposite hills across the little brook which flowed between them.

In the afternoon du Croc, the French ambassador, rode to the rebels and declared his readiness to act as a mediator between the two forces.

'We have not,' said Glencairn to the Frenchman, 'come to ask pardon but to give it. If the Queen is willing to withdraw herself from the wretch who holds her captive we will recognise her as our sovereign. If, on the other hand, Bothwell will come forth between the two armies and make good his boast that he will meet in single combat any who should declare he is the murderer of the King, we will produce a champion to meet him, and if he desires it another and another, ten or twelve.'

'You cannot seriously mean me to lay these proposals before the Queen,' protested du Croc.

'We will name no other,' said Glencairn, and Kirkcaldy and Morton joined with him in this. 'We would rather be buried alive than not have the death of the King investigated.'

Du Croc then went to the Queen. Bothwell was with her.

He cried: 'What is it that the lords are at?'

Du Croc answered: 'They declare themselves to be willing servants of the Queen but that they are your mortal foes.'

'They are sick with envy,' said Bothwell. 'They wish to stand in my place. Did they not all sign the bond promising to make good my cause and defend it with their lives and goods?'

Mary said quickly: 'I would have all know that I espouse my husband's quarrel and consider it my own.'

Du Croc told her of the suggestion that Bothwell should engage a chosen champion in single combat. Mary looked fearful. She would not agree to that, she declared. There should be no single combat. What man was there on the other side who was of high enough rank to fight with her husband?

'Unless this is done,' said du Croc, 'there will be bitter fighting.'

'Stay and see it,' said Bothwell. 'I can promise you fine pastime, for there will be good fighting.'

'I should be sorry to see it come to that for the sake of the Queen and for both armies.'

'Why, man,' boasted Bothwell, 'I shall win the day. I have four thousand men and three pieces of artillery. They have no artillery and only three thousand men.'

'You have but yourself as general,' said du Croc. 'Do not forget that with them are the finest soldiers in Scotland. Moreover there is some discontent I believe among your people.'

When he had gone Bothwell and the Queen looked round them at their army and, to their dismay, they saw that du Croc had spoken the truth. Many of those who had marched behind her banner were now visibly deserting to the other side. They did not wish to serve under the banner of an adulteress and a woman who had, they all believed, had a hand in the murder of her husband.

Bothwell then rode forward shouting: 'Come forth! Come forth! Which of you will engage in single combat?'

Kirkcaldy stepped forward.

Terrified for her lover, Mary galloped up to his side.

'I forbid it!' she cried. 'There must be someone of rank equal to that of my husband. I will not have him demeaned by this combat.'

Bothwell cried: 'Let Lord Morton step forth. I will do battle with him.'

But Morton had no wish for the fight. His friends rallied to his side and declared that such a man as himself must not face the danger of combat. He was worth a hundred such as Bothwell.

Bothwell had no desire to fight any but Morton, and when

others were offered he declined to accept them as opponents. And while this farce was in progress Mary saw with dismay that her force was dwindling so fast that there were scarcely sixty men left to support her cause.

She asked that Kirkcaldy should come to her and, when he came, she asked him what terms he would give.

'That you leave your husband, Madam, and the lords will submit to you.'

'You mean that he will go free if I return to Edinburgh with you?'

'Yes, Madam. Those are our conditions.'

She looked about her in despair. Bothwell stood apart with a few – a very few – of his Borderers. She knew that there were two alternatives. She must part with her lover or see him slaughtered before her eyes. She asked that she might be allowed to speak to him.

Drawing him aside she said: 'We must part. It is the only way. You will be allowed to ride off with your men unmolested.'

'And they will take you back to Edinburgh. For what, think you?'

'I am their Queen. They will remember that. I shall force them to remember it.'

'You place too much trust in them.'

'I can do nothing else.'

'Mount your horse. Pretend to bid me farewell . . . and then . . . we will gallop off to Dunbar. There we will fortify ourselves. We will defend the castle while we raise an army.'

'They would kill us. That is what they mean to do. They mean to part us. They will do it either by our willing separation or by death.'

'I demand that you do as I say.'

But she shook her head and gave him her tragic smile. She was the Queen and he could no longer force her to his will. She longed to ride with him, but greater than her desire for him was her fear for his safety.

'I shall go with them,' she said.

Kirkcaldy rode up to them. 'The time is up, Madam,' he said. 'Unless you make an immediate decision I shall be unable to hold my men.'

Bothwell held her in his arms. In those last moments she was aware of an exasperated tenderness. She had decided, and he was opposed to her decision. He believed that once more her emotions had played her false and that she was delivering herself defenceless into the hands of her enemies. His last kiss held a plea. Do not trust them. Leap on to your horse. We will snap our fingers at that mighty army. We will ride together to Dunbar.

But she, who had been so weak in love, could also be strong.

Let them do what they would with her, let them deceive her; he had an opportunity of riding away unmolested. He would find his way to safety.

One more kiss; one last embrace.

A terrible desolation came over her, for she had a sad premonition that she would never see his face again. She wavered and clung to him afresh. But Kirkcaldy was impatiently waiting.

He helped her into the saddle and she turned her horse.

Bothwell had shrugged his shoulders; his spurs pressed into his horse's flanks and he was away.

She turned her head, straining for the last glimpse of him; but Kirkcaldy had laid his hand on her bridle and was leading her away.

◈ ◈ ◈

How right he had been! How wrong she was to trust them!

She knew that if she lived twenty years she could never live through such horror, such shameful humiliation, as now awaited her.

Seeing her thus, mounted on her jennet, stripped of her royalty, a conquered queen in a red petticoat, the rebel soldiers, remembering and repeating the rumours they had heard of her, inflamed by the vilification of years which had been hurled against her by John Knox, jeered as they gloated on her humiliation.

The whispering first started among the low soldiery. 'Who murdered the King?'

The rest took up the cry. 'Burn the adulteress. Burn the murderess.'

The soldiers crowded about her and Kirkcaldy had to hold some back with his sword.

'Bring her to the city – the scene of her shame!' they cried. 'Let her see what the citizens of Edinburgh have to say to her.'

So she was led towards her capital, and two soldiers, bearing a banner extending between two pikes, marched before her; the banner was turned towards her that she might read the crude inscription thereon. On this banner had been painted a figure of Darnley lying murdered, and beside him was a smaller figure which was meant to represent Prince James, Darnley's son and hers. The little Prince was on his knees praying: 'Judge and revenge my cause, O Lord.'

'Make way! Make way!' cried the soldiers. 'Good people of Scotland, we bring you the murderess. We bring the woman who, with her lover, slew her husband. We bring you the whore of Scotland. Make way for the adulteress.'

She was alone; she had lost her strong man and had given herself over to traitors, but as always in terrible adversity she found great courage.

She took the hand of Lord Lindsay of the Byres who was beside her and cried: 'By this hand which is now in yours I swear I'll have your head for this outrage.'

'Madam,' said Lindsay, 'look to it that you do not lose your own.'

For hours it lasted, that terrible ride. She was exhausted and only pride kept back the tears of heartbreak. Never had a queen been treated so. If her lover had been with her now, how different it would have been. Then they would not have dared to treat her so. She should have obeyed him. Then he and she would now be riding to Dunbar . . . together.

She kept her eyes fixed on the hideous banner. She had lost everything – her lover, her child, her throne.

It was twilight when they came to Edinburgh. Crowds thronged the Canongate to watch her pass; and there was not one friend in the city to give her a word of comfort.

'Here comes the murderess,' they cried. 'Let us burn the whore.'

Morton had arranged that the procession should take an indirect route through the city. Mary did not at first understand why. Then suddenly she realised what they were doing; they were taking her along the road which led to Kirk-o'-Field. They halted for a moment before the ruins of that house in which Darnley had been murdered. There the banner was brought close before her eyes, and the people crowded in on her.

'Burn her! Burn her! Now . . . *now*! Why do we wait? She betrays her guilt.'

'Good people,' cried Mary, 'I beg of you let me speak.'

But her words were lost in the howls of derision. And as the people closed in on her Kirkcaldy once more drove them off with his sword. Lindsay, Morton and Atholl were forced to join him.

Almost unconscious with strain and exhaustion she was taken to the provost's house and there put into the strong room, the window of which looked straight on to the street. About the window the rabble clustered and the banner was set up outside so that every time she lifted her eyes she could see it.

But for Kirkcaldy she could not have lived through that night. Kirkcaldy had not foreseen what would happen; he was a general who had promised safe conduct to the Queen, and since he had given that promise he meant it to be kept. Morton had no such scruples and had it rested with him he would have let the people have their way. He knew that Moray was on the way back from France. It was true that Huntley, with some of his Catholics, was half-heartedly preparing to rally to the Queen, but the people were all against her. They believed her to be guilty of adultery and murder, and they cried: 'Take her to the stake. That is the place for sinners such as she is, be they queens or commoners.'

There was no food for her in the provost's house; there was no bed; she had no means of bathing her face or changing her clothes.

She paced the room, moaning softly to herself, worn out with fatigue, distressed and hysterical. All through the night people thronged the streets and the fiery light of torches filled the room.

Again and again she tried to speak to them; she tried to win their sympathy. She stood at the window, her hair loose about her shoulders; in her great agitation she plucked at her bodice until it was in shreds and her breasts bared. She beat against the walls; she wept; and at last she sank to the floor, moaning and whimpering.

Outside the cry of 'Burn the adulteress! Burn the murderess!' was chanted through the streets.

❀ ❀ ❀

Another day came. She went to the window, her long hair covering her bare shoulders.

'Good people . . .' she cried. 'Good people . . .'

But their only answer was: 'Burn her. Burn the murderess of her husband!'

The dreadful banner was before her eyes. She wept and stormed. Then she saw Lord Maitland passing along the street. She called to him. He would have looked away but the sight she presented was so terrible that out of pity he was forced to turn back.

'Come here, Maitland,' she cried. 'Come here.'

He knew that if he followed his inclination to hurry away he would be haunted by the memory of her eyes for ever.

She looked at him – the husband of her dear Flem – and one of those who had betrayed her. How wicked was the world, how cruel!

'So you are with them now?' she called. 'So you are with my enemies, Maitland?'

'Madam,' he answered, 'I served you well until you chose others who you thought would serve you better.'

He had never forgiven her for supplanting him with David.

He would never forgive her for her marriage with Bothwell.

She cried: 'Did *you* not know then of the plot to murder Darnley! Were you not in the plot, my lord?'

His answer was: 'Madam, you destroyed yourself when you took Bothwell for husband. Had you not become his slave and the slave of your own passion, you would not now stand guilty of murder.'

The crowd roared: 'Burn the murderess!'

Maitland averted his eyes and passed on.

In that moment she knew that all who had planned to murder Darnley were against her. They would – as Maitland would – revile her, doing their utmost to put all the guilt on her shoulders and those of her lover, that investigations should not be made concerning themselves. The murder of Darnley – like the murder of Rizzio – would be shown to the Scots and the world not as a political murder, but as a *crime passionel*.

She was lost. She knew it. Maitland had had some honour in the old days. He had been one of those whom she could trust; but Maitland was ready to save his own life and his political rewards at the cost of the reputation, and perhaps the life, of the Queen.

She lived through another day of torment, and that evening, because they feared for her reason, they took her from the provost's house to Holyrood. She was forced to walk as a captive with Morton on one side of her, Atholl on the other, while the soldiers marched with them to protect her from the murderous rabble. As she walked the odious banner was held before her eyes and she prayed for death.

But in Holyrood some comfort awaited her, for there she

found some of her women, and among them those two loved ones, Mary Seton and Mary Livingstone.

She wept in their arms and they swore that they would not leave her; they would die with her and for her if need be.

But her captors did not intend her to stay at Holyroodhouse. Late that night she was hurried out of the palace and, hysterical and exhausted with misery and fatigue, she was taken through the darkness to Lochleven where her jailors would be the Douglases – Sir William and his wife who was Moray's mother.

And there, in the ancient castle on an island in the centre of a lake, Mary Stuart came to the end of her turbulent reign, for that night she passed into the half-light, a prisoner. She was twenty-four years of age and had many years left to her, but her life as Queen was virtually over.

Mary, Queen of Scotland and the Isles, had become Mary, the captive.

✿ Author's Note ✿

It is probable that no historical character has ever aroused more ardent supporters or more fierce detractors than has Mary Stuart. Strangely enough these admirers and detractors extol or defame irrespective of their religious faith. This is most unusual and is no doubt due to the fact that, in contrast with the disputes which almost always involved those who lived in the sixteenth century, those which concern Mary are not, in the main, about religion. The questions so fiercely debated in Mary Stuart's case are: Did she write the Casket Letters? Was she a willing partner in her abduction and rape? Was she a murderess?

My research for *Royal Road to Fotheringay* led me to discover a Mary who was sometimes quick-tempered, sometimes gentle, always charming, tolerant and warm-hearted; but because I have been unable to exonerate her from implication in the murder of Darnley I want to stress that when assessing Mary we must not weigh her deeds and behaviour by present day standards. She lived in an age when life was cheap and cruelty part of daily existence. Many men and women of the past who were considered during their day as patterns of virtue would receive a very different verdict if they had lived to-day. For example: Michelet says that Gaspard de Coligny was the most ennobling character of his times; yet the discipline he imposed on the battlefield would be called cruelty to-day, and it is by no means certain that he was guiltless of the murder of François de Guise. It is very necessary to remember this when considering the part Mary played in luring her husband to the house in Kirk-o'-Field. In her generation she was kinder and more tolerant than most of the people around her; but she herself faced death more than once, and in the sixteenth century, the elimination of human obstacles was not deemed a crime of such magnitude as it is to-day.

Other questions asked are: How could a woman, having lived as virtuously as she had (even Brantôme had no scandalous gossip to record of Mary) suddenly indulge in an adulterous passion, and take part in the murder of the husband who stood between her and her lover? How could she, beautiful and cultured, suddenly become the slave of Bothwell, the uncouth ruffian from the Border?

I have sought explanations by posing questions of my own. Mary was not healthy and her pictures do not support all we hear of those outstanding attractions; so what was the secret of that immense physical charm which she undoubtedly possessed? I believe it was largely due to an extremely passionate nature which was but half awakened when she met Darnley and not fully so until it was recognised by that man – so experienced in amatory adventures – the virile Bothwell. I believe that dormant sensuality to have been the secret of her appeal. And why was it so long in coming to fruition? I think I have found the answer in Mary's relationship with the Cardinal of Lorraine, that past-master in all things sensual, whose closeness to Mary would have given him every chance to understand her; and, being the knowledgeable man he was, he could not fail to do this. The scandal – the origin of which was traced to Bothwell – that Mary was the Cardinal's mistress, cannot have been justified; yet theirs was no ordinary relationship, and I am of the opinion that it was the reason why the passions of such a passionate woman were so long dormant.

The Casket Letters and the poems are perhaps the most discussed documents in British history. If they were actually written by Mary, there can be no doubt of her guilt. But are they forgeries? It is impossible to answer Yes or No, for the mystery of the Casket Letters has never been solved. It seems clear that some of the poems could have been written by no other hand than Mary's, and it is equally clear that some parts of the letters could never have been her composition. (I refer in particular to the crude reference to Darnley in Letter No. 2, the most incriminating of all the Casket documents.) Yet might it not be that the letters were in some part forgeries, in others Mary's actual writings? Because a part is false it does not follow that the whole is. Who else could have written those revealing poems? Who among the Scots was sufficiently skilled in the French language? Maitland of Lethington? He was a cunning statesman, but was he a poet?

Mary was raped by Bothwell. Those who would proclaim her an angel of virtue are ready to concede that. An important question is: When did the rape occur? Was it in the Exchequer House or later at Dunbar after the abduction? Was Mary herself in the plot to abduct her? If so, she and Bothwell must have been in love before the staging of that extraordinary affair, and it is more than likely that the rape took place at the Exchequer House. Buchanan's ribald account is clearly exaggerated. The story of Lady Reres being lowered into the garden in order to bring Bothwell from his wife's bed to that of the Queen might have been written by Boccaccio and is too crude to be believed; but Mary *was* at the Exchequer House, and Bothwell's servant *did* live next door. Why should not Buchanan's story be *founded* on truth?

I have discarded, selected and fitted my material together with the utmost care and I hope I have made a plausible and convincing picture of Mary, the people who surrounded her, and the circumstances which made Fotheringay the inevitable end of her royal road.

I have studied many works and am indebted in particular to the following:

Anon, *Feudal Castles of France*.

Gore-Brown Robert, *Lord Bothwell*.

Gorman, Herbert, *The Scottish Queen*.

Guizot, M., *History of France*.

Hume, Martin, *The Love Affairs of Mary Queen of Scots*.

Lang, Andrew, *John Knox and the Reformation*.

Letters of Mary Queen of Scots (Vols. I and II), with Historical Introduction and Notes by Agnes Strickland.

Preedy, George R., *The Life of John Knox*.

Smith Aubrey, William Hickman, *History of England*.

Strickland, Agnes, *Lives of the Queens of Scotland and English Princesses* (Vols. III, IV, V, VI, VII).

Wade, John, *British History*.

Williams, H. Noel, *Henri II*.

Zweig, Stefan, *The Queen of Scots*.

J.P.

ALSO AVAILABLE IN ARROW IN THE TUDOR SERIES

The Shadow of the Pomegranate

Jean Plaidy

Whilst the young King Henry VIII basks in the pageants and games of his glittering court, his doting queen's health and fortunes fade. Henry's affection for his older wife soon strays, and the neglected Katharine decides to use her power as queen to dangerous foreign advantage.

Overseas battles play on Henry's volatile temper, and his defeat in France has changed the good-natured boy Katharine loved into an infamously callous ruler. With no legitimate heir yet born, Katharine once again begins to fear for her future . . .

arrow books

The King's Secret Matter

Jean Plaidy

After twelve years of marriage, the once fortuitous union of Henry VIII and Katharine of Aragon has declined into a loveless stalemate. Their only child, Mary, is disregarded as a suitable heir, and Henry's need for a legitimate son to protect the Tudor throne has turned him into a callous and greatly feared ruler.

When the young and intriguing Anne Boleyn arrives from the French court, Henry is easily captivated by her dark beauty and bold spirit. But his desire to possess the wily girl leads to a deadly struggle of power that promises to tear apart the lives of Katharine and Mary, and forever change England's faith. . .

arrow books

ALSO AVAILABLE IN ARROW IN THE TUDOR SERIES

Uneasy Lies the Head

Jean Plaidy

In the aftermath of the bloody Wars of the Roses, Henry Tudor has seized the English crown, finally uniting the warring Houses of York and Lancaster through his marriage to Elizabeth of York.

But whilst Henry VII rules wisely and justly, he is haunted by Elizabeth's missing brothers; the infamous two Princes, their fate in the Tower for ever a shrouded secret. Then tragedy strikes at the heart of Henry's family, and it is against his own son that the widowed King must fight for a bride and his throne . . .

arrow books

ALSO AVAILABLE IN ARROW IN THE TUDOR SERIES

Katharine, the Virgin Widow

Jean Plaidy

The young Spanish widow, Katharine of Aragon, has become the pawn between two powerful monarchies. After less than a year as the wife of the frail Prince Arthur, the question of whether the marriage was ever consummated will decide both her fate and England's.

But whilst England and Spain dispute her dowry, in the wings awaits her unexpected escape from poverty: Henry, Arthur's younger, more handsome brother – the future King of England. He alone has the power to restore her position, but at what sacrifice?

arrow books

THE POWER OF READING

Visit the Random House website and get connected with information on all our books and authors

EXTRACTS from our recently published books and selected backlist titles

COMPETITIONS AND PRIZE DRAWS Win signed books, audiobooks and more

AUTHOR EVENTS Find out which of our authors are on tour and where you can meet them

LATEST NEWS on bestsellers, awards and new publications

MINISITES with exclusive special features dedicated to our authors and their titles

READING GROUPS Reading guides, special features and all the information you need for your reading group

LISTEN to extracts from the latest audiobook publications

WATCH video clips of interviews and readings with our authors

RANDOM HOUSE INFORMATION including advice for writers, job vacancies and all your general queries answered

Come home to Random House

www.randomhouse.co.uk